JEANETTE GR

HEARTS' HOME

RANSOMED HEARTS, PART THREE

Previously.

Back when rock and roll was young, twin werewolves fled from France to Northern England to escape a mortal danger to their family. They hid their true selves, found love, married, and each had a son. When the children were still young, the twins returned to Europe to take the fight to the enemy, leaving their boys, Mark and John, in the care of their mothers.

Mark and John grew up to find they were also werewolves – a fact they hid from their mothers and everyone else. They formed a band with two rich boys, Andrew Ransome and Xan Kendrick, and along the way to fame and fortune they infected Andrew with the werewolf trait, but Xan's infection failed to take. Soon after, they met Diana, a female werewolf and scientist whose fate became entangled in theirs.

And then, Xan was murdered.

Chapter 1

Xan Kendrick was dead.

Mark Preston hung up the phone. His new bride, Katie, was asking him what was wrong, and there weren't enough words in the world to express what was wrong, and how wrong it was.

'It's Xan.' Mark swallowed. 'He's dead. Murdered. In Ibiza.'

'Are you sure?'

Mark shook his head. The news of the drummer's death had come to him from a very reliable source. 'That was Andy on the phone, he was with Xan at the end. There's no doubt.'

'But why?'

'Don't know. Andy just about managed to give me the basics before he broke down. I'd better ring Andy's father, he'll know what to do. They're cousins, distant cousins, you know? Andy and Xan. Andy's mum and dad helped to bring Xan up. Yeah, I'll ring Andy's dad.' He stood up, heading for the phone. His throat was weirdly dry, and his legs were suddenly unreliable. He sat back down.

'Stay there. I'll make the call.' Katie grabbed a bottle of water from the fridge and poured it into a glass. 'Here, sip this.'

Mark sat, silent. It was early evening in New York, where they were honeymooning. Back home in Lancashire it would be the middle of the night, and somewhere in the

Ransome house a phone would be ringing. Mark released a long-held breath when Katie started to speak, in measured, sympathetic tones. After a few moments she gave the phone to him. 'Mr Ransome would like to speak to you.'

Mark took the phone and tried to explain that he didn't know anything, not yet, but Nat Ransome broke in gently. 'Mark, please, look after yourself right now. I have people in Spain. They will make sure Andy and Helen are cared for, and that Xan's body comes home as soon as possible.'

Mark held back a sob of relief. 'I'm sorry, Nat. I know you were close.'

'My cousin's lad, but my wife and I pretty much brought him up. Look, I have to wake my wife and tell her, then let Helen's mother and Xan's father know. The press will be involved soon, is there anyone else who needs to know?'

Mark took a deep breath. 'My mum. I don't want her waking up to press at the door. Could you…?'

'I'll ring her now, and arrange a car. She can stay here as long as she needs to. I know she was fond of Xan.'

'He … he called her Auntie Fran,' Mark stammered. 'Look, I need to let John know…'

'Of course, I'll keep you informed.'

John, Mark soon discovered, was not at home. Katie said that it was hardly surprising. Mark's cousin and bandmate was often away from his flat for several days. Mark cursed, and tried John's mobile phone, which switched to voicemail. He couldn't bring himself to leave the news of their friend's death as a message.

There was someone else who needed to know the news.

'I'm going for a walk … just need some time…' he muttered to Katie as he left the hotel room. He found a public call box and rang a number from memory. When Diana answered, he closed his eyes and spoke.

The chair was plastic and cold, the walls a drab combination of mustard and olive. John returned his attention to his book. He'd been in the middle of *Crime and Punishment*, again, but had picked up *War and Peace* when the request came that he present himself at the police station.

Nobody knew he was there. He wanted it that way.

He glanced up from the book, distracted by his reflection in the glass of the doorway. He had Changed several times since Xan's death, and had been horrified to realise his new, close blond crop had gone, replaced by his usual long black curls. He'd cut them off, flushing them down the loo, then used his electric razor to trim the remainder back even shorter. At short notice, there was nothing he could do about the colour. He wondered if Diana would have liked the blond look.

He told himself not to think about Diana, and returned his attention to the book. Minutes later, the door opened.

'We're ready for you,' a WPC said politely. 'Could you come through?'

The interview room was small, stuffy and stank of old cigarettes. A full ashtray sat in the middle of the one table. John took a seat and waited.

Five minutes passed, and nobody came. He hid his amusement, and took out the book again, opening the well-read pages to where he'd left the story. Within seconds, the door to the interview room opened and a detective sauntered in, shadowed by the same uniformed WPC.

'Detective Inspector Grey. WPC Austin. You are known as John Preston?'

'I am John Preston.' John kept his smile low-key, glancing at the WPC first, then returning his attention to the detective. 'I take it this is about Xan Kendrick's murder?'

'It is. Do you want to have a lawyer present?'

'Why on earth should I want a lawyer present? I thought I was here to help you find the killer?' John frowned. 'No, I don't want a lawyer.'

The detective nodded, and pushed a photograph across the desk. 'Recognise these two?'

John glanced at the photo. 'Am I under arrest?'

Grey shrugged. 'No, you're helping us with our enquiries. Who are the people in the photo?'

John knew. 'The woman is Jen Conway. The guy is, I think, Evan March. I've met Jen before, we're acquaintances. Evan I never saw until the other night, when he stabbed Xan.'

'Are you sure?'

'Of what? That's definitely Jen. I'm not certain about the guy. Like I said, I've only seen him once, other than in newspaper pictures. He's the one you should be looking for.'

'Trust me, we are.'

Silence. John refused to fall for it, adopting a respectful silence of his own. He didn't feel any need to speak first.

Eventually the WPC spoke up. 'Would you like a cup of tea?'

'Thank you, that's sweet of you, but no. I had one before I left.'

Silence, again. Grey cleared his throat. John looked at him, but Grey said nothing.

Eventually Grey spoke up. 'Did you have any reason to want Alexander Kendrick dead?'

John blinked, genuinely surprised. That was OK, it was a surprising question. 'No. What makes you think that?'

'Jen Conway. We did some research. You rescued her from an assault, some years back. Xan Kendrick slept with her, a while ago, and then broke up with her. Is it possible that you were angry with him, because of how he treated Miss Conway?'

'Jesus.' John stared at the wall. 'Someone has one hell of an imagination. OK. Jen and I didn't keep in touch after she was attacked. She didn't know me, I didn't know her. We met again at Xan's place, coincidentally, when she spent some time with him. He did not "break up" with Jen because there was nothing to break up – it was a one-night thing, which both of them understood, and enjoyed. I had no problem at all with it. I like Jen, and respect her, other than her recent crap taste in men. By which I mean Evan March, not Xan.' He looked at the detective. 'There were dozens of witnesses who saw March stab Xan.'

'You were in Ibiza in disguise. Did you meet up with Jen Conway and Evan March at any time before the murder?'

'No.' John flushed, angry now. 'The first time I saw March was when he killed Xan. As for "disguise", I cut my hair. That's hardly a disguise.'

'And the last time you saw Mr March?'

'He ran out of the club. I stayed with Xan until the Ransomes arrived. Then I tried to follow him, but I was too late.'

'He's not on Ibiza. We're sure of that. Local police have searched the island, thoroughly. He's gone. Someone helped him to get away.'

'Not me. Xan was my friend.'

Grey tapped the table with a packet of cigarettes and took one, offering the pack to John, who shook his head.

'Don't blame you, it's a filthy habit. Of course, you rock stars, you know all about filthy habits.'

'I don't smoke. I don't take drugs. I get drunk, now and again, but I was sober the night Xan died. Does that rule out a line of questioning?'

'Did you know Evan March's dealer?'

'I didn't know Evan March. It's fairly clear that he had a dealer, from what I've read in the papers. Since I don't know who that dealer is, I can't tell you if I know them or not.'

'So, you may know him?'

'Him, her, whatever. I'm in the music business, I know people. I know people I'd rather not know. So, tell me March's dealer's name and I'll tell you if I know them.'

Grey hissed, and ground out his cigarette. 'Why were you in Ibiza?'

'Holiday. My cousin got married last week. We can't do much work as a band without him, so I decided to go away.'

'Why Ibiza?'

'I know the place, you can have as much fun as you want. We've had group holidays there in the past.'

'Andrew and Helen Ransome were at the resort too, but they said you weren't with them?'

'I was in a bad mood, I didn't want to spoil their holiday.' John didn't take his eyes away from the detective's.

'Did you know they were there?'

'Yes. I spotted them a couple of times, but I stayed away from them. Like I said, I was in a bad mood.'

'Xan Kendrick travelled to Ibiza to look for you. Did you know?'

'No. If I'd known he was looking for me, I'd have met up with him. I wasn't hiding from him. Like I said, I was feeling grumpy and wanted to get away for a while.'

'Why the bad mood? Why was Kendrick looking for you?'

John sighed. 'A woman. Not Jen. Another woman. Stupid situation. The barmaid at the wedding. He chatted her up. I could see she really liked him, but the next day he'd forgotten about her. He does it all the time. Did. We argued about it. A band is like a family, small things get blown out of all proportion. Usually I don't care about stuff like that, but I was feeling tense because of the wedding and all the family stuff around it, and I lost my cool. I didn't want to upset anyone, so I left. I'm told that

Xan felt guilty about it and was looking for me, to apologise. I was cooling down by then anyway. If he'd found me, we'd have been fine. He didn't find me. He found Jen. Unfortunately for him he also found a nutcase junkie called Evan March, who was carrying a blade in a fucking nightclub. That's what happened.'

He sighed. 'I saw Jen and March at the same time, just before the stabbing. I was a few feet away and spotted Xan first, he's tall – he *was* tall. I headed towards them and witnessed the stabbing. I stayed with Xan until Andy and Helen arrived – they were in the same club. Not that much of a coincidence. It's a great club and we've all partied there before. I went outside the club, frantic. I looked for March, to stop him from running, but he was gone. I saw Jen. She was crying, outside. We talked. She said she'd not known him for long, she'd met him a few days earlier, and they were in Ibiza with a group. He was kind of with her, but it was early days, and she was going to finish with him. Maybe he knew that. Maybe that's why he was so hostile to Xan? She said she was going to talk to the police. I went for a walk. There didn't seem to be anything they'd want to talk to me about. Around dawn, I went to the station to see if there was any news. The island police questioned me and let me go. I met up with Andy and Helen Ransome there, and we stayed together until Andy's dad could arrange for us to come home with Xan's body. I've spoken to Jen since, she's pretty cut up about it. I've told her it's not her fault.'

'Jen Conway tells the same story.' Grey blinked. 'You didn't have any contact with her before the killing?'

'Not for months. I saw her a couple of times – we move in similar industry circles. Our paths crossed, but usually nothing deliberate. I had coffee with her, about a year ago, maybe more. Her and her sister. We bumped into each other in London.' He closed his eyes. 'Really, that's it. Maybe we exchanged Christmas cards? Like I said, she's someone I know, and like, and get on with, but she's not a close friend.' He sat forwards and stared at Grey. 'Not like Xan. Xan was like a brother to me. We're the same age, but he was like a kid brother, you know? The annoying kind, who winds you up but you love anyway. Xan was good at getting into trouble, and me and Andy, we were used to getting him out of it. This time, we couldn't.' He paused. 'Any more questions? We've got a funeral to organise.'

John stopped off at a supermarket after leaving the station, quietly losing the young officer who had been assigned to follow him, and walked the few miles to Diana's house.

She said nothing when she opened the door; she looked haunted and exhausted.

He offered a hug, then realised that he was asking not offering, and fell into her open arms. Ah, this was what it felt like to be home at last.

She broke away, moving to the kitchen and the twins, who were watchful and quiet. She was silent as she made two mugs of tea and handed one to him. She sat at the kitchen table and waited for him to sit opposite her.

'What happened?' she asked calmly. 'All I know is that Xan was murdered. Mark rang me. He didn't know much, but I've not heard anything since, other than what's been on the news. The guy … the murderer, he's not been caught yet.'

John took a deep breath. 'He won't be. I tracked him down. Broke his neck. He didn't suffer, didn't even know I was there until the last second or two. I went wolf most of the time, to track him, but Changed back for the killing. It didn't seem fair, otherwise.' He waited, watching her face.

She nodded. 'And the body? I haven't heard about a body being found.'

He took a deep breath. 'Yeah, well, then I went wolf. Back and forth, wolf to man, using up those calories, emptying my stomach … you know? Took a while, but I did it in the water, and the fish helped.'

'Nothing left?' Her tone was flat.

He swallowed. 'Tore him up, made the bones unidentifiable. Made sure the fish got every scrap that I didn't. I buried his clothes deep, they won't be found. Are you… Do you think… Do you hate me?'

'Hell no.' She shrugged. 'You saved me a job.'

He stared.

'What?' She smiled, just a little. It didn't reach her eyes. 'Xan is dead, and I can't change that, and I'll grieve him for the rest of my life. The guy who killed him would have been caught and tried and locked up, and all of that would have been more pain for everyone who loved Xan. And one day some parole board would have decided that he was safe to be out again, and one of us would have had to kill him. Not to make a point, or for justice, or any of that, but because it wouldn't be right for him to be alive and Xan to be dead.'

John shook his head. 'I'd never have thought you were a death penalty kinda girl.'

'Fuck no, that's just cruel. State murder, isn't it. Making someone wait, with that over their heads, it's sadistic. And what if they're innocent? No, you weren't punishing him, or dispensing justice, were you? You were simplifying things. Yeah, it was murder, and we'll spend the rest of our lives worrying if you'll ever be caught, but if you hadn't done it, I would have.' She smiled wryly. 'But not for a while, because something's wrong with me. I can't Change.'

John stared at her.

'I'll make another brew, shall I?' She walked away.

Chapter 2

There was a cautious knock on the door – an announcement, a warning – then a key turned slowly in the lock. Mark slipped into the house, hung his black duffle coat on the newel post at the bottom of the stairs, and stood quietly, taking in the silence of the house, the expression on Diana's face and the subdued noises coming from the babies.

He swallowed. 'I'm on my way to see my mum, officially. The press are all over us, but I managed to shake them off. We've got a few minutes. Can we talk?'

'Sure.' Diana waited.

'I can't stay.' Mark stumbled over the words. 'Hell, I always seem to be saying that. Diana, you need more than I can give you, I know that. I kinda gave the green light to you and John, at my wedding, but I forgot to tell you. And I maybe forgot that it's not up to me.' He shrugged. 'You and Xan though, that came out of nowhere. I believed him when he said you were just friends. Do you want to talk about it?'

'Just friends, eh? That doesn't really cover it. He was my best friend and he's gone, and I'm empty. I didn't know what I'd found until I lost him. Until we lost him.'

'You were lovers?' Mark kept his voice carefully neutral.

'Once. It was a mistake, and we both knew it. But it wouldn't have been an issue if John hadn't walked in on us. Xan and me, we had a row, and we were both on edge, and…'

Mark sighed. 'And he got what he'd wanted from the start. Oh, you're right, you would have both moved on and it would have been fine. He was always bloody brilliant at managing expectations.'

Diana stared. 'It wasn't like that. I wasn't a conquest.'

'No, I never meant to imply…' Mark sat on an armchair. 'Shit, I don't want to fall out. We need each other, more than ever. All of us. We've all lost Xan. That's really what I came to say, that I know you are hurting, and that I'll be here as much as I can. But it won't be easy – the press are all over us right now. My mum's had to hide out with Andy's parents. That's where Andy and Helen have gone too, until we're yesterday's news. Katie … she's stayed in New York for a while, with friends. Better that way, we both thought. Have you seen John?'

Diana nodded. 'He slept here last night. In his room. A long, deep sleep – he needed it. Then he went back to his flat.'

'Are you going to be OK? I mean, I'm feeling like we've been apart for too long but…'

'No. Not yet. I mean, yeah, I'm feeling the addiction, but I can hold off. It's not what I want, right now.' She smiled and shrugged. 'I never thought I'd ever say that, but I've been feeling a bit weird recently. I can't Change. I feel ill when I think about it. There's something wrong.'

'Since the boys were born?' Mark frowned.

'No, I've gone wolf since then. It's since…' Diana sat down on the sofa. 'Mark, I think I might be pregnant

13

again. Think about it… If Xan is the father, then it's not going to be a Shifter, is it? And if I Change, and the embryo doesn't, well… It could kill the baby. The nausea when I try to Change, it's a warning.'

Mark moved to sit next to her. He took her hand. 'What are you going to do?'

'Bloody hell, I don't know. Take a test, I guess, to make sure. If I go ahead, then that's my career gone, isn't it? I could just about get away with taking a few months out with our babies. My boss is sympathetic, but I'm on a fixed-term contract, and … shit. If I'm pregnant, it's all we have of Xan. I have to go through with it.'

Mark shook his head. 'He wouldn't want you to do that, not if you didn't want to. I'm sure.' He shook his head. 'He was always so careful.'

'I told him not to be.' Diana shrugged. 'I didn't think I could get pregnant again so fast.'

Mark started to speak, then stopped.

'What?' Diana said.

'If you go ahead, count me in. I'll do the dad stuff, as much as I can anyway.' He glanced at the clock and winced. 'I have to go. I'll be back as soon as I can. Can I have a quick peek at the boys?'

'They're your kids, help yourself.' Diana gestured behind them, to where the boys were asleep in their new pram.

Mark managed a smile, and spent a while looking at the twins wistfully before sighing and leaving the house.

Diana walked over to her sons and stared at them. 'What the hell are we going to do?' she asked them. They slept on.

Andy was the last to turn up. The band's bass player arrived at Diana's a week after Xan's murder. He was hollow-eyed and pale. He nodded a greeting, went through to the kitchen, sat at the table and opened a briefcase.

'Coffee?' Diana asked. 'Sorry, no cake…'

'I've had enough cake to last me the rest of the year. My mother and Helen's mum are grief-baking, and it's been my job to dispose of the results. I swear my blood is half syrup. But yeah, coffee sounds good. Strong, black…'

'Three sugars?' Diana managed a small smile.

'What?' Andy stared at her, then smiled back. 'No sugar, thank you.'

He waited until she'd joined him at the table with the coffees, then nodded. 'I'm here about Xan's will. And to check up on you and the boys, of course.'

'Of course.' Diana nodded soberly.

'Um, first of all, we all changed our wills, when you were pregnant. We all left a significant sum to the rest of the band, on the explicitly spoken but unwritten condition that it was to look after the boys, and you, of course. Xan left everything. It's rather a lot, because he had some family money, and of course Ransomed Hearts is a profitable concern these days, so there will be royalties—'

'I never asked for this.' Diana was staring at him.

'Oh, we know, but Mark suggested it when we were setting up that consultancy business to get funds to you. Xan said flat out that Helen and I didn't need more money, and his dad is comfortable enough. So, it's all gone to the Ransomed Hearts Trust, which is run completely by the band. It means we can disburse it without anyone else really knowing what's going on. There are issues though, in getting funds to you without raising questions about who you are. And I'm assuming you still want to lie low?'

Diana repeated. 'I didn't ask for this…'

Andy cleared his throat. 'I realise that it's really none of my business, but Mark did mention you might be expecting again,' – he looked at the table – 'and that it would be Xan's child, if you were. And this has nothing to do with the inheritance, obviously, but if you are, and you think you'll struggle with three little ones, then … well … Helen and I have been trying for a baby, and I'd be happy to talk to her about adopting. Obviously I wouldn't reveal who you are, or what you are to Mark…' He stood up and backed away. Diana's expression had changed from confusion to cold-eyed fury.

'I'll leave you to think about it then.' He gestured at the papers on the table. 'Forget that last bit, obviously, it was just an idea. I thought it might help. No offence intended.' He blinked. 'Diana, I am sorry. Just read the stuff I've drawn up about the money. I'll leave.'

'Goodbye, Andy,' she growled. He left.

Diana went to her room and picked up the positive pregnancy-test stick. She shrugged. 'I reckon I know how I feel about you now,' she murmured, then turned to the sleeping twins in their cot. 'You two are going to be big brothers,' she said quietly.

Chapter 3

The band decided to sell Xan's lake house; they'd visited the place together and decided that, without Xan's merry presence, it wasn't somewhere they wanted to be. For the time being, they'd rent rehearsal space. In mid-October they made a final visit there, inviting Diana along to say her goodbyes. Diana had made it clear that she wasn't going to claim much from the house, other than a few items of sentimental value, and it was already looking stripped-down, with paintings, art works and photographs already gone.

The big dining table was still there, and the four of them each took a seat. Diana had parked the carrycot in a corner, but Mark walked over and took the boys out, cuddling one in each arm. Andy stood up and spoke quietly to Mark, then took one of the babies to hold, glancing over at their mother, who nodded her permission. She watched the men with amused interest and looked at John, who was leaning back and yawning.

Mark started off.

'OK, now we're all here. First item of business. Do we split up? As a band?'

Nobody spoke.

'We have to talk about this. The label want to release the album, and they want to do it with our blessing. It's finished, bar a bit of tarting up, you all know that. And the tour is booked. We're supposed to be in Plymouth at the end of next month.'

Andy spoke. 'Tour? Without Xan?'

'He was cremated, you know. It's a bit late to have him stuffed and mounted behind the drums,' Diana said drily.

Andy glared at her, then grinned. 'Are you channelling him by any chance? That was a real Xan comment.'

She smiled back, accepting the olive branch.

Mark coughed. 'I need a decision.'

John spoke up. 'I vote that we release the album, tour, look at the lyrics he's left behind and decide if we carry on from there. Also, I have lyrics.'

They all turned to look at John.

'Don't mock. I do. I can write lyrics. They're a bloody sight more cheerful than Xan's though, I'm afraid.'

Mark nodded. 'My feeling is the same. We carry on. I have lyrics too.'

Andy put his hands under his chin, and looked dead ahead, at John. 'I guess we carry on then. I'll phone the tour manager now, let her know. By the way, I don't have lyrics.'

He handed the baby to John, who held him comfortably, and left the room.

When Andy returned, he rumpled Diana's hair as he walked past then casually stole the other child from Mark. Diana shook her head and flashed a conspiratorial grin at Mark.

'Second item,' said Mark. 'We have two kids with no names.'

Diana shrugged. 'I've had other things to worry about. I know which is which.'

'Still, we should name them,' said their father. 'If you agree, I would like to name the eldest one Seth, the second born, Noah.' He looked a little lost. 'Now I've lost track of who has which baby,' he admitted.

'John's got Seth, Andy's got Noah. Just tell me that you can tell them apart,' Diana begged.

Andy joked. 'I'm the tall, gorgeous natural blond, John's the muscle-bound ape.'

Mark smiled. 'I can tell them apart. It'll just be easier to talk about them now they have names. Are you happy with those names? I was kinda waiting for you to decide, but…'

Diana shrugged. 'Yeah, whatever. I've been calling 'em Poopy and Stinky, but was reluctant to make it official. I'll register them, now it's decided.'

They were all a little more relaxed now, until Mark's next words.

'Now, next point on the agenda… Whatever we are is dysfunctional, and it's making me miserable. Is anybody actually happy?'

There was an uncomfortable silence.

'I thought so. I'm sorry. Xan's death, Seth and Noah's birth, they've brought it home to me: I'm not a good leader. Does anyone want me to stand down?'

Diana interrupted. 'I'm sorry, that's not something that goes by majority decision. You're my … I don't know what to call you … my mate? You always will be. And I have total confidence in you.'

'You have too much confidence in me, but I accept that. OK. Next question… John, Andy, you're in a …

something … a pack? … with a crap leader and a loony woman.' He looked at Diana and smiled. 'If you want to leave, say so now.'

There was silence.

'Right, let's get down to it. I want to know what you're all thinking, and what you're not saying. Then we'll lay down some ground rules. Go on, girl, you first.'

She looked at him, wondering if he meant it, then spoke.

'OK, you and Andy make me feel like I'm not really a person. When we first met, you were lovely to me, then you cut me off. You tell me it will be OK, and it never is. It never will be. I love you, you don't love me. It's that simple.'

'What can I do?'

'You can talk to me, get to know me, stop treating me like a bad habit that you can't break.'

'OK, I'll try. What do you want to say to Andy?'

She turned to Andy. 'We've talked about this before. I feel like you don't want me around. You ignore me unless you want access to the babies. It pisses me off. I know you are married, but I'm not asking for you to sleep with me, just to accept me as part of your life. Treat me like a person.'

Andy scowled. 'Xan would still be alive if it wasn't for you.'

Mark looked like he was going to wade in and John was standing up, but Diana was there first.

'That's not it. You treated me badly when Xan was still alive. You're being unfair.'

Mark spoke up.

'She's right. She has no reason to trust you. The pack we need to be must trust each other. What are you going to do about it?'

Andy drew back. 'Are you giving me an ultimatum?'

John spoke up. 'I am, even if Mark isn't. I love you, Andy, you know I do, but you have to climb down off your high horse. We've had some great times, but I have a family now, and I'm going to put them first.'

'Family? What bloody family?'

'My mate, my children,' he said.

'Fuck it, have you gone mad? She's Mark's mate, they're Mark's children.'

'No, they're mine too. Aren't they?' He looked at her. She looked back and smiled.

Mark looked at Andy. 'If this is how you feel about Diana, I don't feel safe with you in the pack. It's not a playground any more, we've got Seth and Noah to think about, and Xan's baby.'

Andy flinched.

Mark continued. 'If you want to leave, we won't be able to trust you any more. We'll split the band now, I mean it. We'll never have a better excuse. And John and I will have to find somewhere secret with our children and Diana. I'll have to leave Katie, and you will never see any of us again.'

'So what do you want from me?' Andy whispered.

Diana spoke. 'Andy … please don't think that this wouldn't have happened if Xan had been here. You're still among people who love you, I promise. We just need you to commit to us.'

He met her gaze. 'I understand, but I made a commitment to Helen.' He held Noah a little closer, and whispered, 'He does feel like mine, though. It's crazy, but he does. OK, you win.' He looked relieved. 'Being a total shit to you was grating on my nerves a little, I must admit. What do I tell Helen?'

Mark leaned forward.

'You tell her nothing. She won't understand. You understand that, in your guts, that's why you're holding our child like that. You are going to have to spend the rest of your days hiding half of your life from Helen. I understand what that means, but there's nothing that I can do about it. I'm bound to Diana and responsible for our kids. You still have a choice. You can stay with the band, stay with the pack, and lie to your wife, or tell her the truth and live the rest of your life without us.'

Andy sighed. 'No, I have no choice. If Xan's child is going to be born into the pack, I'm in. I'll lie to the woman I love, and I'll be damned with you all.'

John smiled with relief, and left the room. He came back with four beers.

Mark nodded. 'John, say your piece.'

'OK, I want my own kids. I know they'll all be mine, in a way, but you know what I mean. I don't know how this is going to work, but if it's just going to be you and Diana, I'm not going to be happy.' He was blushing.

Mark shrugged. 'It's up to her, but I know what she'll say.'

All eyes were on Diana, who shrugged. 'You know how I feel. I want you.'

Andy kept his face blank.

John drank his beer straight back, left the room and returned with a second bottle. They waited silently until he got back.

'And you, Mark, what do you want?' Diana asked.

'I want a peaceful life, lots of money, a dozen kids, my band, my friends, my wife and you.' He smiled. 'Not necessarily in that order, and I know I probably can't have them all.'

'I'll work on it for you,' she promised. 'Now, if there's nothing else you need me for, I'll take the kids home.'

A few minutes later, with the babies safely in the car, she watched as three wolves trotted out of Xan's house. They were going to run together, in this safe place. She watched enviously, then drove home from the lake house for the last time.

Chapter 4

The album was released: *Songs from A Lost Heart.* The tour went ahead, with a session drummer. It was inevitably and ghoulishly sold out, and extra dates were added. Mark and Diana snatched whatever moments they could between mainland British dates, and after the short European tour. The North American tour would take the band out of the country until mid-January, with a few days' break between the US dates and the Canadian ones. Hoping it would be enough, Diana and Mark set up a system of exchanging their worn clothing via airmail; perhaps each other's scent would be enough to dull their craving for each other. Before the band left for America, Diana told John she loved him. He cursed her timing but promised her that he felt the same way.

Mark managed occasional phone calls from anonymous call boxes, asking Diana about Seth and Noah. They were still skinny, but long and a good weight for their age.

The Canadian tour was due to start on the 4th of January. On the 2nd, Diana was listening to the new Therapy? album and eating cereal when the front door flew open, and a bulky shape in black motorcycle leathers and a helmet strode in. She put herself in front of the babies and tensed, ready to fight. Seconds later she relaxed, and laughed as John removed the helmet and started to unzip his jacket.

'You scared the living shit out of me. Aren't you supposed to be in Vancouver?'

'Do you want me to be?' he asked, uncertainty in his eyes.

'God, no. I'm just … surprised.'

He was with her in seconds, wrapping her in a bear hug. He was about to fall with her on to the sofa, but her frantic yelp alerted him to the tiny babies sleeping there, and he laughed and put her down again.

They were grinning at each other.

'I take it that you're glad I'm back?' he teased.

'Hmm, yes. Is this a short visit?'

'Unfortunately. We've got tonight, then I have to fly back tomorrow.'

'Go out or stay in?' she asked.

'Oh… One then the other?' He grinned.

'We'd better make the most of it then. I'll ring around for a babysitter.'

'If they're reluctant, promise them lots of money,' he suggested.

John went back out into the cold night. He delved into his panniers and brought out a second set of leathers and a spare helmet.

When the babysitter arrived, they were both dressed for the road; John had his helmet on already, hiding his face. Diana hurriedly checked the house to make sure there was nothing there to link her to the Hearts.

'You do know how to ride this?' Diana asked.

John nodded. 'I know what I'm doing.'

She climbed on behind him and wrapped her hands around his waist. He trembled, then started the bike and they were off into the night.

Soon, they were on the back lanes to the moors, racing along the tarmac. John understood the machine, and Diana understood him. They rode for about an hour; then he pulled off the road, propping the machine up against a tree, and began to strip off his leathers. She followed suit, and they began to walk through a small woodland, hand in hand. Once they were out of the trees, the wind was fresh and cold, but she could feel the heat radiating from John.

She half stumbled on the dark path, and he caught her arm and pulled her back up.

'Do you want to Change?' he asked.

'No, this is a human thing. And I can't Change with Xan's baby growing in me,' she reminded him.

At the top of the hill, they stood and looked around. They could see the lights of towns and cities and villages all around Lancashire. A line of moving lights was the M61. How could a motorway look so romantic? John's arm was around her waist, and he was breathing quickly.

'Is this OK?' he said.

'This is wonderful,' she sighed.

She realised he was still nervous and turned to face him, standing on tiptoe to kiss him, to rub her face against his stubble.

He shivered as she removed his sweater and T-shirt. He undressed and waited.

She stepped out of his reach and looked at him for a long moment. She'd seen him naked many times, but always in that comfortable, pack-friendly post-Change moment when nakedness isn't really an issue. This was different, and she looked at him appreciatively for several seconds.

Their eyes met, then she undressed too.

'Come here, hon, I can't wait another second. I swear I'm dying here,' he said.

She closed the few yards between them, and stood next to him, feeling the heat between them, slipping her arms around his waist and breathing in his scent.

He was still hesitating. 'Do you really want me?' he said.

'Yes. Why are you stalling?'

'You don't understand. I love you. I can't bear it if you don't feel the same way. So many girls, so many women, and it's always been so easy…' He was shaking.

'John, this is *me* now. I know you, I love you, I want you, I need you.' She wanted that Shapeshifter hit again, not thinking about what she was saying or doing – aware of the feel of his skin, his still-short dark hair under her hands.

Then they were on the wet cold grass, and he was inside her, and his face was buried in her soft red hair, and he was screaming her name as they both came so fast, falling into the sky and out the other side, shaking in relief as the chemistry started to work.

She touched his face. 'John, it's OK. This is where it starts being OK. Nobody can take me away from you now, not in this life.'

'They'd better not try. I love you.'

'Yeah, you said that.' She smiled again. 'I'm hungry, hon. Shall we go home?'

He nodded, and they dressed, then found the bike again. They stopped halfway home at a chip shop that was open late. She bought fish and chips and mushy peas, and two cans of dandelion and burdock, and joined John, who was sitting in the shadows at the front of the shop, on a low wall.

'Ah, Lancashire soul food,' he sighed and dug in happily. He looked up and frowned at her. 'Should I have taken you to some fancy restaurant?' he joked.

'Yeah, probably, but it wouldn't have been as good as this,' she replied, licking salt off her fingers and throwing the greasy newspaper in the bin.

When they got home, he waited outside until she'd overpaid the babysitter. Then he prowled back into the house and watched her feed Seth and Noah. They bathed them together, and put them to bed, then finally showered off the mud and the grass of the night's adventure, and burrowed into bed. This time, he needed no reassurances.

Mark was standing outside the hotel room, hesitating. The hesitation in itself was a new thing; he couldn't remember a time when it hadn't been natural to be with John. 'They're closer than brothers,' his mother had always said. He knocked on the door. How difficult could it be, to talk to him, to be his friend?

He heard a thud as John's feet hit the floor and he came to the door. Mark smiled wryly. John liked to make his presence felt; doing anything quietly was an alien concept. The door opened wide, and he found himself swept into the room and seated on the edge of the bed, barraged with questions about the last few days.

John wanted to know how Andy was. Had he been missed? How was the session drummer behaving? At last he quietened in the face of Mark's increasing impatience.

He grinned. 'Well, I'm back,' he said. He looked sheepish, pleased with himself, and nervous.

'And is it love?' Mark snapped. He tried to keep the sarcasm out of his voice, but some of it filtered through.

'Love? Mark! You know her, how could it be anything else?' John was more subdued now. 'Are you jealous?'

Mark stood up, paced around the room, before grabbing a chair and sitting back down. He glared at his cousin. 'It could be a chemical addiction, a natural instinct, an effort by your body to fool you, to make you feel that she's the right woman for you just because she's the *only* woman for you. And for the record, I'm certainly not jealous. I don't expect her to have any notion of fidelity – she'll do what her instincts tell her to.'

'Well aren't you the cynical bastard today?' John muttered. 'It's nice to be welcomed back so joyously. She sent you something, although I'm not sure you deserve it.' He reached into his suitcase and drew out two sealed plastic bags. He threw them across the room to his cousin. The first one held a dark green sweatshirt, one of Diana's. The second one held two baby-sized T-shirts.

Mark looked at them hungrily. 'She sent them? Or did you ask her for them?' He'd been ill for a couple of weeks now, deprived of his mate. He'd been bad-tempered, missing meals, barely sleeping.

John smiled gently. 'She sent them. She talked about you a lot. She's sick too, nothing I could do could change that. Be good and send her something stinky from you. She's panicking that if she gets really ill, she'll lose the baby.'

Mark answered immediately. 'I'll do it tomorrow. I'll send her my T-shirt from tonight's gig. Will that be enough?'

John shook his head. 'She needs *you* – you know how it is. Is there any way you could get away for a day or two between gigs?'

Mark had already opened the first bag and had the sweatshirt close to his face. He felt his despair ease a little as his body learned that his mate was not lost to him, that she still existed somewhere, so far away. He yearned for her, to hold her, kiss her, make her his again. Eyes closed, he breathed in one more deep draught of her scent, then returned the clothing to the bag and sealed it.

He waited for clarity, fought for it, achieved it. 'I can't. No. Katie is coming over tomorrow. Diana and I will just have to cope a while longer. This tour will be over in thirteen days. I'll have to spend the first night home with Katie, of course. I'll be with Diana first thing the next morning.' His smile was a little cruel. 'You'll have that night.'

'Fine. Look, just talk to her. Tell her that you're sending something for her, give her something to hold on to. You can be as cold-hearted as you want, but the fact is, she's in love with you.'

'I thought she was in love with you?' Mark sneered.

'Some people don't have to be exclusive, you know?' John tried to smile.

'Yeah, I know. Your mother certainly spread her affections around. That must be why you find Diana so attractive.' Mark regretted it as soon as he'd said it. His aunt Miriam had been a second mother to him, and he felt a dark stab of guilt.

'You'd better leave,' John said, turning away, his back straight.

Mark slammed the door behind him, making his way down the corridor to his own room. Locking himself in, he threw himself on to the bed, swearing to himself. He relived the scene again and again, blushing deeper with shame each time. After the third time, he picked the phone up and rang his cousin's room. John didn't pick up. Mark waited until he did.

'I apologise. That was shitty of me. You know I didn't mean it,' he said.

'Fine. I'll see you later. Leave me alone,' John snapped.

Mark relaxed. He'd made his apologies, and John would forgive him. John always forgave him; it was a natural law. Perhaps, this time, it might take a few hours for John to calm down, but by evening they would be speaking again, close enough to make the gig a pleasure for both of them.

He curled up on the bed, reaching out for the plastic bags he'd thrown there. He took out Diana's sweatshirt and held it close, breathing in her scent again, aching for her. He couldn't even keep it in his room, he couldn't risk Katie finding it. That went double for the baby clothes. He gently opened the second bag and caressed the creased and worn T-shirts stained with dribble. He wanted to Change, to get every nuance of the scent of his sons, but he didn't dare, didn't feel safe. He replaced the clothes in their bags and made his way out into the city, finding a payphone and ringing Diana's number from memory. It would be late in England, and he was surprised when he found her number engaged. He frowned, and rang his own hotel, asking to speak to John.

'I'm sorry, sir, that line is engaged,' the receptionist told him.

He slammed the phone down, his eyes blazing. How could John be so stupid? Any overseas call would be logged. He breathed deeply, then dialled Diana's number again and again until he got through.

'Was that John you were speaking to?' he demanded.

'Mark?' she said. 'Mark? Is that you?'

'Of course it's me. Did John ring you from the hotel phone?'

She laughed. 'You are in a mood, aren't you? No, as it happens, I was talking to someone I used to work with. But it's nice to know that you're thinking about me.'

'How can I not think about you when you send your dirty laundry to me? You're sick in the head. Are you trying to drive me mad?'

'It was meant to help you. Send me something of yours. I'm dying without you,' she replied, her voice low and desperate.

He bit through his lip in frustration, the blood falling on to his shirt. He wanted to scream, wanted to be with her so much that his brain hurt. He couldn't speak. She was saying something, asking if he was all right, if the clothes had helped him. He breathed deeply.

'Diana, I'm not myself. I'm going mad without you. I'm saying awful things to people, and I can't help it. It scares me, you know? I don't like being out of control.'

'Oh Mark, you sound miserable. It won't be long now. We can manage a few more days … just a few more days.'

'You sound in better shape than me,' he said bitterly.

'I've got to look after myself,' she pointed out. 'There's the boys, and Xan's baby, to think about.'

He remembered what John had said, and spoke more gently. 'Look, I'm going to send you something of mine tomorrow. I'll send it express, OK? How are my boys?'

'Oh they're wonderful, not a bit of trouble. Did you get their Ts?'

'Yeah, and I miss them.' He smiled a little. 'I'm looking forward to seeing them again. And you, of course.' He found himself making his voice gentle; the sound of her breathing was calming him. 'Look, it's OK you know? About you and John. I know I sounded angry a minute ago, but I'm not. I'm just … frustrated.'

'Well, Katie's joining you tomorrow, isn't she?' Diana's voice was light, casual.

'Not that kind of frustrated. It's not sexual, is it? What we have?'

'Not primarily, no. It's a bonding mechanism. Sexual intercourse seems to strengthen it, and it's also the fastest way of soothing the effects of withdrawal.'

'You sound like you're giving a lecture,' Mark observed. He realised he was smiling.

'Well, it's interesting, isn't it?' she said, somewhat defensively.

'It's bloody painful, that's what it is. You do understand that I won't be able to come straight to your place when we get back from the tour?' He realised belatedly that he'd told her the same thing in every conversation they'd had that week.

'Yes,' she said.

He struggled to find something else to say. *I love you* was what he wanted to say, but, of course, he couldn't ever say that; it raised too many questions he couldn't answer – even to himself.

'Diana? Are you still there?' he said, after a long while had passed.

She made a small sound, then cleared her throat. 'Yes, I'm here. Sorry, got distracted by the boys.'

'Are you crying?' he said cautiously.

Her voice had become brisk. 'No, of course not. Don't be silly. Are you eating properly? John said that you were losing weight, and you're too thin to start off with.'

'I'll have a big lunch, I promise,' he said gravely.

'It's way past lunchtime!' she protested. 'Haven't you eaten yet?'

'No. But I will, for you.' He realised with a smile that he would, for her.

'Good. Do it now. I've got to go. Seth and Noah … you know?'

'I know. Tell them I love them.' He cursed himself as soon as he'd said it. Once more there was silence at the end of the phone, then a click, and she was gone.

The end-of-tour party was hell. John had been offstage and out of the door before the first fans had milled their way outside, and Mark had visions of him boarding the late flight back to England even as Mark, Andy and Helen put smiles on their faces and joined the aftershow party. Of course there were questions. 'He's not well.' 'He has a sick relative.' So many stories were going around, all evidently claims from John himself. Andy eventually took charge and told everyone very firmly that John had urgent personal business that he'd been away from for too long already. He kept his eye on Mark as he said it, and was satisfied his pack leader was holding himself together.

Mark circulated, doing his own job and John's: clumsily flirting with those who wanted to be flirted with, and talking about music and the business with those who wanted that from him. Some people fell silent as he passed by, and he realised that his deteriorating physical condition was a point of gossip. He wasn't inclined to argue the point, but he had a word with Helen. Helen was a born socialite, and casually found her way into every group as the night progressed, mentioning the mild viral infection 'poor old Mark' had been battling for the last month. It helped that she believed him.

Eventually he felt that it was late enough for him to retire gracefully. He didn't sleep at all, but found distraction in a book until it was time to shower and dress and join Andy and Helen for the trip to the airport. He found the drummer who had toured with them, and thanked him for his professionalism. They'd already decided Mark would drum on the studio stuff. Xan would not be replaced.

Katie was waiting for him at Manchester airport. She looked smart and awake and beautiful, and he felt a dull self-loathing as he sat in her car and gazed at his reflection in her mirror. His hair was lank and split, his skin pale and slack, his eyes reddened. He knew his breath stank, and he searched her glove compartment for mints or gum. He knew that she was glad to have him home, but, as always, she seemed to be vaguely embarrassed by his activities of the past month. She'd never quite accepted his profession, and he had the impression that she thought it was something he should have grown out of. There was a classical music CD in the car, and he slept as they crossed the Pennines and made their way home.

In his own house, surrounded by the familiar, Mark at last felt relaxed enough to talk to Katie. Within minutes they were laughing, and within half an hour they were in bed, making love deliciously slowly. He refused to think about Diana, about his hunger for her wildness. He was home, with his wife, his beloved.

Afterwards, they put on their robes and drew the curtains, and cooked a meal together. She scolded him for his lack of appetite and threatened to make an appointment for him with his GP. He assured her it was just jet lag and distracted her by making love to her again. As he touched her, marvelling at how perfectly they fitted together, he found himself asking her when she thought she'd be ready to start a family. She was amused. She told him she'd never suspected he wanted to be a dad and that she was busy with her career. Motherhood wasn't an ambition of hers; she thought he'd understood that. He accepted it gracefully, and she relaxed again in his arms.

He fell asleep there, on the sofa, and she woke him up gently in the early hours and led him to bed, where he lay awake until the alarm went off. He watched her as she dressed and styled her hair and put her make-up on. He loved to watch her get ready for the day, to watch her rituals and female sorcery. They exchanged their magic words, as they did every morning when they parted, wishing each other a good day, a safe day, a happy day. And then she left, and he listened as she drove away to her job.

He showered and dressed and shaved, and with each step he put Katie out of his mind. He drove carefully back across the hills, listening to a new album by his favourite new band, amused by some of the musical references to his own work, and pleased by some of the innovation they showed. He made a mental note to get to see them when they next toured. He didn't think about his destination.

The best place to park was in a supermarket car park a couple of miles away from where Diana lived. There were no cameras, and he was unlikely to be recognised. He put on a duffle coat and pulled the hood up, and walked towards the street of tall Victorian terraced houses where she lived.

The door was a different colour than he remembered, freshly painted, with a new letterbox and knocker. He found himself smiling; she'd probably done it as a distraction in his absence. He let himself in and was unsurprised to walk in on a scene of almost laughable domestic bliss.

Diana had her feet up, reading a scientific journal, while John sat next to her, bouncing Noah on his lap. They looked up as he came into the room, and he took in more details. Diana had lost at least fifteen pounds in the last month or so, and her face was almost gaunt. Her pregnancy was noticeable now, almost obscenely so on her thin body. John's feet were dirty, and he wore nothing but a loose robe. He'd evidently spent some time Changed earlier that morning, taking advantage of the privacy of Diana's high-walled garden. He looked relaxed and happy.

John winked at Mark. 'I'll look after the babies. I think you two need some time together. Before you both fade away or something.'

Diane was already standing, and Mark followed her in a daze, stumbling up the stairs behind her, taking her hand as she held it out for him. The physical contact made him jump. The clammy sweat that rose from her palm seemed to soak into his skin instantly. He moaned.

At the top of the stairs, out of John's sight, she spun and pressed him against the wall, reaching up to kiss him savagely, insistently, her tongue hungry in his mouth, her teeth scratching at his lips, just enough to draw blood. He picked her up and carried her into her bedroom. He felt better, stronger, already.

He was naked and inside her. She was slick and wet. He was holding her tightly. Her eyes were open wide, and she was laughing, exhausted.

'Again?' she was saying. 'Or shall we get something to eat?'

'Again?' he said, dazed.

'It's been a couple of hours, I was starting to wonder when you'd say hello.'

He looked at the clock. Somehow, hours had passed. He knew he had no energy left, but his body was demanding more of him. He withdrew, caressing her almost tenderly. 'Hello, Diana,' he said.

'Hello, Mark. Again, or food?'

'I think we should eat. It's the first time I've actually been hungry for weeks.'

'Do you feel OK?' she said cautiously.

'I feel perfect.' He grinned. 'You look good too, apart from the general malnutrition thing. Now talk, I need to hear your voice.'

'You are a bossy git today, aren't you?' she teased. 'I'll get my revenge later.'

'I can't stay,' he replied, appalled that she'd even thought so. 'I have to be home before Katie gets back. You can't have thought that I'd stay? You didn't, did you?'

Her face fell. 'I'll take what I can get then. We should eat, really. If you've not got long, you'll probably want to spend some time with the twins.' She rolled away from him, landing lightly on her feet, grabbing a robe and heading for the bathroom. 'Strip the bed, will you? It's definitely ready for fresh sheets.'

He obeyed, feeling guilty again. He wondered if he could ever do anything right ever again, and felt a sudden rush of jealousy for his cousin, for whom things were always simple and well defined and easy. In a sudden hard desire for simplicity, he Changed and prowled the room, deliberately letting his human-self fade, satisfying himself that only he and his pack had been in it since his last visit. He growled at the thought of any other man touching Diana, and his fangs showed. He padded downstairs, and sniffed curiously at the babies, recognising them as his own sons.

John was holding them, and he put them gently on the floor, where they snuggled closer to the thin black wolf and grabbed on to his fur as he curled himself around

39

them. The woman came downstairs; she smelled clean and good and healthy. She seemed happy to see him, and brought him meat from the kitchen – gamey meat, from a pantry rather than a fridge. She spoke to John; they made happy noises, and she got more meat than he could possibly eat. Then his cousin was a wolf too, big and strong, able to protect them all.

They fought a little over some of the choicest bits of food, but the woman shouted at him when he got too boisterous near the children. He wondered why she didn't Change too; he wanted his beautiful red mate who always smelled so good. He nuzzled at her, and remembered that the new cub inside her was not like them, that it couldn't Change with her. The most important thing was to protect his mate, protect the cubs, and protect his pack. He had to keep them secret, keep them hidden.

He gave a great sigh and sniffed enthusiastically one last time at the twins, then stretched and Changed again. He picked up the boys and settled back on to the sofa. Diana seemed to be happier.

'I can stay a few more hours,' he conceded. 'What's for lunch?'

Chapter 5

It was the mug that set her off. The red and white mug, a
petrol-station freebie, that had held every cup of tea that
she'd ever drunk at her desk at the university. Her secret
research was safely downloaded on to floppy disks; she
had testimonials from the postdocs and professors, and
she'd handed over her official research to a newly minted
postgrad. All of that was fine. It was the mug, on her
kitchen table, in her home, that made her cry. It had
happened gradually. She hadn't seen the massive fracture
in her life for what it was until now. Of course, meeting
the Shifter men had been a huge event, but she'd never
dreamed she would lose so much, while they continued
with their careers and lives. A moment of reckless passion
had left her addicted to Mark Preston, and stupidly in love
with him. After the birth of her twin sons, she'd been
thinking about going back to work quite quickly, to her
official research, to her colleagues, and to that red and
white mug that had sat untouched in her desk drawer for
months. Then Xan had been murdered, and she'd realised
she was pregnant again, and buried under her anger at her
own stupidity was a slowly realised relief that Xan was not
lost, not entirely, that he would have a child. But there was
a price to be paid. She worked from contract to contract,
and the university would not countenance two periods of
maternity leave within one year. She'd given her notice, left
the babies with John for the afternoon, and gone to the

department to collect her things. While she was in a practical mood, she'd rung her mother to tell her that she was a grandmother. Diana hadn't been surprised by the cold reception to her news; she was a disappointment. She'd thrown everything away for some feckless man who wouldn't even marry her, and if she expected her mother to take time from her own career to help with two illegitimate children, she had another think coming. Diana had replaced the telephone receiver carefully and walked into the kitchen. John had just left, and her only confidantes were the sleeping twins, just a few months old. A cup of tea would help, and she picked up that red and white mug, sighed, and dropped a teabag into it. Seconds later, she was sobbing.

John was frantic. 'Seriously, mate, you need to be here. She won't go to the hospital, and she says she wants you here.'

'I'm not a midwife, I'm a guitarist. And what do I say to Katie?'

'Any lie will do, so long as Katie believes it. And Diana says you're *her* midwife, and honestly, I'm beginning to think you've both lost your marbles. I'm going to tell her that you're on your way. You'd better be.'

John ended the call and sighed. Diana was in labour, and was listening to 'Neon Knights' by Sabbath, on repeat. The twins had been bathed, fed and bathed again. They knew something was happening and were doing their best to get their mother's attention. She and Mark both had a knack for encouraging them to be quiet, that John hadn't yet mastered. He would also like to master the knack of persuading Diana to change the record; he adored Dio, but this was repeat number thirty-one, by John's count, and there were limits. Diana was doing it the hard way too, playing that poor old seven-inch bit of vinyl again and again, picking up the arm at the end of each play and dropping it carefully back to the intro. By repeat forty, she wasn't speaking to John. Midway through repeat fifty, the front door opened and Mark stepped in, looking annoyed and frazzled.

Diana turned down the volume on the stereo system and took the needle off the record.

'I was enjoying that,' John murmured, watching with relief as Mark and Diana exchanged a long and desperate kiss.

Miranda, they named her. Born bigger than either of the twins, yet somehow frailer – a long, skinny baby with startling blue eyes and a weak cry. The twins were fascinated by her, and Seth's first word was 'Baba'.

Miranda's birth brought Andy and Diana closer, his lingering distrust of her fading as he watched her with Xan's child. He visited every week, turning wolf or big cat in the privacy of the house, to accustom the kids to the kind of family they'd been born into.

Diana found that she could Shapeshift again immediately after the birth, much to the surprise and delight of her sons, who laughed whenever she approached them as a wolf.

Diana converted the cellar into a small but powerful genetics lab – she'd set up a research company, funded by Xan's estate. Most of her time was spent gathering data about her own children and the Hearts, but she managed to spend some time on paid sequencing work, subcontracted from the university. Her chosen field of work was changing fast, and she was determined not to be left behind.

Diana reluctantly socialised with John. He'd nagged at her, telling her he wanted her to know some of his world. He liked to go out, he liked dating, he liked parties, and he wanted her to have fun. He already knew she wasn't jealous of any of his brief relationships: they were short, intense and fun, and almost always with his peers in the entertainment business. Diana, by contrast, was lost in this kind of social situation. She'd navigated office and lab politics with ease and had no problems taking over a classroom, but parties were an unlearned skill, and she was visibly anxious when John left her chatting to a group of young women while he wandered off to speak to someone else.

A dark-haired girl smiled at Diana. 'He does that, brings women to parties then disappears. He thinks everyone is just effortlessly sociable. What's your name? I can't quite place you.'

'Debs,' Diana lied. 'And you?'

'Mary really, but I prefer Marilyn, as in Monroe. What do you do? Is this a first date?'

Diana hesitated, then nodded. 'Yeah, first date. And I used to be a researcher, but I'm a full-time mum now, two boys and a girl. They take up most of my time.'

'Research? Like TV and stuff? And does John know about the kids? I bet he doesn't, he likes to keep things simple. Have you met the others?'

Diana was getting annoyed. 'The others?'

'Mark, Andy. John's band.'

'He's in a band?' Diana blinked. 'I met him in the library. I didn't know he was musical.'

'Well, it doesn't sound like you two know very much about each other at all. Excuse me, I've just seen my friend, I need to talk to her. Nice to chat.'

Diana forced back a smile as 'Marilyn' headed straight towards John, placing a hand possessively on his arm. Marilyn spoke and they both glanced towards Diana, who turned away and picked up a drink. Seconds later, John was by her side, laughing.

'Scandal! Hearts' front man unwittingly dates single mum of three!' he laughed. 'Marilyn's a nice girl, but she does love a bit of drama.'

Diana had her own card to play. 'Mother of five, soon,' she told him quietly, with an intimate smile. That shut him up. He put his hand on her shoulder, and steered her into a quiet corridor.

'Whose?' he asked.

'Mine,' she said.

'I'm taking you home...' His voice broke, and he lifted her in his arms. She wriggled. 'Put me down, you idiot, I'm pregnant, not crippled.'

And somehow, in the next year or so of childcare, research, writing, tours and recording that kept them all busy, Andy and Diana at last grew close. John's children were born – twin boys – and then there was a hot, expectant wait, anticipating that last union.

Chapter 6

Mark's mobile bleeped, and he excused himself from his conversation with Andy. It was her.

'Mark, I'm really sorry to disturb you, but I can't get hold of John…'

He grunted. 'John's still hungover. He's probably switched off.'

She spoke quickly. 'Ah. Look, I'm desperate here, we're going stir-crazy. You did say I should shout if I needed help?'

Mark frowned: it was inconvenient; he was busy. Also, he'd visited only three nights ago, staying for several hours, sharing the fix and making sure the pack was healthy and well cared for.

'I was there on Monday,' he pointed out. He listened to her breathing. He could almost see her expression.

After a while, she spoke again. 'Yeah, I know. It was good to see you. But we didn't go out of the house, did we? And you didn't come until after the kids were asleep. It's a fortnight since they saw any face but mine – it's not good for them, Mark.'

Andy was sprawled on a sofa next to him, idly picking at his bass. He raised an eyebrow. 'Diana?' he mouthed.

Mark nodded briefly and returned to the phone. 'Look, we're really busy here. I'm working on the drums for the album this afternoon, and John's meeting me later to tweak some lyrics.'

'OK, I understand that. But is there any reason why you and John can't tweak lyrics at my place?'

The Alpha shut his eyes tight. 'I'm sorry, Katie's throwing a dinner party tonight. John and I are going to work on the lyrics afterwards. We really can't come.'

'Oh.'

Andy saw Mark wincing, put the bass down and took the phone. 'Diana? Hiya, titch, it's me. Is everything OK?'

'Andy? Oh, no disasters. Just sick of the sight of these four walls. Nothing for you to worry about, really.'

'Shall I come round? I'm just excess baggage at the studio today. Besides, I'm sick of the sight of Mark's ugly face.' He neatly dodged a flying newspaper and laughed at Mark.

'What are you laughing at?' Diana sounded wistful.

'Mr Short, Dark and Grumpy is throwing things at me,' Andy explained. 'So, shall I come round now, or do you need an hour or three to prepare before I grace you with my gorgeous presence?'

He heard her laugh, low and wicked. 'Oh, don't worry about preparation time. By the time you arrive, I should be well stocked up with missiles. Make sure you're wearing a crash helmet or something.'

'If I thought you meant it…' he started.

'You'd be here in five minutes, I know. I'll see you soon then?' Her voice had lifted.

'Yeah, leaving now. Do you want to speak to Mark again? OK, I know, silly question. Here you go.'

He gave the phone back to Mark, who had cheered up when it became apparent that he was off the hook. Andy picked up his jacket and keys, and glanced back at Mark, who was still chatting. Andy rubbed at his chin, watching his friend smile and gesture as he spoke to Diana. Mark didn't seem to realise she made him happy, and Andy knew that pointing it out would be a bad move.

He let himself into the house quietly, wanting to sneak in. It was dark and cool; all the curtains were closed, making the house into a haven from the heat of late August. The hall was almost filled by a large pram. He sidled past, through the dining room and into the kitchen. The washing machine was on, as usual. The view to the garden was blocked by two washing lines strung across its width, bedding on one, clothes on another. He went out of the back door and ducked under the lines. He emerged on to the lawn, and stood, watching.

Diana had heard him and was already standing up, calling to Seth and Noah. Miranda had evidently been dozing under a tree, but the sudden movement woke her up. She rubbed her eyes grouchily.

Diana was already moving. 'Andy, you are an angel. I have to get out. I'll take the big boys out to the nature reserve for a ramble around. I'll be two hours, no more, I promise. Absolutely promise. They've all been fed. Make sure they drink lots of water … keep them in the shade, OK? Bye, sweetie.'

Before he could get his bearings, she had pulled on her shoes, grabbed a bag, stuffed her purse, keys and a wad of tissues into it, and was on her way out, closely followed by a pair of whooping three-year-old redheaded boys.

Andy listened to the sound of her car starting up and sat down on the grass. His glum expression attracted Miranda, who toddled over to him and made herself at home on his lap.

'Daddy sad?' she asked.

'No, honey, Daddy's just fine. Mummy just went a bit more quickly than I expected. How are you, baby?'

'Beautiful,' she said with a sunny smile. 'I've got sisters now. Come and see them.'

He looked around, checking for the youngest boys. Bill and Frank were in 'the cage'. They were equipped with squeezy bottles full of coloured water, a paddling pool full of sand, and some old yoghurt pots. Whatever they were doing involved long periods of quiet absorption, followed by equally long periods of excited flailing about and shouting. They were sensibly naked, and there was a bright blue potty inside the cage. Andy peered in and was pleased to see it was empty. Miranda led him to a carrycot next to the cage. It was covered with a net, and he gently lifted it away, picking Miranda up and letting her look at the babies. He hadn't seen his tiny daughters for two weeks and was surprised by how much they'd changed already. He considered, for a moment, lifting them out and holding them, but decided to let them sleep for a while. He had hours with them yet.

Miranda distracted him, playing with his shaggy blond hair. 'Brush Daddy's hair,' she said.

He took his place in the chair, and tolerated it until he realised they were being observed by the suddenly quiet twins in the cage. Francis and William were a year old already, and he barely knew them. He unfastened the cage and let them out, to their delight. They crawled quickly to the fence, and hauled themselves upright, pulling themselves along via bushes and fence posts, chasing each other around, shouting loudly.

A loud cry from the carrycot drew Miranda to it. She looked back to Andy, who at last felt that he could pick up and hold his new daughters again. They quieted in his arms, looking up at him with deep blue eyes.

When Diana returned, she found Miranda earnestly teaching the boys how to play with her building blocks, and Andy sprawled in the sun, stripped to his shorts. The babies lay on his shirt, sleeping in the shade of the now-dry washing.

Andy's eyes blinked open, and he stretched, catlike. She looked down at him. 'You look like you want to have your tummy tickled,' she said drily.

'Ah, well. We know where that would lead,' he flirted.

'Do we indeed?' She tried to sound stern, but couldn't keep the smile out of her eyes.

He realised that Seth and Noah were looking at them, and he sat up. 'Did you have a good time? Do you need some time to yourself? I can look after seven as easily as five.'

She nodded. 'Yeah, I used to think that, but I didn't factor in that they get older and more mobile. Thank you for the offer, anyway, but I spend enough time alone when they're in bed. As for our little trip, it was wonderful. They ran wild, met some ducks, and played with some other kids. It did them the world of good.'

'And you? Did you get to play with the other kids?'

She narrowed her eyes at him. 'Tease. Actually, I did speak to some nice people. Twins are a bit of an icebreaker, I must admit.' She flicked her hair back. 'Actually, I got chatted up by a bloke who noticed I wasn't wearing a wedding ring.' She smiled as Andy's eyes clouded over. He looked away, unwilling to admit to jealousy.

'And did you enjoy that?' he asked lightly, digging into the lawn, concentrating on removing a dandelion by its roots.

She didn't answer, and when he turned, she was gone. He stood and looked round, a little annoyed. Wherever she was, she'd taken the babies. He pulled on his trousers and made his way back into the house. He found her in the cool darkness of the living room, feeding Sara, her eyes closed.

He cleared his throat, and she smiled but didn't open her eyes.

'I can stay,' he offered. 'Hel's at a conference again. Nobody needs me...'

'Stay if you want to – this is your home too,' she replied, not taking the bait.

He looked at her, stumped both by her attitude, and by his reaction to it. For years, she had actively courted him – subtly, it was true – but *she* had been the seducer, the spoils of her victory lay in her arms. The conception of Sara and Darlene had been the final seal on the ties between the four pack adults. During her pregnancy she had been hungry for him, and he for her, but they'd barely seen each other since his daughters' arrival.

He felt vaguely irritated. He wanted to hold her, to breathe in the smell of her. He knew that it would ease the restlessness inside him. He glared at her, and she looked up, smiling knowingly. 'Feeling twitchy, are we?' she asked.

Andy shook his head, denying it, and she nodded understandingly.

'I wondered when it would kick in. You can't say you weren't warned, though. It's the addiction, isn't it? Don't worry, we all feel it.' She looked down, into the wide-open eyes of her daughter.

'So that's what it is … I expected something more painful,' he mused.

'Oh, trust me, it can get a lot more painful. Well, for Mark and me anyway. Maybe it will be less so for me and you. Do you regret it?'

'I don't like the lack of control,' he snapped.

'No, me neither, but that's what we have to live with. Here, hold Sara while I feed Darlene.'

He stepped up to her without thinking and took the baby from her. As he took a chair next to her, he fought down his annoyance at her air of authority. He continued to fight back. 'If you know I'm addicted to your … presence … does that mean you expect me to beg to stay here tonight?'

She looked up, hurt. 'Andy, how many times do I have to say it? This is your home, you don't need permission to come and go.'

'You know what I mean,' he growled, sulky.

'Ah, you want to fuck? Andy, this will only work if you make yourself clear. If you want me, say so!'

'You mean you *do* want me to beg?'

'No! Oh, for heaven's sake. We should have sorted this out years ago! Look, every time you've slept with me, over the last nine or ten months, I was the one to make the first move. Yes?'

'Of course.' He sat up stiffly.

'Well, all I'm saying is, I want you to acknowledge that this isn't one-sided, that you want me too. I don't want you to feel humiliated, but I am getting tired of always being the one to ask.'

'But I don't want you.'

'Andy, don't be so obstinate. You've made it abundantly clear over the last four years that "short, pale and ginger" doesn't do it for you. I understand – you're married, you love Helen. Hey, I get it! Now grow up and play nice. Here's the deal. We could make each other miserable until you give in, or you can put a smile on your face and treat me sweetly – like you did when I was pregnant. It wasn't so hard then, was it?'

'I was being chivalrous,' he muttered.

'So carry on being "chivalrous". I'm still who I was then.' She stood, and carried Darlene with her out of the room. She glanced over her shoulder. 'Bathtime for babies. Will you bring Sara?'

He nodded, sidetracked, and followed her up the stairs, carrying the sleepy baby carefully.

'Do you want me to bathe them?' he asked as she ran the bath.

'Oh, let's do it together, eh? Those five will be fine for a while. They can't get out of the garden, and if there's trouble, Seth will shout. Loudly.'

'You're doing a nice job of sidetracking, by the way. I'm still pissed off.'

'But horny,' she observed.

'I'm not your toy,' he sulked.

'Nor I yours. If you don't like it, walk away.' She had finished running the bath, and was bathing Sara.

Andy looked helplessly at her. 'How can I walk away? They're my girls. And Miranda … and the boys. You know I can't leave.'

'So what, exactly, is pissing you off? And can you answer that without getting angry at me?'

He counted to ten silently. 'It's not personal enough, it's animalistic. I resent that. You could be anybody. I could be anybody.'

'Sure, that's possible. But I actually like you – all three of you. I thought you liked me.'

'That's not the point. My body is telling me what to do.'

'It's forcing you into something you don't want?'

'Yes! No! I want it to be my idea.'

'And with Helen and Xan, when you first made love, was that a pure passion, a meeting of intellects? Or was it three horny teenagers doing what their bodies told them to do?'

'You're impossible! You know what it's like when you're a teenager … all those hormones.'

'No, actually, I don't. I wasn't interested in sex until I met Mark.' She spoke quietly.

'I forget that. I guess I see you as…' he trailed off, lost for the right words.

'The pack whore?' she said, suddenly bitter.

'Oh, no. I didn't mean… Oh shit, Diana, I didn't mean that.'

'Will you put your daughters to bed, please?' she said coldly, carefully placing Darlene next to her twin, and turning her back and walking downstairs. Andy took a step to follow her, but a loud, affronted shriek from Darlene stopped him. Diana didn't hesitate, just carried on down the stairs.

'OK, now I've really pissed your mother off. Let's call it a talent of mine and hope you haven't inherited it. Come on, babies, I guess you sleep in the big bedroom still?' He picked them up and carried them cautiously into what he thought of as Diana's bedroom. A double cot next to the bed confirmed his guess, and he put the babies carefully in the middle of the bed before searching for nappies and nightwear. He had them dressed and laid down quickly. Sara was still grumbling, but he rocked her for a while until she was sleeping. 'Ah, beautiful child, it's a pity you're ginger,' he told her, amused by the faces she pulled.

When they were asleep, he ventured downstairs again. The washing was folded or hanging next to the ironing board, and Diana was sitting in the garden, her back to the house. She had Seth and Noah cuddled up to her, and was reading to them. He stood at the back door.

'I'm staying tonight,' he said.

'Fine. Do what you want,' she called back.

'What's for tea?' he asked.

'Oh, for fuck's sake,' she said, turning round. 'Can't you see I'm busy?'

Miranda was quietly playing with bricks, and she looked up, upset by Diana's tone of voice. Diana breathed deeply. 'I'm sorry, Andy, are you hungry? Miranda, don't cry, mummy's just grumpy.'

Miranda had stood up and run to Andy, hugging his legs. 'Kiss Mummy better,' she said urgently.

Andy laughed nervously. 'I don't think she wants me to.'

'She's sad,' Miranda said. 'Daddies kiss her better.'

'Ah, is that what daddies do?' Andy laughed, in spite of himself, and hauled Miranda up into his arms. He carried her across to Diana.

'Look, I was just asking, that's all. I'll ring and get something delivered, OK? And I've got a nice crate of wine in my car – that was going to go home with me, but it's staying here, now. And…' he kneeled down. 'Will it help if I do kiss you?'

She turned her face away. 'Not really.'

'They were your words, Diana,' he pointed out. 'Not mine.'

'And yours would be?' she said quietly.

'I've never seen you as a blushing maiden, I suppose. You're just overwhelmingly … Diana … I suppose. How can I describe a phenomenon?' He gestured grandly, and she laughed, relaxing again.

'Flatterer.' She allowed herself to smile.

'I speak only the truth,' he intoned. 'Now, curry or pizza? Wine or beer?'

'Pizza, wine, music and time with the kids? William and Francis barely know you.'

'I've been trying to fix that this afternoon, you're right. And then, can I sleep with you? I need you – we can't deny that – but I really want to hold you too, put things right between us. Is that OK?'

'Yeah, I guess so.' She took a deep breath. 'Where are we going, Andy?'

'I really don't know, hon. Maybe we'll know when we get there?'

'Maybe. Your daughters are beautiful, you know?'

'So are yours,' he teased. 'Surprisingly.'

She smiled and stood up. 'So, the night starts with pizza, does it? You'd better get it ordered.'

He stood and went into the house, to the phone. He looked back. She had called for Seth and Noah to come back, and was reading to them again, pointing out before she started that the story was on the page, in the book, and that, if they learned to read, they could tell each other stories. Andy sighed; the babies were growing up.

Later, with the children in bed, they shared a bottle of wine. Andy stopped her hand when she reached for a second bottle. 'Don't get drunk, it's insulting,' he whispered.

'You still make me nervous,' she confessed.

'Yeah. Ditto. Twitchy, nervous, pissed off, helpless.' He drifted into silence, looking at the bottom of his empty glass, wondering if that second bottle might not be a good idea.

'Helpless! Don't start that again, please!'

'Sorry.' He watched her; she was rummaging in a bag by the side of her chair. She drew out knitting needles and yarn.

'What are you doing?' he said curiously

'D'oh!' she snapped.

'No, I'm serious,' he said.

'I'm making sweaters for Seth and Noah,' she said.

'It looks familiar,' he commented.

57

'Yeah, the yarn is from an old hand-knitted sweater Xan was always wearing around the house. I thought it would be nice to recycle it for the kids.' She looked at him, wary. 'Is that OK by you?' She looked at him carefully.

'My gran knitted that sweater, I remember now. She used to knit for all three of us.' Andy moved over to sit next to Diana, touching the unravelled ball of yarn. 'This is really weird, watching you use the same wool.'

'I didn't realise. I'll do something else if it bothers you?'

'No, it's good.' He pulled his feet up on to the sofa, curling up, watching her carefully. 'You don't have to, you know?'

'What?'

'You don't have to recycle old clothes. We're hardly short of money.'

'We don't need to listen to music or read books, for that matter. I like doing this. I like the idea of Xan's clothes being recycled for the kids. Your gran was a good knitter, by the way.' She spoke with an almost professional air, and he watched her for a while, reminiscing.

'I miss him,' he said quietly. 'I mean, we talk about him, Helen and I, but he fades, you know? It's been three years now.'

'Will you talk to me about him? I miss him too,' she said.

'Did he ever tell you about how the Ransomed Hearts got together?'

She looked up. 'No, he didn't.'

'Well, long, long ago, in a galaxy far, far away…' he started. She smiled and nodded to him to continue.

'Xan always, always, wanted to be the greatest drummer in the history of the world. He tried to get me to play guitar, and I got pretty good. We pissed around for a while at school, with other bands, guitarists, singers and stuff, but they were all, truly, crap. Xan was very demanding.'

'I can imagine,' Diana said, deadpan.

'Pay attention, wench, and stop interrupting. Well, we all left school, and went to the local sixth form. Me, Helen and Xan hit the ground running, so to speak. We were the in-crowd. There was an element of confusion among the masses as to our precise relationship with each other, and we enjoyed muddying the waters. We told everyone that we were "just friends". Of course, that left Xan and I without a leg to stand on when a certain cocky long-haired ape was noticed looking at Helen with interest.'

'John? John and Helen?' Diana dropped a stitch, and swore mildly as she picked it up again.

'Only in his dreams. She laughed him out of town. But it put him and his quiet little friend on our radar. Xan was particularly interested in them – they had their own self-contained little mystique going, and he was convinced that they were a couple, so to speak.'

Diana snorted with laughter, and looked up. Andy was enjoying the attention, and carried on.

'Yes, as I was saying, Xan took an interest in them. When he found out about the music, and the fact that they were trying to put a band together, he talked Helen into throwing a party and inviting them … and the rest is rock and roll history.'

'Tell me more,' she begged.

'There's always more,' he sighed. 'Well, Xan was intrigued by them. He was convinced they were gay, but they were absolutely oblivious to his attempts at flirtation. He caught them a couple of times, back home, naked in the woods or whatever.'

'Oh dear.'

'Yeah. For some reason Xan told me, but not Helen. It was around that time that the band became just as important to us as what we had with her. She had her own hobbies and interests, and took it pretty well. Actually, she seemed relieved to get some time to herself! Anyway, Xan told me about the naked thing, and I proceeded to tease John until he lost his temper and told me absolutely and categorically that he wasn't gay, and if I didn't shut up he'd kick me into the middle of the next century. So I let it drop.'

'For how long?'

'Not long, actually. We got a lot closer, writing the songs that would be the first album. We knew we were something special, and we got a few gigs. We finished our A levels, and much to our parents' disgust, we announced that we weren't going to waste our time going to uni – we were going to make music. And we did.'

'Yeah, I remember. I remember it all.' She looked at him fondly. Their music had been one of the highlights of her teenage years.

'Yes, well, there was recording, and rehearsals, and touring, and writing. We all got pretty close. And Xan stayed nosy. He just wouldn't let it drop. Eventually Mark and John got careless, and Xan saw them Change.'

'And how did he react to that?' Diana asked. It was something she'd never got around to asking Xan about.

'He never talked about that with me, but he asked if we could play too. He included me automatically. By that time, we were a close unit, and Mark and John eventually got talked into it. You know the rest – it worked for me, it didn't for Xan.' He took a deep breath. 'I hated it when you and Xan got so close. I didn't understand what the hell he was doing. It was like a betrayal of me and Helen.' He stopped, suddenly aware of the bitterness in his voice. He glanced guiltily at Diana, who had lowered her head, absorbed in her knitting. When she looked up at him, her face was composed, almost sympathetic. He managed a weak, apologetic smile, and held his arms out to her.

'He was just finding a home. You and Hel were settling down, and he felt like a fifth wheel. That was all.' She put her knitting down and moved closer to Andy. He stretched his legs out along the length of the sofa and nestled back into it, drawing her close, her hair in his face. He reached up and freed it from the schoolgirlish plait she was wearing, gently smoothing it out across her neck and shoulders, loving the bright fire of it.

She spooned up to him without urgency, and he knew she was content to be held, to enjoy his strength. His arms were around her waist, and he stroked her belly for a while, enjoying the slight convexity of it. For a second he thought of Helen, his love, his life, then banished the thought. Diana would always be part of his life now, and he found himself accepting the thought, finally associating her with happiness. As his hand drifted to her hip, gently pulling at the soft fabric of her skirt, he surrendered a part of himself to her. She must have sensed that sudden release of tension – he felt her purr with pleasure – and she pushed herself closer to him, signalling her desire. Her scent reached him: musky, strong, irresistible. He realised that she was learning to control it. Appreciated that she'd waited until she was sure he wanted her before allowing her own arousal to take control of them both.

Hours later, he stood, shakily, next to the sofa. She was asleep, her skin still flushed. He tried to remember what had happened, how she'd acquired the bloody scratches and bites on her hips and shoulders, the deep bruises on her backside. He shuddered and staggered to a mirror, seeing matching wounds on his own body. When he turned, she was watching him carefully.

'They'll heal quickly, don't worry,' she told him.

'It's never been like that before,' he whispered. 'What happened to us? It was … wild.'

'I know. Did you like it?' She joined him at the mirror, inspecting her own injuries almost with amusement. 'I think you bring out the beast in me,' she teased. 'That was new for me too.'

'Did I hurt you?' he said cautiously.

'Only when I asked you to. And vice versa, I think I remember. It's a side of you I never suspected.'

'Ditto.' He looked into the mirror, seeing two naked, bloody, long-haired creatures. 'That itch has gone,' he commented.

'Mine too.' She turned away, stretching and picking up her clothes. 'I'm going to bed. Do you still want to join me? Or do you want the sofa?' She glanced back.

'I want to sleep next to you, if that's OK?'

'More than OK. How do you feel now? About us?'

He considered the question. 'More relaxed, I think. When I looked in that mirror, we looked like we fit together, you know? I feel like a creep for having to hide this from Helen, but I guess I have to live with it. I look at you now, and you're a part of my life.'

'That's good enough,' she said, and led him upstairs, to sleep.

Chapter 7

John held Diana, who was sobbing. 'It's cruel.'

'I know.'

'I'm not crying for me, I'm crying for her. I wish she could've met her grandkids. This is horrible, horrible. I'd hoped so much that we could go public before she died.'

John held her close. 'Shh. I've known for weeks, we all have. We should have told you before now.'

'I know he doesn't love me, but I thought we were friends. You'd tell a friend, if your mum was dying. You would, wouldn't you?'

'He wanted to, but Katie was so distressed that he was worried about her pregnancy, and he's worried about yours too. He cares about you, I promise.'

Diana wiped her face and sniffed. 'I don't want to make it about me, but I'm hurt. I know I shouldn't be…'

'I wanted to tell you, and I was angry with Mark for asking me not to. You know, she's like a mum to me too.'

'I know love, I know. Is there anything I can do?'

'Hold me. Hold me enough for all of us,' John whispered.

Frances Preston died three days before her fifty-sixth birthday. The breast cancer that'd been defeated just a few years earlier had made a fast and furious return, stampeding through her body and burning through her resources. She'd stubbornly held on just long enough to hold Mark and Katie's baby boy, Jacob Preston, in her arms.

'Oh, he's just like you!' she whispered to Mark. 'Just like you were. Your father adored you, you know. I should have told you long ago. He loved you so much.'

That was all she gave to Mark at the end, and he held the words close, held Jacob close, and as he looked into his infant's eyes, he wondered again why his father had left.

Mark followed his mother's wishes and her body was buried in a churchyard in Ulverston. Even at the end, Frances had refused to tell him her maiden name. She still had a family to protect in Bardale.

A month later, Anthony picked up a British music magazine in a Danish supermarket. He read that Ransomed Hearts had postponed a TV appearance following the death of Frances Preston, who was Mark's mother and John's aunt. There was a brief mention of Mark's new son, but no mention of the child's name. Anthony took himself to his rented room and spent several hours considering his new status as a widower and grandfather. Before long he was packing his bags. He knew there were White Pack men stationed in Bremen; he'd left them alone for a long time, but he suddenly felt like reminding them of his existence.

Chapter 8

It was three in the morning, and John was perching on the lab stool in Diana's basement laboratory. She was doing something technical on the other side of the lab, and he was looking at the shelf full of ring binders.

'You have one for Xan,' he observed.

'Yeah, not much info. Just cross references to his DNA samples and Miranda's gestation and birth, and notes on my reaction to his absence. I thought I'd be thorough, I mean, I didn't expect a bond to form, as it had done with Mark, but I kept notes anyway – appetite, pain, stuff like that. Turned out it was grief. You know?'

'And what about me and Mark, and Andy? Did you keep records of your 'bonds' with us?' He spoke to the back of her head; she was absorbed in her work.

'Yeah, sure. Mark and Andy are fairly reliable data points – they usually only want to fuck when the addiction kicks in. You … well, have we ever gone long enough apart to get ill? You're a rubbish experimental subject.'

He could hear the laughter in her voice and smiled. 'Is it different? I mean, does it feel different?'

She sighed and finished what she was doing. She turned round. 'It's actually chemically different. I take samples, sometimes, after we fuck, or even after we kiss. There are molecular changes in us when we're apart. They build up over time, make us lose our appetites, feel low. They can even affect our normally brilliant immune systems if we're apart for long enough. When we're together again, when saliva or mucus or semen mix, there is a whole raft of response molecules that flood our bodies, wiping out what I've been calling the 'absence biochemistry'. I've had to up my biochemistry game, you know, to study all this. Anyway, most of these chemicals are formed whether it's you, or Mark, or Andy, but there's also – and this is really interesting – genetic markers that seem to activate when I take a new Shifter lover. I produce a specific addiction molecule for each one of you. Isn't that amazing? That's why I still get miserable and miss Mark and Andy even when you're around. It's not personal. And I guess it's why I feel like superwoman if you all visit within a couple of days.' She smiled. 'But get this, with one caveat, all three of you produce exactly the same addiction molecules in response to me. I wonder sometimes what would happen if another Shifter woman joined us.'

John raised his eyebrows. 'How would you feel about that?'

'Ask me when it's a possibility. I mean, there must be more of us out there.' She shrugged. 'But there's a very specific chemical that isn't even related to the three different addiction chemicals I have for you, Mark and Andy, and it's been there right from the start. It's specific to Mark and me. I've been calling it bonding molecule Alpha.'

'So, your bond with Mark... You think of that as the main one? The Alpha bond?' John was curious.

'It's not a matter of opinion,' Diana sighed. 'It's biochemistry.'

'So I'm your Beta bond? And I guess that makes Andy your Gamma.'

She giggled. 'If there are other Shifters out there, I'm going to have to learn that Greek alphabet, aren't I?'

'Gamma is all the Greek you'll ever need.' John laughed. 'Anyway, fancy a midnight snack?'

John must have mentioned that conversation to his bandmates, and gradually Diana noticed they were referring to each other's relationship to her as Alpha, Beta and Third. Andy had snorted at the term Gamma and said it made him sound like a side of bacon. Mark twitched away from the idea of the four of them being a family, he considered 'pack' a good enough term. With a common goal of raising the kids, they all grew closer, but always there was a distance between Mark and Diana: he would draw back from her frequently, unable to reconcile his love for Katie with his infidelity with Diana. Andy was less troubled; he'd decided to draw a line between his life with the pack and his life with Helen.

Chapter 9

Time passed. The folders took up two shelves now, and the lab was bigger, expanding in the basement of a new house. Diana had moved herself and the kids there, leaving the city behind and moving to a detached and secluded house on the northern outskirts of Bolton. It stood back from the road, comfortably hidden by high hedges that gave the family the privacy they needed. The house had been a comfortable size just seven years earlier, but was starting to feel cramped now.

Diana surveyed the folders that held the coded notes about herself, her children and their fathers, and started to take them down, one by one, to add her latest notes.

Seth and Noah, her firstborn sons. They were eight now, still skinny and redhaired, and the image of her own father when he was a child. Mark's genes came through only in their dark, dark eyes. Both boys were curious and intelligent, if somewhat intense. Noah was developing a sense of self-importance that his siblings tried to tease out of him. Seth was reliable and deeply sensible, and Diana struggled to not lean on him too heavily.

Miranda, the fatherless child, was two months away from her eighth birthday and had already outstripped her older brothers in height. Diana suspected her eldest daughter might be an actual genius, but her main concerns were Miranda's tendency to daydream and her susceptibility to any infection that might be around.

John's sons, William and Francis, were just a few months away from their seventh birthday. They were the image of their father and shared his ability to get along with pretty much anyone – the notable exception being Noah, who seemed to have a talent for winding them up.

The second pair of redheads, Darlene and Sarah, were dead ringers for Andy, other than their hair colour. Andy had started to call them 'the Kittens' when they were toddlers, and the name had stuck. They were sociable, charming and ambitious, and the only children in the family to object to Diana's home-schooling policy. It would be a while before they understood that large families and twins drew attention, and the longer Diana could put off the local schools noticing her family, the better.

The parents had thought, for a few months, that seven children were enough, but then Mark talked Diana into another pregnancy. Several months later, he'd blurted out that Katie was pregnant too, an admission that had led to a focussed cross-examination from Diana and the revelation that no, Katie hadn't wanted kids, but yes, Mark had wanted a child with his wife. Diana had not been happy, and things had been cold between the two Alphas until Beatrice and Bridget, usually known as 'the Bees' had been born, and their parents relented towards each other again. Katie's son, Jacob, was represented by a file on the shelf with his name on it, but, apart from his date of birth and parentage, it was empty. Another pregnancy soon followed, the first of the new century, and in the spring of 2000, Mark's sons Caleb and Samuel arrived. Unaware of her husband's other family, Helen Ransome gave birth to a longed for first child, Eva, three years later.

Diana was anxious about yet another vulnerable half-blood child with a mother who could not know about the dangers, but Andy was unrepentant; he adored his Eva. Scant months later, Diana and Mark had two more daughters, Jane and Alice, after the longest gap so far between pregnancies. With thirteen pack children and two others outside the pack, they were kept busy, fondly thinking their biggest problem was the outside world gossiping about Diana's large and twin-heavy family. But the outside world had other surprises for them.

Chapter 10

What's the best thing that could happen at this point? Joyce wondered. She was tired of everything in her life; she felt jaded and vaguely dirtied by her time in LA, and still stressed from the last hit – it was time to relax. She left her Paris apartment and took the train out to the suburbs, treating herself to a huge meal before making for the woods, carrying a rucksack and a shotgun for camouflage. Once in the shelter of the trees, she shoved the gun into the rucksack, undressed and packed her clothes, and Changed. Clumsily arranging the rucksack around her neck, she broke into a trot, feeling more relaxed with every moment as she made her way to sanctuary and peace.

The cottage was self-sufficient but by no means primitive; the door was operated by a keypad, but she had to Change back to operate it. For some reason, number skills seemed to fall away when she was a wolf. She shook her hair back and shoved the door open, hauling the rucksack behind her. So close to a Change, her senses were heightened, and she stopped dead on the doorstep, hearing quiet breathing in the next room, noticing a strange smell. She challenged the intruder.

'I know there's someone here. What I want to know is, who and why?'

She waited, poised and motionless, hearing a chair scrape against the floor in the small living room – it sounded deliberately loud, as if the intruder wanted to make it quite clear what he was doing.

'I'm coming out with my hands up. Stay calm, I'm not here to hurt you.' The voice was deep, musical, confident.

'You'd be surprised if you tried,' she muttered.

The stranger was standing in the doorway between the kitchen and the living room, his hands were in the air, but it was clear from his stance that this was his idea, not something he'd been forced into. He looked to be in his late forties, about five six, glossy black hair reluctantly fading to grey, muscles still well defined under his thin woollen jersey. He didn't bat an eyelid at Joyce's nakedness.

'Why are you here?' she demanded.

'To talk to you. If I'd wanted to rob you, I would have brought transport.'

That was a good point; there were no vehicle tracks near the house.

'How did you get here?'

'The same way that you did. I walked. Well, you probably ran, but I prefer to walk whenever I get chance these days. It's less tiring on the old legs.'

Joyce cursed liberally. She had been careless, not checked around the house for footprints or strange scents before going in.

'Don't beat yourself up. I've been here for days. The rain would have washed away all signs of my arrival. By the way, you're out of whisky.' The man's smile was becoming more confident.

'Who are you?'

'I'm someone who wants to be your friend. If you let me. I know stuff that you really do need to know.'

'What sort of stuff?'

'Wolf-related stuff.'

She nodded, and dropped the rucksack to the floor, closing and locking the door behind her. 'You're a Shapeshifter?' she demanded.

'Since I was so high.' He grinned, indicating a height barely three inches shorter than his actual height.

She smiled involuntarily, then winked at him and Changed again. Normally she avoided such rapid Changes, but she knew she had lots of food in the cottage, and could replenish her energy easily. She growled low as she approached the man, warning him not to move, not to Change. He understood, and stayed quiet and still as she sniffed him cautiously, checking for the smell of ammunition, drugs, anything that could possibly be a danger to her. Finding him harmless, at least physically, she walked past him and checked out the cottage. The smell of him was overpowering in this form, but not distracting enough to stop her finding anything new or different. Once in her bedroom, she Changed back and dressed in a simple black skirt and top. Barefoot, she descended to the living room, and poured two glasses of brandy.

'You can relax, I've decided to listen. Have a drink,' she offered, settling into a battered armchair and resting her legs on a cracked and ancient leather footstool.

He looked around theatrically. After several days in the cottage, he was well aware that there only one chair in the room. Joyce wasn't big on the idea of visitors, and hadn't seen the point of over furnishing the room.

'There's another chair in the kitchen, as you well know,' she pointed out. He shrugged and went to bring it in. It was heavy, but he seemed to carry it with ease. 'Do feel free to start,' she invited.

He paused for a while, looking at her long and hard. 'You're only the second female werewolf I've seen since I was a child.'

'And you're the first male I've ever seen. If you are one.'

In reply he blinked at her, his eyes changing from a deep gentle brown to feral yellow, then back again. He extended a hand to her, and she watched wide-eyed as it Changed to a grizzled black paw.

'Lesson one. You don't have to go all the way.' He smiled.

'That doesn't prove to me that you *can* go all the way,' she challenged.

He looked taken aback. 'That was supposed to be an impressive display of skill and control!' he said.

She shrugged. 'Maybe I'm not easily impressed. Show me the whole thing.'

'Fuck. Bloody women, you spend sixty years looking for 'em, then wish you hadn't bothered.'

He undressed, carefully folding his clothes and laying them out on the chair. She liked him for that. Then he Changed, padding over to her, resting his chin on her lap and inviting her to scratch between his ears. She obliged, suddenly overcome with emotion. She was shaking.

He Changed back and dressed. 'I know, I know. It's weird. Thank you, by the way, it's many years since someone scratched me there.'

'Who are you? How did you find me? What do you want?' she managed to say. She shook her head and poured more drinks.

'Thanks…' He clinked glasses with her in a toast. 'My name is Anthony. I've had surnames, but Anthony serves well enough. I found you the hard way – it's taken years. I knew you were out there, and it's been my purpose to find you. But it's not been easy, because I had to find you without alerting the Whites that I was still alive, that I was looking for you, and that there was a "you" to find. And, as I said before, I want to teach you what you need to know to survive.'

'I'm doing a pretty good job,' she retorted.

'Due to your luck, your natural secrecy and the fortunate familial trait of stupidity in the White Pack members.'

'Whites?' she queried.

'Look, Joyce, how many of our kind do you think there are?'

She blinked, unwilling to give away too much information.

He nodded. 'Good girl. Well, whatever you're thinking, you are wrong, very wrong. I'm the first male you've met, but there are hundreds of the bastards in Europe, possibly other packs globally that I've not heard of.'

'Females?' she queried.

'They're all with the same pack. All that I know of, anyway. Inbred, not throwbacks like you. The White Pack Alpha – that's what they call their leader these days – he controls population growth, interaction with the human world. Ha! Interaction, they're not big on that.' He reached for the brandy bottle, then checked himself and turned on a charming smile.

'I'm far too relaxed,' he commented.

'So who are the Whites, and why don't I know about them?'

'Secrets and lies, fair maiden. They're the majority of the werewolf world, run by the pack Alpha and his top lieutenants, all male, of course. They believe they have the right to control all aspects of Shapeshifting. They've been hiding themselves away from the world for centuries, coming out of cover now and again to purge the world of "rebels and collaborators". That's you and me, in case you hadn't realised.'

'Why?'

'The oldest reason in the book … religion.'

'These creeps are Christians?'

'Hell no!' That smile again, then his voice dropped an octave, and he intoned, 'In the beginning, thrice a thousand years ago, the gods came to us, and gave us the gift of Changing. They charged us to keep the secret safe, to stay pure in body and soul, and to wait for the time to be right.'

'Pure in body and soul?' she laughed.

'Yeah, means that we've to keep ourselves to ourselves, and not get involved emotionally or sexually with any of those normals. Of course, not everyone thinks like that, which is why there are people like you around, born of parents who look and seem totally normal, but are half werewolf. Not a lot though, most of them are pretty infertile, and usually only have one child.'

Joyce managed to keep her face straight. This guy seemed OK, but he didn't really need to know about her sister.

'I've met other women though. Why haven't you spoken to them?'

'Trisha Harrison?' he asked.

Joyce was taken aback, and nodded silently.

'Born 1963, brought up in Cornwall, by all accounts. Journalist by trade, and not as good as you at keeping secrets. She died eighteen months ago, car bomb attack on a diplomat she was interviewing … at least, that's what was assumed. Trisha was the target.'

Joyce winced. It had been a while since she'd heard anything of Trisha, but this was brutal. 'Any others?' she asked.

Anthony raised an eyebrow. 'You tell me.'

She shook her head. 'No, not yet. I need to get to know you a lot better.'

She was flirting. The guy might be older, but he was the most attractive man she'd met in a long time.

'No. We don't do that,' he said, avoiding her eyes.

Joyce was hurt. Rejection had always come hard to her. She was rarely attracted to any man, so rejection from someone she might actually want was doubly hard. She looked down, biting her lip, trying to push down the fury. This man had come to her home, broken her barriers so easily, and now…

'Joyce, let me explain, please. Whatever we are, we've had a cruel trick played on us. You've never known a true pack, obviously. We call the first male and female in a pack "Alphas" – they rule a pack, sexually, politically and psychologically. They have a bond between them, keeping them together. It's not necessarily love, it's an addiction to each other. The bond forms automatically whenever two Shapeshifters mate, although I've heard rumours that powerful Alphas nearby can prevent it. Once it's there, there is no going back, so if you want to be an Alpha, you choose your first mate very, very carefully, because there's no going back on that decision.'

'Shit. Thanks for telling me,' Joyce whispered. 'I've been studying myths and legends about us all my adult life. Why has that one slipped by me?'

'Possibly because it doesn't involve biting innocent virgins, or bathing in the blood of babies?' Anthony shared a small smile. 'My brother and I were the children of the only non-White pack I knew of. We looked, we searched, but we couldn't find mates. We found a compromise. We looked for women who carried the trait, who might be able to give us Shapeshifter children – even one child would be a blessing in an empty world. We moved to England, following rumours and legends from my great-grandmother's side of the family, and traced family trees until we found a village with several possible carriers. But not a Shapeshifter in sight, unless they were too young to Change. We were lucky, we found we could love the women we chose. It was hard, knowing that they were so vulnerable, that the very trait we needed from them would cause their early deaths, frailty in old age …. but we did, truly, love our wives. But they weren't Shapeshifters, the Alpha thing never happened.'

'So you've never fucked another Shapeshifter?'

'No, and neither have you, unless you've got a pack hidden away somewhere.'

Joyce nodded. 'Is there any way…'

Anthony sat back, affecting amusement, but interested. 'Any way?'

'Any way we can still fuck but avoid this addiction?'

'No. The Alpha bond is permanent. Separate an Alpha pair and they die. The bonds between other adult pack members isn't always fatal when broken, but it's still an addiction. Even if we were lucky enough to find a friendly pack who'd take us in, we'd be stuck with each other, and with them. We'd still be bound, I promise you that, just not to the same extent as the Alphas. Shapeshifters don't leave each other. Realistically though, the only existing pack is the White Pack, and they want to kill us. Look at us … we've got trouble written through us like Blackpool through rock.'

She looked up. 'Your accent is French, but your English is excellent. And "Blackpool through rock"? Have you been to Blackpool?'

'A few times, with my wife, when we were young.' He looked at her eyes; they were somehow familiar. He felt memory nudging at him, something interesting his mind wanted to tell him. He let it go; there were more important things to discuss. He needed her help.

Chapter 11

Standing at Euston Station, waiting for the time and platform of departure to appear for the next train to Manchester Piccadilly, Joyce hid her impatience well. She was appearing on a TV show about Brits in Hollywood, and had arranged a short tour of British local radio stations to promote the show and her latest book. It was excellent cover for a trip to the North West, her first visit in years.

She was travelling light, and had left France with the minimum of fuss. Although Anthony had reassured her that she was unknown to the White Pack, she felt safer leaving the country with a bare minimum of luggage, indicating a short trip to Britain rather than her intention of returning for good. If Mark or John were true Shapeshifters, she had a duty to tell them their history, and to make sure they knew of the danger they were oblivious to. She would have to track down Diana too; there had been no word from her for years, other than the routine 'still alive' codes on the Usenet boards they both followed.

She was still thinking about her redhaired sister when the movement of the boards above her caught her attention, and she made her way to Platform 3, finding her seat. The journey north gave her a feeling of lost familiarity: a journey taken so many times in the past, clouded by the years and interspersed with lightning flashes of memory. Fields just waking up from winter, signs of spring receding visibly as the train moved further north, tugged at her memory and heart. She was going home.

The train drew in at last to Piccadilly, and she closed her eyes and rested for a while as the carriage cleared. Collecting her overnight bag, she stepped off the train and walked along the platform. Piccadilly had changed beyond recognition: it was a modern, busy and clean station, transformed by shops and fast-food outlets. As she stood on the concourse, trying to match memory with the new reality, a young man stepped forward, politely introducing himself as a representative from the radio station and offering to drive her to the studio. He was charming, attractive and very informative about local celebrities. Without even mentioning the Ransomed Hearts, Joyce learned that John Preston had a flat in Manchester. It was a start. Before her guide could leave, Joyce laid a hand gently on his arm, and asked if he knew of any good restaurants in the area. She could see in his eyes that he was mentally clearing his diary, and she allowed a small smile to reach her eyes for the first time since she'd met him.

'Nothing too fancy, just a nice comfortable place to enjoy a good meal, perhaps enjoy some intelligent Northern conversation?' She allowed a trace of her parents' Geordie accent to filter through, and the charming young man found himself charmed.

He suggested he drive her to her hotel and wait for her to change, but she wouldn't hear of it, insisting he meet her at the restaurant at 8 pm. He left to make a reservation, making a mental note to speak to the station's researcher. He'd been expecting a forty-something academic, not a thirty-something confident woman who was obviously not ready to spend the evening watching telly and eating room-service pizza in her hotel.

When he met her in the lobby, he was relieved that he'd judged her mood correctly. She was wearing dark jeans and a crisp white top, with a jacket slung over her shoulder in preparation for the cold spring night. Her black hair was loose, and reflected the glow of the soft lighting. She turned and grinned at him, totally disarming him.

'So, Ross, is this a regular chore for you? Taking talk-show guests out to dinner?'

'It's not a chore, not this time anyway. Believe me, there's nothing I would rather be doing.'

'Really? I thought young men your age like to spend all night chatting on internet forums or doing that multiplayer game thing?'

'LOL!' he said, and she laughed.

'I believe that ROFL is the correct reply?' she said.

They made easy small talk as they walked the mile to the restaurant, both enjoying the crisp air. She answered a couple of questions about the films she'd been involved in, before turning the conversation back to Ross.

'I guess you must meet lots of celebrities?'

'Oh, not really, this is Manchester, not London. There are only so many local celebrities, and they're spread pretty thin. Most of them move away.'

'No scandals to report then? No juicy gossip?'

'You're kidding? The ones that stay in Manchester are here because they like their families. They're the ones least likely to be the cause of gossip. Of course, there are the footballers, but they have very little imagination, and their managers tend to rein them in these days.'

'So you don't know of any parties we could go on to later?'

He stopped short; they had reached the restaurant, and she was watching him, amused, waiting for his reply.

'Well, I have an ex-girlfriend, Marilyn. She had invited me to a party tonight, but I was going to give it a miss. I thought you might…'

Her cool stare silenced him.

'I'm sorry, I thought you might like to take your time over dinner,' he finished politely.

'A meal and a party sound like just the thing. I might be staying in the North West for a few weeks, and it would be good to meet some people.'

Ross nodded, and wondered how Marilyn would react when he turned up at her party with Joyce. Strictly speaking, she *was* his ex-girlfriend, but it had only been a matter of days, and he wasn't sure her invitation had included a guest.

They arrived at Marilyn's flat at close to midnight. Their hostess was mollified when Ross explained who Joyce was, and Joyce was amused to see her pointedly turn her back on the young man while asking Joyce about her work, who she'd met and what films she'd worked on. Joyce subtly scanned the room, but saw no familiar faces. Marilyn was still talking.

'Of course, men have no tact. It's amazing how many of my exes have turned up at my parties with new girlfriends.'

Joyce shook her head. 'You think Ross is my boyfriend?'

Marilyn blushed. 'God no! Oh, I'm so rude. I was speaking in general. I suppose I'm hoping to get back with Ross really – he's one of the nice ones, and there are damned few of them.'

'So tell him.'

'Yeah, I suppose I should, before he turns up one day with a little wifey.'

Joyce was getting bored. Jealous women bored her. Marilyn was getting very tipsy.

'Bloody John Preston, anyway. I should tell him to fuck off next time he wants company. He's fooling nobody. I know he's got a wife and kids hidden away, even if he tries to keep it secret.'

Joyce almost jumped at the mention of John's name. 'Is he a footballer? Or an actor?'

'Oh, I thought you'd have heard of him. He's a singer, pop star … whoops, I mean *rock* star.' She tried to drip venom, but was too drunk and succeeded only in dribbling a little red wine. 'We dated for a couple of months, then he dropped me. Then a few years later he got around to me again. He acts like we're good mates, but he doesn't give a shit about me really. Bastard.'

'Well, if he's married…' drawled Joyce, as if she wasn't really interested.

Marilyn was in full flow. 'Oh, I met her. He never said he was married, but she had that look about her, as if she was sure he was hers. He brought her to a few parties. She was always bloody pregnant – it was so funny. Eventually she got the message that she wasn't wanted and stopped coming. He's still with her. I know that because every time I mention her he gets very defensive … won't hear a word said against her.'

Joyce nodded. 'It must be very hard for you if you're still attracted to him. Perhaps he wanted someone who was less of a challenge to him, intellectually?

Sometimes that's all a man wants, someone who will keep quiet and have babies and look pretty.'

'Pretty! Well, if you call short, pale and ginger pretty, I suppose she was. But she had brains coming out of her bloody ears. I talked to her once, she said she did research. I thought she meant TV research at first, but I think she was sciencey, you know? She had that look about her.'

Joyce nodded. 'Yeah, I know. Ah well, there's no accounting for a man's taste. So he's still with this … did you say her name was Gina?'

'No, I said she was ginger. It's noisy in here, isn't it? I think her name was Dot or Debs or something with a D. Anyway, there are some new arrivals. I'll introduce you to them.'

Joyce fixed her party face on and went to mingle.

Joyce had finally got the hotel room she wanted; it overlooked the lobby of the block of flats where John lived. She'd pulled a chair over to the window, and was sitting with a book, patiently watching the door. Some days John didn't leave the flat at all. On the few occasions he had left, it had been on foot, to go to the mini-market or takeaway. She'd followed him on foot to a pub a couple of nights earlier, but decided against following him in. It was clear there wasn't a werewolf pack living in those flats; nobody had mentioned that John had a woman or kids living with him, and the main priority now was to find out where John had hidden this supposed family of his. She was almost sure the 'little wifey' was her own sister. She'd checked out the old terraced house she'd lived in, so long ago, and found it occupied by a bunch of students. Diana was long gone.

Early one morning she heard a car and looked out of the window. The driver slipped out, and Joyce took half a step back, recognising Mark from the video Anthony had shown her. He was of medium height, with long straight dark hair and a pale complexion. He looked as if he needed a good meal or ten. The second man hauled himself out of the passenger seat; it was the band's bass player, Andy Ransome. Six feet of athletic good looks, his blond hair was cut just long enough to give him an angelic appearance. He leaned on the car roof, lazily looking across at the lobby. Mark shut the car door carefully and scanned the area; his gaze moved upwards, and Joyce stepped back fully into the darkness of the room, grateful that she hadn't switched the light on. She ran down to the car park.

The hire car was small and nondescript, and she pulled in around the corner, turning the lights off and watching Mark's reflection in the window of the hotel restaurant. He was pacing impatiently now, speaking into a phone. Andy was sprawled back against the car, ankles crossed casually, staring around the street. His legs seemed to go on forever, and Joyce had to drag her attention from him to monitor Mark. She could see Anthony in him, that same focussed intensity.

At last the lobby door opened, and John strode over to his friends, giving each of them a bear hug before throwing an overnight bag into the back seat and following it in. He sat there for a few seconds, before sticking his head out of the window and looking enquiringly at Mark. Mark raised his head to look despairingly at Andy, who laughed and opened the passenger door, folding himself into the car in a way Joyce found mesmerising. Mark took one last look around the street, then got into the car and drove off. Joyce moved off after them.

The city was just waking up, cleaners were busy cleaning shop doorways and windows, delivery vans were moving around, and there was just enough cover for her to stay back and keep the men in her sight.

Within fifteen minutes they were on the motorway, and she cursed as Mark stepped on the pedal, cruising up to eighty and staying steadily there. Her little car wasn't happy at this sort of pace, and she was well aware that the last thing she needed was to be pulled over for speeding. She knew how to tail someone, and kept as far back as she could without losing sight of her target.

After fifteen miles or so, she began to feel anxious, and paid attention to what her subconscious was trying to tell her. While she'd been following the three men, someone had been following her. A white van, about four years old, visible as it overtook the car behind her and slotted neatly into the gap. There was a driver and a passenger. She slowed down a little, and registered that the occupants were male and blond. She sighed, put her foot down and overtook her target, coming off at the next exit and stopping at a nearby retail estate. She shopped in four different stores, and hoped she was boring her pursuers. Anthony's enemies may have eyes on her, but she wasn't going to lead them to his son.

She wondered how long they'd been tracking her and why they hadn't attacked yet. Maybe they needed proof of her abilities; Anthony had made it clear that killing normals was bad form. If the White Pack had followed her, then they knew where she was staying. It was time to move away from John.

The following day she returned the hire car, packed her bag, and went for a wander around Manchester. She was definitely being tailed, and if she could see one blond Shifter, there would be others nearby. A crowded pub gave her a chance to lose the tail, and three random bus journeys brought her to a small town just outside Chester. She booked into a bed and breakfast under a false name, and decided it was high time she warned her sister about the White Pack situation.

The room had Wi-Fi, which was surprising but welcome, and Joyce logged into one of her Usenet accounts and brought up a Barbie message board. There was a short thread, buried several weeks deep, which she brought up. She replied to a message from Pity In Pink:

> *Yes, Barbed Grrl agreed with her — if she agreed with her once, she agreed with her eight times. Wasn't there a post from last June along similar lines?'*

Joyce logged out, grateful for the codes they'd agreed on years ago. Diana would get the message.

Two days later, Diana checked her Usenet groups. Messages were rare between her and her sister,- the lines of 'still alive?' and 'yes'. This one worried her. The choice of the Barbie group meant that Joyce was deadly serious, and something dangerous was happening. Could Diana meet at the agreed June-coded location at 8 pm one evening next week? Sunday was the probably the best evening to rely on one of the guys to look after the kids. Diana replied:

> *Pity In Pink thought that there were at least seven posts on the subject.*

The reply came back fast:

> *Pity In Pink, you're always right.*

It was confirmed.

'So, where are you going again?' Andy was aiming for casual, but not quite hitting it.

'I've told you, just meeting an old friend. All I need from you is for you to watch the kids for a few hours. I'll be back before dawn. You and John will be fine.' Diana frowned and raised her voice. 'Seth, Noah, please go back into the kitchen. I don't like being spied on.' She waited until her eldest children had disappeared, then sighed. 'Just because I never go out doesn't mean that I never will go out. This is fine.'

'I'm going with you,' John said.

'No.' Diana sighed. 'Please, this is just a quick meetup with an old friend. There's no need for drama.'

John leaned against the wall and folded his arms. 'You're wearing that quick-release dress, slip-on shoes and no underwear. You're planning a Change. Who is this friend?'

'I told you, an old friend, and if you ever need more information than that, I'll give it to you. I promise. You two are going to have a nice quiet evening – they're all toilet-trained now, except the babies, they're all in bed, except Seth and Noah, and all you need to do is stay sober and keep the noise down. Right, I'm off.'

'Diana … I don't like this,' Andy said, his voice low and firm.

'I appreciate that, but I'm still going.'

John shrugged. 'Fine, have fun. We'll be here when you get back.'

Diana left, and as the dull sound of her car crunching down the gravel driveway reached the men, Andy shrugged. 'You or me?'

'You. I'm on the motorbike – she'll spot me. Stay well back. Don't interrupt.'

'What if it's some guy?'

'We don't own her. Just keep an eye on her.'

Andy picked up his car keys and left the house. His Saab was on the drive, a back door still slightly ajar from when the older kids had helped him take out some shopping. He slammed it shut and set off.

The house was on a road that ended in a dirt track a quarter of a mile to the right. He turned left and sped up until he recognised Diana's tail lights ahead of him. He felt a tingle of excitement – this was something new, and he really wanted to know what she was up to. He reached into the glove box for his mobile phone and swore again as he remembered leaving it on the dining table. Too late to go back for it. He relaxed; Diana had a right to a night out, but this felt weird, and as the miles rolled by, he felt increasingly uneasy.

Diana noted a muddy white van parked half a mile before the end of the track to the marsh. She was tempted to stop, to have a sniff around, to see if the years had brought any changes to Joyce, but she was already running slightly late and it would be poor manners to turn up in wolf form. She turned the engine off and let her car roll to the end of the lane. She took a deep breath and stepped out across the narrow strip of field. She knew the rendezvous – the sisters had been here before. A low hedge separated the field from the marshes beyond. It was a lonely spot, the kind of place that had always appealed to both Diana and Joyce. Diana smiled with anticipation, it had been a long time, and although they'd parted on bad terms, she was starting to realise how much she'd missed her sister.

The old gap in the hedge was still there, and Diana pushed through it, pausing on the other side, looking for Joyce. Would she be wolf or woman?

Diana wrinkled her nose at the sudden smell of blood, and stood quietly, wondering what Joyce had done. She scanned the ground, her attention caught by a patch of white that glistened in the darkness a few metres away. There was something else, black and wet, not far from the white. Further on, another white patch. She fought against the sudden tightness in her chest, and crept forwards. The white patches resolved into wolves: one dead, one dying. They were white-furred, stained with blood and thick river mud. The black shape… Ah, the shape was another wolf. She kneeled and looked closer. Joyce. It was Joyce, and she was dead, dead beyond all hope, all reason. So many wounds, so many terrible tears and bloody holes where flesh should be. Diana struggled to understand, and moved closer to the dying white wolf. A male, was this Joyce's mate? Were these white wolves Joyce's pack, the reason for the meeting? The wolf bared his teeth, and Diana took a step back. She heard a sound and spun round. Two blond men, one of them bleeding heavily from a shoulder wound, were between her and the hedge. She froze, focussing on movement in the field behind them, someone running towards her. Someone small, who squeezed through the gap and stood still, looking at the scene. Someone with red hair, someone wearing green pyjamas. She watched, frozen, as Seth took in the scene: three dead or dying wolves, two strange men and his mother. He looked directly at the dying wolf and called out. 'Mummy, who is that?'

It was the 'who' that damned them all. She knew that instantly, and started to run towards Seth, but the uninjured blond was closer and had already started to move. Instinct kicked in, and the Change took Diana. She moved like a bullet between her child and the stranger, knocking Seth to the ground beneath the hedge, recovering to spin around in front of him, snarling as the two men burst out of their clothing and embraced their own Change.

One was limping still, but the other was big and strong and heading straight for Diana. She snarled her defiance and took position in front of her child. A righteous fury descended on her; these men had killed her sister. These men had turned up, four of them, to kill her beautiful, vicious, crazy sister, and they'd done it; they'd taken Joyce's life and it had cost them two of their own, because Joyce hadn't left much to stitch together of that dying white wolf out on the mud.

They were bigger and stronger than Diana, and Diana had never hurt anyone in her life, but her child was behind her and … there came a low snarling cough, repeated louder. The white wolves paused, sniffing the air, then backing away as a creature flew over the hedge and landed on the injured one, biting deep into the already torn shoulder and half ripping the leg from the body. The wolf screamed and died as the tiger tore out his throat. The last white wolf snarled and took advantage of the distraction, leaping at Diana with death in his eyes. She screamed in fury and stood her ground, protecting Seth, taking long, deep scratches along her flank as she used all her strength to turn her enemy away, to hold him away from the still, silent child until the tiger moved in, casually batting the white wolf's hind leg, scoring it with bloody runnels in the flesh. The white wolf didn't pause, launching forwards again at Diana, only to find himself caught, his haunch fast within the tiger's jaw. He screamed as the tiger bit down, and Diana flew forwards, finding the throat by pure instinct and tearing with her own strong jaws until hot blood flowed. Red fury took over, and she tore at her enemy until she heard her name spoken, again and again. 'Diana. Diana. Di love, it's done.'

She Changed, and retrieved her dress and sandals. The shoes were a write-off. The dress would need a new zip but the belt was intact, and she pulled the dress on and belted it tightly. She picked Seth up and held him close. He wasn't moving.

'What the fuck was that?' Andy whispered.

'I don't know … I don't know. Seth…?' She laid her child back on the ground and pushed his hair back, repeating his name. Andy kneeled beside her and took the boy's wrist, then leaned closer.

He straightened up. 'He's alive, probably in shock. Let's get him home, and hope he didn't see any of that.'

Diana nodded, wretched. She glanced behind her. 'We can't leave things like this,' she whispered.

'You get Seth home. I'll deal with this.'

'The black wolf, she's my sister. Be kind, if you can.' Diana closed her eyes. 'Her name is Joyce.'

Back home, John opened the door as soon as he heard the gates open. He stood in the porch, Noah a pale figure behind him in the doorway.

Diana dragged herself out of her car, swaying, bloody and exhausted. She opened the back door and was lifting Seth off the back seat when John gently moved her aside and took the boy in his arms. He bent his face to the boy's, and looked at Diana. 'What happened?'

Diana shook her head.

'Where's Andy?' John asked.

'He's OK, he's fine. Get Seth inside, please.' She summoned strength from somewhere. 'Noah, it's OK, go to bed. Your twin is just very tired. We'll bring him up to you soon.'

'Why are you bleeding?' Noah asked.

'I fell, we both fell. Go to bed.'

Noah glanced at John who dragged a reassuring smile from somewhere. 'Do as your mother says. And not a word to the other kids — we don't want them coming downstairs at this time of night. Be a good boy.'

John laid Seth on the sofa. 'He's alive, he's breathing OK. He has a strong pulse, but he's out for the count. How long has he been like this?'

'Getting on for an hour. I drove as fast as I could…' Diana burst into tears. 'What do we do?'

'Hospital?' John asked.

She shook her head. 'They'll do tests, I can't risk it. We can't risk it. Do we know anyone who can help?'

John squeezed Seth's hand. 'Katie. She'll come if Mark asks her to. We'll tell her that you're my girlfriend, and you've been in an accident. You're religious, won't go to hospital. She won't like it, but she'll do it for Mark.' He looked at the pale, skinny, redhaired child on the sofa. 'She won't believe he's mine, but he doesn't look that much like Mark either. I'll ring them now.'

Andy glanced at the tattered remains of his clothes and sighed. He kept a spare pair of jeans, a pair of cheap trainers and a T-shirt in his car, but there was bloody work to do before he dared to get dressed again. The moon gave enough light to work by, but the tide was trickling in; he could hear it running through the mud channels, rising by the minute. He retrieved a picnic blanket and some bungee cords from the boot of his car, and dragged the body of the black wolf to drier ground, where he wrapped it securely and carried it to his boot. 'Her sister,' he muttered. 'She never once mentioned a sister.' He shook his head and looked back along the lane, noting the white van. He let the Change take him again, this time choosing his wolf form, and sniffed around the van. Just four scents, similar to each other. No sign of a female wolf or a woman. Joyce hadn't been near this van; it had arrived after she had, or from a different direction. He sniffed around, widening the circle. No sign of anyone else. Just the four blonds then.

He took human form, his fourth Change of the night, and opened the van, noting the evidence that the men had been sleeping there. A large leather holdall held guns, ammo and some vicious-looking knives. Andy sighed and took a long, thin knife and a meat cleaver, and headed back down to the mud flats.

Water was lapping around the body of the furthest white wolf, and Andy butchered it there and then, removing skin from flesh and flesh from bones. The water took the fragments, and Andy thought about fish and crabs and gulls, and hoped that they would do their work quickly. The second wolf was now respectably dead, and was soon reduced to scavenger food. Andy was tiring now, and the tide was rising fast. He needed to do his bloody work below the tideline, but time was running out. He worked faster, and by the end of it he was standing in waist-deep water, the mud sucking at his legs. He waded back towards land with real difficulty, falling more than once, exhausted.

He made his way back to his car, and stared at the van behind it, at his tyre tracks, and Diana's. Almost too tired to think, he leaned for a moment against his own vehicle, closing his eyes. The roar of an engine tore through the night, and he forced himself into alertness, aware of his nakedness and the thick river mud that covered him. He dropped down behind his car, hiding from sight, until he recognised the bike and the rider.

John stood his bike in a wheel rut, dropped his kickstand and carefully placed his helmet on the seat. 'Diana sent me. She said you might need some help.'

Mark was driving and Katie was talking. No, Katie was questioning, and Mark really needed her to be quiet; he had to think. They'd left Diana bandaged and exhausted. She'd had soup and tea, pints of water, and Katie had found biscuits and juice which she'd left within easy reach. Seth was conscious but silent. Katie had diagnosed shock, but no injuries other than a few scratches. Diana had told a tale of going out for a walk, not realising that Seth had followed her. There'd been a dog, a large one, that had attacked. Diana had protected Seth, who had fallen. Katie had been furious; some of Diana's wounds, she said, needed to be stitched. Katie had talked about antibiotics, maybe a scan for the boy in case of hidden injuries. Diana had looked at Mark, then John, and shaken her head. And Katie had seen that look, that moment when Diana's and Mark's eyes had met, and then she'd looked at Seth, and back at Mark. And Mark was worried.

'So, it's John's kid, and you've never mentioned him to me?'

'Diana likes to keep things private – she's a quiet person. It's a funny relationship, her and John, and if it was public she'd be plagued by the press and John would get pilloried every time he was seen with another woman.' Mark took a deep breath.

Katie pushed. 'But you could have told me.'

'Why? You've made it clear that you don't particularly like John. Why would you be interested?'

She was quiet for a while, then cleared her throat. 'He must have been born around the time that we got married. Was that why John was so moody back then? Was he feeling cornered? A new baby, us getting wed, could he feel the walls closing in?'

Mark forced a laugh; it sounded natural, almost. 'Possibly, but he never said he felt trapped. He's always adored that kid, and he and Diana are close. He visits a lot. Kinda on and off, the two of them.' Mark decided that he'd said enough, no need for embroidery.

'Seth looks a bit like you…' She left that, hanging.

Mark blinked. 'He looks like his mother, he's the spit of her.'

'His eyes, they're like yours. And something around his jawline reminds me of those old photos of you when you were nine or ten.' She waited.

'John and I have our dads' eyes, so we've been told, and they were brothers. And the jawline, well, my mum and John's mum were distant cousins, and sometimes these things come out in the wash, don't they.' Mark frowned. 'Are you actually asking if Diana went behind John's back and her kid is mine?'

Katie shrugged. 'If it was before we were married…'

'John met Diana after I met you. I was in love with you back then. I'm still in love with you. But you know, I'm not that chuffed about these questions. Look, we're close, me and Diana. We both love John, and the circle of people who know about her and Seth is pretty much her, John and me. You now, I guess.'

'The Ransomes?' Katie asked.

Mark hesitated. 'No. They don't know. Please don't mention it to Helen – she'll be hurt and so will Andy. Thing is, Diana is very, very protective of her privacy, and she's probably absolutely appalled that John went to you for help. Come on, Katie, I know you're not John's biggest fan, but Diana's a decent woman doing her best. Can we just leave it? Think of it as medical confidentiality…'

Katie shrugged. 'OK, let's just get home before my mum starts panicking. It was good of her to babysit Jake at such short notice.' She glanced across at her husband, and saw him relax. She knew him, and she knew what she'd seen. 'Oh, and I didn't like the way that woman looked at you. Humour me a bit, and stay away from her and her kid for a while. Please.'

'Sure, I'll tell John I'm too busy to visit. He'll be cool.' Mark nodded and mentally reviewed his lies as he drove home. He needed to talk to Andy before Katie did.

John watched as Andy wiped his mouth and finished off the bottle of water. Andy had been filthy, bloody and exhausted, but not too tired to immediately eat two of the four huge pizzas John had brought with him. John had watched him steadily as Andy Changed twice, returning to his human form in a decidedly skinnier body than the one he'd started the evening in. The blond ate both of the remaining pizzas, drank down a litre of water, then dressed in the spare clothes from the back of his car. John waited, watching, until Andy nodded and looked at him.

'What do you know?'

'Diana's injured, Seth's unconscious. I've left them with Mark and Katie, which was probably not my finest moment, but she didn't leave me with much choice. She said you needed help and told me where you were. What the fuck happened here?'

Andy took a deep breath. 'OK, so far as I can figure out, Diana was meeting her sister here.'

John interrupted. 'Sister?'

'Yeah, I know. Well, I don't actually know, but that's what she said. So, I follow Diana here – I'm a minute or two behind, in my car. What I don't know is Seth has hidden himself in my back footwell. I get out, and hang back. I can see Diana squeezing through a hole in a hedge. The river's on the other side, tide's out. I have no fucking clue what she's up to. Then I notice a couple of guys moving towards her – she's looking at something on the ground. I start walking, but Seth's behind me, and he's running, and I'm so surprised I stop and stay stopped while I try to figure out where the fuck he came from. Next thing I know, there's howling and snarling, and I think Shifters and I think wolves, and I think at least two wolves and I know what scares wolves, so I go tiger and jump the hedge ... and next thing you know, Seth's out cold, Diana's bleeding enough to scare both of us, and there are five dead wolves on the bank. Four white, male. One black, female. Diana gets me to bandage her up enough to slow the bleeding, tells me that the black wolf is her sister and buggers off home with the youngling. I've got the dead sister – Joy or Joyce or something – in my boot wrapped in a picnic blanket, and I have no fucking idea what I'm supposed to do. But Diana said to be kind, so I guess I have to find somewhere for a decent burial. The four white wolves, well … I disposed of them.'

'Disposed of?' John raised an eyebrow.

'No, I didn't eat them, although by the time I'd finished slicing and dicing and feeding them to the local aquatic scavengers, I was so hungry and tired I did give it some consideration. They're gone. And now there's a van and a bag of weapons all covered in my prints and someone else's blood, and frankly, John, this is not what I'm trained for.' Andy's voice rose in pitch at the end of his rant, and he jiggled his car keys in his hand.

'Go back to my flat and get some sleep. I'll finish this.' John gripped Andy's shoulder for a second. 'I don't know what this is, and I don't think Diana does either, but it looks like her sister had enemies, Shifter enemies. And if this is what Shifter enemies do, then I think we might actually need some training. But for now, eat and rest. OK?'

Andy nodded gratefully, and reversed his car out of the narrow lane and on to the road.

John bagged up the clothes that Andy had left piled by the hedge. There were four pairs of shoes and socks, and enough ragged, torn clothes for four men. Diana had taken her own clothes home, but there was no sign of anything that might have belonged to the black wolf, not even a car. He surveyed the ground again, finding a couple of scraps of riveted denim, which he added to the bag before stashing it in the van. Inside the van he found a bag of cash in used notes – somewhere between a thousand and two thousand quid. A plastic bag under the mat held a mobile phone and four German passports, all in the surname Haraldson. The vehicle registration and a receipt were in the glove box; it had been bought three days earlier, for cash. Apart from a couple of changes of T-shirts and underwear, and some empty soft drink cans, there was nothing else. He hauled his bike into the van, laying it down and bracing it with whatever he could find, then returned to the river in wolf form. He picked up four trails from the van. He tracked the known scents of Diana, Seth, himself and John, and he excluded them all. Then he found and followed a fifth, strange scent towards the sea. A mile downstream he found a bicycle, and a plastic bag containing women's clothes and shoes. He carried them both back upstream and stowed them in the van. There was no sign of further disturbance, and no new scents, so he Changed again, dressed, and drove the van up and down the lane, obliterating any tracks that didn't belong to it. He pulled on a beanie hat, and after some thought dug out a clean T-shirt and used it to mask his face. He drove a hundred miles south, avoiding the major roads, where he stopped near a housing estate, wiped the bicycle down carefully, and left it next to a park. A few miles further along, he parked on the edge of a small town. He retrieved his bike, the cash, the bag of weapons and the tattered clothes and shoes, wiped the van down thoroughly, then headed back north on his bike. He dumped the guns and ammo in a river, and everything else into skips and wastebins. He thought about the cash; it was unlikely to be traceable. He decided to keep it – he had kids to feed.

Chapter 12

Diana's injury and bereavement hit hard, and John stayed with her for a few days. The kids were unsettled, and although Seth didn't seem to have understood what he'd seen that night, he was clingy and nervous. Having John around helped a lot. Andy, shocked by the carnage, stayed away, brooding. Mark sent a message that Katie was suspicious – she'd rung the Ransomes to ask if they knew about Diana. Fortunately, Andy had answered, and said that John's love life was a mystery to him and he was happy for it to stay that way.

Eventually, John was happy enough with Diana's state of mind to go out to meet Mark and Andy in his Manchester flat.

Andy headed straight to the whisky bottle and poured a large helping. He offered the bottle around, but the cousins declined.

Andy drew a deep breath. 'We need to talk.'

'No shit, but we need to include Diana,' John replied.

'You'll have to represent her.' Mark shrugged. 'Katie is suspicious as hell. She's still gnawing at the idea that Seth's mine, and she knows I'm shaky but not why. I can't go anywhere near Diana and the kids for a while. Possibly months.'

Andy spoke up. 'I killed a man, helped Diana kill another, butchered them and two others. I buried a black wolf on the moors behind my house because Diana said it was her sister. What sister? What's happening?' He looked at John.

'She's not talking,' John replied. 'She's withdrawn and hurt, and jumpy as hell. She'll tell us the story at some point, I know she will, but until then we'll just have to trust her. All I know is she'd arranged to meet this sister and that, as far as she knows, Joyce didn't know about us or the kids, just that there was something Joyce really needed to tell Diana. We have no idea who the blond Shifters were, or where they came from. Diana keeps saying we need to be prepared to fight, for us and the kids, because if we *do* have enemies, we can't rely on Andy suddenly turning up at the right time. We all need to be able to defend our family. Hell, the children need to know how to defend themselves. We don't know when or where we'll be attacked again.'

Silence, broken eventually by Mark. 'She's right. We'll learn how to fight, privately, just the four of us. There are books, videos, for when we're on two legs, and we'll figure it out ourselves when we're on four. For now, I'm afraid Andy and John will have to practise with Diana. I don't like it, but we can't risk Katie getting any more anxious about me. As for the kids, make it a game with them, all of them. We need to agree where they try to run to if they're attacked at home.' He swallowed hard and looked round.

'That house isn't defensible,' Andy said quietly. 'I've been suggesting to Diana for a while that she should find somewhere bigger. There's plenty of money sloshing around in her accounts, we can build safe rooms and tunnels maybe, at a new place?'

'Good idea.' Mark flashed a smile. 'I never thought I'd be having a council of war. I never thought I'd have people who wanted to kill our family, but that's where we are. I'm grateful to both of you, and I know what you've both done to protect us all. I won't forget that. Now, I need to get home – Jake has a cold and Katie has a conference to go to. Next meeting, we need to talk about the band – I've got ideas.'

'I have blood on my hands and he has ideas,' Andy intoned. 'OK then, when shall we three meet again?'

Diana pushed John away, gently. 'Do you want this story?'

'The story of Joyce? Definitely. You've told me about your uncle already, about him abusing Joyce and her saving you and spreading him around the house. And about your parents' reaction. I'm not sure my mum would have been so calm. Auntie Fran, maybe…'

Diana sighed. 'Am I telling this story or not?'

'Werewolf big sister, disassembled uncle, shellshocked parents,' he summarised.

'Yeah, that's about it. Well, we moved back to the North East.'

'Where you got that gorgeous accent,' he commented.

'Where I got this gorgeous accent,' Diana agreed. 'Mum and Dad both found new jobs – Dad as a deputy headmaster, Mum as head of science. More money, less expenses, so life was easier. Joyce became much more outgoing, and she spent a lot more time with me. She was a different person to the quiet, moody big sister I'd always known. She didn't make friends, and she didn't have any boyfriends, but she did join lots of clubs.'

'What sort of clubs?' John asked.

'Chess, drama, language clubs. She went on every exchange and skiing trip she could. She was obsessed with learning other languages, but there was a purpose behind it. She was committed to being a folklorist. She'd exhausted all the stories our family and their friends could tell, and she wanted to be able to follow stories and their history beyond Britain. She learned Welsh in three months, when she was sixteen. She persuaded our parents to spend holidays in North Wales, so she could practise.'

'Clever girl,' John muttered.

'Yeah. Then one day I Changed. I was thirteen, we were on holiday in Whitby. I don't remember the Change itself, I just remember trotting along the wharf in the early hours, scaring the shit out of a courting couple. Joyce had been out too that night. It was a nice warm night, and she'd been up on the moors, hunting. She heard me howl, and ran to me. She ushered me back to the holiday cottage and started to teach me the basics.'

'How did she feel about it?' he asked.

'Happy, exasperated at my stupidity, proud.' She grinned. 'We were both so lucky. I had Joyce, you had Mark. How would we have coped without them?'

'I wouldn't,' John whispered. 'Drop the subject, it creeps me out. What happened next?'

'Well, I was pretty much alone. Joyce was already at uni – she went a year early, we both did. She was in Manchester, and I was back at home, so it wasn't as if I had someone to run with. But the holidays were good. She always came home to look after me and talk to me about what she'd found out.'

'Which was?' he prompted, genuinely curious. 'Come on, hon, you've never told us anything about this before.'

'I couldn't, could I? Not without telling you about Joyce. You would have wanted to look for her, and I know her, remember. I always knew that nothing good would come of it.'

'Tell me.' he whispered.

'Oh, nothing very interesting at that stage. No definite evidence anywhere that werewolves were anything but a myth. Where there had been reports of Shapeshifters, the "accused" disappeared before proof could be found. Lots of stories about wolves in places where they shouldn't have been, but they could all be explained away as big dogs, or escapes from zoos and private collections. The most interesting stories were from our own family. Dad had a great aunt who never married. It was considered unlucky to cross her – you were apt to wake up to find your chickens missing. Mum had a great uncle who died in his thirties. Suicide.' She frowned. 'Joyce suspected he was a Shapeshifter who gave up hope. It must be a lonely life if you think you're the only one.'

'Any cousins of yours?' he asked.

'Believe me, we checked out every living relative. Cautiously, y'know? We'd sniff around their homes, but no luck, no trace of any other wolf scents. Thinking about it, it's about time I went back home, to check up on the next generation.' She widened her eyes. 'John, I really ought to do that. It's a responsibility, really, isn't it?'

He grunted. 'You've got thirteen responsibilities here! I see your point, but someone else should do it.'

Diana privately decided to give it some thought. 'Anyway, then Dad died. I was fifteen. Joyce was twenty-one. She'd graduated and was doing postgrad work at Manchester Uni. She came straight home when she got the news, and stayed with me and Mum for a fortnight. I was a mess. I'd grown up in one of the most perfect nuclear families you could imagine. My parents loved each other, and they knew kids inside out. They spoiled me, but not enough to ruin me, y'know?'

John grinned. 'My mum was like that with me and Mark,' he said. 'I miss her, every day.'

'What was she like?' Diana asked, curious.

'Me.' He laughed. 'Just like me. She drove Auntie Fran up the wall sometimes. She was forever partying with some guy or other. I was fifteen when she died. She was only thirty-nine, you know? She managed to see me to my fifteenth birthday, but she didn't see that Christmas. Auntie Fran just took me straight home from the hospital. There was never any discussion, it was just obvious that I was going to live with her and Mark. When Mum's will got read, she'd left everything to Fran.'

'Including you,' Diana said.

'Including me,' he agreed. 'What happened when your dad died?'

Diana shrugged. 'She didn't want me around, she closed off completely. She took it very hard. I tried to help, but it was as if I wasn't there. I was grieving pretty hard myself, but we couldn't comfort each other – there was no connection at all. It didn't feel like a shared loss, it felt like she blamed me.'

'I'm sorry,' John whispered.

'Joyce rang one night, and they talked for about ten minutes. The next day Joyce turned up in a hired van, packed up all my stuff, and told me that I was going to live with her. I think Mum rang every month, to check that we were OK. Once I was eighteen, that stopped. We rang each other at Christmas, and on birthdays, for a while, but we've only actually seen each other about half a dozen times since I moved in with Joyce.'

'That's horrible,' John said with conviction. 'How could she not want you?'

'She had a family, then Dad died. She hurt horribly, and she wanted a life without anyone to remind her of that. Joyce said I reminded her of Dad, and she really didn't want to be reminded. I'm sure if Joyce hadn't taken me away, we would have found a way of living together, but Joyce just wanted me to be somewhere where I could be happy. You see? She wanted to look after me. She took me in and made me welcome. She got me through my A levels and made sure I got a place at Manchester Uni so I could stay with her. She found a house with a sheltered back garden so we could Change and run around without being seen.'

'I loved that house,' he said quietly.

'Yes, it suited us. We talked a lot, mostly about Shapeshifting. It was the only thing we had in common really. She'd left the uni by then and was setting up as a folklore writer and consultant. My job was getting my A levels, getting access to a decent genetics lab so I could try to figure out what made us what we were. I pointed out that it was unlikely we were the only Shapeshifters in the country, and we talked about finding others.'

'How?' John asked.

'Well, she had the perfect cover, didn't she? She was working as a folklorist, and she travelled around the country, uncovering stories about werewolves. If she heard something juicy, she'd Change, and go sniffing around in likely spots. Within six months she brought back a young woman who was between the two of us in age. Lyn had been convinced for years that her Changes were just weird dreams – she was strongly in denial about the whole thing. Being found by Joyce changed her life, and ours. I was fascinated by Lyn, somehow she made the whole thing a lot more real.'

'And the others?'

'Joyce found them, one by one, and brought them back to Manchester. Never any boys, though. She heard stories, but she missed them by months or years. After I found out about Joyce's hobbies, and asked her to leave, the whole lot of them eventually decided to go to France. One thing I established was that we all had French or German ancestors, three to five generations back. It was the only thing we all had in common, so they thought it was worth taking the chance and travelling abroad to look for guys.' She sighed. 'And all the time, there you were, prancing around on stage.'

'Why didn't you go with them?' he asked.

'I was happy where I was,' she replied.

'And that was all? Come on, hon, why would you choose to be alone, when you could have been with the others?'

She looked at him; he was gazing at her earnestly.

'We'd been together for about ten years, I suppose I thought I could manage without them,' she said.

111

'Truth?' John said quietly.

'Mostly,' she admitted. 'There was the fact that I didn't want to be associated with Joyce any longer. Look, you know Joyce was a killer. It was half hobby, half business. She was a busy woman. The front was the folklore work, the film work, the books … but she also killed rapists and child murderers who hadn't been arrested or convicted for their crimes. Their victims and their families contacted her anonymously, and paid her anonymously too. She rarely left bodies. No body means it's a missing persons enquiry, and there's not going to be much public pressure on the police to investigate the disappearance of someone who's been accused of those sorts of crimes. She kept files, records, which I stumbled upon. She confessed all to me, and left. The records, well … I destroyed them. I had a career ahead of me – I didn't want some workman in the attic finding out about my killer sister.'

'If she was killing anyway, what's the problem with collecting a bounty? Do you think she carried on? When she moved abroad?'

'Yeah. I do. I've no proof. I didn't have time to comb through foreign newspapers for evidence, because I met you guys soon after she left. But I don't see why she should have stopped.'

'And that's why you didn't tell us about her?'

'Well, if you remember, I wasn't quite sure of you and Andy for a year or so, was I? I was being selfish, and I wanted to keep us all together. And I honestly didn't know where they were. I could have tracked them down if I'd put my mind to it, but there was a lot going on. Then the kids started to arrive, and the whole thing just got pushed out of my head.'

John sighed. 'From what you've told me about Joyce, it's probably just as well we didn't all meet, but I'm curious about these other women.'

Diana nodded. 'Me too. I'm going to try to track them down.'

Chapter 13

'It's called Silverwood,' the estate agent said. 'It's been empty for a few years now. It was a hotel. There's three floors, a big basement and extensive grounds with several outbuildings, including an additional four-bedroomed house and a housekeeper's cottage. The woodland at the back belongs to the estate, there's a working farm next door and moorland grazing to the rear, owned by another farm. There have been offers from developers, but the owner doesn't want it to be turned into a housing estate.'

Diana nodded. 'We're interested in renovating the hotel as a family home. We're a group of friends with a few kids between us, and we need a lot of space. It makes sense to pool our money. We've looked at a couple of places, and there's another one in Yorkshire that looks interesting, but once we've decided, we're ready to go.'

'Mortgage in place?' the estate agent asked.

'Cash. We have savings, legacies – enough, between us, to cover it. Of course, this one is going to cost a lot to renovate. The last place I looked at is a lot newer. I mean, that cottage … it's practically derelict.'

'It's in better shape than it looks, and the annexe – the four-bed house next to the hotel – that's ready to move in to right now. It would make an ideal base for someone to oversee the renovations from. The price is very reasonable.'

Diana wrinkled her nose and shrugged. 'Then there's the location. We have school-age kids and there's no bus stops for miles.'

'Blackburn, Bolton, Preston and Chorley are all within easy reach, and there are several local villages with primary schools and health centres.' The estate agent sighed. 'But I'll contact the owner and see what they can do, price-wise.' He glanced at the baby in the pushchair. 'How many do you have?'

'Between us, or just me? This is Jane, my baby girl. She's named after my mum. Do you have any?'

The guy smiled. 'Not yet, but I see how a place like this would be great to grow up in – so much space. She'd love it.'

'Or somewhere like it.' Diana was laughing now, and the estate agent conceded defeat and made a phone call.

He came back ten minutes later. 'Five grand lower?' he asked.

'Make it eight and we have a deal,' Diana replied.

He nodded and they shook on it.

Back at the house, Andy was waiting. 'Yes?' he asked.

'It's perfect!' Diana said. She gave Jane a kiss and said, 'You and Alice are going to have your own bedroom!'

Mark rang a few days later, calling from a new mobile number.

'Where are you?' Diana asked, desperate to hear his voice. The Alpha addiction was kicking in with a vengeance.

'London. Waiting for John and Andy – we're doing press for the next album.'

'Great,' she said quietly. 'Tour?'

'Tour, festivals, signings, whatever it takes. Andy keeps an eye on album sales, and we've been out of the loop for a year now. And … and Katie doesn't quite trust me at the moment, so it's going to be difficult, getting to see you. I might as well make myself useful and earn some money if I can't be with you and the kids.'

'When can you come here?' she asked.

'I don't know,' he whispered. 'Look, make a note of this number. Don't call me on any other. This phone is dedicated to you, OK? If you need me, leave a message.'

'Leave a message? I can do that now. Just get here as soon as you can.'

'We'll do the best we can,' he said, and hung up.

The kids were sitting around, watching TV and eating cereal. She turned the TV off.

'What on earth is going on? It's mid morning! You can't just veg out y'know!' she yelled. 'What happened to the study schedule? Darlene, Sara, Bridget, Trixie, get your reading books and join me in the dining room. Seth, get that number work out and do some sums with Caleb and Sammy! Noah, it's Wednesday – it's your day to clean the kitchen. Miranda, I want a report by three o'clock on why we don't drink out of puddles! Bill, Frank, didn't I set you a geography project weeks ago? Where is it?'

There was a moment of stillness, then Seth stood up. 'Cal, Sam, come on. I've got some sums ready for you in my room.' They disappeared.

Bill looked at his mother anxiously. 'When did we have to finish that project?' he asked.

'Let's be generous and say tomorrow?' she replied. 'Use my computer, but I want references for everything you use, OK?'

'OK.' He and his twin frowned and went to the study.

Miranda flashed Diana a big smile and ran to the bedroom she shared with her sisters. The other four girls found their books and gathered around, taking it in turns to read. Noah went into the kitchen and started to clean up.

Home-schooling the kids was fun, but took a lot of time. Diana decided that it was time to try to make some changes. She rang John.

'Hey gorgeous, are you planning on coming home any time soon?' she asked.

'Next week, as it happens.' She could almost see him smiling. 'Mark says I'm getting on his nerves, so I was thinking about staying with you for a few days.'

'How many?' she asked quickly.

He was quiet, not used to being pinned down to a schedule. Eventually he agreed to three or four days, and promised to bring some of Mark's worn clothing to help Diana's cravings. When she asked him to bring Mark instead, even for just an hour, he laughed nervously. 'Hey, Katie's ringing him on landlines three times a day, to make sure he's where he says he'll be – there's no chance of him getting away.'

'Why is she so suspicious?' Diana complained. 'I thought she'd accepted the story that I'm with you?'

'Ah, she was OK for a day or two, then she started brooding. She still doesn't like the way Mark was looking at Seth and you.'

'Shit,' she muttered.

'Well, I put on a good act. I got all possessive and territorial and said that you'd never even look at another man, and pointed out that I'm distantly related to Auntie Fran through my mother – they were third cousins or something – which would explain the family resemblance. Katie bought it, eventually, enough not to come storming back to your place, but she's suspicious as hell.'

Diana breathed deeply. 'John, if she ever comes "storming back" here, I won't answer for the consequences. I appreciate that she helped us, but I've spent the last three weeks getting the stink of her out of the carpets. Make sure Mark understands that.'

'Oh hon, Mark already understands that. Look, gotta go, I promised Mark I'd thrash out some lyrics with him this afternoon, and you know what he's like when he gets stood up.'

She sighed and put the phone down, then started to make plans.

When John arrived, the kids were more than usually clingy with him. They'd already started to notice that Mark and Andy weren't around as much. He'd brought presents from their two other dads, which distracted them long enough for Diana to discuss her plans with him.

The next morning she gathered the kids round. 'OK, JohnDad's going to be in charge for a few days. I have to go away to see someone. I'm taking the babies with me, and Noah. The rest of you will behave for your dad, I know that.'

There was a small riot as everyone started asking questions. She sat patiently until they quietened, then continued. 'Three days and I'll be back, don't panic. I've decided who I'm taking with me, so don't argue. And no, Mark and Andy won't be coming here, and I'm not going to see them. Sara, I'm not bringing presents back – it's not that kind of trip.'

The kids went quiet, mulling the situation, it was the first time she'd ever left them for more than a few hours and they were clearly anxious, but John distracted them and she made a quick getaway.

In the car, Noah spoke up. 'Why me?' he asked.

'Because I need someone who will make a good impression and be polite and intelligent,' she told him. That shut him up for about an hour, after which he started to take advantage of having his mother to himself.

Noah was a bright lad, eager to learn, and very impressed with himself and his place in the pack. He didn't have much of a sense of humour, but he cared for the little ones, and voluntarily took a lot of responsibility. He wasn't impulsive either; he preferred to think things out carefully, and that was the main difference between him and his twin. He and Seth weren't as close as Frank and Bill, but they did stick together under pressure.

Eventually they arrived at their destination. Diana had never seen this cottage before. It was a large, two-storey cottage with a highly disciplined front garden. It was scrupulously well maintained. The front gate was newly painted and still slightly tacky to the touch. No doubt the prospects of rain had been carefully assessed before the project was undertaken.

The curtains twitched, but Diana ignored it, heading for the cottage, with the babies in her arms and Noah behind her. She knocked and waited. A few seconds passed, maintaining the fiction that she hadn't been observed from the moment she pulled up outside the house. The door opened slowly.

Diana put on her best smile. 'Hello, Mum,' she said steadily. 'Get the kettle on, it's been a long drive.'

Jane Foster had changed a lot in the years since Diana had last seen her. She looked like an old lady: grey-haired, but still straight and elegant. She stood aside and let her daughter in. The front door led into a short hallway, with a door on the left, one on the right and a third at the far end. The walls were neatly plastered, and painted in a neutral pink colour. Lamps and tables cluttered the hallway, each one highly polished. She led Diana into an equally cluttered and equally spotless living room. It was decorated in shades of pink and peach.

Jane gestured to the sofa, and Diana made a nest of cushions for the babies then perched on the arm. Noah stood quietly.

'I wondered how long it would take before they threw you out,' the older woman said.

'Noah honey, would you make a pot of tea, please?' Diana asked. 'He's a good lad,' she said. 'And they can't throw me out, it's my house. Speaking of houses, this one is lovely. Did you decorate it yourself?'

Jane understood, and drew herself up to her full height. 'I've lived alone since you ran off to live with your delinquent sister,' she said.

'Are you happy here? Just a minute, I'll just tell Noah how you like your tea. Keep an eye on little Jane and Alice please?'

Diana went back into the corridor, guessing that the end door led to the kitchen. Noah was standing next to the kettle, looking out of the kitchen window at the neatly manicured lawn and flowerbeds. 'There aren't any kids here, are there?' he said.

'No, hon.' She put two sugars in one of the mugs, for her mother, and waited with Noah until the kettle had boiled. She watched him carefully pour the water; he had a look of concentration that was perfectly familiar to her, in an entirely different context. John was right: Noah and Seth did copy Mark's expressions and mannerisms; she'd not really noticed before.

They went back to the living room.

Diana's mother was sitting next to the babies, her finger in Janie's grip. 'Jane, you say?'

'Yes, she's the older of the two.'

'You named your eldest daughter after me?' she asked.

'Well, she's not my eldest, but yes, she's named after you. Can we talk?'

Jane sighed. 'What do you want? Because you don't turn up out of the blue unless you want something.'

'I want a grandma for my kids. I can't cope, and I can't trust anybody else.'

Jane looked from Noah to Diana. 'Didn't you say you were expecting twins, last time we spoke?'

'Yeah, there's Seth too. They're identical. All the twins are identical.' She took possession of the sole armchair, leaving her mother sitting with Jane and Alice.

Noah perched on the arm of Diana's chair, sipping his tea carefully, watching them.

Jane looked at Noah. 'How old are you?'

'I'm eight,' he said.

'You seem nervous,' she said.

'I am,' he admitted, moving closer to Diana, who laughed and hugged him. 'Mum, putting it plainly, we don't get out much. I can't take them all out together, people would talk, so I'm limited to taking them out in twos and threes whenever one of their dads is able to babysit. I'm home-schooling them too, so they're really not used to other people.'

'You said "all the twins"?' she queried, still enraptured by baby Jane and her twin.

'Seth and Noah, Bill and Frank, Sara and Darlene – we call them the Kittens – Bridget and Beatrice, who are usually Bee and Trixie, or the Bees for short, Caleb and Sammy and these two. And Miranda – she's a singleton.'

'Good grief,' Jane said. 'No wonder you didn't have time to keep in touch!' She frowned. 'Fine, stay tonight, we'll see how we all get on. Then we'll talk some more tomorrow. How does that sound? Or do you have to get back urgently?'

'We're fine. John's looking after the kids.'

Jane looked up. 'John? Is he one of the...?'

'Rockstars? Werewolves? Weirdos?' Diana smiled. 'Yeah, he's one of 'em. He's a good dad. I'd like you to meet him.'

She nodded, and Diana understood that she didn't want to talk about that.

They cooked a meal together, for the first time since Diana was fifteen. They made up the spare bed, and together put the girls in their carrycot to sleep. Noah stayed up for a while; Jane had the TV on and he watched the documentary channels avidly until bedtime.

After he'd gone, the two women looked at each other. 'He's like your dad,' Jane said.

'Yeah. He takes after me, in his looks. Does it upset you?' she asked.

'Ah, I thought it would, but it doesn't. Seeing him brings back happy memories.' She summoned a smile. 'Seeing *you* brings back happy memories. Why did you leave?'

Diana blinked. 'Mum, you wanted me out of the way!'

'Yes, for a few weeks, while I grieved. Not permanently! But you seemed so happy with Joyce, and she was adamant that she knew how to care for you better than I did.' Her voice was steady, and she seemed calm, but she wasn't fooling anyone.

Diana paled. 'You should have said something. We were happy, until Dad died. You were a great mum to both of us.'

Jane laughed, low, mocking. 'Yes, so great a mum that I didn't know my eldest daughter was being raped by the man I entrusted both of you to. It never occurred to me that Joyce was in any way unhappy.'

'That wasn't your fault. Steve was a manipulative bastard, and he got exactly what he deserved.' Diana bit her lip, wondering how much to tell. She decided to keep quiet about Joyce's fate, for the time being. 'Really, if you wanted me to come home, you should have said something.'

'I had no idea how to deal with you, my love. Your dad was the one who was willing to learn, to adapt to what you were. You know that.'

Diana remembered lying on the floor of the landing, quiet as a mouse, listening to her parents arguing about Joyce's Shapeshifting. Her mum had wanted to talk to the vicar about it, to ask where in God's Creation her daughters belonged. Dad had convinced her to stay quiet, pointing out that Joyce was a wanted child, conceived and born in a Christian marriage, and must fall within God's plan. Dad confessed to Diana, when she was about fourteen and newly, fiercely atheist, that his own faith had taken a huge dent when he came home to find his brother shredded on the carpet, but he kept up the pretence to keep Mum happy.

Diana looked at her mother, and at the beautiful tidy home she'd made for herself. 'When did you retire?' she said, changing the subject.

'Three years ago,' she said.

'Bored yet?' Diana asked.

Jane smiled thinly. 'Deadly bored. It's amazing how quickly people forget you. My colleagues kept in touch for a year or so, but it's down to Christmas cards now.'

As the night went on, they talked about family, and Diana made a mental note to chase up younger cousins who'd had hit adolescence since Joyce made her last investigative trip back home. Eventually Jane stood up.

'I'm going to bed. I tend to go early these days. Goodnight, my dear.'

Diana stood up too, and moved a step closer, then stopped, feeling absurdly self-conscious. They looked at each other, then moved into an embrace that ended a separation of two decades. When Jane drew away at last, she was smiling but composed. 'You're good company – it's a pleasant surprise.'

They stayed for another two days. Jane took to Noah immediately; she'd always wanted a little boy, and Noah was polite, smart and willing to learn to play cards and board games with her. Like all the kids, he was confident with adults, but unused to strangers; it took him a while to accept that Jane was family.

On the third morning, Jane watched as Diana packed.

'Will you come again?' she asked.

'It's not easy. All the guys are really busy. There's only John who can reasonably stay overnight, and I don't like to leave the kids with him for so long. Why don't you come to stay with us for a few days?'

Jane frowned. 'I don't know. I have things to do here.'

'Mum,' Diana said gently. 'I've been here for three days, and the phone hasn't rung once. What things?'

'Housework, gardening,' she said.

'They'll wait. Come and meet your grandchildren,' Diana suggested. 'Just a few days? And if you get bored, there's housework and gardening at my place.'

Jane gave her daughter a cynical smile. 'I just bet there are,' she sighed. 'You really are struggling, aren't you? You wouldn't have come here if you weren't.' There was a note of self-pity in her voice.

'Mum, I need you. Please just come for a day or two and meet the kids, then make your decision. We both made mistakes, and we paid for them with twenty years apart … but it's not too late to be a family again.' She hesitated. 'Look, whatever help you can give, I'll take, and I won't ask for anything else. If all you can do is collect Noah and Seth once a month and bring them here for a long weekend, then that's fine.'

Jane looked around at the house, at the sofa that had been pristine only days earlier and now bore several suspiciously sticky marks, at the empty space on the coffee table that had held a vase until Noah had run into the room at full pelt and tripped over a rug, at the nose prints on the windowpanes. 'Oh, bother it. I'll come back with you and meet the rest of my grandchildren. It looks like I'm a grandmother whether I like it or not.'

'Ace,' Diana said, hugging her. 'Pack a bag.'

Diana rang John when she was halfway home, and warned him. When they got home, things seemed to be under control. John looked almost respectable; he was wearing a new pair of jeans, an actual shirt, rather than a tour T-shirt, and shoes and socks. His hair was clean and brushed, and he had apparently indulged in a mid afternoon shave to clear the usual two o'clock stubble he was cursed with.

He was on an instant charm offensive: offering to make tea, taking the babies and putting them to bed for a nap, jokingly asking Jane if Diana was a changeling as well as a werewolf, because he couldn't understand how an elegant and charming woman like her could produce such a hopelessly untidy daughter, then allaying her anxiety by making it very clear how much he liked that same daughter.

Jane asked him about his career, and he told her about the band, how it had always been his ambition to make music with his cousin, and how happy he was with his work. He talked to her about her career, and drew parallels between her and his own Auntie Fran. He spoke frankly about his own mother, and the way he'd lost her far too early, because of the carrier syndrome, then gently turned the subject to Diana's father, and how he knew how much she missed him.

That naturally led to questions about his own father's whereabouts. He shrugged. 'My father and Mark's were twins. Diana has looked at my DNA, and Mark's, and she thinks they were identical twins. Mum and Auntie Fran didn't talk much about them – they both left at the same time.' He shrugged. 'They must have had a hell of a good reason, because I can't think of anything on this earth that would make me leave my kids and never come back.' There was a raw edge of hurt when he said that, and Diana caressed his shoulder soothingly.

Diana's mother sighed. 'Things happen, parents make mistakes,' she said. She turned the subject a little. 'Which of the little ones are yours?' she asked.

'All of them,' John said. 'But I know what you mean. Didn't our Diana tell you?'

'Considering the situation, she has been very discreet on the matter of my grandchildren's paternity,' Jane said primly.

John cheered up. 'Guess,' he said.

'Oh, without meeting the other … gentlemen … concerned, it would be difficult,' Jane said, becoming somewhat flustered. 'But I assume that the oldest three girls aren't yours?'

'Nope. Our Miranda is Xan's baby. He died before he even knew he was going to be a father, but anyone who ever met him would know that she's his child. Our Kittens carry Andy's blood, God help them.'

Jane frowned. 'Why?'

John recovered, remembering who he was talking to. 'Ah. It's just my little joke. Andy and I been winding each other up since we were sixteen – it's a bad habit of ours. He's a good bloke really. A good dad to all our kids, a great band mate and my closest friend, after Mark.'

'What about me?' Diana demanded.

'You aren't my friend, you're my heart and my soul,' he said, laughing.

'Fair enough,' she said.

Jane looked at them carefully. 'And when are you two going to get married? In the eyes of God?'

'We're not,' Diana said firmly. 'John's famous. If he got married, there are a lot of people who would want to know everything about his wife, and this family can't take that sort of scrutiny. Do you understand?'

Chapter 14

Silverwood. A pretty name for a haphazard and ungainly collection of buildings. The main building looked good after the renovations, and Diana was happy with the new security features. There was plenty of room for everyone, with three floors and two solid, brick-built wings that sheltered a garden area. The cottage and annexe stood on the other side of the garden, framing the woods that reached to the far edge of the property. Set further away, hidden from the house by a small copse, were two outbuildings that had been repurposed into a music room and a laboratory.

Andy now lived just fifteen minutes away by road, and twenty minutes via the moors as the wolf runs. He visited frequently, but his visits were short and he spent more time with the kids than he did with Diana. Mark still hadn't visited. He and Diana had been apart for six months, and it showed in their health and appearance, despite almost daily exchanges of well-worn clothing. They knew the other one lived, they spoke to each other as often as they could and they had hope, but still Mark was terrified of Katie finding out about his other life. He wasn't ready to face the world with his secrets yet.

Diana's mother had decided to move in with the family once Silverwood was ready. She'd transferred the decor and contents of her old house directly to the Silverwood cottage, which was slightly smaller and much more cluttered. John kept his flat in Manchester, but spent as much time as he could at the new house. Diana reserved three bedrooms for the adults, two of them with a linking bathroom. She surveyed her new home, and made her plans.

'Mum, I need to you to take charge here. John will help, the older kids are really, really good at helping out, and Miranda seems to want to impress you, so it won't be too hard.' Diana tried to smile.

'More surprises?' Jane asked. 'Because it's only a fortnight since you told me that Joyce was dead, and there's no grave, no marker, no death certificate …'

'There's a grave. Andy will take you there, if you need to go.' Diana took a deep breath. 'And if you want to report Joyce as missing, then I'm fully in agreement with you. But can you wait until I get back? What I need to do right now is carry on with Joyce's work.' Jane raised her eyebrows and Diana took a breath. 'I mean, her work looking for other Shifters.'

'Well, please be careful, and get back as often as you can. I'm getting old, you know.'

'Honestly, just ask Seth and Noah what to do if you get confused,' Diana teased.

Travelling was a distraction for Diana; she was pregnant again, and heartsick for Mark, but her new project helped. She set off for the North East and, within a week of starting her search, she found a young male werewolf trotting through the midnight streets of her father's home village, a dead fox in his jaws.

He stopped when he saw her, and growled, dropping the carcass. She Changed and chased him down, holding him down and restraining his struggles until he went back to human form and started to beg for mercy. He was nineteen and terrified.

She taught him the basics for survival, and took his details. He was called Duncan Moss. She gave him a phone number, and told him to keep in touch. He told her that a couple of years earlier, he thought he'd seen a wolf sitting in a field in Hoxton, watching the world go by. She thanked him for the tip, and moved on.

She prowled the country, finding a scattering of young werewolves, but none of her age or older. Where were all the adults? She went back home, finally, to give birth to John's daughters. For the first time ever, Mark wasn't there to midwife the birth, and his absence seemed to cut away Diana's last remaining hope and energy. She named them Susan and Anne, but within hours they were Susie and Nancy.

Andy set to work networking the young werewolves Diana found, impressing on them the need for secrecy and caution, but at Silverwood, things were falling apart. John couldn't help Diana's withdrawal symptoms; Mark was reportedly listless and tired, and the children started to behave badly. A practice fight between Frank and Noah turned vicious, leaving Noah with a broken arm, and John finally snapped, and told Diana to do whatever she had to do to get Mark back.

She waited until she knew that Mark and Katie would be out of their house, and parked her car a mile away. She

Changed, and slunk through gardens until she reached their home, confirming by scent that her beloved lived there.

John was waiting, anxious, with his spare key. He unlocked and opened the back door, then walked back to the car. As the red wolf pushed the door wide open, the alarm went off. She put her head down and ran through the house, rolling on the sofa, the beds, the rugs, getting her smell everywhere. She'd timed it well; she heard a car pulling up outside and Mark's anxious voice saying something about the alarm, asking Katie and Jake to stay in the car. As he walked into the house, through the open back door, Diana bowled past him, a russet blur. Mark watched as she ran, as she skidded to a halt and turned, staring at him. He grinned, and turned as she did, he for the house and his wife, she for her car and John. He told Katie that 'some Mark-shaped idiot' had forgotten to shut the back door, and somehow a dog had got in and got trapped. Luckily no real damage had been done.

Diana and John got to Silverwood about half an hour before Mark arrived. He'd been clever, deliberately escalating the row over the open door into an excuse to storm out and drive off. If Diana was any judge of Mark's sulks, then Katie would be more than happy not to see him for the rest of the day. Mark stormed in, his colour high, looking for Diana.

John was in the hallway, holding Alice down and tickling her while she screamed in fake terror. Mark grabbed her off him, getting her scent again for the first time in a year. She stared at him, her lip trembling, not recognising him. He saw Diana, standing by the stairs, smiling. She went upstairs and he followed her.

There was a clatter of feet as word got round, and kids appeared from all directions.

'Who is that?' demanded Diana's mother.

John went over and gave her a delighted hug. 'It looks like the boss is home,' he told her.

In the bedroom, door locked, pandemonium outside, Mark pulled her close. 'That took some guts,' he said. He undressed her greedily, then stopped and closed his eyes. 'I love her,' he said.

'It's OK,' she replied.

'But I don't love you...' he added.

She swallowed. He'd never said he did, but he'd never made it so clear that he didn't. The world fell away. She closed her eyes and let her body sense him, moving close to him, rubbing against him, holding his hair, breathing in the overwhelming scent of her Alpha. He stood still, inhaling her scent so deeply he felt that they were already inside other. 'This isn't love?' she whispered.

'It's need,' he answered.

She saw in his eyes a dawning understanding that it had been the same for her, of how close they had come to losing everything.

He touched her hips, the bones outlined sharply against skin, and scowled. 'You're too thin,' he blurted out.

'You too. You've lost weight. You were skinny before, but...' She stroked his arms; the sinewy strength of his upper arms was almost gone. She drew back, noting the dark shadows around his eyes, the dullness of his hair. He didn't speak, just looked at her, his breathing rough and shallow. She could see pity in his eyes, for both of them, for what their addiction had brought them to. A line of sweat on his lip drew her close again. She licked it away, her cells grabbing on to every trace of his scent and starting to scream out for more.

He touched her face, gathering a tear on to his finger. He tasted it, a wild hunger flashing across his face. And still he held back.

'It's been a long year,' he said. 'I'm a stranger here. You and John have new daughters, he's been here a lot. If things have changed for you, if you don't want me anymore, I understand. We'll get our fix and I'll go, leave the two of you alone.'

'No! That's not what I want! Is it what you want? Tell me the truth. I deserve that at least.'

'Ah, the truth? I want what I've always wanted, everything. But I'm trying to be fair to you. I stayed away to try to protect you and our family, and look where it got us. I would have died of stubbornness, but you came to get me. I'm sorry. I just didn't realise that it was just as bad for you. I thought John would make things better for you.'

'No, I need you.' She sighed. 'I always need you.'

He reached across, took both of her hands in his. 'Tell me you want me. Tell me that this is about more than the addiction. We both know how it goes, how it will be, and I don't want you to feel you're being used.'

'Used? We're together, we're meant to be together. How can we be using each other? Unless you hate me? Unless you hate the fact that you can't stay away from me?' She looked at him cautiously; could things really be so bad between them?

'No, never. I don't hate you. Sometimes I resent the situation, but it was always my choice…' He broke off, his thin lips twitched into a nervous smile. He didn't break the eye contact, and she couldn't look away. 'Oh, my wolf girl, it's been so long. Can I kiss you?'

'Of course.' Since when had he needed permission? She kept her eyes open for a moment, then the fix started to hit, harder and stronger after the time apart, and they gave themselves to the wild.

Twelve hours, that's what John told them. For twelve hours they'd been lost to the world, caught up in the scent and feel and sound of each other. Afterwards, they showered and dressed, and revelled in their renewal, their clear skin and glossy hair, the absence of pain and fatigue. They ate and ate, then Changed and ran in the woodlands of Silverwood. It felt like a holiday, and they both spent the rest of the day with the children.

Mark was captivated by the new babies, Susie and Nancy. 'I've missed having babies,' he told her. She reminded him that Alice and Jane had no idea who he was, and he nodded and wandered off to play with them and talk to the throng of kids who had missed him and needed to know that he had missed them.

Before he left, Diana took him to the cottage to meet her mother. They got a cold reception from Jane, who openly wondered where Mark's wife thought he was. Mark drove away in a sombre mood.

The Alphas knew they couldn't spend so long apart again. Mark spent another night away from Katie, going out clubbing with John and leaving with a woman that he'd been flirting with all night. He'd said goodnight to the woman on her doorstep, his main goal was to be seen with her. As a distraction, it was perfect. Nobody wanted the end of his marriage; Diana felt an instinctive revulsion at the very thought of it. In some weird way, the marriage was pack business. Mark turned around every single accusation that Katie made, saying that the more jealous she got, the more he needed to get out. John and Andy backed him up, and eventually they made up. Katie had been as miserable as anyone else. Mark was free again to spend the occasional day or night with John and Andy.

Diana and her mother began to deal with Joyce's affairs. Joyce had also been reported as missing by her assistant. Diana set up a PO box for redirection of Joyce's mail. It wasn't long before the phone rang; the police had found a body close to where Joyce had last lived. It was a woman, headless, similar in height and age to Joyce. Without a qualm, Diana went and falsely made a positive identification, swearing that she recognised jewellery on the body. Armed with a death certificate, they visited her solicitor, who drew out her will. She'd left everything to Diana. Joyce hadn't accumulated so much wealth and real estate around the world by writing books about the folklore of Estonia, or even by acting as a consultant for half a dozen Hollywood films. The legacy repaired the considerable hole in Diana's finances, from buying and renovating Silverwood, and what was left over was donated to a charity that Diana knew Joyce had supported.

Chapter 15

In Silverwood's garden, Andy was reading *Gulliver's Travels* to the older boys, Miranda and the Kittens. Sara had forced herself under his arm, desperate to get closer to him. Darlene was sitting in front of him, so that every time he raised his eyes, he saw her. The Kittens were seven now, and were going through a favourite parent phase. On this late September day, it seemed that Andy was it.

Diana rescued Janie and Alice from the toddler cage, and carried them over to where Andy was reading. She left the new babies, Susie and Nancy, in a buggy in the shade. She found a garden chair, hugged the toddlers close, shut her eyes and listened to Andy, his voice washing over her like sunlight. When she woke up, she could hear the girls practising piano in the music room. Andy was watching her, smiling.

'The boys are in the library with your mum,' he said.

Janie and Alice had gone to sleep. The weather had turned colder, so she took them to their beds and laid them down quietly. She tiptoed out and found Andy in the kitchen, drinking tea with her mother, who left the room when Diana entered.

'She still disapproves of us,' Andy said.

'You're still married.' Diana shrugged. 'She adores the kids, although she'll never admit it, but it's hard for her to accept my life with you guys.'

'We all love the kids. And by the way…'

Diana grinned. 'By the way, you've waited your turn and I'm glad for your patience. And yes, I reckon Darlene and Sara have proved that we make exceptionally amazing human beings when we put our heads together.'

'Hardly "heads", but I agree.' Andy smirked, and Diana shook her head. 'Don't make me change my mind,' she said. 'But yeah, whenever you're ready. But first, I need a report.'

Andy nodded. His first words were very cautious. 'Have you heard that Katie is pregnant again?'

'Smelled it on Mark weeks ago,' Diana said briskly. 'Don't worry, I'm not going to lose my temper. He's a good dad to Jake, and I understand how Katie might think another kid would be nice. She doesn't know about us, and she doesn't know the implications of a single W chromosome, but neither of those things are my fault or really my business. When's the due date?'

'Next April,' Andy said. 'Probably around the same time as Caleb and Sammy's birthday.'

'Inconvenient but can't be helped.' Diana shrugged. 'And you and Helen, are you still trying?'

A flash of anger from Andy. 'We are. Eva was wanted, and Helen wants another, so yes, we're still trying.'

'Again, your business,' Diana sighed. 'OK, how are our finances?'

'Ridiculously healthy,' Andy said.

'And the other Shifters?'

'Ah. I was coming to that. Right. First of all, Duncan's Pack. They're too young to be mated, I told them that, but they seem to be gelling together. Laura's pregnancy is going fine, definitely twins, so it's not just you. It was lucky we found Laura and Chloe so soon after tracking Duncan down. They all seem happy together. I've got Chloe enrolled in a Business Admin apprenticeship with a Ransome Industries company. So far she's not pregnant, which is a bit of a relief.'

Diana nodded. She really had hoped the younger Shifters she'd found and mentored would be sensible, but Laura and Duncan had fallen hard for each other and mated with little thought for the consequences. Laura had a younger Shifter friend, Chloe, who had latched on to her years ago when they'd found each other in the city one night. Chloe and Duncan were also mated, despite Diana's misgivings, the girl was only seventeen and still had a lot of growing up to do. Laura, Diana found, was very capable and reminded her of a young Joyce.

She listened carefully as Andy went through his list. It was a short one still. She made a mental note that their latest young Shifter discoveries, Raj Drake and Hannah Byrne were of a similar age, at sixteen and fifteen respectively, and decided to wait a while before introducing them; she didn't want another Duncan / Laura situation. It would be enough to let them know they weren't alone.

Andy had gone quiet. 'There's a woman.'

She looked up. 'Not a girl?'

'She's thirty. Name's Zoe Bradwell. I found her through the clippings service ... remember, you told me to look for suicides who were orphaned young? Well, she tried, and changed her mind – jumped off a cliff and managed to grab a tree on the way down. Knocked out and found by some walkers the next day. Looked half dead to them but she came round in the ambulance and discharged herself before they got her through the hospital doors. I followed up. A week later she was back at work, looking just fine. She's been married and divorced, no kids. Are you OK, Diana?'

'Fuck. These are the ones I should have found, but I just sat around, being selfish. Have you made contact?'

'I've found out where she lives and had a sniff round. Definitely a Shifter and definitely very, very careful with it.'

'Any other scents?'

'You're thinking of our blond friends? No, just her.'

'Just her.' Diana bit her lip. 'Do you think Duncan and Laura would accept her?'

'She's ten years older than them, they're just kids.'

'OK, leave it with me. We can't lose her, and if she's tried suicide once, she might try again. Write her address down, please.'

'Sure. You want the reports on fight training and looking for our blond friends?'

'Yeah, but I'll put the kettle on first. Can you or John help Mum here while I go to visit this Ms Bradwell?'

'We'll work something out.' Andy took a deep breath. 'About those new babies?'

'Sure hon, let me get this Bradwell woman sorted, and I'm all yours.'

The hired meeting room was cosy and small, with three comfortable chairs and a small table. Diana spotted Zoe Bradwell at reception and introduced herself before showing her to the meeting room.

'What's this about?' Zoe asked. 'I mean, I got an email saying someone might be interested in hiring me. You know I already have a job?'

'We know, we're just exploring possibilities. You've done some good work over the last few years, and you've been noticed. My boss, Ms Tasker, is running a bit late, are you OK for an hour or two? We've ordered coffee and cakes, they'll be here soon.'

'An hour, then I really have to get back. I've told work I have a dental appointment.' Zoe shrugged. 'Unless you really want the cakes, you should cancel them. I'm trying to lose weight.'

Diana looked at the woman who stood at the window, looking at the car park, waiting for the mythical Ms Tasker. Zoe was tall, taller than Mark and John. Her blonde hair was short and artfully styled, and her make-up was subtle and very office chic. Her clothes were indeed rather tight, and Diana suspected that any weight gain was recent. Clothes a size up would solve the problem.

'Oh, once you're out of your twenties, it's a constant struggle, isn't it?' Diana laughed. 'But you know, for women like us, it's easy to make a few changes and then we can go back to wolfing our meals down. Body shape isn't fixed, after all.'

Zoe masked a frown, looking at Diana properly for the first time. 'What do you mean? Cardio? Weights? I'm too busy for all that.'

'Sure, but there's always time for a run, isn't there? Maybe a few times round the park, or even out in the countryside. Maybe at night, when it's quieter…'

Zoe blinked. 'Do you run?'

'Sure. I put my running coat on, take a few laps round the woods. Of course, all that gets my appetite going, so I'm apt to tear into a good meal straight after. You know, get my teeth into something tasty.'

Zoe took a step closer to Diana. 'Any special kind of running coat?'

'Oh, I've had it for years. Keeps me warm, great fit, suits me perfectly. I was wondering if you had anything similar.'

'There's no Ms Tasker, is there?'

'No. Just me, Diana Foster. Wondering how you like to run. In a friendly way, of course.'

'Is there a job?'

'Oh, if you want one, there probably is. I have connections. But this is really a way to get you somewhere where we can talk. Do you want to talk?'

Zoe bit her lower lip. 'I do. But not here. Let's go back to my place.'

'Your dental appointment?' Diana smiled.

'Work can wait. I'll tell them I needed a filling and I'm taking the rest of the afternoon off.'

A young man knocked on the door and brought in a tray of coffee and cream cakes. Diana thanked him, and told him to add them to the bill but take them to the staff room, as the meeting had ended earlier than planned.

Zoe's home was clean and well organised. She made a pot of strong coffee and invited Diana to sit down.

'How long have you known?' Zoe asked.

'About you? A few days. About as long as it took to organise the meeting.'

'And how did you find out?'

'Enough of that,' Diana said, kindly but firmly. 'Tell me about yourself. Tell me your story. Tell me about the wolf.'

Zoe took a deep breath, then released it in a sudden sob. Diana reached across and took her hand, waiting. The sobs came faster and louder, and Diana moved across to hold the younger woman until she'd tired herself out.

Zoe wiped her face and looked up. 'Sorry, I'm sorry. I thought I was alone.'

She told of a childhood where she was free to do what she wanted. Her dad had died of an infection when she was an infant, and her mother had been chronically sick and trusted Zoe to run the household. 'I was a young carer, and when the dreams came, the dreams of running and being free, I accepted them. It was months before I realised they weren't dreams, that I really was Changing. It was terrifying.'

Diana nodded. 'Of course it was.'

'Mum died when I was eighteen. We lived in a council house and I could have stayed, got the tenancy transferred, but I moved away, got a uni place and hardship grants, worked a full-time job too because... Do you need much sleep?'

Diana shook her head. 'No, none of us do, after first Change.'

'Yes, well, got through uni, first-class degree in English Literature. I wanted to be a writer but had nothing to write about in any way that I could write, so I fell into PR, corporate for a while, then a couple of years with a big charity, then back to corporate. Not much difference, to

be honest. I married young. He didn't want kids, I did …
maybe hoping for someone like me?' She looked at Diana,
questioning.

'Carry on.' Diana smiled. 'It's OK.'

'Yeah, well, last year he left me, someone younger.
I wasn't even thirty. Do you know about the fall?'

'I do.'

'It was on purpose.' Zoe closed her eyes and
swallowed.

'I guessed that. It's not unusual for us to give up
when we think we're alone. It's probably our biggest cause
of death. It's OK, you're not alone now.'

'Thank you. Well, I recovered physically, but was
still shaky. I stopped Changing as much, it made me
nervous. I went down to just once a month. I was thinking
of maybe moving somewhere else, finding a new job, then
I got the call, about you … Ms Tasker … the job offer.'

'Anything else?' Diana asked. 'Did your ex know
about the furriness?'

'Hell no, he slept like a log, and, anyway, he was
away with his job a lot. Or he said he was. It wasn't a good
marriage. Nobody knows.'

'Brothers, sisters, cousins? Aunts and uncles?'

'Grandmothers are both dead. Grandfathers are
both alive, but I've sniffed around both their houses and
there's no sign of anything … erm, wolf-related. Mum and
Dad were both only children. There are second cousins
through both my granddads, but not my grandmas, they
were only children too, as was I.'

'Close friends?'

'An ex-girlfriend, from years ago. We were together
for six months, never moved in or anything, but we still

talk. She doesn't know about the fur or the … the fall. So, not that close, I suppose?"

Diana nodded. 'OK. Now, in the privacy and safety of your own home, I'm going to ask for something. I'm absolutely sure we're both talking around the same thing, but if we're going to move on, I need proof. Can you Change for me?' Diana's voice was firm, but she'd never asked this of an adult before.

'Now?'

'I'm a busy woman.' Diana smiled.

'Well, I've got work tomorrow and, you know, hair and stuff…'

'Please?' Diana let her smile harden. Zoe nodded and undressed. The Change came quickly, smoothly, and the brindle wolf that stood before Diana lowered its gaze and then its head.

'Come,' Diana said softly, and caressed the wolf around the ears, digging her fingers into the thick fur. 'You are beautiful,' she whispered. 'Now, Change back.'

Zoe, human again, looked very different. The make-up was gone, and so was the short blonde hair. Zoe's default setting, it seemed, was shoulder-length, mousy hair of a similar texture to Diana's own.

Diana was grinning. 'Oh, you are a wonder. I wish I'd found you years ago. It's my fault. You should never have been alone for so long. I have to go home now, but I promise you, your life is going to change.'

'She did *what?*' Mark stared at Andy in horror.

'She invited this Zoe Bradwell to visit Silverwood, to see how we work together, and to meet the kids. She reckons it'll be good for the little 'uns to see another Shifter adult.'

Mark shook his head. 'And how do we know this woman is friendly? That she's not in league with those blond bastards who killed Diana's sister? What if she leads them to Silverwood? What if she attacks one of the kids while she's there?'

Andy frowned. 'Diana will be there. You think anyone could get to our kids with Diana there? Besides, Diana says we have to show trust, we have to make allies and we have to find more friends.'

Mark bit at his thumb. 'Can you be there, Andy? I can't, I really can't. I'm only home for a few days and Katie has plans. Shit. Diana should have talked to me before she went to meet this woman.'

Andy sat down on Mark's sofa and put his stockinged feet on the coffee table. 'Look, she tried to. She left messages, but you didn't reply. Zoe has attempted suicide once, and Diana was frantic to get to her as quickly as she could. And I can't be there – there's a party with Helen's work friends and I promised weeks ago. Just poor timing. Anyway, it's been a long drive, Mark, any chance of a coffee?'

Mark shook his head. 'She has to give me more time! Bloody Diana. Everything was going OK, and then she pulls this. Fine. Get your own coffee, you know where it is, and make one for me while you're at it. I'm going to phone John, and ask *him* to be there when this Zoe person gets to Silverwood.'

Andy sighed and got to his feet. 'Seriously? John?' he said. 'Well, on your head be it.'

Diana met Zoe at the gate and escorted her to the large catering kitchen. A battered oak table sat in a corner near the door to the rest of the house, with four mismatched wooden chairs around it. Zoe took a seat and looked around as Diana sliced home-made cake. 'I hope the cake is OK, my daughter Miranda made it. She's only nine, so please be kind.'

'This is a big kitchen,' Zoe observed.

'It was a catering kitchen, for the hotel. There are a lot of us here.'

'How many?' Zoe asked.

Diana blinked and took a deep breath. 'We can trust you, can't we?'

'You know what I am, and you came to me to offer help and friendship. Yes, you can trust me.'

'Well then, there's me, my mum, who is a carrier – she lives in the cottage. There are three men – they're like us – who are the fathers of my kids, but they don't live here. They're public figures and maintain separate lives. They visit. Anyway, I have fifteen kids – seven sets of twins and Miranda, who isn't a Shifter. That's what I call us, Shifters. The youngest twins are nearly five months old, the oldest are just ten years old. Six boys, nine girls, so far. Miranda's a carrier too. Her dad died before she was born. Not Shifter-related, just something … horrible. So yeah, seventeen living here, three regular visitors. Oh, one of the men has a daughter with his wife, another of the men has a son with his wife, and she's pregnant again, so I suppose between us we have seventeen kids, going on eighteen. It's scary when you think about it, so I try not to. Ah, here's Seth, he's one of the ten-year-olds. I asked him to come to meet you because the kids are dying to meet another adult

Shifter, but I didn't want to overwhelm you. He's here to brew up and report back to the others. My mother will probably wander in at some point to look you over. She's supposed to be here to help me look after the kids, but she seems to spend most of her time in the cottage, which I honestly can't complain about because she steps up when I ask her to. Whew, that's a lot. Sorry. Tea? Coffee? Milk? Sugar?'

Seth cleared his throat. 'There was a phone call. MarkDad asked JohnDad to come by, and AndyDad rang to let you know.'

'And … it's impossible to keep anything quiet in this house.' Diana laughed. 'Yes, their dads are called Mark, John and Andy. We don't particularly pay any attention to actual paternity, it's more of a case of three dads and a mum parenting fifteen kids and trying to be fair to all of them.' She glanced at Seth. 'I'll have tea, black today, I think. Zoe?'

'Oh, black tea too, with lemon if you have it?'

Diana took a sheet of paper from the back pocket of her jeans. 'I made a list, of things to go through with you. OK, genetics, other Shifters, enemies, basic biology, history as we know it … we'd better get started.'

'Enemies?' Zoe raised an eyebrow.

'I'll get to that, I promise.'

Zoe spent the morning at Silverwood. Diana left her a couple of times, to deal with the youngest babies and unavoidable domestic tasks. Jane Foster wandered in via the back door, and introduced herself quickly before leaving again before Diana could find a job for her.

As Diana was explaining what she knew about how the mate-bonding process worked, John stepped through the back door.

'Here to report back to Mark?' Diana asked, smiling.

'Yeah, can't stay long. We're supposed to be working on new stuff but Grumpy and Lanky keep disappearing.' He glanced at Zoe. 'Hi. You the new girl? Welcome to the madhouse.'

Zoe leaned back in her chair and took a sip of tea from her mug. 'John Preston. And I guess that Grumpy and Lanky are Mark Preston and Andrew Ransome?'

'Ah,' John said, blushing 'We're not that famous outside rock music. I didn't expect to be recognised.'

'I can keep a secret. I met you when I worked in corporate PR. You flirted with me.'

'Really?' John smiled.

Diana closed her eyes and sighed.

'I was blonde that night, and dressed-up. But you probably don't remember.'

'I flirt a lot, but my heart is here.' John smiled. 'I bet you look amazing blonde. Although I'd put your natural shade as dark blonde, you know?'

'Mousy, that's what my ex called it.' Zoe grinned.

'An ex? If he let you go, he's obviously a fool, so forget the mousy thing. Dark blonde, yeah. Zoe, is it?'

Zoe glanced at Diana, who had stopped rolling her eyes and was paying close attention.

Diana's mother wandered into the kitchen. 'I saw that John was here. I wondered if he could have a look at my bathroom tap. It's dripping.'

'On it, Mrs F,' John said, and left via the back door.

Jane started to follow him, then glanced back at Diana and Zoe. 'Be careful,' she told Diana as she left.

Diana's phone rang and she picked it up.

It was Mark. 'No,' he said.

Diana took a deep breath and ended the call. Thirty seconds later the phone rang again. She answered.

'Diana here,' she said.

'I know it's "Diana here". It's your phone. Don't hang up on me. It's hard enough sneaking around keeping this phone charged and finding a spare minute to ring you. Don't hang up on me.'

'Hiya, Mark, how are you?' Diana put the phone on speaker and settled back with her knitting. The kids were in bed; she'd spent three hours in the lab, and the house was in a mostly satisfactory state. The early hours were a quiet time when she could listen to music and enjoy some peace. She glanced into the basket where her babies slept. 'I've put you on speaker, but Nancy and Susie are asleep next to me, so keep your voice down.'

'Take me off speaker then, because I just might shout.'

'I'm knitting new sweaters for Caleb and Sammy, so I don't have a spare hand, so you're on speaker. If you shout, I end the call. When are you visiting? I'm getting really itchy for you.'

'You are the most annoying woman I've ever met.'

'Sucks, doesn't it.' Diana was glad it wasn't a video call, and worried for a moment that Mark could actually hear her grinning.

'Is it true? That you want to move this woman in with you? As part of the pack? Because I vote no.'

'Noted. I wish you'd said that yesterday, because then I might have been able to do something about it. I rang and texted to tell you John was smitten, but got no reply. And I'll remind you that it was you who asked him to come round. As it was, I had to guess how you'd respond to having another adult around the place to look after your kids, to protect them if we're ever attacked at home, and to stop me from going bonkers with loneliness when the three of you disappear on tour next month. So, I made the assumption that you give a shit about me and the kids, and I told Zoe and John that they had my blessing. They went into the woods, they are well and truly mated, and she's gone back home to start packing. She's probably pregnant too. Oh, and Andy and I started off those kids I've been promising him for years, so all three of you will be daddies again. Isn't that nice?"

There was silence, and more silence.

Diana leaned over and looked at her phone. 'Call Ended' it said. She kissed her sleeping baby daughters and shrugged. 'Someone is in deep shit, and it might as well be me.'

Her phone beeped. There was a text.

> *Your mother lives there, isn't that enough? Congratulations on the pregnancy. I am so*

> *angry with all of you that I can't speak. I miss you.*

She sighed and replied.

> *I miss you too. This will be fine, I promise. I'll see you soon.*

Zoe fitted into Silverwood life as if she'd always been there. Diana marvelled at how quickly the children accepted her as a second mother. Zoe had resigned from her job; it was too far away to commute. She set up her own PR company and soon found that work was trickling in as Andy quietly recommended her to various Ransome Industries companies. He was Creative Director of the family business now, a role that merged easily with his band responsibilities.

Jane Foster found it harder to accept another woman at Silverwood, and at first was frosty to Zoe, seeing her as a threat to Diana and John's relationship. Slowly, seeing how fond Diana was of the younger woman, Jane thawed. A month into Zoe's acceptance into the pack, Diana made a cautious pass, late at night. Zoe responded with enthusiasm.

John joined Diana in the lab the following night as she examined samples. She responded to his unspoken question. 'Your bond with her is a different chemical to mine, it shows that each bond is unique. There's no big difference between my bond with her, and the bonds with you guys. They're not gender-specific in any clear way. Are you OK with this? With me and Zoe being together?'

John laughed. 'You're kidding? I'm just waiting for an invitation to join in.'

Diana pulled a face. 'I'm not sure I'm ready for that quite yet, but yes, one day.'

Andy made it clear that he wasn't going to have a sexual relationship with Zoe, but he welcomed her to the pack with small gifts, career support and encouragement to start writing again. The pair of them were obviously fond of each other, but Andy explained that he had everything he needed and he wasn't prepared to add another secret to the ones he was already keeping from Helen.

Mark was frostily polite to both Zoe and Diana on his increasingly short visits to Silverwood. He'd disappear with Diana for a few minutes to slake their addiction, then spend the rest of his time with the children. Zoe was amused by his obvious reluctance to engage with her on any level.

'He thinks I'm going to seduce him! He is *so* not my type,' she confided to Diana. 'I can't abide a moody bloke.'

'He's not moody, he's just got a lot to worry about,' Diana replied.

'He's got a lot to enjoy too, but he chooses to worry rather than have fun.' Zoe shrugged. 'But you're obviously besotted, so I'll shut up.'

Zoe was all about fun, and things changed in subtle ways. Household chores became games and competitions. There was more music, more spontaneous laughter, and Diana found she could trust her new mate.

It finally seemed possible to get the older kids enrolled in high schools. Miranda, Noah and Seth were due to start the following year, and Diana was determined that her eldest daughter would not be at the same school as her eldest sons. Twins excited comment – three kids from the same family in the same school year would raise questions she wasn't prepared to answer. With Jane and Zoe both available to help with school runs, things looked much easier. Preparing her free-range kids for the constraints of high school was going to be interesting, but her mother already had things in hand, preparing a small classroom and spending three days a week training the older children to stick to a timetable and not wander off whenever they felt a lesson was done.

There was a feeling of charged excitement at Silverwood, with the prospect of four new babies arriving at once. Mark had accepted Zoe as a family member, and although he was surprised when she asked him to act as her midwife, he readily agreed. His second child with Katie, a boy named Matthew, was nearly three months old when he was urgently called back to Silverwood to welcome the new pack kids into the world.

'Are they born yet?' John's voice was clearly audible from behind the bathroom door, and Mark spared a moment to look up and grin at Zoe.

'He's always been like this,' he assured her. 'Come on, woman, one good push … ah, that's the first one. The second won't be far behind. I'll give … him … a minute or two to realise the traffic jam has cleared. Here's your eldest son.'

Zoe still had her eyes closed. 'I want Diana.'

'Now? This minute?'

Her eyes shot open, and for a moment she suspected that the Alpha might have some kind of embryonic sense of humour. The grave look on his face convinced her otherwise, and she nodded seriously. 'Yes, will you call for her, please? Please?'

'John, get Di,' Mark called out. 'And don't panic. Everything's fine.'

'Why can't John be here?' Zoe asked after taking several deep breaths. She peered down to see what Mark was doing, but shut her eyes again as a contraction took her.

'Because he faffs,' Mark murmured. 'And that'll wind you up and it's not good for babies. Did I say you have sons?'

'I don't care what they are, just get them out,' Zoe muttered. She glanced towards the door, which banged open. Diana strode in, looking anxious.

'Problem, hon?'

'No, just wanted you to see what I can do,' Zoe said.

Diana had already taken the first baby from Mark and was cleaning and weighing him. She had a small bag with her, and Zoe winced as Diana took a few drops of blood from the baby's heel, then handed him back to her.

'What do I do?' Zoe asked.

'Whatever feels natural,' Diana said absently. 'Mark, how's that second one?'

'Crowning. No probs. Zoe, you sure this is your first birth?'

'I think I would have remembered.' The new mum took a deep breath. 'Push?'

'Whenever…' Mark said.

'Are they here yet?' John's voice, behind the door, held an element of suppressed panic.

'Let him in…' Zoe sighed. 'Or send him to the pub, I don't care which.' She closed her eyes and concentrated hard.

Mark gave a stifled yell as the second baby came out fast. 'Little 'un. About four pounds?' he said quietly. 'Is that enough?'

'He's fine,' Diana said within a couple of seconds, as the second child gave a small cry then accepted the comfort of the Alpha's scent.

'He knows you,' Diana said.

John was standing behind her. 'Lemme see. Is that the first one?' He looked up at Zoe, and realised that she was nursing. 'Oh, oh. He's *cute*. Gimme?'

'Let them feed!' Diana laughed, then hugged him. 'Congratulations, hon, they're fine and healthy and everything good.' She took the second child from Mark, to clean and measure him, and held him close.

'You're crying,' John said. 'Are you really OK with this?' His voice was pitched very low.

'I'm very OK with this. It's just that this is the first time I've ever held anyone else's brand new babies.' Diana cleared a smear of mucus from the tiny twin's lip. 'He is adorable, isn't he.'

John, reassured, had moved away and was kneeling by the chair, holding Zoe's hand. 'Can we call them Pippin and Merry?'

'No,' Zoe said.

'OK. How about Harry and Sirius?'

'Over my dead body.' Zoe smiled sweetly. 'I was thinking Isaac and Ian, actually.'

'Perfect,' John said instantly. 'Look, I'll go and get you a glass of water while you do the yucky bit.'

He disappeared out of the bedroom, and Mark shrugged. 'He claims he's allergic to afterbirth. Come on, lass, we're not finished yet. Isaac and Ian eh? I like those names. Di? Have you named those little blonds yet?'

'Andy asked me to name them Nathan and Joseph, after his dad. I didn't really have anything else in mind.'

Diana finished cleaning Ian and sat beside Zoe, allowing her to nurse the newborns. 'That's OK, hon, you can feed them both together, or in turn, whatever feels right. Make sure the little one gets his share.' She laughed. 'Oh look at that – Isaac just smacked Ian in the face. Nat and Joe are exactly the same. We're going to have fun with these four, I can see. It'll be like having quads. Yes, they're the Quads, aren't they?'

Time passed for the pack. Undeterred by the rush of two sets of twins arriving together, Diana and Zoe repeated the feat the following year. They had the money and the space, and the older pack kids were enthusiastic about new babies. Andy, his other family expanded by the birth of Naomi, his second daughter with Helen, cheered Diana on, but told her he was happy with his contribution to the pack and wouldn't be asking her to give him more Shifter kids. The arrival of the pack's second lot of 'quads' brought the total number of children up to twenty-seven.

Mark shook his head as he and John cuddled their new daughters. 'What have they called them?' he asked.

'Yours and Diana's are Elizabeth and Margaret, but they're already Beth and Meg. They're gonna look like you, sorry. I've seen it before. Mine and Zoe's are Tara and Louise. Looks like we've got Quadettes hot on the heels of the Quads.'

Mark took a deep breath. 'Twenty-seven,' he said. 'Twenty-bloody-seven.'

'You gonna ask 'em if they wanna stop?' John asked.

'Nope, we're coping.' Mark tried to hide his grin, but John saw it and laughed.

Six months later, in the deep midwinter of 2008, nine-year-old Bill Preston went to his grandma's cottage to find out why she wasn't answering the phone. He found her cold in her bed. He sat and held her hand for ten minutes, listening to the wind howl at the windows, before he rang the big house and asked for Diana.

She ran over, bursting through the door and holding him tight for a long time. It was the first death the kids had experienced, and they were allowed to visit the body and say goodbye before it was taken away.

A post-mortem revealed a stroke; it had been fast. The funeral was held in the North East, and was well attended by old colleagues and ex-pupils. Diana received the mourners alone. Jane was buried in the same grave as her husband, according to her wishes.

And still, the pack grew. Diana gave birth to Mark's daughters, Leah and Deborah, the following June, and in May 2009, Zoe gave birth to her and John's third set of twins. She named them Liam and Patrick, after her grandfathers.

Chapter 16

Noah was the first of the kids to Change. He and his twin had both been impatient for it since they were eleven, but it didn't come until they were almost fourteen. Noah had been restless since he got back from school, pacing around the house, looking in the fridge, checking the TV, radio and his favourite websites. He was looking for something, but he didn't know what. He was driving his mothers up the wall, winding up Bridget and Trixie and generally being a teenager. Finally, he picked a fight with Seth, and they ended up in the back garden having a screaming match with each other. Diana was too close to them, and too wound up by them, to see what was happening. But Zoe had been watching them both closely, and was Changed and outside as soon as Seth's shouts turned to screams and Noah's shouts turned to growls. Seth got away with nothing more than a deep scratch on his arm, and Zoe had Noah pinned down before he could do any more damage. He calmed down pretty quickly, having managed a clean and fast first Change.

Staying in wolf form, he danced around Seth, taunting him a little. Seth shrugged, knowing that he couldn't be far behind his twin. Before too long, every kid that could as much as toddle was out there, looking at Noah with wide-open eyes. Frankie and Billy were especially impressed. Diana caught a constipated, cross-eyed look about them both that made her smile.

Diana took Noah for his first run. To her joy, he was also a red wolf. He took a while to get used to being four-legged, and fell over his feet a couple of times before he got the hang of running properly. After an hour, Diana encouraged him to Change back, and led him back to the bedroom he shared with his twin.

He was excited but exhausted, jumping into bed and pulling the covers up, dark eyes shining with excitement. 'I never really believed it would happen to me,' he confided.

His mother sat on the bed, squeezing his hand. 'It's hard for me to take too. You're on your way to growing up!'

He looked worried. 'Will I have to leave home?'

She hugged him. 'No, not until you're ready, and certainly not before you're able to cope by yourself.'

Seth bounced into the room, throwing a bag of crisps at his brother, who ate them ravenously. 'I thought you'd be hungry,' he said. 'Mum and Zoe always eat like pigs after a Change.' He gave his twin a big hug. 'Congratulations!'

'You need to speak to MarkDad,' Diana told Noah. 'It's OK, I know that Katie is out tonight – he's looking after your half-brothers.'

The eldest two boys were aware of the complex family history; they'd been old enough and mature enough to trust with it for a couple of years now. Diana dialled Mark's landline and when he answered she handed the phone straight to Noah.

'I did it, Dad!' Then he couldn't say anything else, just held on to the phone tightly, listening. His eyes were shining, and a big smile was spreading over his face.

Seth was doing his best not to be jealous, and Diana whispered to him that she was proud of him too, for handling it so well. The scratch that Noah had given him was already scabbing nicely.

'Dad wants to talk to you,' Noah said after a few minutes, handing the phone to Diana.

'What colour wolf?' was his first question.

'He's red,' she answered.

Mark sighed happily. 'I'm on my way down the first chance I get!'

He arrived three days later. Diana watched from the window as he walked towards the house. He spotted her and grinned, and she smiled back, then started to laugh as two red wolves darted out of the house and ran at Mark. He undressed, leaving his clothes on the drive, and Changed, following the boys around the side of the house.

Diana ran to the back of the house, and saw the three wolves disappearing into the woods. She was desperate to join them, but was halted by Sara, who was an obvious minor casualty of her brothers' excitement and Seth's first Change. Her jeans were torn and covered in wolf slaver, but she was unharmed.

'Boys! They are disgusting!' she was muttering. 'Wait 'til I can do it, I'll show 'em.'

'You'll be amazing,' Diana said, then spotted Miranda standing at the window, staring wistfully at the woods. She walked over to her tall blonde child and took her hand. 'And you'll be amazing too.'

'I'll never have what they'll have,' Miranda whispered.

'There are other things to look forward to.' Diana promised her.

Mark found her later that night. When they came together, there was a rare tenderness to his touch, and afterwards he told her that he and Katie would be moving closer to Silverwood. Katie had been offered a prestigious new job north of Manchester, and Mark had taken the chance to steer their choice of a new home to one that was less than half an hour away. Diana understood. Leeds was only an hour or so away, in theory, but traffic was getting worse every year, and it was getting harder and harder for Mark to make a quick visit and get home without being missed by Katie.

The pack continued to grow. Mark and Diana's third set of sons were named Henry and Michael, while Zoe and John's second pair of daughters, Julie and Leanne, arrived a year later. Diana started to wonder if she was getting too old for more pregnancies; she'd taken a day or two to recover from Harry's and Michael's birth. She was in her mid-forties now, and starting to wonder how much more she could reasonably expect from her Shifter body.

First Changes had become a matter of regular celebration, with Bill, Frank, Darlene and Sara all finding their wolf selves as their hormones surged. To everyone's surprise, Bridget and Trixie managed their first Changes at the tender age of twelve. The Change brought the expected benefits to the older children; they enjoyed the ability to heal faster, recover from injuries quickly and manage with very little sleep. These were all secrets they had to hide from their schoolfriends and teachers, but they had their parents to help and advise them, and more importantly, they had their siblings to confide in and learn from. They learned to fight and to run, to make the most of their every ability, and to a child, they were determined to protect their pack.

Chapter 17

Despite all their precautions, Silverwood's outreach work with lone werewolves had led to rumours of a large pack somewhere in Britain. Andy had changed his mobile number; he was getting too many calls that he didn't trust. Zoe had taken over as the main contact for loners; she had an instinct for the truth. If someone claimed to be a werewolf needing to be matched up with a pack, they were given a remote location to travel to and Change, while a Silverwood Pack member watched from the shadows. Diana started taking one of the older kids with her on these trips; they needed the experience. Miranda and Diana had had several heated discussions about the whole thing, and eventually the Alpha had consented to Miranda coming along occasionally. She might not be a Shapeshifter, but she was still pack, and she desperately wanted to help. Seth and Noah were reliable, but Darlene and Sara made the best company. Billy and Frankie were far too aggressive with strangers to really trust in these situations, but they were favourites of Diana's, and she fought for their right to get the experience they needed. Bridget and Trixie were not invited. Diana judged them still too young to trust on a mission.

Zoe was spending more time in the outside world. She'd found a talent as a writer, and Diana got used to dozing off to the glow of the laptop screen as Zoe typed away. Her first book had been a slow burner that had gone bestseller, with a helping hand from Andy's contacts. She was pleased that she could help to support the family with the proceeds. The pack was wealthy, but with nearly three dozen kids to support, every penny was welcome.

The first hint of trouble was the blond salesman at the gate. Diana had realised that she couldn't see Susie and Nancy anywhere. She went to look for them, and called for Zoe, who joined her outside. At six years old, the girls were fairly trustworthy, but Diana had a bad feeling. She Changed and found their scent easily. They had walked up the drive. Diana ran towards the gate, Zoe in human form close behind her. The little girls were looking through the railings at a tall blond guy who was chatting to them pleasantly enough.

'Mum,' they said when Diana arrived, grabbing hold of her fur.

Zoe took their hands. 'Yes, Mummy's here,' she said. 'We don't want any, whatever you're selling,' she told the guy.

He was staring at Diana and the twins. 'That's a nice dog. Part wolf, is it?' he commented. Diana's hackles raised; she didn't like the smell of him, and she really didn't like the look of him. It had been eight years since Joyce's death, and Diana's struggle with the white wolves had been conducted in darkness and confusion, but there was a strong resemblance between the men on the riverbank, and this stranger at the gate.

Zoe turned on her heel, ignoring him, walking back to the house with the girls in tow. Diana remained, pacing back and forwards in front of the gate. After a short while, the blond walked away.

Diana ran back to the house and Changed, dressing as simply as she could, and running to the living room, where all the children had been gathered together by Zoe. Caleb stood behind Zoe, looking very serious. He was the image of Mark, and knew it. His twin, Sammy, was joking and playing with the younger kids, keeping them calm.

Diana's gaze swept the room, counting kids. She took a deep breath. 'OK, you're going down the basement and into the tunnel. We've practised this. Sammy, it's your job to lock the tunnel to the annexe from the inside once everyone is out of the main house. Alice and Jane, you're in charge of the others. You all need to stay in the tunnel and keep quiet. I want Zoe, Cal and Sammy to go straight through the tunnel to the annexe, with mobile phones set to silent. Stay away from the windows and don't go upstairs. There's food and water there. Use the downstairs loo in the annexe if you have to, but don't flush. Keep the lights off. Keep all the doors locked. Alice, I need you to be a big girl today, lock the tunnel from the inside please when ZoeMum and Cal and Sammy are through to the annexe. Show me our special knock that says you can open the door.' She watched as both Jane and Alice rapped out the rhythm. She smiled. 'Don't worry, we're just being careful. Zoe, ring the guys, please. Caleb, Sammy, can you carry Michael and Harry for us? Alice and Jane, can you manage Julie and Leanne? I want Zoe to have her hands free.'

She watched them head for the basement and the escape route she'd planned years ago, then she messaged her older kids. Seth, Noah, Sara and Darlene were at one school, Miranda, Bridget and Trixie at a second and Bill and Frank at a third. Miranda usually took the bus home; the others cycled in good weather.

'Plan 2' Diana messaged all of them. There wasn't time to drive around three different schools; she had to get them all safe as quickly as possible.

Replies came from all nine kids almost immediately. No details, just 'OK Mum'.

She took the people carrier, noting that there was no sign of anyone lurking by the gate. As she arrived at the first school, taxis drew up carrying her kids from the other two schools, stopping separately. She made eye contact with each child, and waited, approving as they all casually checked their surroundings.

Miranda bent to tie a loose shoelace, her younger sisters flanking her, alert. They drifted towards their mother, casually getting into her car. One of each twin lay down, hidden from view. Even now, Diana was wary of gossip.

The journey home was quiet, and a mile from home Diana suggested that all the kids hide themselves from view. Only then did she hear a sound from them, as Bridget got the giggles. A chorus of 'Shush!' made Diana smile, then all was quiet.

A rusty van she'd not seen before was parked half a mile from the gate. There was a footpath nearby, into the fields that bordered Silverwood. A blond guy was leaning against the wall. Diana drove quickly through the gate, locking it behind her. She drove the car to the big house and moved her older children inside via the back door.

She rang Zoe, who answered instantly. 'You got 'em?'

'Every one, safe and sound. You OK?'

'Perfect,' Zoe confirmed.

'Guys?'

'John's on his way. He set out about five minutes after you did. I gave Andy that coded message you told me to use, and he just said, "OK". I think he's with someone. Mark isn't answering. I sent him a coded text but…'

Diana hung up and rang the number that Mark kept for her use alone.

'I'm in the loo!' he said. 'Is it urgent? We've got Katie's parents coming for dinner, and I can't get away.'

'I think we're being watched, and I don't think it's friendly. There are strangers around,' she said.

'OK, I'm on my way,' he said calmly. Diana was taken aback.

'I just wanted to let you know…'

'I'm on my way. I've expected something like this for a long time. If there's trouble before I get there, deal with it, kay?' He hung up. Diana's phone rang again instantly.

It was Andy. 'I'll be there,' was all he said.

Diana gave her instructions. The older kids were to stay in the basement, to provide a last defence to the tunnel if she failed. 'Look after the little ones,' she told them. She spoke to Zoe next. 'Stay in the annexe. Only drop the shutters if you're targeted. Let's keep attention away from the annexe as long as we can. Stay human, stay smart.'

'I can fight. I can fight as well as you.'

'One of us has to stay with the kids, and it's going to be you,' Diana said. 'I love you, Zoe, but just do what I ask. Please.'

Diana took a breath, without knowing enemy numbers, she couldn't make more plans. The longer she could stay human, the better it would be. She thought about the kids sitting in the dark. They would stay quiet, she knew that, even the babies. She sat on the porch, her back to the house, and waited. She'd never known a silence like it. It was broken by a distant noise: a van door shutting, multiple murmured voices, carried to her by some freak of the wind. More than two then. Time was passing, and she needed information.

She knew her territory, and crept around the estate, establishing that there were nine intruders, all male, all related to each other. She caught John's wolf scent and glanced towards him.

He was deep in the undergrowth, watching her cautiously. His eyes flickered to her left, and she spotted a tall blond guy, in his early twenties, downwind of her, leaning against a tree. He was speaking into a mobile, in German. She caught a few words, but couldn't understand.

She growled low in her throat, hackles rising. The guy heard her and instinctively fell to all fours, starting to Change. Two more men appeared, saw her, and began the Change. The first one was at a vulnerable stage – it was coming slowly for him – and she didn't hesitate. She sprang. His blood was in her mouth in a sudden fountain. He twitched and died.

More men arrived, and John grabbed her tail in his mouth and pulled. They were outnumbered, and he wanted to leave. They ran full pelt towards the house. The pale-coated wolves were checking their fallen comrade.

Halfway to the house, Diana and John found themselves face to face with eight sturdy young wolves.

Diana stopped dead. Her wolf saw allies. Her human saw her children. She glanced behind her; the grounds were clear, for now. She Changed to human, and signalled to them to stay wolf. They were right: this was the best way for them to protect their younger siblings.

'Seth, I need you to find Mark. He's on his way, but alone. Tell him we're under attack. Get back safely, both of you. I don't want any heroics, but kill if you have to. Noah, go back to the annexe and stay with Zoe. We need at least two lots of teeth and claws if anyone breaks through. Frankie, Bill, you're off the leash. You know what to do.' The fourteen-year-old boys were tough and powerful, already taller than their father.

She addressed her girls, who were alert and ready. Beatrice and Bridget had suddenly grown up. She looked at them, and decided that if they were old enough to Change, they were old enough to fight. 'Sara, Darlene. Fight with your sisters, don't let them out of your sight. Andy will be with you as soon as he arrives.' She looked round once more, then Changed.

They took their positions and Zoe let Noah into the annexe. Seth disappeared silently into the woods. He knew them as well as anyone. As the Silverwood wolves spread out across the lawn, there was a gunshot. Frankie went down instantly, his foreleg shattered and bleeding. Bill was distracted and moved towards him, but Diana headed him off, away from danger. She looked in the direction the shot had come from and saw Darlene there already. Sara was following her. Frankie's jaw was clamped shut, and he was limping in agony towards the annexe.

The door opened, and Caleb and Samuel ran out, grabbing Frankie by the scruff and dragging him inside. All but one of the steel shutters on the annexe windows went down; Miranda was keeping watch through that one. Zoe was screaming in fury through the door. She'd had to Change back to human form to deal with Frankie's injury.

Diana looked around, another gunshot, and Sara skipped out of the way, superhuman reactions saving her. Darlene was at the first gunman now, and was facing him down. He was raising the gun. She was cautious, not experienced enough to take him down.

Bill was in a fury, heading towards the scene in a boiling frenzy of black fur and burning orange eyes. As he reached them, a net fell from the trees, snaring Darlene.

The gunman turned his weapon towards Bill, as two other men came from the trees and started to drag Darlene away. Their fates were sealed in that moment. The Bees were behind Sara, flanking her, looking wary.

Diana ran faster than ever before, towards Bill, ready to die for him, and buried her jaws in the stomach of the gunman before he could press the trigger. Hard muscle resisted for a moment, then she was in, tearing at intestines and losing herself in the sheer lust of the kill.

John was behind her, growling in her ear. The gunman was dead, and she was wasting time.

Bill had joined his sisters – instinctively protective, but a mistake. Together they made a better target.

Zoe appeared at the door. 'Scatter!' she screamed as two more gunshots rang out. Zoe slammed the door shut again.

Beatrice fell, stunned by a shot. Diana ran to her, it was a minor headwound, but she was helpless for the moment. John wanted to guard her, but she had the good sense to play dead. John winced as another bullet flew over his head. Bridget lay beside her twin, unwilling to leave her side, but Diana snarled at her and she moved.

Sara was looking for Darlene. Not seeing her, she started to howl. Two more blond men, another net, running for the Bees, from the woods. John nipped in and slashed their legs. Bill was with him, growling with pleasure, tasting blood.

Both of the intruders Changed; it helped to stem their blood loss a little, and they were good enough to do it quickly. They were as tough as John, but also had the air of experienced fighters. Bill was not going to be a match for them. Sara joined them; it was a stand-off.

Bridget was terrified; she wouldn't be able to help, she went to her twin and lay down next to her. She was out of the fight. Too young, too scared. Diana looked around for more of the enemy, wanting desperately to chase after Darlene, to check on Frankie, to go to her Bees and protect them. Two guys were at the annexe door, firing at the lock and the panels repeatedly. They must have come through the woods.

Noah and Zoe would have to deal with the two at the door. Bridget and Beatrice were safe, for now, but would need protection if more men appeared. Darlene was gone, and that was something that Diana had to put out of her mind for now. John was the one in the most trouble; he was the biggest threat to the enemy and the one they would want to take down first. She joined him, Bill and Sara as three more white wolves trotted out of the woods, hackles raised.

Every one of the white wolves outweighed the Silverwood wolves, and they outnumbered them too. They could see and smell their brother's blood on Diana's muzzle, and advanced towards her. The Silverwood wolves backed up, guarding each other's rear, four snarling mouths ready to fight and die for the pack.

Diana caught sight of John; he was loving this, not an ounce of fear in him. Two of the white wolves came at her together, one for the throat, one for her belly. She bit into the muzzle of the first attacker, and he screamed. Bill grabbed for the ear of the second one, and put a lifetime of fury into his next move, ripping the ear off and spitting it to the ground. He hadn't been quite fast enough. Diana felt a wound opening up on her side, but ignored it.

They tried another tactic: threatening Sara, who moved closer to John. Diana was back to back with her, trusting her daughter. Sara shot forward and grabbed the other ear of the bleeding white wolf, tearing enthusiastically and proving that Bill wasn't the only one to take trophies. Diana felt John relax next to her; he pushed himself against her for reassurance.

Two wolves shot into sight – one red, one black, both of them lithe and well-muscled – running out of the woods, unseen yet by the whites, both landing together on the back of the biggest attacker, bearing him down with their combined weight. Seth climbed over the head, and went for the throat; Mark twisted underneath and buried himself in the white leader's belly, castrating him in one tearing bite. Diana saw the dying, affronted look in the leader's eyes, and the shock as his brothers turned to see him go down.

Four against six now, better odds for Diana's family, but the white wolves were still stronger. Diana was contemplating the odds when she realised that Mark hadn't paused since castrating the leader, and had now spun around and ripped out the throat of another of the white wolves. The remaining three started to turn, to meet the new threat, and Mark flew headlong at the biggest and strongest of them, who lowered his head and turned away, evidently terrified. Too late, Mark had him; he was dead before he hit the ground. Bill and Seth had one of the other whites in their jaws, and all Diana saw was a whirling of white, black and red fur as the three of them thrashed around on the ground. The remaining enemy wolf launched himself at Sara while she was distracted by the fight in front of her. Diana ran in, low, knocking him off his feet, then danced back as John growled, wanting the kill, getting it.

Sara whimpered. Andy and Darlene were walking out from the trees, human, grinning.

Andy called out. 'I killed two, we're sure there's no more. Where do you want the bodies?'

Diana signalled to him to wait, and ran to the annexe, remembering the two men that had been at the door. They were dead. Zoe was on the floor, a horrible bite taken out of her thigh, pale and with her mouth shut tight against the moans she would not make in front of the kids. Noah had tied a belt around her thigh to slow the blood loss. One white wolf lay with his throat torn out. The other was still human, with a knife in his heart. Caleb was looking solemn and frightened. His arm was red to the elbow; it wasn't his blood. Samuel was still gripping his own knife and shaking with fear. Miranda was scowling as she joined them, surveying the damage. She shared a long look with her mother.

Diana Changed, and called to the Bees. 'You two, get up and get the kids out of the tunnel. And put the kettle on.' She smiled as they got to their feet and made for the main house.

The group in the annexe were joined by Andy and Darlene, who stopped smiling when they saw how badly Zoe and Frank were injured. Diana gave Darlene a long hug. 'Report please.' Diana said.

Darlene cleared her throat. 'They got me in the net, hit me on the head, thought I was knocked out. I wasn't really. One of them wanted to kill me straight away, the other one wanted to take me away somewhere. I think he wanted to try to mate me. I would have liked to see him try.' Diana glanced at Andy, who was gazing into space with a blank expression. Darlene continued. 'So they were arguing and paying no attention to me at all, and I managed to claw through enough of the net underneath me to get out and run away if they ever put their guns down. Then I saw Dad hiding in trees, and I Changed but I pretended to be unconscious still. That got their attention and they started arguing again. Dad jumped out and bit one through the back of the neck, and the other through the throat. I got out of the net and went wolf again, and we had a quick sniff around to find out where they all came from. There's a rusty old van on the other side of the wall but there's loads of traffic right now so we'll have to wait to check it out.'

Diana hugged her again. 'Good girl, you did everything right.'

Later, Andy commented that it had been harder work to bury their attackers than to kill them. He'd just finished helping Miranda, who had carefully taken tissue samples from each enemy corpse. The adults dug a deep pit near the top of a small hill on the edge of the property, while Seth and Noah dug up some holly and oak saplings to plant in the freshly turned earth that hid so many bodies.

With all wounds bathed and dressed and all casualties fed and cared for, the adults and teenagers sat around the table. Diana wouldn't leave Frankie's side, and kept touching him to make sure he was really alive. She'd found the bullet and set the bone herself, not trusting anyone else near him, fear taking hold of her at last. Caleb was sitting very quietly on her lap, Sammy at her feet. Zoe was pale and still trembling. Darlene was sitting on Andy's lap, her arms around his neck. Sara was stood behind them, her hand on Andy's shoulder, watching everyone. John was still grinning; he and Bill had just had the time of their lives. Mark was effortlessly alert, calm, watching the rest of the family. The younger girls were subdued, despite the words of praise from their older siblings.

'Next time, we'll kill some of 'em too,' whispered Bridget.

Mark glanced at her. He was trying to hide his approval of her, and Andy tried to hide a smile. Seth and Noah sat a little apart.

Seth spoke for both of them. 'Mum, they tried to take Darlene. That's not how packs work, is it?'

Diana shook her head. 'That's not how we work, and that's not how the packs we help to put together work. It's given us some very useful information about these white wolves though.' She turned to Miranda, who had been busy after the fight. 'Thank you for taking the tissue samples from them. You were so cool-headed to think of that.'

Miranda shrugged. 'I tried to avoid bite wounds. Saliva contamination, you know?'

Mark shook his head. 'If this one was a Shifter, she could've probably dealt with the lot of 'em by herself.'

Darlene spoke. 'Aunt Joyce was the expert on this kind of thing. I want to carry on with her research.'

Diana promised to find Joyce's academic notes.

Darlene was already a promising intellect. 'You can help me,' she said loftily to her twin, who wrinkled her nose at her.

Andy looked calm, but his mates could see the anger in his eyes. His blood was up. His girls had been threatened. He'd already said that he was going to sleep outside their door that night.

Mark looked up, clarity in his eyes. 'This pack isn't a secret any more, is it? I'm going to tell Katie before she hears from someone else.' It was a quiet bombshell.

Andy's eyes widened, and then he nodded. 'In that case, I'll have to tell Helen.'

They left to make quiet phone calls to their wives, explaining they weren't coming home that night. Both of them came back grim. *I'll tell you everything tomorrow* was the gist of what they'd said.

Seth and Noah went to the white van, finding German passports, a lot of cash, guns and ammunition. They burned the ropes, weapons, ammo and drugs ceremonially in the back garden. The pack kept the cash – several tens of thousands of pounds. Diana drove into the hills with the van, wiped her prints, and dumped it by the side of the road without the keys. It took her hours to get back, even as a wolf; the wound in her side was paining her. It wasn't healing fast. When she got back, everyone was asleep except Noah, Seth and Bill, who were patrolling the grounds. Andy was curled up outside the Kittens' room. She woke him up and persuaded him to take a mattress from a spare room, at least. She kissed him goodnight, and made her way to the main bedroom. She passed the room John and Zoe used sometimes, and heard them talking in low voices. In the main bedroom, Mark was asleep in the big bed, and she lay beside him. He stirred and wrapped a strong arm around her. 'Goodnight, killer,' he muttered.

Chapter 18

The next morning Andy was in the kitchen first, getting food on the table for the little ones, changing the babies and reassuring the kids that everything was going to be OK. He caught Bridget and Trixie getting ready for school, and made it clear nobody was leaving the house that day. Then he went and rounded the adults up. The babies needed to be fed, and he wanted to get the day's business over and done with.

John and Zoe were adamant they weren't leaving Silverwood that day. The others left John at the computer, researching security systems as Zoe limped around managing the household. She looked pale; her wound was knitting together, but it would be a while before it was fully healed.

Diana's injury was a wide and shallow one that had scabbed but not yet quite healed. She'd already taken samples from both wounds, interested in the biology of a Shifter inflicted bite wound.

Andy, Mark and Diana headed through the woods to Mark's car, Andy took the passenger seat, Diana dozed in the back seat as Mark drove.

Andy shook her awake when they arrived at his home. 'Are you coming in?' He looked miserable. Diana climbed out of the car, swept her hair back and rubbed her eyes. Taking his hand, she squeezed gently and tried to smile. She could see a figure at the window, looking out at them. She dropped Andy's hand and followed him to the front door.

He walked into his home, looking back briefly to check Diana was following; she was a few steps behind him, and stood in the hallway, uncertain. Helen stepped into the hall, looking at Diana a long moment and nodding.

'So, you've finally decided to take him for good?' she said. She looked exhausted. 'I've known, all along. I know him, I know when he's lying to me. Thirteen years, isn't it?' She was desperate and furious.

'Over sixteen,' Diana told her. 'And this isn't about him leaving you – it's about the truth.'

They sat in the living room, like civilised human beings, as Helen poured the tea she must have prepared when she heard Mark's car drive up.

'Mark knows, does he? That means John does. You've all been lying to me. That makes it even worse.' She was rightly angry. She stared at Andy, her eyes burning.

He looked down. 'Never that, love. We never mocked you. If it was my secret alone, I would have told you.'

'If we're really here to tell the truth, then here we go,' she challenged, standing and walking to loom over Diana, who stood to meet her, forced to look up as the tall blonde spoke.

'Have you asked him to leave me?'
'Never.'
'Do you love him?'
'Yes.'
'Do you know that I love him?'

181

'Yes.'

'Does he love you?'

Diana hesitated. 'Yes, I think so.'

Andy spoke up. 'Yes,' he said clearly.

Both women trembled, but didn't turn to him.

'Does he love me?'

'Oh yes,' Diana replied with no hesitation.

Andy shot up, and crossed to his wife, his arms around her, tears on his face. 'Yes,' he whispered. She shrugged him away, not wanting comfort.

She turned and went for her purse. Opening it, she pulled out a dog-eared photograph and handed it to Diana. Six-year-old redheaded twin girls, laughing at the camera. Andy buried his face in his hands.

'Who are these children?' Helen demanded.

'My daughters.' Diana stood her ground.

'Whose daughters?'

Andy spoke up. 'Our daughters ... my daughters. Helen ... please, sit down. We can't explain this by question and answer.'

She looked at him, and her courage collapsed.

Diana instinctively moved towards her and led her to the sofa, where Andy caught her and held her while she sobbed.

He looked at Diana. 'She knew, all along, she knew.' Then he was crying himself. Where to start? She knew nothing, and thought she knew everything. 'Hel, do you remember when we were kids? And I promised there was nothing I would ever hide from you? I was wrong, there was a secret I had that I could not tell you, because it wasn't just mine to tell. Mark and John are ... different. I wanted to share that difference, because it was exciting and tempting. Right now, I almost regret that choice. If I hadn't been so greedy, this wouldn't have happened. They shared, but I should've been stronger, not asked for what they so willingly gave.'

Helen snapped her head up. 'I haven't a clue what you're talking about. Explain.'

Andy nodded at Diana, who stood and turned her back, undressing quickly.

Helen gasped as the transformation began. Within seconds a red wolf lay on the living room floor, tongue lolling out.

Andy breathed out. It was done, the secret almost told. 'That's what Mark and John can do, that's what I can do.'

Helen fainted.

Diana stalked over and sniffed at her, looking at Andy, worried.

When she woke again, Diana was in the corner. Helen stared at her. 'Is she dangerous?' she asked.

'Oh yes, very.' Andy managed a smile. 'But not to you. She wouldn't hurt you.'

She looked at him. 'OK. You're a fucking werewolf. I'm married to a werewolf. You're real. But why didn't you tell me, trust me?'

Andy was dumbstruck. He stared at her. 'Well, I don't think…'

'It never occurred to you, did it?' she asked, her voice hollow. 'It never occurred to you that I could have been a part of this? And Xan? What about him?'

He shook his head. 'No, it didn't ever occur to me. And it might not have worked. And to be absolutely honest, the idea of letting John and Mark bite you…' he trailed off, a possessive look on his face. He shook his head. 'No, even if I'd thought of it, I wouldn't have let you go through it. It wasn't easy for any of us, getting me infected. And … you are *mine*.'

The illogic and double standards he was showing were painfully apparent to him, and he shut up.

'Xan?' she repeated coldly.

Andy briefly and drily outlined what had happened to Xan.

For a moment, there was a small spark of joy in her face, at the news that Xan had a living child, then jealousy took over again. She nodded towards Diana. 'So, she's the pack bitch, is she? Nice.'

'Helen, she's my mate. She had even less choice in this than I did. She was born with the genes. And it was Mark who went to her, not the other way round. And none of us knew what was going to happen. None of us knew about the addiction until it happened.'

Diana Changed back.

'Cover yourself up,' snapped Helen, throwing her clothes at her.

Diana winced and got dressed. The wound was half healed, but still hurt when she reached to fasten her zip. She coughed, to get the Ransomes' attention; she needed to move things along. 'The point is, now you know, what are we all going to do?' It was the wrong thing to say.

Helen snapped. 'You bitch, you come to my home, throw all this in my face, and expect answers here and now? Who the fuck do you think you are?'

Diana backed down. 'I'm sorry.'

Helen stopped and thought. 'Why now? After all these years? Andy, if this isn't about leaving me, why are you telling me now? I guess it isn't love, or conscience.'

Andy shook his head. 'Someone knows about us. The pack was attacked last night – two of the kids were injured, our mate was nearly killed, our daughter was nearly kidnapped… We're telling you because we don't want you to find out about this from any other source. And because I want to spend more time with the pack, at least until I'm sure they can deal with the danger.'

Diana shook her head. 'No, Andy, we can manage. We don't need you to be there.'

'I need to be there. I've let you all down, I see that. We were only attacked because they saw two women and the kids alone. They thought you were vulnerable.' He had a point.

Helen didn't miss a trick. 'Two women?'

Diana wasn't going to start lying again. 'Yes, Zoe is our packmate. We're a family, the five of us. But she and Andy don't fuck. She and Mark don't fuck. But you need to know that Andy and I have four kids. There are a pair of five-year-old boys—'

'I thought as much,' Helen said viciously, throwing a dirty look at Andy. 'Is one of them called Nathan? Because I lost count of how many times you called Naomi that when she was a baby.'

'Helen. Why didn't you say something sooner? If you knew I was lying to you?'

'I was waiting for you to tell me the truth. If you loved me. Although I'm beginning to understand why you didn't. Werewolf!'

He blushed again.

'What do you want?' she said. There, it was out.

Andy and Diana looked at each other. Diana spoke first.

'We need to know if you will support Andy if anything happens … if all this goes public.'

'Bitch, I'd support Andy to hell and back, what makes you think I wouldn't?'

Diana couldn't help but smile and wish for a moment that Andy had considered trying to turn Helen. 'I think the whole werewolf thing isn't going to be a secret for much longer – there's too many of us now. Genetic testing is getting more sophisticated and common. I need to know who we can count on, and who is going to stab us in the back. Do you realise *your* daughters are half Shapeshifter?'

Helen paled again, then recovered. 'What does that mean?'

It wasn't time to tell the harsh truth, Diana told a half-truth. 'If they have kids with another carrier, or a Shapeshifter, some of your grandkids might be like me.'

She nodded. 'OK. Andy, you are in deep shit. I needed to know about this. You know that?'

He nodded. 'How deep am I in it?'

'I'll tell you in a month or two, when I've calmed down.'

Things were looking promising. Helen had stopped crying, and was taking the whole thing in. Her eyes were clear and her expression calm. She was ready to negotiate. 'You've told me what you want, this is what I want. I want Andy to tell me the truth about you and your pack, from now on. No secrets, no protecting you from me. I want to know who this second woman is, and what she means to my husband. And I want to know today.'

Diana flinched. After so much secrecy, this was asking a lot. But she was right. If they were going to ask her to protect the pack, she deserved to know everything. Could they take the risk?

Helen was smiling, a wild, vicious smile that made Diana wish she'd been with them the day before. She was a fighter.

Andy stepped in. 'I'll tell you everything.'

Helen and Diana looked at each other; they understood each other now.

'Andy, what do *you* want?' Helen asked.

'I want everything. I don't want to lose you and our kids and my home. I don't want to lose her and the pack. I will do anything to keep both of you.'

Helen touched his face. 'If you think I'm going to chuck you out, you're mad. I think I understand this, and I can tolerate it, occasionally. But no more lies. When you go, you tell me that you're going, OK?'

Andy realised how difficult it was going to be, but agreed. Diana was more than happy. She'd expected to have to give him up completely, and was dreading the hole it would leave in the pack and her soul. She'd been anticipating the emptiness of life without him, and the relief must have showed on her face.

'I can't take the pack leader away, can I?' Helen said.

'Oh, that's me, and Mark,' Diana answered casually.

Helen blinked, then nodded. 'Yeah, that makes sense. If I needed someone I could absolutely rely on, I'd choose Mark, no doubt.' She walked to the window and looked out to where Mark was sitting in the car. 'Does Katie know yet?'

Diana spoke up. 'No, that's the next task. I have to go with Mark to tell her.'

Helen looked at Andy. 'Are you going too?'

Diana reassured him. 'You don't have to, Andy. I'll cope.'

He shrugged. 'OK. Do you mind if I stay here tonight?'

His wife glared at him. 'I mind you asking her.'

Diana's lips twitched. Somehow, she thought it had all gone rather well. She left them hugging each other, Helen demanding explanations, Andy knowing that he had a lot of making up to do. So far as they were concerned, suddenly she wasn't there. She left the house. Mark was leaning against the car; he looked thin and pale and fragile. He hugged Diana and asked how it went.

'OK, but that was the easy bit,' she told him. 'Shall I drive, or shall you?'

Chapter 19

Katie wasn't at the house when they got there. They'd moved since Diana's desperate visit in wolf form all those years ago, and Diana didn't recognise the new place. Mark searched the house. He found a note.

'She's gone to her friend's house with the boys,' he told Diana.

'What do you want to do? Do you want to collect her?' she asked.

Mark shook his head. 'I'm going nowhere without you.'

Their eyes met, and they stood in his living room, kissing hungrily for ages until they broke away. 'I'm sorry. I'm *so* sorry about yesterday. I should have been there earlier. I should have been there already. If Seth hadn't been wasting his time looking for me… If I'd got there when John did…' He threw his head back and groaned. 'Why didn't you ask me to leave Katie? Years ago. When this started. I needed to be with you, to protect you.'

Diana knew why she'd actively encouraged the marriage, coldly using it as a smokescreen for the growth of the pack. Ultimately, though, she'd believed him when he said he loved Katie, that he didn't want to give her up. Diana knew him. She knew he would always instinctively be with the woman who needed him most, and right at that moment, he thought it was Diana. But like Andy, he believed he needed his wife *and* his mate.

'Mark, when you fought, I knew why we were together. If we're threatened again, I'd want you there. But we're not all that vulnerable – the boys and the Kittens proved that. And you can't be there all the time anyway, you have work to do.'

'No, I should have been there.' He said no more.

Diana moved through the house like a tourist, commenting on the neutral decor, the tasteful paintings and statuettes, the subtle lighting and expensive furnishings.

'Did you choose this? It's nice,' she said, inspecting a coffee table.

He shrugged. He barely noticed his surroundings, although he appreciated the difference between the quiet comfort of this place and the hectic confusion of Silverwood, where the walls were filled with photographs and portraits of the pack, and the only sculptures were made of plasticine.

Diana had no shame; she was looking through the kitchen cupboards, marvelling at the fact that all the crockery matched.

Mark suddenly realised he was being teased, and he pulled her to him affectionately. She winced, and he took charge immediately, finding that her wound had broken open again, and that she was bleeding. He felt the wetness and broke away, her blood on his hands. He led her to the bathroom for bandages and something to bathe her side with.

They were there, tending to her wound, when Katie arrived home. She found them in the bathroom, opening the door to see Mark tying off the bandage he'd wrapped around Diana's ribs as she reached for her bra. Katie slammed the door shut and ran downstairs.

'Shit,' Mark said. He went after her.

Diana dressed, and followed more slowly.

Mark was blocking the front door.

Katie was flushed and furious. 'Let me out. You bastard. You scheming, lying, treacherous little bastard. I'll kill you. I'll kill her. I'll bring your world down so fucking far you'll be wandering in the wreckage for years. You are dead in the water, believe me.' She glared at Diana. 'And I hope it's been worth it. I hope she was a good fuck, because, believe me, it's going to be the most expensive one in history.' Her voice trailed off. 'It's you, isn't it? The woman I helped? I fucking knew it!' She turned on Mark, hitting him hard with an impressive right hook. He spun back and staggered into the wall. 'All that bullshit about needing space, I can't believe I fell for it. You've been seeing this tramp for years. Haven't you? Oh right, this is *it*. If you're going to leave me, pack as much as you can right here and now, because it's the last time you step foot in this house.'

'He doesn't want to leave you,' Diana offered mildly. Mark was still leaning against the wall, rubbing his chin reflectively. He was bleeding from the mouth. 'But carry on, do. I love to see a woman get good and angry. It's good for the soul.'

Mark glared at her, she wasn't helping. But then she'd never had much patience with drama – she got enough of that at home with Sara and Darlene.

Katie screamed. 'We have kids, you cow! Do you know what you're doing to us? Because if you had kids, you'd know, you wouldn't do this.'

191

Diana stared at her, hard, until Katie nodded.

'John's kid. I remember. You do understand then. How can you do this to me when you know what it's like to have a man who sleeps around? And why both of them? You couldn't keep John, so you get to him through Mark? Is that it?'

Diana weighed the odds of Helen telling Katie about the pack, and decided the risk was too great. They had to tell her. She looked pointedly at Mark. He took charge so well at home, but here he seemed ineffectual. 'Mark?' she said.

He took Katie by the hand. By now she was past the worst of her fury, and was beginning to settle into a shocked grief. They all went to the study, and Mark turned the computer on.

'Katie, I had to lie. I had to protect my family … my other family.' He slotted a disc into the computer. He'd been busy in the Silverwood computer room that morning, and Diana realised what he'd been doing. He sat his wife down and showed her hundreds of pictures.

The first was one Diana had forgotten about: she and John in the back garden of the terraced house in north Manchester, Mark's unmistakeable shadow in the foreground. They looked so very young. More photos: Mark holding the eldest twins up for the camera, the mirror in the background reflecting Andy taking the picture; Zoe and John with Isaac and Ian, their eldest sons; family pictures, years of them; Mark and his family. He clicked forward until Katie had got the message.

'My kids, Katie, all of them. Whether they are my blood or not, every one is mine. They're my responsibility, even the twelve of John's and the four of Andy's. Even

Xan's daughter … especially Xan's daughter. Just like I'm responsible for our children.'

Katie was trembling. 'This whole thing is crazy. You've been lying to me all these years, messing with my head, telling me I was too suspicious. Now *you've* finally flipped. It's all in your head. Nobody has that many kids!' She looked at him, then at Diana. 'You were seeing her when we got married, weren't you? You stood in front of all those people, and some of them knew, and you did it anyway.'

He closed his eyes. 'I married you because I loved you, to make you feel safe and secure. You are safe with me, you always have been. I've never wanted to leave you, but I have to be with my other family sometimes. It's not something I have a choice about.'

Diana was watching from a corner of the room. She was exhausted. Too much danger and fighting and killing, too much emotion, too much travelling and too much blood loss in the last twenty-four hours was fast taking a toll and she struggled to keep her eyes open.

Katie turned to look at her. 'I'm glad you can sleep. I'm glad you can sleep while my marriage collapses.' Her voice dripped poison. 'Seriously, I think I'm going to have to kill you.'

Diana started to speak, but Katie shook her head, heading for an ancient and heavy digital camera that sat on a shelf like a museum exhibit. Diana ducked out of the way as it came flying towards her, denting the wall behind her and showering her with fragments of brittle plastic, glass and aluminium.

'Fuck this, Mark. I'm going home. She's nuts. I'm too tired for all this.'

Katie howled, and the next thing to fly at Diana was a chair. The woman was strong, and had been pushed past her limits.

Mark moved across the room to stand in front of Diana. 'Katie, I'm going with her.'

That stopped her.

Katie took a deep breath. 'No, don't go. Let's talk. I've left the kids with Siobhan. I knew something was up. Let's talk.' She looked at her husband. 'Can we save this marriage? Will you leave this woman?'

'I didn't want to hurt you,' Mark said 'Katie, I've never, ever stopped loving you. But this is different. I need this woman in my blood, in my bones. It's not a human thing.'

'Not a human thing? What do you mean?' she challenged.

So they both Changed. There and then. It had been building up between them for hours, the emotional tension, the danger, the closeness. And there they were, sitting on the carpet, two wolves, haunches pressed close to each other for comfort.

And Katie stared at them, hand over her mouth, eyes wide and terrified, until they Changed back. And she sat numbly as Mark told her the whole story. He told her he should never have committed himself to her, not knowing what the future held for him, but he'd given up waiting for a Shapeshifting girl. Then Diana had come along, and he'd made a choice that changed his life. They were bound from the start, from that very first night. The pain of being apart had scared him, but he couldn't bring himself to leave Katie. Every day since then had been a lie, and he'd had enough.

The look of horror on Katie's face was matched only by the sorrow on Mark's face.

'So you see, I can't and won't leave my pack. Before you give me any ultimatums, or make any demands, you need to know that I physically need to be with this woman. Even if I hated her, I would have to be with her, or die.'

'Are you in love with her?' Katie demanded.

'No, I'm in love with you,' he told her.

Put in her place again, Diana closed her eyes and ached for Silverwood, where she belonged, where the kids were, where Zoe and John were. She wondered if Andy had been in touch with them. He probably hadn't. She was so lonely it hurt. She wanted to be in the woods with Zoe and John, with her uncomplicated lovers, in a warm and furry pile with them, not here, waiting to hear her fate from a woman who would never understand how she lived or felt or loved.

Katie had tasted blood and wanted more.

'Do you like her? Is she good company? Is she good in bed?' She was turning vicious again.

'I'm not going to answer any of that. I care about her, I need her, and she needs me. And if you attack her again, I'm leaving with her.' Mark stood up, tired and drained, and moved over to Diana. He noticed for the first time that she'd closed her eyes, and saw the tears on her face. He wiped them away, unconsciously raising his hand to his mouth and tasting them. He sat next to Diana.

'Please, the two of you are killing me with this. Katie, you have to understand, I'm not leaving her.'

'What if I go to the press?'

'Then I'd have to deal with it. I can't believe you'd do that though,' he said mildly.

Diana felt him, inches away, the heat of his body, the smell of him.

Katie quietened. 'So what happens now?' All her anger was suddenly gone. Diana's silent tears unnerved her. Mark's response to them scared her.

Mark sighed in relief. 'Can I stay with you tonight? Talk about this, where we go from here? I know things will never be the same, but I still love you, still want to be with you, still want to be married to you, to be a father to our boys. But I need to be with the others too, much, much more than I have been. And I know I need to do a lot to rebuild your trust in me.'

'You can say that again… I can't stand seeing this though. I won't tolerate seeing *her* next to you in my home.'

For the first time she really looked at Diana. 'Will you leave?'

Diana nodded, and left the house. Standing on the step, she wondered where the nearest bus stop was and realised her purse and phone were in Mark's car. She heard the door open and close again, and felt Mark's hand on her shoulder.

'I'm taking you home, but I'll have to come back here tonight. I think this is going to work, you know. Perhaps we should all have told the truth a lot earlier.'

'Perhaps. Look, I need some time alone, Mark. Just take me to the nearest train station, I'll get home OK. I can look after myself.' She managed a weak smile.

He looked at her long and hard, then decided she meant it.

'OK, but I'll drive you back to Silverwood. It's only an extra ten minutes for me but it's two trains and a long walk for you. Tell the kids they can ring whenever they want to. I'll square it with Katie.'

They drove towards Silverwood. The sun was going down already. As they passed a small wood, he stopped the car. They walked into the trees and undressed each other, hungrily satisfying the yearning that had built up between them.

Back in the car, Diana rang Zoe and said she'd soon be home. Zoe sounded odd, reserved, but Diana dismissed it; it had been a hard couple of days for them all.

Mark dropped her off at the gate, where Zoe was already waiting. She looked serious.

'Is everything OK?' Diana asked, worried.

'Yes, I think so.' She cleared her throat. 'We want you to be the first to know. John and I have decided to get married.'

Chapter 20

Mark arrived back home. He knew he was scratched and dirty, and he didn't care.

The windows were wide open and Katie was ostentatiously cleaning the house. She glared at him.

'I get it. I'll be in my study,' he told her. 'I'll sleep in the spare room until … until further notice, I suppose.'

'You screwed her, just now. Didn't you? What kind of animal are you?'

'A wolf,' he muttered, making his way upstairs. Diana's scent on his body and clothes was powerful, and he was torn between the comfort he found in it, and the offence he knew it was to Katie. He turned his computer on and mindlessly browsed the web for a while, knowing he had to deal with things, that he couldn't hide away like this. Eventually he decided to be polite, to shower Diana away. She didn't belong in this house anyway.

On the way back from the bathroom, he passed the main bedroom. He heard Katie sobbing in there, and stood outside the door. He knocked, and she stopped. He knocked again, and he heard her say, 'Come in.'

She was very, very quiet.

He glanced at his wardrobe. It was wide open, and his clothes were cut to shreds. Fair enough. Katie was lying on the bed, face down. He saw with horror that she'd scratched her own face, blood still ran on to the quilt.

'OK, that's enough. This isn't your fault,' he said, sitting next to her and stroking her shoulders.

'I know that. Bastard,' she whispered.

He was taken aback. 'I'm sorry,' he managed.

'Then prove it. Stop seeing her.'

'Oh, Katie, I can't. I'm sorry I lied to you. I can't be sorry about Diana. I can't be sorry about my family.'

'We're your family,' she spat. 'Me, Jacob, Matthew. We're your family.'

He reached out to touch her, to comfort her, and she lay, tense, under his caress. She was questioning him, questions he didn't know the answers to, asking him what came next. He stroked her gently, trying to soothe her.

'Honey, I don't know. I've been living with this for so long. This is where I'm happy, with you and our sons, our life together. This is what I'd choose, if I had a choice.'

'Who was first?' she snapped.

'You. You were first. I waited and waited. I wanted a woman like me, someone who could run with me. I didn't know if someone like that existed, but it seemed wrong to be with someone who wasn't a Shapeshifter. I held back, you know I did. Then I saw you, and I couldn't resist any longer. You are perfect for me, you know that?'

'And when did she come along?'

'Too late. You already held my heart, it's always been yours.'

'So why?' She twisted around so that she lay on the bed, face up. Her eyes accused him.

He shrugged. 'She wanted me. She'd waited for me. She'd not surrendered. She'd not given up. I felt I owed her something for that. I admired her.'

'Do you still? Admire her?'

He was silent. Katie persisted, her voice growing shriller. Eventually he stood. 'I do. I'm in awe of her, when I think about it. I try not to think about it.'

'Fuck off, Mark,' she spat, and he sighed and went to the guest room.

The next morning Katie told him where Jacob and Matthew were, and he went to collect them.

Jacob waited until they were home, until Matthew was in his own room, then asked, 'Dad, are you going to leave us?'

'Not if I can help it,' Mark said, surprised. 'Why?'

'Mum told me, before she sent me to Auntie Siobhan. She said that you had another woman.'

Mark fell silent, furious with Katie. He looked at Jacob, whose face was completely inexpressive.

He sighed. 'Look, I'm not the sort of man who leaves his family, OK? I love your mother. I want to stay here.'

'Are you going to leave?' Jacob persisted.

'That's up to your mother,' Mark said. He kept his voice mild. 'I don't want to go, but she might not forgive me.'

'So, you did have an affair?' There was no trace of judgement in Jacob's voice.

Mark studied him carefully. He decided to tell the truth.

'It's not an affair, it's not like that. It's not something that will end. I've got another family, children. I've had to keep them a secret, and they're still a secret.

I'm not lying here, but you can't say anything about them to anyone else. Can I trust you on this?'

Jacob nodded solemnly. 'I guess I knew. I've heard you talking to them, on the phone, when you thought I was asleep. How old are they?'

Mark looked at him, amazed. 'How long have you known?'

Jacob spoke quietly. 'A few years. I didn't say anything to Matthew. I didn't say anything to Mum either. I thought if she knew, she didn't want to talk about it, and if she didn't, it would cause trouble. I don't want you to go away.'

'You're a wonder. Why didn't you say something to me?'

'You're not easy to talk to,' Jacob said mildly. 'Does Uncle John know?'

'Uncle John and Uncle Andy. Aunt Helen knows now, as well. Look, this has to be our secret. Don't tell Matthew, he's too young to deal with it.'

'OK. Have I got brothers or sisters?'

'Both. One day, when it's safe, I'll tell you about them. I might even take you to meet them.' Mark smiled a little, imagining it. 'It's probably a good idea if you don't bring this up with your mother, unless you really want to.'

'I do want to talk to her about it,' Jacob said hesitantly.

Mark swallowed. 'OK, I can see that.' He was tempted to ask his son to intercede for him but banished the thought; it was cowardly. Jake went to his own room, and Mark cautiously went into the bedroom. Katie was gone.

She'd left a note. 'I've gone to work. Some of us have to.'

He went to check on Matthew, who was settled in his room in front of the TV. Mark left him there, and rang Silverwood.

John answered the phone, and assured him that everyone was safe and recovering well. Then he was quiet. Mark knew that quietness; he could almost see John's grin.

'Well, cousin, what have you done now?'

'I'm moving in. I've decided. And I'm going to marry her.'

Mark took a deep breath. If anyone other than John had said that, they would be dead before morning. 'You are not,' he said firmly. 'You are not going to marry Diana.'

He heard John giggle. 'Gotcha. I mean Zoe. It'll make us all feel safer. Diana's OK with it. Oh, do you trust Seth and Noah to design some safety stuff? Gates and fences and things? Diana seems to have a knack for it, and so do they.'

Mark shrugged. 'John, Silverwood belongs to Diana. She knows that she doesn't need any sort of permission from me to change things. Does she need money, for the security stuff?'

'If she does, she's not mentioned it. I've already put both my flats on the market anyway. I'll clear 'em out when you get here.'

'Ah. Well, I don't know when I can get there.'

'Katie took it hard?' John asked.

'That's putting it mildly,' Mark replied.

'Ah well, it'll all work out in the end. Look, I've got to go – there's toddlers everywhere and Zoe's still down. Take care.'

The connection cut, and Mark was left staring at the phone.

'Shit.' said Mark, and went for a lie down.

The following Sunday night, after one of her dinner parties, Mark followed Katie to the bedroom.

'I'm going to see her tomorrow. When I've dropped the kids off at school.' He waited for her response.

'It's not convenient, the lawn needs mowing. You can go on Wednesday, perhaps.' She didn't turn to look at him, but concentrated on removing her make-up.

Mark scowled, knowing that she couldn't see him. 'Katherine. I'm telling you because I don't want to lie any more. I'm going tomorrow.'

'A few days? Is that all you can manage without getting laid? I thought you were better than that.'

He frowned. 'Better than what?'

'I didn't think your prick was in charge. But see, a week in the spare room, and you're off to see her again.'

'That's not it. I'm going because I want to. I'm going somewhere where people like me.'

'People who you haven't lied to for seventeen years,' Katie said casually, wiping the cleanser away and studying her complexion. She frowned and touched her face. 'Do you think I've developed a few wrinkles this week?'

Mark's legs were weak. 'Don't do this, Katie. I want things to be good between us.'

'If I let you sleep with me tonight, will you stay here tomorrow?'

'No!' He frowned. 'Katie, it's not that. It's not.'

'So you don't find me attractive enough to give up a few hours with the whore?' She started to brush her hair, still not looking at him.

He was baffled. 'You've never been like this before,' he said helplessly.

'I never knew what you were really like before,' she pointed out reasonably. 'You can come back to this room, if you stay away from her until Wednesday.'

He was tempted; he'd missed her. She was looking at him now, smiling. He wanted to lie with her and talk and laugh and tell her about his day, and listen to her stories about the hospital.

'No,' he said firmly. 'If you don't really want me, there's no point. Let me know when you've decided that I've been punished enough. Until then, you know where you can find me.'

He moved with agile grace through the doorway. Some movement in the corner of his eye warned him, and he slammed the door shut behind him just in time to hear the heavy thud of her hairbrush hitting the wood. He breathed deeply, then opened the door again.

'She's called Diana. Not "her" or "whore" or "bitch". She's always been polite about you, think about that.' He shut the door again, and wondered why he suddenly felt less miserable.

Chapter 21

The drive to Silverwood the next day went by in a blur. Mark parked in his usual spot, away from the main gate, on a back road that skirted the edge of the property. The wire fence was still there – a four-foot gesture to privacy – but on the outward side of it there was now a deep ditch. Baffled for a moment, he looked round, then drew himself back and ran up to it. He made one of his best stage leaps, tottering for a moment on the treacherous edge, then pulling himself forwards. He vaulted the fence, and started to make his way through the familiar woods. Fifty yards in, he got the feeling that he was being watched. He stood still and grinned.

'It's Dad. Who's there?'

There was a scrambling noise above him, and a skinny dark-haired boy peered out of a tree. 'Hiya, Dad. Why are you sneaking about?'

'Because I'm sneaky. Why aren't you at school, Sam?'

'Mum said we can have some time off school. We have to help make a new fence.'

Mark frowned. 'I hope Mum is making sure that you're keeping up with lessons?'

Sam pulled a face. 'Of course she is. She's in the kitchen, warming things up for dinner.'

His father frowned. 'Are you OK out here, by yourself?'

The boy laughed. 'I'm not by myself. Bridget's over there.' He pointed, and Mark turned.

A very healthy and well-fed young black wolf lay under a nearby tree, watching him intently. He nodded to her.

She was less than a year older than Sam, but the gap seemed wider now, with her and Beatrice already Changing regularly. She stood up and stalked over to him, lowering her head to be caressed. He hugged her, and moved on.

Diana was in the kitchen, battling with a huge pan of pasta sauce. Frank was sitting on a high stool, straining vast quantities of pasta. They both looked up when he came into the kitchen.

Mark winked at his Alpha and went straight to Frank. 'OK, buster, show me the arm,' he said drily.

Frank rolled up his sleeve and grinned. 'All healed up, but Mum's being mean and making me do kitchen work and be quiet,' he complained.

'I just want to keep an eye on you.' Diana returned Mark's wink. 'Frankie, is that pasta ready?'

'Just about.'

'OK, carry it through will you?' Frank slid off the stool and picked up the bowl with a flourish. Diana watched him carefully as he left. 'I think he's OK now. I wish I could heal that fast. Mark, will you grate some cheese, about two pounds? Quickly. And there's half a dozen pizzas in the big oven. They should be done by now.'

He sighed; this was more like it. 'What did your last slave die of?' he enquired mildly.

'Insubordination. Do I get a kiss?' Mark's face dropped, and she winced. 'That bad at home?' she said quietly.

'Yup. Let's feed the starving hordes. Where's Zoe?'

She paused to kiss him on the cheek. 'Rounding them up. Stick that pie in the oven, will you? It's for John and Sam and Bridget and Seth – they're on guard duty.'

'Guard duty?' Mark blinked.

'Yeah. We've been stupid. We nearly got ourselves killed last week. I'm an idiot. I should have guessed there were more of those blond bastards out there. We can relax a bit once the new fence is up and the security cameras are online, but for now, four on duty, day and night. Can you stay tonight?'

He bit his lip. 'I have to collect Jake and Matt from school…'

'Of course you do. I shouldn't have asked.'

'No, you're right. I need to be in two places at once. Do you think Jake and Matt are safe?' he said.

Her head snapped round. 'Mark, do you want me to take responsibility for them too?' she said sharply.

'Shit, no. Sorry. They're at a private school anyway, Katie insists on it. Security is pretty good there. Speaking of schools, why are the older kids at home?'

She looked away for a moment, pouring the pasta sauce carefully into serving dishes. She kept her voice low. 'Look, Mark, I have them at three different schools to keep the size of the family a secret. It's getting harder every year. Right this moment, I'm not sending any of my kids out there alone. Just give me a bit of time, OK?'

Mark nodded. 'Noah and Seth are seventeen in September. We'll get driving lessons for them, then they can help out.'

'Fuck Off. Noah? Behind the wheel? He's bad enough on that bloody BMX you bought him.' She smiled happily, walking out of the kitchen with the pasta sauce and a huge bowl of grated cheese. Mark followed with two heaped plates of pizza slices.

In the dining room, Susie and Nancy were putting plates and forks out. Mark took the seat next to Diana, heaping food on to her plate without thinking.

She looked at him affectionately. 'I can feed myself,' she said.

Chastened, he looked away.

She reached out, taking his hand. 'Mark?'

He shook his head. 'Can we talk later?'

'Sure.' She raised her voice. 'Susie hon, are those babies getting fed?'

Susie, at the bottom of the table, between two highchairs, looked up guiltily. She'd given Harry and Mikey a slice of pizza each, and they were gumming them messily and enthusiastically.

Diana sighed and went to pick the pack's youngest boys up. She chopped some pasta and sauce in a bowl, handed Mikey to his father, and started to feed Harry. Mark settled back, his own food ignored for now while he supervised Mikey's lunch. The child protested a little at how tightly he was being held, and Mark relaxed.

He caught Diana's eye. 'I'm sorry I missed their first birthday.'

Diana looked at him for a moment, puzzled. 'Mark, that was five months ago!'

'I know. I won't miss Julie and Leanne's, I promise.'

His mate shrugged. 'Try making it to Cal and Sam's, eh? The babies don't care if you're there or not, Cal and Sam do. Oddly enough.'

Mark pulled a face and changed the subject. 'Have you heard that new Whispercats album?'

Diana laughed at his transparency. 'OK, I'll bite. Is it any good?'

After the meal they spent an hour in the kitchen. All the kids wanted to see Mark, and they came in, mostly in pairs. Trixie established herself on his lap early on, and made it clear she wasn't moving. Eventually Diana stood up and lifted her daughter to the floor.

'That's enough Daddy time, hon. He'll be back soon. Right now we need to be alone.'

She started to lead Mark upstairs, and he balked at first, then realised some of the kids were watching.

In the bedroom, he stood with his back to the door, his hands behind him, playing with the handle.

'I'm not going to bed with you,' he blurted out.

'Oh. You've promised her that, have you? How long can we manage that for?' Diana sat on the edge of the bed, her face turned away from him.

'It's not a matter of promises. She expects me to come to you. She won't sleep with me, she expects me to come to you when I get horny. I won't fulfil her expectations.' He spoke stiffly.

'Great. She won't fuck you, and you won't fuck me.'

'I want her back, but I don't know how to manage it,' he whispered.

'Mark, please. Don't ask me for advice on how to win her back. There are some limits.' She was looking out of the window now.

He sighed. 'She knows about the pack. I need her on my side. I … we… need her to understand that if she doesn't keep quiet about us, we're in danger.'

Diana shrugged, still not turning round. 'Her own kids are half blood. Point that out to her. Tell her she'll be putting them at risk too.' Her voice was cold.

Mark made a nervous noise. 'That would protect us, yes. But it hardly improves things between me and Katie.'

Diana spun round. 'Mark, why are you here?'

'To see if you're OK, to see the kids.'

'Well, see the kids then. We all know they'll be glad of it. Just leave me be, OK?'

He looked at her. 'I've pissed you off too, haven't I?'

She managed a weak smile. 'Mark, I'm not pissed off, I'm not angry with you. You're just being Mark. I'm disappointed, that's all. You go and do the dad thing, I'll sit here for a while, if that's OK?'

He took a step towards her, and she shied away. 'No. Don't change your mind. If you do, you'll blame me.' He left the room.

Later, as he drove home, as he collected his sons from school, he found himself thinking about the red wolf woman.

He'd thought that night would be like the last few: a family evening with the boys, and then Katie would read, or chat to friends, and he would spend some time on the computer. At some point he would listen out for her going to bed, that certain noise as the door was carefully and meaningfully closed against him. He'd had to hide his toothbrush away so he could use the family bathroom without the boys knowing.

It wasn't to be. After their meal, after the boys had played games and done their homework, the phone rang, and Katie answered it. Her eyes went cold, and she passed the receiver to him. It was John, just ringing to chat, as he'd done thousands of times during their lives.

When he'd gone, Katie was in the living room, a tray of tea and biscuits in front of her, two cups and saucers ready. He cautiously sat down.

'Of course, it's his fault,' she said. 'You would never have got involved with her if it wasn't for him.'

Mark stayed silent; half amused. John was 'a bad influence'. He always had been. That was one of the many things his mother and Katie had agreed on. The difference was that his mother had loved John like a son, whereas Katie's feelings for him bordered on distaste.

Katie curled up on the sofa, nursing her cup of tea. She looked over the top of it. 'Explain to me again why you can't end this relationship.'

Mark gathered his facts, watching her carefully. 'It's a physical addiction. A terminal one, we think. We get sick when we're away from each other for too long. A week or two is bearable, more and we get bad-tempered, headachy. A month – weight loss, sickness, faintness. We once managed several months apart, although John ferried clothes between us – I think that's how we made it. That and knowing it didn't have to be a permanent separation. Hope kept us going.'

'That was when I thought you had cancer?' Katie said thoughtfully.

'Yes. And when I came back, miraculously recovered, you fixed on the fact that I'd been fucking around, and never commented on the fact that I was healthy again.' He allowed his hair to fall across his face, hiding his expression. 'I wasn't sleeping around, by the way. Not with that woman from the club. It was a smokescreen to divert you away from the pack.'

She coughed, that tiny noise she used to get his attention. He looked up again, blank faced.

'I've decided to believe you. I suppose that, medically, it's possible. I should consider myself lucky you don't have any other vices. We've always had a good marriage, I don't see why we shouldn't try again.'

Mark nodded. 'I want that.'

She put a CD on, and they listened to it together, growing closer, until they made that old familiar shape again, knowing just where their bodies fit well and comfortably together. Her breathing quickened, and she traced figures on his chest, over his T-shirt.

She looked up at him. 'Mark, I still want you. Despite everything. Despite the fact that I still see that creature when I look at you, that wolf. It's scary, but I still want us to be together.'

'I still love you, Katie. You don't have to be scared. I'm the same man I was when we first met.'

'Prove it,' she said, almost shyly, and he lifted her in his arms and carried her, like a bride, to their bed.

Chapter 22

Eventually, of course, he had to go back to Diana. He couldn't find her in the house, where Zoe had a nice little reading circle set up for the young kids. John was in the music room, making a din. Andy was in the office, answering emails.

'You OK?' Andy said.

'Yeah.' Mark leaned against the wall. 'Where is she?'

'Diana? She's been in the lab for hours. She's fascinated by those samples that Miranda took before we buried those white wolf bastards.'

Mark sighed. 'You seem pretty relaxed anyway. How did Helen take it?'

'With tears, shouts and then… Well, then she got interested in the whole thing. She wants to invite Darlene and Sara over for dinner. She's always been broad-minded, you know that. It was the fact that I'd lied to her that upset her. Once she looked at it from my point of view, she was OK about it. Then I looked at it from her point of view, and fell in love with her all over again.'

'Not enough to keep away from Diana,' Mark observed.

Andy licked his lips. 'You know how it is. I get an itch for her.' Andy gave his Alpha a lazy smile. 'I'm staying tonight, I've got a pass. Helen's off to her mother's with

Eva and Naomi. Are you staying too? It's been a long time since we were all together.'

Mark was tempted. The feeling of having all his mates with him, especially running with him, was exhilarating. There was nothing at home that could compare with that. He shook his head. 'No, things are good with Katie right now. I don't want to piss her off.'

Andy closed his eyes in mock despair. 'Will I ever have my Alpha back again?' he cried in theatrical tones.

Mark smiled gently; he understood that Andy was only half joking. 'Hey, we'll all be together again, I just have to get the timing right. Is that Hearts business that I need to know about?' He gestured towards the laptop.

'No, Ransome Industries. Dad's talking about me taking over, again. He's ready to retire.'

Mark nodded. Andy would always make time for the Hearts, he knew that. He went to look for Diana.

Mark spotted Diana getting into her car, glancing over her shoulder. She'd obviously seen him, but she shut the door and started to move away. He glared as the car headed down the drive, and ran indoors to the main control panel of the new security system. He hit the gate override button and waited.

The screen next to the panel blinked to life; Diana was looking straight at the camera.

'Is there a problem?' she said evenly.

'Where are you going?' he asked in return.

'Just for a drive. I was feeling cooped up. Open the gate, hon.'

'I've not seen you for ages,' he said quietly.

'No? Well, I've been here. Open the gate, Mark.'

'Not when I've been here. You're avoiding me.' He was managing to keep his voice even.

She sighed. 'Look, last chance. Open it.' She looked straight at the camera, her eyes icy. He shivered and his hand hovered over the override switch.

'I don't want you to go out. I've come to be with you. Diana, I miss you.'

Her face softened. 'I'll be back in time for tea, OK? Will you still be here?' He could see a trace of devilment in her expression.

He shook his head. 'I'll be here if you're back in an hour.'

She couldn't see him, but he could see her lips narrow. He felt his cock twitch and was amused at his own reaction to her anger.

'Diana, I want you.' He made his voice low, just loud enough for her to hear. He watched as the colour rose to her pale cheeks.

'But?' she said.

'No buts. I'll make it worth your while.' He smiled unconsciously. They rarely flirted, but today he wanted to.

Understanding flowered in her eyes. 'Katie gave in? You can climb off your high horse now?'

'Sort of. Are you coming back?'

She shrugged. 'Open the gate. I'll think about it. I just need to get out – I've not been out for a week.'

'I'll come with you then,' he suggested, and she grinned.

'OK.'

'Back up the car,' he suggested.

'You idle sod, you can walk down the drive.'

He didn't run, but he didn't dawdle either.

He eased himself into the passenger seat. 'Where are we going?'

'I thought I'd have a drive over to Manchester. We could have a look round the shops, go to a few bars, then I could drop you off at home.' Her mouth twitched just a little.

'Yeah, and then you can come and choose which bits of me you want buried at Silverwood after Katie's finished with me. No dice, babe.'

'I love it when you call me that.'

Diana drove through the gates, she didn't turn to look at him, but she was smiling.

'I love calling you that. Katie hates it.'

Diana giggled. 'I know, John told me. Anyway, let's not talk about her, please? Where do you want to go?'

He was rummaging in the glove box. He retrieved a battered old CD and put it on. He leaned back. 'Oh, wherever. Somewhere quiet.' He glanced at her, then licked his lips slowly, and took a longer look. He turned the music off and sat upright, looking straight ahead.

'When were you going to tell me?'

'Tell you?' Diana negotiated a curve a little too fast, and Mark frowned.

'I've known you long enough to be able to tell that you're pregnant again. I thought we discussed these things, me and you? Who's the father?'

'Definitely not Andy,' Diana said. 'It was that day when we told Katie. It could be you, or John. I was kinda distracted.' She concentrated on the road. 'Are you mad?'

He thought about it. 'No, I was going to ask if you were ready. They'll be mine anyway.' He spoke with such assurance that Diana laughed.

'So we're OK?' she asked.

'We're fine, hon. Back to normal.' He shut up as she slammed the brakes on and reversed into a side road. 'Where are we going?'

'Home,' she said happily.

Chapter 23

He was doing his best to blend in with the crowds, going with the flow, attracting as little attention as possible. His trademark long hair was hidden under the collar of a thick jacket, and a scarf hid most of his face. So far, he'd gone unnoticed. That couldn't have happened twenty years earlier, he reflected ruefully, at the height of the Hearts' fame.

So this was the shop. He recognised the logo instantly: a long-established purveyor of expensive bridal wear. His attic at home held boxes with that logo on it – Katie's treasures. He wrinkled his nose, reacting to the memory of that dusty room.

He glanced through the window, and realised the glass was polarised. He moved away, suddenly convinced Diana was looking straight at him from within the shop. He'd not seen her for a couple of weeks, 'being good' he told himself. It was his mantra. If he could be good for long enough, maybe Katie would start to love him again, maybe he could wake up in the morning without the memory of the red she-wolf haunting his dreams.

He'd quarrelled with John on learning that 'the girls' were going to London to shop. John had been confident he could manage the house and kids just fine alone, at least for a day or two. Mark hadn't been able to decide what was more stupid, leaving the entire pack in the care of one adult, or allowing both of the pack women to go to the city together.

John had laughed. 'Hey, "allowing" isn't a word you use with Diana. You know that.'

Mark had been on the verge of explaining things to Katie, of telling her he had to be at Silverwood overnight to protect the children. Something had stopped him: some dark voice that murmured it would be better if she didn't know Diana and Zoe were in London. That voice had continued to whisper to him, telling him that if anything happened to the women, the pack was doomed anyway, that he'd failed them too often; he had to protect them.

He'd mentioned a Canadian producer friend who was in London for a few weeks. He'd been clinging to Katie like a child, wanting to know when she'd be back from work, if he could go shopping with her, what she was doing. When he'd mentioned the producer would be going back home in a few days, Katie had given him one of her brilliant smiles and suggested he go to visit. That smile scratched at his soul; she was so willing to be rid of him for a while, so long as he wasn't with his pack. He'd found out, via John, what Diana and Zoe's plans were, and driven to London without any further thought. The stereo played loudly enough to stop him thinking.

He left his car on the outskirts and got the train into the centre. He staked out the bridal shop hours in advance, and retreated to a doorway opposite, as still as any of the mannequins in the surrounding windows. When the women came out, he was caught unawares; out of context he almost didn't recognise them.

Diana stood for a moment on the step, checking out the street carefully before she allowed Zoe to follow her. She was wearing a tailored black trouser suit. Her hair was done in some sort of complicated plait he just knew she'd had help with. Zoe's hair was perfect. The Beta woman was wearing a short dress and matching jacket with high heels that made her tower over Diana.

He followed them, waiting outside a jewellery shop. He was surprised when Diana came out wearing a silver and amber necklace that he could see from across the street; he'd never known her to wear jewellery before. They hit several more shops, and he began to relax. They would go back to their car soon and set off home. He planned to catch up with them on the motorway, follow them to Silverwood, make sure they were safe then drive back to Katie.

Diana had glanced back a couple of times, and he was beginning to worry she'd spotted him. He'd shortened his stride and was walking differently. His hair was hidden and he was hanging too far back for her to recognise him under the thick jacket, but he suspected that she was sensitive to his presence, whether she knew it or not.

He watched as they stopped at a cafe for coffee and cakes. They were approached by a good-looking man whom he distrusted on sight. Mark was amused by the smooth way that Zoe dealt with him. Mark's eyes lingered on his Beta; she was a hundred times more assertive away from the pack, more capable of dealing with life outside than Diana ever had been.

Eventually they went back to the car, and he hid in the shadows, watching them chatting and laughing. He drew a deep breath as they glanced around, then, satisfied that they weren't observed, kissed each other deeply. He was well aware that their bond was sexual as well as emotional, but usually managed to keep that knowledge filed and locked away under 'Things Mark doesn't need to think about'.

Zoe got into the driving seat, and Diana leaned against the door, talking to someone on her mobile. She'd thrown her jacket into the car, and he took a moment to appreciate her figure. When she'd hung up and got in the car, he waited for them to draw away, then made for a Tube station to take him back to where he'd parked.

He rang John. 'Hey, heard from the girls yet?' he asked casually.

'Yeah, they're stopping in the city overnight. Diana said they were having fun. I can cope, the older kids are a big help.'

Mark's guts clenched. 'Staying? Where?'

'A hotel, they've not decided which one yet. Why don't you ring them? Does it matter?'

'No. Look, did you recommend anything to them?'

'Yeah, two or three places.' John listed them, and asked Mark why he wanted to know.

'Oh, I don't want them staying in some fleapit, that's all.' He ended the call, and stood in the car park, flummoxed. He thought of going home, then realised he couldn't rest until he knew they were safe. He knew he had responsibilities.

'OK,' he said to himself. 'Where do middle-aged women go when they're in London?'

He made his way to the theatre district, scanning the crowds. As he pushed his way through a group of denim-clad teenagers who were going in the opposite direction, he stopped. He turned around and went with the flow. He quizzed one of the youths about the band they

221

were on their way to see, and got a description of a young rock band with a long-haired, skinny guitarist. He laughed and bought a ticket from a scalper just outside the door.

The band had just taken the stage. He pushed his way towards the front, stopping two rows back from where Diana's red hair advertised her presence like a war banner. His anxiety fell away, and he allowed the crowd to come between them a little more.

The band were good, and among true fans. The crowd surged and jumped around him, and he struggled to keep sight of his purpose in being there as the music took hold of him, the lights swept around, and the bass grabbed at his insides and started to turn his brain to jelly. He blinked hard, centring himself, looking for the women. They'd moved further forwards, and he followed, taking advantage of each surge to move forwards a couple of rows, planting himself firmly and not allowing any of the younger, bigger guys to push past him.

He was recognised, but that didn't matter. If Katie heard that he'd been to a gig, she wouldn't be surprised. The boy who'd recognised him grinned at him wildly, mouthing his name. Mark smiled politely, then the crowd moved again and he was lifted off his feet for a moment and swept far too close to Diana. She was laughing, caught up in the surge too, hanging on to Zoe for dear life.

The set ended, and he headed for the doors. He looked back, seeing Diana and Zoe standing quietly as the rest of the audience left. He paused, wondering what they were up to. He realised that they were hyped up and a little drunk – Zoe was barefoot, holding one shoe in her hand. Diana was scanning the floor as the crowds left.

As the venue cleared, he moved to a doorway, standing in the shadows. He watched as Diana strode to the barrier and spoke to the security guy. He shook his head a time or two, and Mark grinned as he saw Diana stand taller and put her shoulders back. The security guy was unhelpful, and Diana vaulted over the barrier and started to search behind it, ignoring him. Mark smiled. Zoe had approached the barrier now, and was keeping the guy busy with a very effective outraged-matron act. Eventually Diana surfaced, slightly dusty, raising a shoe aloft. She vaulted back over the barrier and handed it to Zoe, who put both shoes on with a display of immense dignity. The two women headed for the door, and Mark fled.

He fell in behind them as the crowds scattered. They were obviously high on the music, and a little drunk; he could tail them easily. Away from the venue, the crowds grew thin. They were the only ones on the street. He sighed; Diana had never been one for keeping to well-lit areas – she seemed obscurely attracted to dark alleys and dubious side streets.

A car drew up next to them, and he heard the word 'taxi' mentioned. His lip curled back. Taxis didn't have two drivers and no sign, even in London. Diana waved the car away, and it dropped back, parking in the shadows.

He caught up to it just as the doors opened, and he waited for one of the men to get out before he moved. He slammed him against the car and whispered some heartfelt advice to the guy, treating him to a smile that was too full of teeth to be entirely human. The guy was shaking, and Mark bundled him back into the car. He watched, satisfied, as they drove away, then hung back to report the registration number to the police.

He looked up just in time to see the women turn decisively into an even darker and lonelier street. He rolled his eyes. Three youths had followed them.

'Fuck, London's a pigsty,' he muttered. He undressed behind a skip, hid his clothes and Changed. The street stank of rats and piss, and he stalked to the entrance. The women were still laughing, and singing loudly, making no attempt to keep themselves safe.

He saw Zoe caress Diana's neck, lifting her hair, the silver of the new necklace catching the moonlight. Even from here, he could smell them; they'd been dancing hard, and the sweet musky smell of the pair of them was familiar and interesting. Mark found himself wondering why his mate was walking on those stupid two legs – she was much more beautiful when she was a wolf. She was pointing to a young human male, and she and the Beta were making appreciative noises. He growled, jealous, although he didn't take his eyes off the three men who were just in front of him. One of them jumped and glanced back, but the black wolf knew he was invisible in the dark shadows.

He watched carefully, looking for his chance, as the four men surrounded the two women. He would have preferred not to act, but they had knives, and one of them was approaching his Beta. He looked at Diana. If she Changed, she would have to kill them all. Zoe was a successful enough writer to be potentially recognisable, and if Diana let any of the men live, she would be living in fear of them one day making a connection between Zoe Bradwell the romance writer, and the weird woman whose friend had turned into a wolf one dark night in a London alley.

Mark made his move. He only drew blood once, but that was enough, and the men scattered in terror. He could look like an evil bastard when his temper was up. The blood tasted bad to him, poisoned. He shuddered and swallowed it down nevertheless – his body would deal with it.

Diana was very quiet. He could smell that she was angry, and he quietly led her to his clothes. She gathered them up, carrying them to the hotel in a bundle.

Zoe checked in, and opened a service door, letting him and Diana in. The women were sharing a room.

Mark felt a vast relief as soon as he'd got them to safety. He Changed and found himself yelling at Diana, berating her for her stupidity. He found himself even more angry when she accepted it without complaint; she was clearly shocked and furious with herself. He was off balance. Diana wasn't supposed to do stupid things; she was supposed to hold everything together, wasn't she? He changed tack, attacking her for leaving the children alone.

She shot back that he wasn't a paragon of parenthood himself. Behind her, Zoe was ignoring the fight, getting ready for bed. She'd showered quickly, and came back into the bedroom with a towel wrapped around her hips, her upper body naked.

Mark felt himself responding, and got even more annoyed. He'd seen her naked hundreds of times. He'd delivered her children, and she'd never had an effect on him before. She met his glance and looked away, smiling a little, turning round and towelling herself dry with her back to him.

Diana was oblivious to the way that Zoe was flirting with him, and he found himself retreating in confusion. Zoe was dressed now, in a silky nightdress that clung where it touched her. Damn. She was saying something, suggesting he tell Katie where he was, that he was with both the pack women.

It made sense, Katie would find out eventually after all. He tried to be rational, but the night's events were catching up with him. Diana was angry with him now, as if the attempted mugging was his fault. Her eyes … her eyes always caught him out if he spent too much time with her, and tonight she was on fire, aroused to fighting pitch.

He rang Katie there and then, wincing as she yelled at him, accusing him of planning all this. He told her again and again that he'd had no idea his packmates would be staying in London tonight, and that he'd obviously had no idea they would be mugged. He had to stay. Katie's voice was like a January morning when she said goodbye.

He booked a room for himself. He knew what Katie was imagining, and stubbornly decided to confound her expectations. As he left Diana's room, she took his hand and drew him towards her, kissing him gently. He relaxed, but drew away and left. The last thing he saw was Zoe's reflection in the mirror. She was looking at him, and smiling. She snuggled down into the sheets and turned away. He made his way to reception and paid for a room just down the corridor from Diana's.

Back in his room he undressed and showered, getting the stink of sweat and cheap beer out of his hair. He replayed the conversations with Katie and Diana, getting more and more irritated. His phone rang, and he snatched it up.

'What now?' he snarled. It was a response, he felt, that was appropriate to either his wife or his Alpha.

'Hey, calm down. What's up?' It was John.

Mark breathed deeply. 'I'm in London. Two rooms away from two stupid careless women who have pissed me off big time.'

John sounded puzzled. 'What did they do?'

'They got drunk, went to a gig, then would have been mugged if I hadn't stepped in.'

'You were *following* them?' John said incredulously. 'What the holy fuck did Diana say to that?'

'That's not the point—'

'Shit, Mark. If you'd asked, I would have told you where they were staying – they rang to give me the address.'

'John, they were *attacked*.'

'Did they kill anyone?' his Beta asked with disturbingly casual interest.

Mark breathed deeply. 'It was a mugging, not an attempted rape. I could tell that much.'

'So, they give up their credit cards and cash? Report it to the insurance and the police, and no harm done. Why did you butt in? I bet Diana's mad as hell. It's bad enough being caught out, but having you see it all must have been really embarrassing for her.'

'She was drunk, John,' Mark said weakly.

'Yeah, we've been drunk. We've been mugged a time or two. And I've lost count of the number of times I've woken up in a cheap hotel bedroom without my wallet. Mark, it's life, it happens.'

'I saved them,' he sulked.

John took a laconic tone. 'Whoopee doo. Well, I bet that's how Diana will see it in the morning, once she's had time to put you back into your role as Mr Perfect. Now, will you say goodnight to Trixie? She had a nightmare and wants you to make things right.'

It turned out Trixie's nightmare had involved Diana and Zoe being carried away by huge white wolves, and he was able to reassure her that he was with them, looking after them. 'Now, honey, go back to sleep. It's very late, and you should be in bed. Be good for JohnDad.'

'OK, Daddy. When are you coming home again?'

He managed not to make his sigh audible, and told her he'd be there soon.

John picked up the phone again. 'How did you get to be her favourite? You're never bloody here,' he joked.

Mark ignored the jibe. 'Any more problems? I could go and wake the women up if you want?'

John giggled. 'I bet you could. I bet they're all snug and warm together, aren't they? I'd go for it.'

'Oh, fuck off,' Mark snarled, and hung up.

He pulled at the damp towel that was still around his waist, and hung it to dry on the bathroom radiator. He was tired and angry, and needed to be comforted. He rang Diana. When she spoke, there was a coldness in her tone that threw him. She was still angry. He could feel the hostility coming off her. He was tempted to put the phone down and ring Katie, then remembered she was at home imagining he was involved in some salacious orgy with both of his mates.

He spoke carefully. 'You know, Katie already knows about Zoe…'

'And?' Diana snapped.

'So if I sleep with Zoe, it won't make any difference to Katie, she already assumes I'm doing it anyway.' He licked his lips nervously, wondering if he was destroying his pack or bringing it together. One thing he was sure of, Zoe had acted as if she wanted him. John had given him the green light, and he was horny as hell.

Diana was waiting for him to carry on.

He did. 'So you and Katie are mad at me, and Zoe's obviously not, and maybe it's time we all brought this pack closer together.'

'I'm coming to your room now,' Diana spat, and hung up.

He opened the door just in time, before she started banging on it. She was furiously protective of Zoe, and he realised with a pang that she didn't trust him not to hurt her. She knew him too well, it seemed. He tried to reassure her, but she wouldn't listen.

'You were going to fuck her tonight! I've been watching the two of you all day,' he complained.

Diana coolly admitted it. 'Difference is, I love her,' she spat. 'You don't, you don't even…' she clamped her mouth shut, before she could take the argument into ever more dangerous realms.

The hotel room phone rang. It was Zoe. Diana switched the speakerphone on and answered it.

'What's up? Are you two arguing?' Zoe sounded upset.

'Yes,' Diana said, her voice choked.

'What about?'

'Mark wants to fuck you,' she snapped.

Zoe asked why that was a problem. She assured Diana that of course she wanted Mark, he was the Alpha;

229

it would be unnatural not to; it would be good for the pack.

Diana had one last arrow in her quiver. 'You never said that you wanted him before,' she whispered, outgunned.

'Couldn't have before, so why make waves?' Zoe sounded very reasonable. 'I figured it was up to him to make the first move.'

'Fine, bloody fine.' Diana slammed the phone down and stormed out of Mark's room. He watched the door bang shut – the world suddenly seemed very quiet. He spoke to the space where she had stood.

'Diana, my love, this is for us. I need to know if I feel the same way about Zoe as I do for you.'

He lay back on the bed and let out a deep breath. There, it was said, out loud. 'Diana, my love.' He smiled ruefully, perhaps it didn't count if there was only him to hear it.

There was a tiny knock at the door, and he opened it and let Zoe in. She sidled in, looking round. 'I figured I'd be the one left alone tonight,' she said.

'Yeah? You did your best to change that though.' Mark gestured to the nightgown. 'That thing affects people, you know?'

Zoe was relaxed. 'I know,' she said, and winked. 'Look, Mark. Is this about Katie? Or Diana? Or both?'

'It's partly about Diana, partly about you. Is that OK?' he said gravely. 'I care about you, don't doubt that.'

'And afterwards? You're barely around for Diana, will you remember that I need you? It works differently for Betas – we need the Alpha more than they need us.'

Mark wiped his mouth with the back of his hand, biting his knuckles nervously. 'Zoe, I can't promise you more than I can give to Diana, you understand that?'

'I do. And this will be good for the pack. The children will be happier, they'll sense that you're not ignoring me any longer. It's been a little … humiliating, let's say.'

Mark's eyes widened. It had never occurred to him that the children might know who was sleeping with whom, and interpret his refusal to sleep with Zoe as a personal rejection of her. He blushed. 'I'm sorry, Zoe. I can change that, at least.' He patted the bed next to him. 'Come here.'

He studied her, knowing the first kiss would bind them, start a lifelong addiction. He also knew that she was as familiar to him as John or Andy, the scent of her part of the pack scent. He already knew every curve of her body, the most intimate and secret parts of her, the scent of her hair. He reached out, and she took his hands and raised them to her breasts, drawing away from the kiss he offered. They felt glorious under silk. He kneeled on the loose fabric of her gown, and pushed its shoulders halfway down her arms. She couldn't move. He was watching her expression with a wary eye, examining her reaction, ready to free her at the first sign of protest. He gathered her to him, cradling her in one arm while the other worked cleverly at her clothes, trapping her hands beneath her. He bent down to kiss her throat, her breasts, her nipples. He remembered a cold December night in a scruffy student bedroom, how his body had changed irrevocably when he first kissed Diana. It could happen again. He knew he'd wanted this, at some level, since the first time he'd seen Zoe.

He was interrupted in his reverie as Zoe wriggled a hand free and used her fingertips to stroke the inside of his thigh. He lifted his head, licking his lips and smiling at her.

'You're mine now. Do as you're told. Don't move. At all.' He carried on looking at her, her eyes suddenly glazed and rolled back, and he let his hand stray between her legs, touching her inquisitively, gently.

She shuddered and protested. 'Too much,' she whispered.

'I've not even started,' he laughed. 'You like this? You like being told what to do?'

She nodded, helplessly, and he shook his head in wonder.

'Well, that's a nice change, I have to say. Is that why they say you're so sweet? Is this how you like it?'

She nodded again. He was delighted. He bent again to her breasts, a perverse thought making him concentrate on one breast and ignore the other. He enjoyed the way she moaned.

He felt generous. 'Do you want me to tie you down?' he whispered.

She shook her head.

He put his mouth to her ear. 'You can speak.'

'No, just tell me what to do. You're the Alpha. Your voice is enough. I don't need you to tie me down.'

He teased her earlobe with his tongue again. 'Who do you need that from? Tell me. Tell me all about it. You're mine now, remember?'

She came again, and he sighed. His prick was so hard, he couldn't ever remember feeling this strong. Who would have thought their bright, confident Zoe was so utterly submissive.

She was whispering. 'John, he ties me up, he likes to use belts. Diana…' she blushed.

'Tell me,' he said.

'Diana likes to play too, but she uses ribbons, something I could break if I wanted to. I never want to.'

'Shh,' he said, and leaned back down to nuzzle her, unable to resist nipping her slightly with his teeth. She yelped again, and he stroked her stomach, his hand dipping a fraction of a centimetre further down with each circle. He threw his head back, examining the way he felt. He sat still for ten long minutes, restraining Zoe with one hand while he caressed her with the other. She was starting to wriggle, believing she didn't have his full attention.

He considered the situation. He'd not been Katie's first lover, but she had been his, and their first encounter had been a fumbled mess. When he'd come to Diana, he had been barely more experienced, but they'd come together as if they'd been lovers for a decade or more. He'd been desperate to please both of them. And he'd thought this would be easy, this first time with Zoe – she was sexually experienced, mate to John and Diana. And she'd surprised him. There was something about having a totally submissive partner that brought out the inventiveness in him, a new slant of imagination that he seriously thought he hadn't possessed until after the fight with the whites. That day had changed him.

His arm was getting tired, supporting her head, so he released her arms and lifted her, taking her weight off his legs, and taking advantage of her surprise at this sudden change to rip her gown away. The sound of tearing hit him straight in the balls, and he groaned. He helped to free Zoe from the rags of her gown, and massaged her arms until she sighed with relief.

She sat up, kneeling in front of him, watching his face intently for a signal.

He caressed her face. 'Zoe, this is it. I'm stuck with you now, the addiction has started for me. This is *your* last chance to back out.'

She shook her head, and leaned forwards. Their lips met and he jumped a little at that sudden, familiar, electric, shock. Her lips were firm on his; she was forcing him back towards the wall. He reached down between her legs, finding her still hot and dripping wet.

She was equally eager to get to his cock, and pushed his hands away from her, pushing him to the bed and straddling him, getting around him and squeezing tightly as he looked up in astonishment.

'Bloody hell, that ironed out your kink!' he managed, then was quiet as her lips sought his and the chemicals started to flow backwards and forwards. He watched as she fucked him, glad to be with her at last. He lay back, sliding down the bed so he could lie still and watch her working on him.

She was moaning, needing something that the fucking wasn't giving her, and she left him, rose above him, losing him, twisting around, taking his prick in her mouth. Her hands were on his balls, and he cried aloud in ecstasy. She stopped, and glanced back, looking vaguely annoyed, and he wondered whose name he'd shouted. Then she was working on him, and he let himself come, hard and long, feeling her mouth, her throat, around him, feeling her tongue licking greedily at his cock. He got hard again as she cleaned him with her tongue, as she swallowed and tasted his come, making tiny, satisfied noises.

He asked her gently to stop, and she looked around, so erotically feral and alert that he couldn't resist, and he pushed her forwards, on to her stomach. He guided himself inside her again, finding her tight and responsive. He started to move again, his head next to hers.

'Changed your mind about ... you know?' he asked.

'About wanting you to be in charge?' she whispered. 'Oh no. I was just taken by surprise. Make me come, please. Hold me down and make me come.'

He grinned, and fucked her for half an hour, telling her that he was enjoying himself, telling her not to move an inch. Whenever she started to moan, he changed his position a little, and she quietened again. Finally, he let himself go again inside her, and she lay quietly. He crouched next to her. 'Thank you, we can do that again. Now roll over, open your legs.'

She shivered and turned over, giving him a long knowing look that made him feel faint.

He spoke, wondering what he was going to say. 'You're such a gorgeous little werewolf. Mine, I'm the Alpha, right?'

She smiled slowly.

'Zoe, you get your legs wider than that, I know damn well you can And put your hands behind your head. Do I have to tie you up?'

She shivered again. 'No, never.' She winked. 'But you can if you want to.'

He licked his lips. 'Don't wink like that, it's sluttish. Just do exactly as I say, and ... be quiet. Whatever I do, don't make a sound.' He looked at her cautiously, she seemed pleased. He stood up.

'I'm just going to look at you. Don't move unless I tell you to.'

He circled the bed, studying his new lover from every angle. She started to turn towards him as he stood still, as a flower turns to the sun. He whispered an admonition, and she quivered and lay still.

'I'm going to start touching you now. I'm not going to stop until I get bored. Or until I decide I want to fuck you again.'

He kneeled beside her, caressing and kissing her breasts and thighs and stomach, her legs and arms. He licked her inner arms, and behind her knees, then moved so that he sat between her legs. He started to touch her slit, gently, then more insistently. He slid in one finger, then two. She moaned, then clamped her mouth shut, and he explored inside her, watching her face. Three fingers, and she squeezed down tightly on his hand for just a second.

'Lift your arse,' he said quietly, and as she did, he slid a pillow underneath. He bent to kiss and lick at her, and felt her legs come together. He moved away. 'Bad Beta. Don't move. This is for me, not you.'

She opened her mouth, and he felt a rush of delight.

'I thought I told you to stay quiet,' he said gently. He pushed her legs wide apart again, and told her not to move, as he rubbed at her slowly, deliberately. He waited for her orgasm before he slid into her again, and laughed as she gave a muffled scream. He knew he could continue like this for hours; the urgency was gone now, the bond was made, never to be broken. This was just for fun.

He looked at her. 'Enough?' he asked.

'I'm getting tired. What happened?' she whispered.

'It's the bonding, I guess it's more tiring for you.' He smiled fondly at her, and concentrated on what he was doing. This time he didn't hold back, and when she started to come, he called her name in his clear, low voice, holding her gaze. As he felt her orgasm, he followed with long slow strokes that hovered on the brink of leaving her every time, but didn't. When he was satisfied she was finished, he allowed himself another half-dozen fast strokes and came again, almost painfully.

He sighed and rolled away, looking at the ceiling. Zoe was asleep. She'd turned over and was pressed against him trustingly, and he realised he liked it.

Just before dawn, she woke him up as she got out of bed.

He was instantly awake. 'Where are you going?' he whispered.

'Back to Diana. I'll have a quick shower first. Can I borrow a robe?' She spoke matter-of-factly.

He lay back. 'What if I say no?'

'Then I'll take it anyway.' She grinned, and disappeared into the bathroom.

She was very pink and damp when she came out, wrapped in a man-sized bathrobe. She glanced ruefully at the expensive silky rags on the floor. 'Diana bought that for me.'

He smiled. 'I'll make it up to her.' He really wanted to spend the rest of the night with his Alpha, but Zoe was already halfway through the door. He flinched away from

237

the thought of joining the pair of them – there were some limits still. Then she was gone, and he snuggled over to her side of the bed. The scent there was interesting. He was familiar with hers, but it mixed with his own in a pleasing manner. He was asleep again before he knew it.

A phone call from Diana woke him up, inviting him over for room-service breakfast. There were only two chairs in the room, so he perched on the edge of the bed while he shared their huge meal. He watched Diana carefully. She looked well-rested and calm. Her phone rang three times during breakfast. The first time it was John, 'just checking in'. She passed the phone to Mark after a minute or two.

He bit his lip. 'Hiya, John,' he said quietly. 'You OK?'

'I'm good. I hear you took my advice. Sort of.'

Mark looked at Diana and frowned. 'How did you know?'

'Diana rang me last night. How is she?'

'They're both fine,' Mark managed. 'You?'

'I wish they'd bloody get home, it's not easy running this place single-handed. I rang Andy for help, and he said he has friends over for tennis today. Bastard.'

Mark said he was sure the women would be on their way home soon, and hung up.

The next call was from Noah, complaining that Caleb had put itching powder in his underwear drawer. Diana rolled her eyes, and asked for Caleb.

'Hiya, sweetie. Are you behaving for JohnDad? Now, I understand Noah is having some problems with his kecks. Why don't you be a good brother and put his stuff in the wash? And clean his underwear drawer out properly?'

Mark grinned; she was using that tone again. Sometimes *he* couldn't resist it, never mind the kids. He tucked into his breakfast, listening to her voice. This was perfect: good food, good company and the kids were hundreds of miles away.

She was speaking again. 'Cal, if you don't want to clean his underwear drawer, then you'll have to give him yours. Would you rather do that? You can have his?' She waited, frowning. 'Good. I'll be home soon, and if I hear anything more about Noah's underwear today, I won't be pleased. OK?'

She put the phone down and shook her head. 'I never wanted children, you know that?'

Zoe and Mark looked at each other and burst out laughing. Diana looked at them for a minute and then threw a croissant at Mark. It was a perfect hit, and he spent the next few minutes getting crumbs out of his hair. Diana was drinking her coffee and reading the paper when the phone rang again. It was a short conversation. She put the phone down and started to pack.

'That was Sara. Miranda's ill. We'd better get back. Mark, are you coming with us?'

It was a neutral enquiry, and he sighed regretfully. 'Sorry, I can't, you know?'

She nodded, and turned her back.

'I want to,' he said quickly, and he cursed himself again as she glanced round and looked from him to Zoe and back again. He realised there was no way out of that one that wouldn't upset Zoe or Diana or both, so he settled for repeating that he wanted to, but couldn't.

Zoe took the luggage down to the car, leaving him alone with Diana. They kissed, and he knew he'd been away from her for too long; he was beginning to ache for her. Her eyes said that she felt the same way, but she said nothing.

He hugged her. 'I'll come home, soon. I do want to.'

'Home?' she said, puzzled. He didn't call Silverwood 'home'.

'Yeah. Are you OK with, you know? Zoe?'

'Oh, yeah. It's good for all of us. She's amazing, isn't she?'

He wasn't going to fall for that one, and he kissed her again.

'If you say so.' He smiled gently. 'After all, you think John's good-looking.' He was on dangerous ground again. He wanted to tell her how beautiful she was to him, but too many years had gone by, there were too many assumptions between them. She was touching his face, looking into his eyes, and he looked away, blushing.

'I do care, you know?' he said quietly, drawing away from her. He swallowed. 'That's Zoe, coming back. You'd better get off. I'll ring you tonight.'

She looked at him.

He cleared his throat. 'I'll ring you tonight, find out how Miranda's doing. Goodbye.'

He fled back to his own room, and banged his head against the pillow. This wasn't supposed to happen. He wasn't supposed to fall in love with Diana, it mixed things up too much. When had she become so real to him? He looked round the room before he left it. Nothing there to pack; he'd arrived with nothing but the clothes he was wearing. He looked at the torn nightdress on the floor, and was reluctant to leave it there.

He held it to his face, breathing in Zoe's fragrance, analysing his reaction, not allowing himself to lie at all. This was new, this forced honesty with himself. He was amused by how erotic he found her, and wondered if that was because she'd been forbidden to him for so long, or because of the intense nature of the sex between them the night before. He decided she was another force drawing him to Silverwood, a new force, but not nearly as strong as the ever-growing need to be with his Diana.

He bundled the silk into a tight ball and stuffed it into the inside pocket of his jacket. He checked out, and made his way back to the house he shared with Katie.

Chapter 24

The place was empty, as he'd expected. He made himself some lunch, and cleaned away the breakfast things Katie and the boys had left on the table. He felt a sick nostalgia for how things had been, for the days when this had been enough for him. He went upstairs to the main bedroom, and was unsurprised to see his toiletries were gone again from the en-suite bathroom, his clothes gone from the wardrobe. He looked in the guest room, seeing his things in a crazy jumble on the unmade bed. He dressed in clean clothes, then spent a quiet hour tidying up.

He looked at the clock. The boys' school day would soon be over. He rang the school.

The receptionist checked her records and told him Mrs Preston had made arrangements for the boys to be picked up by taxi. He cancelled the taxi and went to collect them himself.

Jake gave him a suspicious look as he got in the car, but waited until they were home, and Matt was settled in front of the telly with milk and some fruit, before he said anything.

'Mum was really mad last night,' he ventured. 'Were you with that other woman?'

Mark shrugged. 'I had to be. I wish I could be in two places at once, but I can't. Most of the time, I can be here. Last night, I couldn't be. Are you mad at me?'

Jake shrugged in turn. 'Dunno. Everyone's mum and dad gets divorced, don't they? You two have done well to last as long as you have, everyone says so.'

Mark drew Jake to him, amused. 'Hey, it's a pleasure to live here, not a chore.'

Jake looked up, oddly wise. 'Most of the time?' he said.

Mark made a face. 'I suppose so. When are we expecting your mum back?'

Jake's eyes widened. 'Oh no, the taxi was taking us to Auntie Siobhan's. She'll have a fit if we don't turn up.'

'No worries, I'll sort it.' Mark went for the phone, and spoke quickly to Katie's best friend. It was a short conversation.

'Auntie Siobhan doesn't like me,' he told Jake.

'Auntie Siobhan doesn't like anybody,' said Jake with huge aplomb. 'She's a bitch.'

This time Mark did choke. He was almost blue in the face by the time he'd recovered. 'JAKE PRESTON! You do not talk about ladies like that. It's very naughty.'

Jake was quiet for a while, then coughed. 'Dad, Mum said it was all right to say your girlfriend was a bitch, because she really is one. What did she mean?'

Mark stood up. 'That's something I'll tell you about when you're old enough to understand. In the meantime, you do realise you shouldn't listen to your mum when she talks about my ... my girlfriend?'

'Is she biased?' Jake asked.

'Very. But so am I, in a different way.'

'Do you love her? Your girlfriend?' Jake seemed to be genuinely interested.

Mark nodded. 'Of course I care about her, we've got children together. Now, I don't really feel comfortable about talking about her to you. Maybe one day, when you're older, you can meet her, and you'll know how nice she is.'

He made tea for them, and they all settled around the telly. Matt wasn't speaking to him, but that wouldn't last long. Mark went to get his guitar from the garage. It was an old electric guitar, the first one he'd owned. All the others were at Silverwood, stored in the music room, but he didn't want this one out of his reach. He'd painted it himself – a clumsy job, but one that evoked memories of learning to play, of finding out that he was bloody good at it.

He scowled as he went into the garage. The guitar was off its stand, face down on the floor. He picked it up tenderly, and stared in disbelief at the strings, which had been cut deliberately. There were huge gouges in the paintwork, some deep enough to scar the wood underneath. He cradled the guitar in his arms, and carried it into the living room.

'Matt, Jake. Which of you did this?'

Matt glanced round, glared at Mark, then looked back at the telly.

Jake's eyes opened wide. 'Dad, I wouldn't do—'

'Quiet. Matt, get up. Now. Look at me. Did you do this? Tell me the truth.'

Matt flinched and looked round. 'I didn't do it,' he muttered. 'I'm going to my room.'

'No you bloody well aren't. Matthew, you're six years old now. That means you're old enough to deal with the consequences of what you do. I know you're a kid, but this is … this is wrong, Matt. I was going to play something for you and Jake, how can I now?'

'I didn't do it.'

'Matthew, don't tell lies. Jake wouldn't do something like this!'

'Neither would I! It's not fair, why do you think I did it? I hate you.' Matthew fled, and Mark stood up in a fury, laying his wounded guitar on the sofa.

Jake spoke up. 'Mum did it,' he said quietly. 'It wasn't Matthew.'

Mark swayed. 'Your mother did this? She hurt my guitar? Katie did this?'

His son looked away. 'Can you fix it?'

Mark looked at the guitar. The damage wasn't major. He could repair it, restringing it wasn't a problem. She hadn't done any real harm. He sighed. 'I can fix the guitar. I'd better go and tell Mattie I'm sorry.'

Matthew was lying on his bed, poring over a children's atlas, when Mark knocked and poked his head around the door.

'Hey, Mattie, I'm sorry. I know it wasn't you. I shouldn't have blamed you.'

'I hate you,' Matt said with absolute assurance.

Mark shook his head and sat down on the bed. He looked at the atlas. 'Do you like maps?'

Matt shrugged.

Mark pointed on the map. 'That's Florida, where we went when you were a toddler. Do you remember going to see Mickey Mouse? And that's Colorado, where we went two years ago. You wanted to go on one of those little horses, but mummy was scared, remember?'

Matt turned the page to South America. 'Have we been here?' he asked.

'Hey, not yet. I went to Brazil once, with Uncle John and Uncle Andy. We played some concerts. When you're a bit older I'll take you there. There's jungles and stuff.'

Matt looked up coldly. 'Why is your hair so long? Everyone at school laughs at it. You look like a girl.'

'Oh jeez, I'm an embarrassment to my children already? Don't say they call me Ozzy, please!' he joked to cover his annoyance. Matt was being bloody awkward.

'I want you to cut your hair,' Matt said. 'Mum wants you to as well.'

Mark stood up. 'I give up. Sulk if you want to, I just bloody give up.'

He stalked out and leaned against the door. After a few minutes, he straightened up to go downstairs. As he moved away he heard a sob from inside the room, and he sighed and went back in, lifting Matthew up and holding him. His six-year-old held on tight, his sobs getting more and more intense.

Neither of them said a word, and Katie found them lying curled up together, fast asleep, when she got home from work later that evening.

They let Matt sleep, and went downstairs together, not looking at each other. Jake took one look at them and went to his room.

Mark gestured to the broken guitar. 'I can't believe you'd do such a childish thing.'

She walked out and came back with a handful of cream silk. 'And I can't believe that you'd bring your trophies home.'

'So, now you're going through my pockets? I told you where I was! Why would you go through my bloody pockets?'

'You planned the whole fucking thing, don't deny it,' she hissed.

He considered lying, then licked his lips. 'So I did. So I wanted to make sure they were OK. What's so weird about that? We've got enemies, she's got enemies. She's vulnerable, I have to protect her and the babies.'

'Babies?' Katie's eyebrows shot up. 'She took babies with her?'

He started to speak, and she opened her mouth wide in shock. 'Ah, you mean she's pregnant again.' She snatched the silky rags off the sofa. 'These are going in the bin. You are sleeping in the spare room.'

She spun as he grabbed the silk and pulled it out of her hand.

He shook his head and picked up his guitar. 'I'll be back tomorrow. Tell the boys I'm having a lie-in or something. Hell, tell them where I am. Tell them I don't want to be in the same house as you tonight.' He stalked out.

He drove too fast, taking the back roads, the darkest, narrowest roads, driving like a demon until he was home at Silverwood. It was late when he arrived, and the house was dark downstairs. He rang Diana, and she opened the gate for him. He asked about Miranda, and was relieved to find it was just a cold, nothing worse. Diana asked him why he was at Silverwood.

'She broke my guitar,' he said simply.

Diana looked at the guitar and hissed sympathetically. 'Ouch. Is it fixable?'

'The guitar is,' he growled. 'Can I stay here tonight?'

'Of course, hon. Shall I give Zoe a shout?' she asked.

He shook his head wordlessly, and followed her up the stairs.

Two days passed. It was the longest he'd stayed at Silverwood for a while. Andy showed up, and they all went hunting together. Their own woods were hunted out of deer, but rabbits still bred plentifully, and they all ate well. Mark realised he didn't fit into the Silverwood routine, and was surprised at how quickly John had made a niche for himself, taking over some of the heavier work, teaching music, making improvements to the place. Mark felt he was in limbo. He half expected to spend the rest of his life there, never to see his wife and sons again. He couldn't bring himself to contact them.

Early on the third morning, his phone rang. He glanced at the caller ID and passed it to Diana, who was in the bedroom with him. 'Answer it, will you?'

She peered at the number and shook her head. 'Don't get me involved in your marital squabbles.' She turned her back on him.

He gaped at her in amazement. 'I think, lady, that you are pretty much involved!' he said with hastily mustered dignity.

'Let me read in peace, and answer the phone,' she muttered.

He sighed and took the call. 'Hello, Katie,' he said.

'You can come home now,' she said tightly.

'Oh, I've suffered enough, have I?' he asked.

'Where are you?' she asked, her voice unusually quiet.

'You know,' he said.

'Oh.'

The silence dragged on, and he let it. He thought of his guitar, lying in the basement workshop, stringless, sanded down to the wood.

Eventually she spoke. 'I shouldn't have cut the strings, it was petty.'

He waited.

'Mark, I'm sorry. I just find this hard to deal with. I don't want a divorce, I want you to come back. Please, for the boys? For me?'

Diana looked up from her book and whispered, 'Don't be such an arsehole, Mark. Go home.'

Katie spoke again. 'Who is that? Oh god, you're in bed with her, aren't you? I can't deal with this.' She hung up, and Mark rolled his eyes.

He looked at Diana. 'Arsehole?' he said.

'Yup. She's offered the olive branch, yeah? You love her, don't you? We need her on our side, as much as she can be. Stop being an idiot.'

He studied her for a long time, then kissed her forehead and got out of bed.

'OK, I'll go. But she went too far, you know?'

'Yeah? You fucked Zoe, and Katie snipped your guitar strings. If I were her, I'd find myself a nice young doctor and shag him senseless. Much more therapeutic.'

'No, you wouldn't.' He grinned. 'You'd track down my mistress and scare her into leaving the country. *Then* you'd find yourself a nice young guitarist and shag him senseless.'

'Wrong. I'd find a bass player. I've always had a bit of a thing for bass players.'

'Hussy,' he said affectionately. He looked at her, considering his options, then sighed and went to get his car keys.

Chapter 25

Back 'home'. Back to what he still caught himself thinking of as 'real life'. Katie had a day off work, and was waiting for him.

'Do you still love me?' she asked.

'Yes, of course I do,' he said. It was the truth, still.

'I need to keep a certain position, I don't think you understand that.' Katie was speaking cautiously. 'We've had a very good marriage. You've been a supportive husband. It's hard, when a woman has a career … but you've been a huge asset, socially and emotionally. Knowing that you've been there for me has helped me to make it.' She smiled wryly. 'And the money's been helpful too – we've always been able to hire help if you've been on tour or recording.'

He raised his eyebrows. 'What are you saying?'

'Well, it's been a shock, finding out about your other life. Your extraordinary other life. I was jealous, of course I was. But is there any reason why things shouldn't carry on as before? The situation is the same, after all, the only difference is that I know now. I still need a husband, the boys still need a father, and so far I can see, you still want to fill both roles.'

'Roles?' Mark said in disbelief. 'What do you mean, roles? I've not been acting a part, you know?'

She dismissed it with a wave of her hand. 'I'd feel more secure if I could be sure you loved me, but I won't be making any more threats. Will you come back? Will you stay?'

'Everything back to normal?' Mark said. 'No more finding my clothes in the spare room?'

'You play your part, be nice to my friends, make it clear that I'm the most important thing in the world to you. That's all I want.'

'You *are* the most important...' he started to assure her, and was shocked by the clear lack of interest she had in what he had to say. He took a deep breath. 'OK, it's a deal. With one proviso...'

'What?'

'My kids can phone me here, without fear of being cut off or hung up on. Not Diana or Zoe, they wouldn't be so insensitive, but sometimes the kids want to talk to me about stuff. It's hard on them when I can't talk to them.'

She considered it. 'Fine. But I don't want John here any more. Or Andrew fucking Ransome and his fucking stupid wife.'

'Helen?' Mark laughed nervously. 'What's Helen done?'

'Oh, didn't you know? She's suddenly a huge fan of that Diana. I rang her to ask if she was planning to divorce Andy, and she *laughed* and asked me if I didn't think it was the most exciting thing ever, real werewolves in my own family. She's a nutcase.'

'OK, the whole pack stays away from the house, and Helen. But the pack kids can phone whenever they want ... and I can take Matt and Jake out with John and Andy sometimes.'

'No,' she said firmly.

'John's their uncle. They love him.'

She bit her lip. 'OK, but you are not to take my sons to her house.'

He nodded, tired out. He'd thrashed out some hard contracts in his time, but this one hurt him deep inside.

She smiled. 'I do need you, you know?'

'Yeah, you've made that clear. When's the next dinner party?'

She had the grace to blush. 'Tomorrow night. Is that OK?'

He stood up and brushed his hair back from his face. 'That's fine. I'll move my stuff back into our bedroom, eh?'

As he walked upstairs, he realised that at no point had Katie said she still loved him. He didn't realise he was crying until he saw the tears drop on to his T-shirts as he put them back in the drawer. He realised with a dull shock that he was mourning his marriage.

He tortured himself by getting the wedding album from the study, and looking through the photos of the day. Katie looked so beautiful and proud, and he was smiling on every single photo. Andy had been best man, a sudden change of plan that they'd explained away as his being much better than John at public speaking.

They all looked so young on those photos. Xan ... Xan had been camera-shy that day, and was only on one of the pictures: a posed picture of the Hearts that John had asked for. John was smiling on that one; it was the only one. That was another thing Katie had always held against his cousin, that he'd not smiled on her wedding photographs. Of course, she now knew why.

He touched the picture of himself and Katie outside the church. Her dress had been perfect, simple and elegant. He wondered idly what Zoe's dress was like, and from there it was a natural progression to think about Diana in a wedding dress. He found himself smiling; he couldn't imagine her tolerating that kind of fuss. Then he realised the chances of Diana ever having a wedding day were pretty low. He'd never thought of it before, and he felt a pang of guilt – everyone should have one day when they can show the whole world that they're loved and wanted.

He copied all the photographs, printing them out. He had a vague idea that he didn't want to be without them. He popped the copies into an envelope and addressed them to himself, then into a bigger envelope addressed to John, at Silverwood. He slipped in a note: 'John, keep these safe, more to come.'

He was crying again, realising what he'd lost. He glanced at the video player in the study; there was a rack of home videos of him and Katie and the kids, and he bit his knuckles as he sat down at the computer and researched how to copy them to DVD. He looked at himself in the mirror. He spoke to his reflection.

'You're going to leave, aren't you? Maybe not this week, maybe not even this year, but you're going to go to her. Oh, you're a sneaky bastard, you've even hid it from me!' He scowled at his reflection. 'Mark Preston, you're a bad bastard. You don't deserve either of them.'

A week later, he was back at Silverwood. He found Zoe in the kitchen with a couple of the older kids. Bill looked surprised when Mark wrapped his arms around Zoe and kissed her, and Mark laughed.

'What's up with you?' Mark teased.

'Just didn't know that you two…' Bill blushed.

'Well, you know now. Zoe, I want to get a bit more involved in things here. Can you show me the accounts and stuff?'

She nodded, and they left the kitchen. He watched her go upstairs. 'Zoe, don't we keep the accounts downstairs?'

'Oh… You really do want to look at them?' Her eyes were very wide.

He shook his head. 'Er, yes. Are you OK?'

She shrugged. 'I'm feeling "itchy". I was hoping for a fix.'

Mark nodded. 'OK, hon. I'm staying tonight anyway, we'll sort it out. But can I look at the accounts?'

He spent the rest of the afternoon alone with the books, shaking his head in disbelief. Diana dashed in just before teatime – she'd been in the lab with Caleb, Sammy, Janie and Alice.

'Mark! Why didn't you tell me you were coming?'

'I didn't want to bother you. What's this?' He pointed to a regular credit in the books, a substantial amount.

She peered at it. 'Ah, that's a payment from a fund that me and Andy set up from Xan's estate. We split the legacy into three – a third to buy and renovate Silverwood, a third for this fund, a third in trust for Miranda. That's what kept us going in the early years. Then Joyce's estate came in, and Andy invested that for us too.'

He nodded. 'And that's what?' He pointed to another sum, a hundred times smaller.

She looked up. 'That's what you set up, right at the start, don't you remember? When I had to give up work after Seth and Noah were born?'

He shook his head. 'I was going to increase that. Why didn't you remind me?'

'I don't need any money from you. It's OK, really. I've got the consultancy income from universities, and from Andy moving band money around via Ransome Industries. Zoe brings in some income, and I've licensed a couple of patents that I developed a few years ago.'

'How much does Andy give?'

'Nothing official, but he mostly takes care of buying clothes for the kids.'

'And John?'

'Well, he didn't used to make any regular payments, but he's always buying toys and books, and he bought my car for me. Daft bugger – I didn't need a new one. Now he lives here, all his income goes into this account, and he takes out what he wants for spending money.'

'And what about this debit? Every month, same account? Big amounts.' He looked wary.

'Out of the current account, into the savings. Zoe's royalty cheques are building up too. She sold some film rights last month – it surprised me how much she got for that.'

He shook his head and turned the pages back. 'Look, this security system, it cost a fortune. Who paid for that?'

'John's Manchester flat. We didn't have to touch the savings.'

He looked at the ceiling and made an exasperated noise. 'Diana, you should have told me that I wasn't pulling my weight. I don't believe it!'

She looked at him warily. 'I kind've assumed that you know where your money goes. Anyway, we don't need more, we've got more than enough already.'

He thought furiously, then nodded. 'OK, I'm going to increase my contribution. I don't need to hide it from Katie any more do I? It can go straight in the savings account if you want, but things are changing. Hell, look at that! It barely covers my keep! And I'm going to pay for John and Zoe's wedding.'

Diana laughed. 'John won't like that.'

'I'll explain it to him. I'm Zoe's Alpha, aren't I? Her dad's dead … I'll be the one giving her away, so to speak. I'll pay for the wedding, as a gesture towards her.'

His mate looked at him. 'How can he argue, when you put it like that? Anyway, speaking of Zoe, she's pining for you.'

'Yeah, I know. I'm sorta pining for her too.' He didn't look up. 'Would it be OK if I took the other room tonight?'

She stood and moved behind him, massaging his shoulders. 'You really like her, don't you?'

'I do, she's an asset to the pack. You were right, I was wrong.' He carried on looking through the books. 'Diana, why the hell did you pay a piano tuner? I've got perfect pitch, and I can fix anything that makes a noise.'

'She was available, you weren't,' she said simply. 'Are you taking over the accounts now? Because that would help me and Zoe a lot more than a few thousand quid a year more in the savings account. How do you feel about Zoe? What did you mean, pining for her?'

He looked up. 'Yeah, I'm planning to be around more – I can do this for you. Are any of the kids interested in this sort of stuff?'

She looked upset. 'Sara loves admin stuff, always has done. She can be your assistant, if you want one. She'd be thrilled to bits. What did you mean, about Zoe?'

The question finally penetrated, and he breathed deeply. 'Ah, I just meant that the bond is kicking in. I recognise it. It's not nearly as strong as it is for you. What did you think I meant?'

'I thought you were falling for her…' Diana said quietly. 'It just doesn't seem fair. All these years and you've been so loyal to Katie, and then you sleep with Zoe and suddenly you're here all the time. I could never get you to spend so much time here. And insisting on paying for the wedding … it made me wonder, that's all.'

Mark pulled her on to his lap. Sometimes it was easy to forget that she didn't know what was going on in his head.

'Look, I'm not falling for Zoe. I'm not in love with anyone except—' He was interrupted by John, who barged in, grinning.

'Sorry to interrupt the fun and games, but I think Mikey wants his mum. I warn you, don't laugh.'

Diana stood up. 'What now?' she sighed.

John smothered a giggle. 'Well, Mikey's got the hiccups, and Sam told him that he'd cast a spell on him, and he was going to start coughing up slugs like in that Harry Potter film. As an added bonus, he showed him the film clip. So we've got a hysterical hiccupping toddler, and nobody can calm him down.'

Diana started to shake with laughter, and hung on to John for a few minutes. Mark watched with a shade of jealousy; there was no doubt that these two had something special.

He spoke up. 'Shall I come? I am Mikey's father after all.'

John sat down next to him, peering at the books. 'Nope, shouldn't think so. Mikey's too young to know who his father is or isn't. He screams when he sees you anyway – Nat told him you were the Devil and you ate Rudolph the Reindeer. Hey, are these the accounts? Have we got any spare money? I want a new radio mike for the music room. And a chip pan.'

Diana left, straight-faced.

Mark put his face in his hands and sighed. 'John, I love you, but shut up. You have the worst timing in history.'

'When are you going to tell her then?' John grinned.

'Tell her what, exactly?'

'All that moon-in-June stuff? Look, I can tell, I've been there myself. I recognise the way you look at her. Are we having a double wedding?'

Mark went white. 'John, I swear, if you say a word about this to anyone, I'll skin you alive and use your pelt to wipe my arse. I'll tell her, when the time's right. OK?'

'OK. And Madame Katie? Does she know yet, that she's for the old heave-ho?'

'John, you're impossible. No, she doesn't. She might not be, actually. She thinks we can have a functional

259

marriage if we act the part until the kids are grown up and she gets that top job at the Trust that she's got her eye on. Thinking I'm still in love with her boosts her bloody ego and keeps her happy. I've stopped pretending to myself that she cares about me any more. Anyway, I don't see why she has to know that things have changed. She doesn't give a shit anyway. I don't think Diana does, really – she's happy with you and Zoe. She was worried then, that I was going to take Zoe away from her.'

John rolled his eyes, but said nothing. He looked at the accounts again.

'Are we rich?' he said curiously, 'cos Zoe said she spends all my money on nappy cream.'

'Yes,' said Mark. 'We've got money. Just don't tell the kids. Diana doesn't want them to grow up spoiled brats. You can have a radio mike if you want.'

'Cool. Why did Zoe tell me we couldn't afford a chip pan?'

'Probably because you set fire to your London flat twice when you came home drunk. She knows all your dirty little secrets.' Mark smiled happily.

John stuck his tongue out. 'Only the ones that you and Diana and Andy know about,' he said smugly.

'I'm offering to pay for your wedding, by the way,' Mark said cautiously.

His cousin flicked through the accounts, and raised his eyebrows. 'OK. Is this really all you've been paying? I'm surprised she's not dragged you through the courts for child support.'

Mark blushed. 'Look, things are changing, all right? Just bring me the invoices, I'll pay.'

John nodded. 'OK, but I'll pay for the honeymoon.'

Mark blinked. 'Honeymoon? You're going away?'

'Damn right we are. She doesn't know yet, I'm being sneaky. I've got passports for the babies – Zoe wouldn't leave 'em behind, would she? I reckon I've got three weeks max with her before we both start pining for an Alpha fix.'

'OK, who's looking after the pack when all this is going on?'

'I, er, thought that you could come and stay, to help Diana, sort of a wedding present?'

Mark stared at his cousin. 'You want me to go to Katie and tell her that I'm going to be staying here with Diana for three weeks? She'll hit the roof. I really don't trust her to deal with that sort of thing – she might tell someone about the pack. That would be a disaster, with you and Zoe away.'

John swore under his breath. 'Well, Andy then? You and Andy could take turns staying with Diana? Helen'll be cool with it, if I turn the charm on – she's always fancied me.'

Mark laughed. 'In your dreams. You've always fancied her, more like. No, it's not going to work. Katie thinks I spend too much time here anyway. Go for a week. I'll stop for a couple of days, then Andy can stop for two or three, then I'll come back. OK?'

'It'll have to be,' John sighed. 'Those girls never get a break. It's not fair.'

He started to walk out, then turned round on his heel and came back in.

'Or, I could take both of them.' He sat down opposite Mark, resting his chin in his hands. 'Problem solved. Katie can't go ballistic about you taking care of your own kids for a while, if Diana's off in the sun with me and Zoe. Even Katie has to admit that you've got responsibilities.'

His cousin looked at him admiringly. 'John, only you could suggest taking two women on honeymoon and expect to get away with it. You seriously think I could manage this place without Diana?'

'Course you could. I did, for two days, and nobody got hurt. Not seriously, anyway. And you're ever so much cleverer than me.' John batted his eyelashes at Mark. 'Please, please, let me play out with the girls, Daddy?'

'Carry on like that and I'll make you sleep in the cottage for the next month. No. It won't work. Diana would never leave the children.'

'She left them to go to London,' John said. 'She left them to take Sara and Darlene to Paris a few years ago. And again to take Seth and Noah to Amsterdam. And she took Miranda to Edinburgh.'

'That was when her mother and Zoe were both around to help. No. She'll refuse anyway. It's a stupid idea.'

John shrugged. 'OK. You're the boss. I suppose you're right. You always have been before, after all.'

He'd danced out of the room before Mark could come up with a coherent reply to that one. Mark closed the books and sat back, chewing nervously at his bottom lip.

Diana came back, carrying a plump eighteen-month-old boy, who was hiccupping slightly, and sobbing whenever he remembered to. Mark waved at the boy, who buried his face in Diana's shoulder.

'Is he OK?'

'Yup. You know, it even made Caleb laugh, for a minute. I think that's why Sam did it, he's not usually so mean to the little ones. Mikey coughed some snot up and screamed the house down for a while, but I managed to keep my face straight. I told him that Daddy knows magic, and had made a spell to stop the hiccups. They've pretty much stopped now, he'd just wound himself up. Anyway, he wants to see Daddy. Don't you, baby?' She lifted Mikey and passed him over to Mark.

Mikey started to scream again.

Diana rolled her eyes. 'Do you want me to take him back?'

Mark shook his head. 'I think I can handle babies by now, don't you? Leave him with me. Maybe if his twin was here he'd calm down a bit?'

Diana looked doubtful and Mark smiled gently. 'Please? Where's Harry?'

'In his room. He's having a nap.'

'I'll take Mikey up there then. Hey, trust me. I'm a good dad.'

His mate smiled. 'Perhaps you could get through to Cal? He's not been himself since the fight, and he doesn't seem ready to talk about it yet. He killed a man, and he's in a mess about it. I don't suppose you could spend some time with him? He might open up to you…'

Mark nodded. He was pretty sure that if he spent some real time with Caleb, he could start to make up for all the time he'd missed with him. It was a chance to do something positive.

'Yeah, sure. I'll take him out for the day, next week. Does that sound good?'

'Will you be able to swing it with Katie?' Diana said doubtfully.

'I reckon I can negotiate something,' he said, bouncing Mikey on his lap and looking into his eyes. 'When's tea?'

'Now, just about, but I think Mikey's overexcited, best wait a bit and feed him later. I'll wait too, if you want. We could eat together, me and you, and Mikey and Harry?'

Mark looked up. 'That would be nice. Really. Do you think he's going to be a redhead?'

Diana stepped back and looked at Mikey critically. 'He's got a look of my dad, you know? Around his eyes. He's got the Foster genes, definitely. But his hair's too dark already to go red. I don't think he's going to have black hair, like you. Cal and Sam were born with jet-black hair. These two started off reddish-blond, but it's darkening fast. Maybe a sort of auburn?'

'We need more redheads in the family. Don't you think?' he said casually.

'Nope. The more my kids look like their dads, the better,' Diana said firmly. She smiled. 'He's settling now. You've always had a knack with babies.'

Mark kissed Mikey's head. 'Hey, it's because they know I'm a big bad daddy who won't stand any nonsense. I'll take him up for a nap now. Then I'm going to have words with Sam. And Nat.'

Diana nodded and walked out of the office ahead of him.

As he went upstairs, she cleared her throat. 'Mark, if Nathan blames Isaac, don't take any notice. When they

264

get in trouble, it's almost always Zak's idea. But Nat should know by now not to listen.'

Mark's face softened. 'Hey, give him a break, he's only five!'

'And I know the pattern. If you give Nat enough of a scare, he'll sort Zak out himself – he's not thick.'

'Okey-dokey. We've still got a date, for tea? I can cook.'

'I know you can, hon, and I'll let you too.'

At the top of the stairs, Mark hesitated. He realised he didn't know which bedroom was Mikey and Harry's. He opened the door next to the room that Andy usually took; it was clearly a little boys' bedroom, but it was empty. He stood in the corridor, cradling his son, feeling quite unreasonably distressed. He heard a door close and looked up; Zoe had just come out of the main bedroom.

She smiled. 'It's the child stealer!' she whispered, and Mark laughed nervously. 'Where are you going with our baby boy?' she continued.

'His room, but I don't know…' Mark shook his head. 'I hate this. I should know which bloody rooms they sleep in. I hate this so much.'

'Ah, don't worry, it changes with the little ones. It's just that Patrick and Liam are so settled in that room that Diana didn't want to move them. She figured it would be easier to move Beth, Meg, Tara and Louise further out into more grown-up rooms and free their rooms on this corridor for these two and Julie and Leanne.' She offered to take Mikey, but Mark shook his head.

'Just show me his room.'

She smiled. 'It's Meg and Beth's old room. You know which one that is?'

He breathed out, happier. 'Yes, I do. Thanks.'

'My pleasure.' She looked at him curiously. 'You're around a lot more these days. I guess things aren't good at home?'

'No,' Mark said briefly, and headed back down the corridor to the next-to-last room on the right. Harry was there, as promised, and he gratefully put Mikey down next to him.

He took his phone out and rang Katie.

'Hiya. I just thought I'd ring to see how you're getting on?'

'I'm fine, busy day. I didn't expect you to call.' Her tone was businesslike.

'Just a quiet patch. Can I talk to the boys?'

She was quiet, and his gut clenched.

'Katie, don't use them against me, that's not fair.'

'You're the one spending the night with another family,' she said coldly.

'Which is exactly why I want to talk to them. Don't they deserve to know that I miss them?'

'Don't you miss me?' she taunted.

'I miss you whether I'm with you or not,' he said, and she went quiet again. He heard her call for Jake and Matt, and relaxed.

Matt just wanted to know when he was coming home. He reassured him that he would be back for Sunday lunch. Jake wanted to know what he was doing.

He smiled. 'I'm sitting with two of my little boys, thinking about what you were like when you were so young.'

'What are they called?'

'Henry and Michael for posh, Harry and Mikey for everyday. They're eighteen months old and they're just starting to talk.'

Jake was quiet, and Mark smiled. He could imagine his son digesting the information. His next question floored him though.

'When I was a baby, did you look at me and think about when your other sons were my age? You know, the teenagers?'

Mark felt an immense pride in his son. 'Yes, I did. I missed them when I looked at you, and I miss you when I look at Harry and Mikey.'

'It's a shame we can't all live together, isn't it?' Jake said hesitantly.

His father shook his head. 'Jake honey, it's a lovely idea, but it can't ever be like that. I'll be home tomorrow, OK?'

'OK, Dad. Can I ring you if I want to talk?'

Mark bit his lip and shut his eyes. 'Jake, do you want me to come home? I will if you want.'

'No, I'm going to the pictures anyway tonight. Can I ring you?'

'Any time. I love you, Jake.'

'Love you too, Dad. Bye.'

Mark found himself listening to a dead line, and pressed the disconnect button. Not for the first time, he was amazed at how alike Jake was to Cal and Sammy: the same precocious curiosity about how other people worked, and how other lives affected their own.

After half an hour, the door opened gently, and Diana crept in. 'I'm knackered,' she whispered.

'Shh, curl up here. I'll go and make something to eat and bring it upstairs for us. Is there anything else that needs doing?'

Diana rolled her eyes and laughed. 'Always. But nothing urgent.' She glanced at the phone on the bed and looked away.

'I rang Katie,' Mark said.

'OK,' Diana said. 'I understand.'

Mark left the room. 'You don't,' he whispered. 'You really don't.'

He searched for Nat and Sam first, and had a chat with them both, then went to the kitchen. He could, at least, find his way around that. He opened four tins of baby food for the boys, and rooted around in the cupboards for something for himself and Diana.

John wandered in, singing. He waited until Mark had straightened up, then said, 'She likes spinach and eggs, when she's pregnant.'

Mark glared at him. 'I know, John. I don't live on another planet. She likes spinach, eggs, sun-dried tomatoes, pickled onions and fresh bread – the fresher, the better. She likes Mackeson stout with blackcurrant cordial too. And green olives, and Wensleydale cheese. But don't give her Cheshire instead, because she'll vomit. And she likes Mars Bars, but they make her sick, so she can only have a fun-sized one. OK?'

John raised his hands. 'OK, OK. Sorry I spoke. But there's frozen spinach in the green freezer in the big kitchen.'

Mark nodded. 'Thanks. Now … eggs, tomatoes, onions, garlic, basil, black pepper, flour, olive oil, mozzarella, yeast and salt?'

'You're making fresh pizza?' John's eyes opened wide.

'You, cousin, ate already.' Mark grinned.

'Make two?' John said. 'Say you'll make two, and I'll tell you where to find the ingredients.'

'Deal. You greedy bastard.'

'Fuel for the machine,' John said blandly.

The smell of fresh dough drew the kids into the smaller kitchen. Mark promised to teach Noah and Seth how to make fresh pizza if they'd all leave him alone to look after Diana. The kitchen emptied out quickly again as the kids surged off to find some other entertainment.

He made his way upstairs again with a tray that held two baby meals, plus a huge spinach and egg pizza, a bowl of pickled onions, a bowl of olives, two fun-sized Mars Bars, a glass of orange juice and a glass of stout with blackcurrant.

Diana was talking to Harry. 'Mama,' she said, smiling as he repeated it. 'Mama Diana,' she said, and shook her head as he made the vowel sounds. 'Duh. Duh.' She emphasised her pronunciation. 'Harry, say "Duh".' She smiled at Mark. 'Duh Daddy, Duh Diana, Duh Darlene, Duh Debbie.'

Harry stood up and waved his arms excitedly. 'DUH! Deyi! Deyi!'

Mark picked him up. 'Was that Daddy?' he said.

Diana shook her head. 'Debbie. He adores her. She gave him a worm from the garden last month, and watched him eat it. He loves her now. She knows the way to a boy's heart.'

'Did he throw up?' enquired Mark.

'God no, he wanted another one. His favourite words are "Deyi", "Mama" and "Wum".' She winked. 'Tell him that food is worms and beans, and he'll eat the lot.'

Mark settled Harry on his lap and started to feed him the first course. 'It's worms, Harry. Nice minced worms, with beans.' He looked at Diana, merriment in his eyes, as Harry shouted, 'Wum!' and grabbed the spoon.

Mikey was still sleepy, and looked at his twin with something approaching disgust.

Diana whispered to him. 'It's not really worms, baby boy, it's nice food.' She handed him his bowl and a spoon, and watched as he fed himself messily.

Their father nodded. 'No wonder Mikey was so traumatised by the slug thing. He's clearly got more of a gourmet palate than his twin.'

'Yeah. Oh, is that fresh pizza? Did you make it?'

'A labour of love,' Mark said, then bit his tongue.

Diana smiled, misunderstanding, taking his hand and putting it to her stomach. 'Hey, they'll grow big and strong on all this good food. They'll know that you love them.'

She ate half of the pizza, and all the chocolate, but refused the onions and olives. Mark frowned, and she reassured him.

'You're right, I do like them, but I'm full up with that pizza.' She yawned. 'This pregnancy is taking it out of me. I'm going to have a quiet evening in front of the telly then get a few hours' sleep before I go to the lab. Will you do the headcount with Zoe tonight?'

'Sure, I'll get the little ones bathed too, OK?'

'Mmm. Come on, let's take these two downstairs for an hour. Did you speak to Nat and Sam?'

They walked downstairs together, each holding one of the toddlers by the hand and waiting patiently for them to get down each step.

Mark nodded. 'Sam was sorry anyway. He won't do anything like that again. He's a sweet kid, he just wanted to cheer Caleb up and the joke backfired. Nat blamed Isaac for the Rudolph comment, just like you said he would, so I've banned sweets and desserts for a week for all four Quads. Do you think that's unfair?'

'No, they plot together, and if you try to punish one, the other three will rally round. Good work.'

'Thanks.' Mark smiled as they got to the bottom step. He was kept busy that night, first of all teaching Noah and Seth how to make pizza dough. He told them that his own dad had been Italian, or French, or Spanish – something foreign anyway. They were fascinated and wanted to know more.

Mark shook his head. 'I don't know any more. He left when I was little. I guess he was a Shapeshifter, maybe he found a true mate?'

His eldest boys dropped the subject, and they worked in silence for a while until Noah said, 'Hey, did you see the football last Tuesday?' and they all started talking again.

Mark opened a bottle of wine and poured a glass each for the boys. Bill and Frank were attracted again by the scent of pizza, and opened their eyes wide when they saw their older brothers drinking.

'Can we have some?' Bill begged.

Mark looked at them. 'You can have half a glass, watered down.' Bill started to protest, and Mark shook his head. 'You're fourteen. You can have a drink, with me, but it's gonna be watered down.'

'JohnDad lets us drink beer. And we're nearly fifteen,' Frank said.

Mark half smiled. 'Fourteen and a half isn't nearly fifteen. You want a beer? You can have a shandy. Wine's stronger, and you have to get used to it.'

'Really? We can have a beer?' Frank looked awed.

Mark laughed. 'Don't bullshit me, Frank. I've heard about you getting pissed after school at Christmas.' He leaned down and whispered, 'And I know about the case of Stella that you hid behind the compost heap.'

Frank looked distressed and Mark laughed. 'So, would you like a beer, Frank? John's told me that he's got a nice case of Stella cooling in the shed.'

'Shit,' Bill said flatly. The boys turned around and left, glaring at Mark over their shoulders.

Seth spread tomato sauce on to a fresh base and nodded wisely. 'You can't kid a kidder,' he observed.

Mark raised his glass. 'Cheers, lads. What's the moral of tonight's tale?'

Noah frowned. 'Don't lie to your parents?' he suggested.

His dad pursed his lips. 'Well, yes. But I was thinking more along the lines of "Don't try to hide beer from John".'

Seth took another sip of wine and waved his hand expansively. 'I think I've got the hang of this now. You can go, Dad. We'll make a few dozen of these bases and freeze them.'

'OK.' Mark started to walk out, then turned back and picked up the wine bottle. He winked at Seth. 'I don't want you guys blaming me for getting drunk.'

Diana was watching TV and knitting baby clothes while John played Trivial Pursuit with Caleb, Miranda, Sammy and the Bees.

Mark glanced around. 'Where are my Kittens?' he asked.

Diana looked up. 'Sara and Darlene are in the music room. They're doing a guitar exam in May – they're practising. Let 'em stay up late, they're being good. For once.'

At eight, Zoe stood up and stretched, picking up the babies. 'Round one, all the little ones, up to and including the Quadettes.'

Mark grabbed Mikey and Harry. 'Shh, bedtime,' he told them. It took half an hour to put the younger kids to bed, then Mark and Zoe sat in the living room for a while, sharing the rest of the wine.

At nine, Diana announced that she was going to bed, and yawned extravagantly, setting everyone else off. She grinned. 'Sorry, Alpha power.' And made her way upstairs.

The Trivial Pursuit game ended soon after, and John followed her upstairs. Mark yawned and looked round the room; most of the kids were there, and he counted heads. Seth and Noah were still in the kitchen, and the Kittens weren't back.

'Bed, you lot. Bridget, Beatrice, don't give me that sad look!'

'One more game of Triv?' Beatrice begged.

Mark smiled. 'Next time I'm here, I promise.' He stood up and wandered over to where Bill and Frank were absorbed in something. They didn't hear him, and jumped when he spoke.

'Oh boys, the underwear pages of the catalogue?' He looked at them gravely. 'Again, next time I'm here, we'll talk.'

Miranda drifted across the room and looked down at the catalogue. 'I've got that underwear,' she said, and her brothers looked at her in horror. 'In black. And red. And white.' She smiled at them angelically. 'I'm going to bed now. And I'm going to take my underwear off, and put a nightie on. That one.' She turned the page and pointed to a lacy white number. She danced away and Bill shook his head.

'Sisters shouldn't be allowed to do that. She's ruined it for me now.'

'I think she intended to. And I'm sure you'll recover. Now, who's patrolling tonight?'

'Me and Seth.' Bill said. 'JohnDad and Frank are taking over once they've had some sleep.'

Zoe was outside already; Mark could see her making her way to the music room. She came back with the Kittens, and locked the doors, sleepily setting the alarms. He took her hand and led her upstairs. She went to the main bedroom and put her hand on the doorknob.

'No. Can we use the other room? I don't want an audience.' He felt himself blushing.

'Sure, but it's just John and Diana, and they're probably asleep already.'

'Ah, one day I might be comfortable with that, but not yet.'

He followed her into the second bedroom, and watched her brush her teeth and take her make-up off.

'What do you…?' He looked at the ceiling and started again. 'I mean, do you want to…?'

She took pity on him. 'Last time was nice, but I'm tired, and I really just want to stop feeling so stupidly desperate for you. Can we just have a nice fuck and then cuddle?'

Mark nodded and brushed his own teeth, reflecting that there were benefits in having a shared bathroom to both rooms: all his own stuff was accessible from both rooms. Zoe was in bed when he came back, and watched him as he undressed and put his clothes in the wash basket.

'You're so tidy,' she said. 'John leaves his clothes everywhere.'

'I know,' Mark sighed. 'I know all about him, believe me. So, shall we not mention him again tonight?'

They made love, and it was as if they'd been together for years, everything felt familiar and safe and comforting, the chemicals in their bodies working to strengthen the bond between them. Satisfied, they went to sleep in each other's arms.

Mark awoke a couple of hours later; somewhere in the house someone was awake. He listened carefully, and decided it was probably one of the older kids, who had rooms at the far end of the house. He realised he could hear John breathing in the next room, and relaxed. He listened more closely until he could hear Diana's lighter breathing, soft and even. He jumped when Zoe poked him in the chest.

'Don't lie there moping, go to her if you want.'

'I wasn't moping. Do you want John? Is that it?'

'I just want to sleep, and I can't with you sending off all those Alpha signals – they woke me up,' she hissed.

'And me,' a low voice called from the next room.

'Diana, you should be asleep,' he said firmly.

'Fucking hell, Mark, we should all be asleep.' John didn't whisper, and he hit the ground with a thud as he got out of bed and walked through the shared bathroom. 'Swap beds and shut up,' he grumbled.

Mark clung to the warmth of the bed for a while longer, then kissed Zoe goodbye, and sprinted across the bedroom, across the cold bathroom floor, and into the big warm bed in the main room. The spot where John had lain was still warm, and he snuggled into it. Moonlight illuminated Diana's sleep-puffy face and tightly screwed-up eyes; her hair was tangled and sweaty.

'Do you wanna fuck?' she muttered.

'I just want to hold you, beautiful,' he told her, and drew her close.

She fell asleep, and after a while, so did he. There was no getting up in the early hours for work that night, she slept right through.

He made gentle, sleepy love to her in the morning. She was looking into his eyes. He decided there was no better moment to tell her how much he loved her. He took a breath. But she started to speak, stopped, and laughed.

'You first,' she said.

'No, you first,' he replied gently.

'OK. I've been thinking about it, and I think it's lamb that gives Patrick and Liam diarrhoea. Next time we have it, I'll give them something else. What did you want to say?'

'Nothing,' he said glumly. 'It's not important.'

'Right, rise and shine.'

She was out of bed and into the bathroom before he could say anything else. He watched her every move that morning, until breakfast was over and he had to leave.

For the next four nights, he slept in a cold bed; Katie as far from him as she could get without falling out.

For Thursday night she'd asked him to make himself look smart and escort her to a retirement dinner at the hospital. They were seated next to a professor of social medicine, and the conversation got around to birth control.

Katie smiled pleasantly. 'Of course, family sizes get smaller as women are given the power to choose how many children they have. It's only in the most primitive social situations that you see large families. Wouldn't you agree, Mark?'

He finished chewing his food and swallowed, washing it down with a healthy belt of wine. 'Not always. You're always going to get the occasional exception, someone who can happily choose to have a large family and manage them very well. Of course, a woman like that would certainly deserve the support of the children's father.'

Katie's smile wavered a little. 'Or fathers,' she said.

Mark shrugged. 'Whatever. Personally, I think there's a lot of hidden self-hatred in all this talk of birth control. A well-brought-up, intelligent, creative kid is always going to be a plus.' He smiled at her. 'Like our own sons – we're not raising them to be idle, are we?'

The professor nodded. 'I agree. It would have been a tragedy if you and Katie hadn't had children. You're a musician, aren't you?'

'Semi-retired rock musician, part-time businessman, part-time producer and hired guitar for other bands.' Mark shrugged. 'I keep busy.'

'He does,' Katie said with a smile that didn't reach her eyes.

'Are your sons musical?' asked the professor.

Mark flinched; it was a sore subject.

Katie replied, 'It's a precarious profession, I'd prefer them to go into medicine or law.'

'Ha, yes. Just a lucky few get to make a living from music, eh?'

Katie agreed. 'Just luck, really,' she said, leaving Mark to fume quietly.

The professor was clearly enjoying their company, and getting a little more drunk.

'I must say, Dr Preston, you're very young to be in the position you have at the hospital.'

'I'm forty-seven,' she said. 'Not that young, really.' She smiled at the professor.

'Gosh, you don't look a day over forty! And your husband?'

'Mark will be forty-seven next month. He's three months younger than me.'

'Really? He looks so much younger. Mark, what do you attribute your youthfulness to? I ask in my professional capacity.'

Mark realised he'd had too much to drink when he heard himself say, 'Red meat, red wine and a red—' he caught himself just in time '—and a red-blooded wife,' he managed to say.

Katie had gone pale, but recovered and kissed him lightly on the cheek. 'You say the nicest things,' she said, then moved closer to hiss, 'Stop drinking or shut up.'

The professor smiled. 'You must have a remarkable metabolism. I know several people who'd love to study someone like you.'

Mark nearly fell off his chair. 'I don't think so. No,' he said, and looked desperately at Katie. 'Change the subject,' he hissed.

She took pity on him and asked the professor if he'd seen the latest article on drug rehab centres.

Mark was drawn into a conversation across the table, about science-fiction novels, and held his own without any further disasters.

They got a taxi home, and paid the babysitter. Katie went to the bathroom and came out wearing a black lace nightdress. She got into bed and looked at Mark.

'Red meat, red wine and a redhead? Are you going off me?'

He summoned a smile. 'Never. It just hurts that you don't want me these days.'

'I want you tonight,' his wife said.

'Why?' he asked. 'All we've done is make digs at each other all night. Go to sleep, Katie.'

He watched in horror as her face crumpled and she turned away from him, clutching the pillow to herself. He made his way to her side of the bed and kneeled on the floor, looking up at her.

'Katie, I didn't … I don't want to … please, love, stop crying.'

'I miss you,' she sobbed.

'I miss you too. We were so good together, weren't we? Katie hon, look at me. Just look at me and tell me you love me. If you can do that, we can still make it.' He held his breath; he knew it was true. She was his first love, and she still had a hold on him.

She sobbed again. 'I don't. I don't love you. You killed all that. I'm so lonely, Mark. I'm so lonely – I want to be held, I want someone to make love to me and make me feel like I'm not some over-the-hill old hag.'

He kissed her tears, his heart breaking. It was the first time she'd admitted it. He didn't reply to the confession; he responded to her plea.

'Hey, I can do that. You're not old, you're as beautiful as you were the first day I saw you. Remember that day? You thought I was going to mug you? Katie, don't cry, honey.'

She laughed, through the tears. 'I did *not* think you were going to mug me. I thought you were selling drugs.'

He sat on the edge of the bed and took her hand. 'See, we got over that, didn't we? Can we get over this?'

She'd stopped crying. 'No, I don't think we can. If it had just been an affair, I could've forgiven you. But this… It won't end, will it? I'll always be thinking that one day you'll stop loving me, and you'll want to be with her, and her family. I don't feel safe with you, I can't love you any more.'

Mark hid his face. He felt like the lowest form of life. When he felt more confident about his ability to lie, he looked back at her.

'Katie, you're my world. I never dreamed someone like you could ever be mine. She's just another Shapeshifter, that's all she means to me, really. I do care about her to some extent. I want to protect her, and I need to be with her, but if she'd been in that park that day, even if she'd been sat right next to you, I wouldn't even have seen her. You know that. You put her in the shade – you always have and you always will. She knows how I feel about you.' He reached out to touch her hair. 'Katie, please don't be unhappy.'

She swallowed. 'Why did you have to tell me about her? We were OK when I didn't know.'

'Yeah, I know. But I'm scared that one day something might happen, and everyone will know. It terrifies me, the thought of my children being hurt and hounded. People don't like anything different. I told you because if that ever does happen, you'll be prepared. You'll be able to say that you knew about it, that I love and respect and trust you enough to tell you my deepest secret.'

She was wiping her eyes, and he was grateful she couldn't see him. Oh you lying, twisted, scheming shit, he told himself. He managed another smile. 'Do you still want me to hold you?' he said.

281

'Yes, please. I'm sorry I can't love you. Is this enough for you? Are you unhappy?' She sounded anxious. 'I do still care about you. You're a good man, a good dad. I don't want you to be miserable.'

He kissed her briefly and sat back. 'I'm not happy, but I can live with this.' He could taste her tears still, just salty water, nothing more important than that.

She tried to laugh. 'Hey, you'd better take that suit off. It's too expensive for me to get all snotty and teary on. I'm sorry, Mark. Come to bed, I really do want you.'

He undressed and went into the bathroom. He looked into the mirror. 'She apologised to you,' he whispered. 'And you let her.' He sat down on the side of the bath, in his boxers, and began to chew at his fingernails. He didn't know how long he'd been there, when Katie opened the door and looked in, almost shyly.

'Mark, what are you doing?' She looked at him carefully. 'Are you crying?'

'I'm fine,' he said, looking up brightly.

'Oh, you *have* been crying. I'm sorry.'

He stood up and hugged her. 'Katie, if you ever, ever tell me that you're sorry again, I'll die of shame. I'm the one who's sorry, forever and ever. I screwed up. I don't think I like myself, that's what it boils down to. If you'd let me make love to you, if I can make you happy just for a few minutes, it would mean the world to me.'

He felt cleaner with that said, but he didn't dare to look at her until he felt her kiss his shoulder, felt her hand on his thigh, let her lead him to their bed.

The next night he booked a babysitter again, and took her out to dinner.

'Katie, I have a huge favour to ask of you. I need to be away this weekend again.'

She put her fork down carefully. 'When is John getting married?'

'In two weeks. I'll be away then, of course. Plus, John and Zoe are going away, so I'll probably have to spend a bit more time at Silverwood at the end of the month. After that, I promise, I'll be there less often.'

'Why this weekend? You were there all day and night last week. You can last longer than that, I know it.'

Mark acknowledged her point by glancing down. 'It's my son Caleb. I want to take him away from the pack, just for the day. He was traumatised when we were attacked, more so than the other children. We thought it would be good for him to get away, fresh perspective sort of thing. He might open up a bit more, away from home.'

'We? We thought?' Katie said.

Her husband pushed away his plate and looked at her. 'Now, you know that's not the point. We're talking about a child who needs me. I would like to spend some time with him, but I don't want a quarrel with you.'

'You have two other children who need you,' she said stiffly.

'I'll take them too,' he offered.

'Ah, so that's it. The integration starts here, does it? No way, pal. I don't want my sons anywhere near those freaks.'

'Katie!'

'I'm sorry, I can just about get my head around you being … weird, but I don't want to have anything to do with the rest of them. And I don't want my kids around them.'

'It's not catching,' he protested, then reconsidered. 'Well, it is, a bit, but only if you try really hard. You've never caught it.' He smiled at her. 'Please, Katie, I won't take Jake and Matt, just Caleb.'

'Why doesn't *she* take him? Or John? Or that other woman?'

'Because they're needed at ho— at Silverwood. If I'm not there, well, what's the difference, I'm hardly ever there anyway.' He shrugged.

'What about Andy?'

'I've spoken to Andy. He said he would if I couldn't. But Caleb is my own child, not John's or Andy's. Caleb knows that. I want to help him, if I can.'

'All right, but you explain it to Jake and Matt before you go. I suppose you'll be off in the morning?'

'Yes. Thank you.' He smiled again, and this time it reached his eyes.

Chapter 26

The following morning he got to Silverwood while the pack were still having breakfast. He waited outside the gates for ten minutes before someone noticed and let him in.

Caleb dropped his spoon when he saw him, and ran upstairs.

Diana looked up. 'Weird kid. I told him you were picking him up, that you were taking him out for the day. He just looked at me as if I'd killed his puppy.' She kissed Mark affectionately, and then lingeringly when he returned the kiss with interest. They were still kissing when Caleb came downstairs. His eyes flashed around the room; he didn't look at his parents.

'I'm ready,' he muttered.

'OK, lad, let's go. Are you ready?'

'Yes, Dad.' Caleb looked at the floor.

'Right, we're off.'

Caleb looked at Diana pleadingly, and she smiled. 'Give me a hug then. Don't worry about money, MarkDad will look after you.'

Mark watched as his son hugged Diana; he was nearly as tall as she was. He didn't seem to want to let go. He was muttering something that Mark moved closer to hear.

'Mum, I've got loads of homework. I can't be out too late.'

'Don't worry, you can do it tomorrow, I'll do your chores. Bye, sweetheart, see you tonight.'

Caleb's head drooped down, and he followed Mark outside. He opened the back door of the car and sat down on the back seat.

Mark frowned. 'Caleb, it's not a taxi. You're big enough to sit at the front with me.' He waited until Caleb had got out of the car again, and ruffled his hair. 'Tell you what, you choose the music. I've got twenty thousand tracks on the music system, I bet you can find something you like?'

'Dunno,' Caleb said. 'You choose. What do you want?'

Mark scratched his head, and got in the car. He set the stereo to Random and started the engine. Diana had her eye on things, and this time the gate opened as he approached it.

'Your hair looks good, Cal. Are you growing it?'

'No,' the boy said. 'Just not cutting it.'

'Ah, I see.' Mark nodded as if he understood. 'We'll have a chat when we get there. Trouble is, I don't know where "there" is yet. Where do you want to go?'

'Dunno.' Caleb looked out of the window, shaking his head so his hair fell across his face and hid him from view.

Mark thought for a minute, then smiled. 'I know, we'll go to Ulverston. I lived there when I was a boy. I'll show you where I grew up, and we can go to some of the places where me and John used to play. I sometimes take my other family there, to show them round.'

Caleb looked up anxiously. 'Will they be there?'

'No, of course not. I wouldn't spring something like that on you.'

Mark struggled, trying to find something to engage his son's attention. He got on to the motorway heading north, turned the music up, and started to sing along. He kept glancing at Caleb, waiting in vain for him to join in.

Eventually they got to Ulverston and parked in a quiet spot. They walked together down the street, past a row of shops. Mark glanced into a window and stopped, grabbing Caleb's hand and pointing at their reflection.

'Good grief Cal, look at us.'

Caleb had to smile; it was too funny. It looked like two versions of the same person, one still a child, the other a grown man. He realised why people had been smiling at them as they walked down the street. Mark looked around, and headed for a café. 'That place looks nice enough. Let's have lunch.'

The waitress blushed as she approached their table.

'Mark Preston? I thought it was you.'

Mark looked at her, trying to guess her age. He figured she was about five years younger than him. He smiled. 'Well, it is. You're too young to be one of my cousin's ex-girlfriends come back to haunt me. Did we know each other?'

'No, no. My sister was in your year at school, but no, I'm just a fan.'

'That's rare enough, these days. What's your name?'

'Kat,' she said, and blushed to her roots.

'That's a nice name. This is my son.'

'I know, I read about him. Hello, Jacob.'

Caleb winced and turned to look out of the window.

Mark smiled brightly. 'What's your sister's name? Maybe I remember her?' He laughed when she told him. 'I remember her, had her hair in a Lady Di cut for four years? We were lab partners in chemistry. Give her my best, will you? What's she doing?'

Kat relaxed and after a short conversation about her sister's year group, took the order and left.

Caleb was nervously moving the salt cellar around. He looked up. 'Jacob?'

'I'm sorry, mate. I'm well known, everyone round here knows I'm married, and most of them know what my lads are called. You're the dead spit of him anyway – we'll get away with it.'

His son had a guarded look about him. 'They only know what two of your lads are called,' he pointed out, glancing up quickly, assessing Mark's mood.

Mark reached across the table to take his hand, but the boy flinched away. Mark stopped, mystified.

'Caleb, shall we talk? You can talk to me, you know?'

The boy shook his head. 'I want to go home,' he said, then looked away.

Mark flailed around for something to say. 'We've only just got here. Look, Cal, I'll show you my old house, and John's old house. Then we'll have a drive up to my old sixth form college and I'll show you the exact spot where I met Andy and Xan and Helen for the first time.'

'OK,' Caleb said dully.

Mark gave him the tour, and then took him to the shops. They found a second-hand bookshop that had a science-fiction section, and for a few minutes they found something to talk about

'What do I have to do now?' asked Caleb, as they left the shop with a haul of 1960s paperbacks.

'Nothing. You don't have to do anything at all. Is there anything at all, in the world, that you would like to do, or talk about?' His dad looked at him for a few seconds. 'No? OK. I'll take you home.'

'Really? Now?' Caleb smiled, and Mark rolled his eyes.

They walked back to the car in silence.

Back at Silverwood, Caleb ran indoors, and had disappeared upstairs by the time Mark got to the front door.

Diana was waiting. 'Well?' she asked.

'Washout. He hates me,' Mark said. Diana started to protest, but Mark put his hand in front of his face. 'Don't. Don't say anything. He hates me, it's as simple as that. I fucked up. I wasn't around when we were attacked, Zoe got hurt, Frank got hurt, we nearly lost the girls. You saw how I fought. I'm a natural, if I'd got there earlier, nobody would have got through to him, and he wouldn't have had to kill anyone. It's my fault. He didn't say anything, but it's obvious, isn't it?'

'Oh, Mark, I'm sure that's not it. He's been fine with you around here. He's wanted to see you. I don't know what it is.' She took his hands in her own and looked up.

He saw that she was tired, and led her into the big living room, sitting next to her.

'Come on, tell me what's up with you. That's what I'm for.' He looked into her eyes, once more wondering how such a delicious green could be natural.

She relaxed. 'I can whinge?'

'Yup. I can't promise that I'll take any notice, but you can whinge.'

She breathed out deeply. 'One. The wedding. It's two weeks away, and you and Andy still haven't got back to me about your suits. I know it's a private do, but Zoe wants you all to match for the photos. Two. The wedding. Are you stopping that night? Because the kids are cooking, and want to know about table settings. Three. Not the wedding. I found a box of condoms in Frank and Bill's room. At least they're being sensible, but they're only fourteen, for God's sake – I'm not ready for this. Four. The wedding. Zoe decided to decorate her own wedding cake, then decided it was bad luck, and it's too late, now, to get anyone else to do it. Five through to ninety-nine. I'm absolutely knackered.' She cuddled up to him. 'Thank you. I feel better now.'

Mark nodded. 'One. Don't worry about the suits. Andy's got it under control, but he should have told you that he had. We'll all match. Two. Yes, I'm stopping that night.' He took a deep breath. 'Bill and Frank... Don't worry about it. I had a packet of condoms when I was thirteen – it's a boy thing. It doesn't mean they're going to use them, but it probably does mean that you've got a good excuse to stop cleaning their room.' He moved a little so that he had his arm around her. 'When Auntie Miriam found a girlie mag in John's room, she said that he clearly needed his privacy, and refused to clean his room or change his sheets ever again. It got pretty nasty for a while, but he learned, especially when he actually wanted to start taking real girls to his room. My mum said the same thing when she found the condoms. They conspired, those two.' He smiled 'As for the cake, it's not important what it looks like, is it? It's a family do. If she wants something for the photographs, I know a guy who does advertising photography, and he can supply a cardboard cake. If it's for eating, let Seth and Noah decorate it. She can show them how to do it, and we'll all eat iced cakes next week until they're good enough, and voila. And your last problem, well, I'll do my best. OK?'

He looked down. All the tension had gone out of her, and she was perfectly relaxed against him.

She muttered something.

'What?' he said.

'I love you,' she said.

He took a deep breath. 'I love you too,' he said quietly, and waited for her to look up.

She smiled in her sleep, and cuddled closer.

An outraged shriek from Debbie woke her up, and sent her running into the garden.

Mark followed her, and looked aghast at his three-year-old daughter, who was covered in mud and screaming at Zoe, who was carrying a cup over to the flower bed.

Zoe emptied several dozen worms into the dirt and looked up.

She glared at Diana. 'She said they were for the babies. It was cute the first time, with Harry, but I'm sorry,

Julie and Leanne are too young for solids. This child is out of control.'

The adults looked at each other for several seconds, then Mark's mouth twitched. 'Zoe, are you quite sure they're too young to be eating worms?'

'She's out of control, quite out of control,' said Diana solemnly, picking up the filthy little girl, who was quiet now and watching Zoe carefully.

Zoe took a deep breath. 'I may have over-reacted. I am not bathing her though. I told her to stay in, out of the rain. She wanted to go out.'

Diana brushed some of the mud away until she could recognise her daughter. 'Why did you want to go out in the rain, my darling?'

'Zak told me that the worms come out in the rain,' said Debbie in a reasonable tone of voice.

'You know, that boy is out of control,' Mark observed, then grabbed Zoe by the arm and ushered her inside. 'Hey, Zoe, are you quite sure they're too young? I'm sure all the best books recommend worms as a good introduction to solids.'

'Drop dead,' Zoe said coolly. She raised her voice. 'Isaac, get your arse down here NOW!'

Mark looked at Diana, who was now fairly mud-spattered herself. 'I have to go. I promised Katie. I just want to have a word with John first.'

'Sure. Bye, hon. See you in a fortnight.' She turned her back to him, and carried Debbie upstairs. He could hear her scolding the little girl. 'Do you like eating worms? No? Well don't feed them to the babies then.'

Mark found John with his feet up in the living room, surrounded by kids. He was reading some big

Russian novel for the first time or the twentieth; he always refused to say. He smiled when he saw his Alpha.

'Get anywhere with Cal?' he asked quietly.

Mark shook his head and shooed the kids away. 'No. I just wanted to say that I think Diana needs a holiday. If I could, I'd take her away somewhere, but that's impossible. I reckon I can cope here for three weeks, even by myself. So you've got what you want – if it's not too late to book a honeymoon for three. Or five, with the babies.'

'Seven, she won't leave Mikey and Harry. Whoo-hoo! This is going to be so much fun.'

Mark cast a dark look at John. 'Are you going to be discreet about this, or am I going to see you all on the gossip pages?'

John grinned, and returned his attention to the book.

Mark wandered out, and drove back to Katie.

Chapter 27

On Wednesday morning Mark dropped Jake and Matt off at school. He was beginning to get distinctly bored. He could feel the first stirrings, in the back of his mind, that meant a new song, and wondered what to do with it. The Hearts hadn't put out an album for years, and it didn't feel right for any of the other bands that he fed. He knew better than to chase the idea; he'd let it simmer at the back of his brain for a while.

On impulse, he put the first Hearts album on the stereo in the living room, and sat back to listen, wincing a little, smiling a lot. Nobody could drum like Xan; he'd had a unique and terrifying passion, and went off on obscure tangents only Mark and Andy had ever been able to understand and master. Andy had been in charge of the band, back then, and he'd allowed his friend two mega solos that had led to pannings from the music papers. Xan didn't give a shit. At the next gig he'd walked on first. He wore a 'Screw the NME' T-shirt, and set up a slow, ironic beat that the audience took up with delight then, when the rest of the band had appeared, had launched straight into the first track off the album before they were ready. Xan had never been an invisible drummer.

Mark haunted the house, wandering from room to room. He settled in the study, and turned the computer on. He looked at the games, but nothing interested him.

He heard the front door open and jumped up, then remembered it was the cleaner's day. He called out, to let her know he was in the house, and she shouted back. The vacuum cleaner started up, and he knew he wouldn't get anything else done until she'd gone. He rang Andy and asked if he could visit, but was told the whole Ransome family had gone out walking in the hills.

He rang John. 'Hiya, mate,' he said, keeping his voice casual. 'I sorta thought I might come over for a jam. I've got some ideas.'

John sounded distracted. 'Not until after lunch, sorry. Diana's in the lab, and Zoe's been seized by the muse. I'm on my own here. Why don't you put something on a tape and bring it over?'

Mark frowned. 'If I get there after lunch, I'll have to come straight back to pick Matt and Jake up from school. And I've no guitars here any more.'

'So come here anyway, there's nothing stopping you, is there? I can't join you, that's all. Come on, Mark, you know you want to.'

Mark heard the amusement in John's voice, and smiled, despite himself. 'I'm on my way,' he said. He picked up his jacket and got in the car, wondering why he needed to make excuses to go home.

John had been keeping his eye on the monitor, and the gates swung open for Mark as he approached Silverwood. He found John in the schoolroom, with sixteen of the kids. John was sitting on the floor with Harry, Mikey, Debbie and Leah. The little boys were playing with building blocks while John showed flash cards to the girls.

Mark squatted down next to them. He picked up one of the cards. It was clearly home-made. 'G is for Guitar?' He approved. 'Good one.'

John smiled. 'Hang around, it's fun.'

Mark knew this project; Jane Foster, Diana's mum, had devised it. It combined English, tech, music, creativity, graphic design and IT. The oldest kids made lists of nouns – collective, concrete and abstract – and the next age group down chose groups from those lists to make alphabet flash cards. Another set of twins chose pictures to go with the words and printed the cards off, to teach the youngest kids. All the children used the cards as prompts for stories and songwriting, and used a simplified recording set-up to make tapes of their stories and songs. It was teamwork, and a series of binders on the schoolroom shelves contained the lists, the flashcards and the recordings.

Jane and Alice were sitting at a table by the window, disagreeing noisily about something. Mark wandered over, and Jane looked up with a righteous zeal in her eyes.

'Dad, will you tell Alice that "nitrogen" isn't an abstract noun?'

Alice piped up. 'The book says that abstract nouns are for things you can't see. You can't see nitrogen, can you?'

Mark wavered for a moment; it had been a while since he'd been forced to consider grammar. 'Well, I think Janie's right. Nitrogen can be observed and measured. An abstract noun is something like "happiness", that can't be observed or measured.'

Alice frowned. 'But you can see when someone is happy.'

Mark nodded. 'Yes, but you can't see the happiness itself, can you? Do you understand?'

Alice chewed her lip and considered it.

Jane had pushed her chair back on to its back legs, and had folded her arms. She was smiling triumphantly. 'See,' she crowed.

Mark looked over at the Quadettes: dark-haired little girls who were rarely seen apart. He made a mental note that they'd be turning five soon, and it was going to be his job to organise their birthday party. They all had microphones and were looking at flashcards.

'What are you lot doing?' he asked.

Tara pushed her hair back. 'We're making stories. We mix up all the cards, and pick twenty, and make up a story using all the words.'

Mark was enthusiastic. 'That is so good! You know, I remember DianaMum playing me one of those stories last year. You're all working really hard. No wonder you do so well when you go up to big school.'

'Will you listen to my stories?' Tara asked, twirling her hair and putting her head to one side.

Mark glanced at John, who was watching. 'Yes, I've got time. Tell me a story then.'

'Oh no. You've got to listen to the *rounding*.' Tara looked shocked at the idea of doing things differently.

John had been listening, and he nodded. 'It's tech as well as English and creative play. They all love the mix-and-match game, however old they are. I caught Bill and Frank playing it just after I moved in, but they were being very rude about it. Taping it too! I don't know where they get it from.' He winked.

Mark laughed. He felt relaxed. 'OK, I'll listen to this tape of the girls', then I'm going to see Diana.' He scowled, realising that something was wrong. 'Where are Patrick and Liam?'

'In the lab with Diana, she's experimenting on them and the babies,' John said blithely.

Harry had got bored with the blocks, and was picking his nose carefully.

John got a big crate from a shelf and said, 'Stickle Bricks! Harry, look at these! What can we make with these?'

Mikey heard and toddled over, frantic not to be left out.

Mark listened to one of the stories the Quadettes had already recorded, giggling helplessly several times. Tara was naturally bossy, and her voice was the loudest, but Louise, her twin, kept interrupting with a loud whisper, saying, 'Make Meg and Beth do something.' Mark was under no illusions about Meg and Beth; they weren't at all shy, but were happy to let their sisters carry them if they thought they could get away with it. He watched the Quadettes as he listened to their tape. Sure enough, his four-year-olds were whispering together while Tara and Louise chose cards. John and Zoe's girls were bigger and stronger than their pack sisters. He could see Tara losing her temper, and Louise getting agitated. Eventually Louise said something to Beth, who looked up and glowered. Louise was smiling agreeably and gave one of the cards to Beth, and another to Meg. The smaller girls took on martyred expressions and joined in with the game. Mark played the tape to the end, and went over to the girls.

'That was fantastic. Tara, you've got a lovely voice, and Louise, you too. I wish I'd heard more from Meg and Beth though. Were you two not on the tape?'

His daughters scowled and looked away. Eventually Meg said, 'Tara wouldn't let us talk.'

Tara was suddenly close to tears, and Mark picked her up and hugged her. 'Meg! We all know that's a lie. Take it back. Next time, I want to hear that you and Beth have helped with the stories. Say you're sorry, please.'

John had wandered over. He was frowning. 'What's up?'

'Little girls telling lies.' Mark looked at Meg, whose eyes were wide open as she looked at John.

'I didn't, Daddy!' She burst into tears and laid her head on the table, sobbing loudly. Mark saw Beth was watching closely, her own lip trembling. Louise was sitting with her arms folded, looking more cynical than a four-year-old had any right to.

Mark hesitated. He had clear memories of Miranda and the Kittens being this age and, to some extent, of Bridget and Trixie too, but none of them had ever been like this. The Kittens had pouted, and occasionally yelled in frustration, but this kind of calculated histrionics was beyond him. He realised John was moving round the table to comfort Meg, and that Beth had noticed and was summoning up a sob herself. He kicked John gently and shook his head. 'She's faking,' he mouthed.

John stopped and smiled. 'I'll let you handle this, eh?' He went back to the littlest kids.

Mark sat down next to Louise, still cuddling Tara, who had calmed down. He watched and waited. When Meg stopped crying for a moment and looked up at him, he shook his head at her. 'Give up, sweetheart, I'm on to you.'

Meg started to sob again, and this time he could tell the tears were real ones of fury and frustration. He told the other three to carry on with the game, and picked Meg up, carrying her kicking and screaming out of the schoolroom.

He took her out into the rain and set her down in the playground. She fell in a crumpled heap at his feet, sobbing her heart out.

'I hate you, you're not my daddy,' she proclaimed dramatically.

'I'm afraid I am, honey,' he said, and waited a while longer. They were both wet through when she looked up again. 'I'm cold,' she said.

'We can go in when you start behaving yourself and promise to say sorry to Tara and Louise.'

'Tara's bossy,' she said quietly.

'And you tell fibs,' he told her. 'I don't care if it works on JohnDad – I'm something else entirely.'

She stood up and threw her hair back, utterly defiant. He fought down a smile; she was so obviously Diana's child. 'You! You don't even *live* here.'

'Doesn't matter. That's not the point. The point is that you were lazy, then you lied to cover it up, and you were very, very mean to Tara. Then you cried to cover up the lie. Are you cold enough yet?'

She narrowed her eyes at him and started to make her way back to the house.

He smiled. 'Meg, get back here now.' He watched, amused, as she came to a halt and turned around, furious with herself and him, but helpless to do anything in the face of a direct order from the Alpha. He'd used *that voice*; she obviously didn't know he could do that. He nodded. 'Good girl.'

'I'm telling Mum,' Meg said.

'I'll tell her the whole story,' Mark replied. He was enjoying himself.

For the first time, he could see an element of doubt creep into Meg's eyes. She seemed to be balancing her known place in Diana's world, against the previously unconsidered place that this relative stranger might hold.

He smiled pleasantly. 'What really annoys me is that you were mean to Tara. You told a lie that could have got her into trouble. That's nasty.'

'I'm not nasty,' she protested.

'So why did you say Tara wouldn't let you talk?'

'I don't know,' she sulked.

'Can you see that it was bad? Do you see that it nearly made Tara cry?'

She looked like she was going to cry again, and Mark was relieved this time. This time it felt genuine.

Meg whispered, 'I love Tara,' and Mark picked her up, realising how cold and wet they'd both got. She clung to him.

'OK, sweetie, what are we going to do about this?'

'Say sorry to Tara,' Meg whispered.

'And?' Mark pushed her hair back from her face, relishing the baffled expression she was wearing. She was having problems understanding how it had come to this.

'Don't know,' she said quietly.

301

'And say sorry to me and John for telling lies?'

'Sorry,' she said.

Mark hugged her and carried her back to the warm classroom. The kids all looked at her as she apologised to Tara and then to John. Mark took her upstairs and ran a bath for her, and had warm towels and clothes ready for her to change into.

He glanced at the clock; it was already noon, and he'd not seen Diana yet. Meg had stopped shivering, and was telling him why the clothes he'd chosen for her were all wrong. He nodded as if he was listening, and led her back downstairs. School seemed to have finished for the day, and he left her in the kitchen with John.

As he headed for the door, he heard her say confidentially to John. 'You're the best daddy, *he's* just mean.'

He didn't miss a step, but smiled when John said, 'Being mean is his job, honeypie. Wouldn't it be horrible if *I* had to be mean to you?'

The laboratory had two doors at the end. The first one led to another lab, which served as a science classroom for the kids. The second one led to an office, and he could see the light was on. He heard children screaming, and opened the door.

The red wolf was growling as she pounced on the toddler. Liam was screaming his heart out as she nosed at his belly then took his feet gently in her teeth and started to pull him across the room. His twin was helplessly laughing, and Mark could see the faint traces of tooth marks on his ankles, where he'd undoubtedly been treated to the same game. Mark glanced at the carrycot on the floor, where twin baby girls slept soundly through the screams and growls.

Mark waited and watched. The wolf was looking at him, and he could see mischief in her expression. She released Liam and sidled over to Mark, burying her muzzle in his crotch and sniffing carefully.

'Hell Diana, I wish you'd say hello like that when you've got your fur off,' he gasped. 'And you've got a bloody cold nose.'

Patrick giggled again. 'She's got a cold nose,' he repeated as Diana moved away from Mark and leaped in the air, turning a full somersault and landing astride the two-year-old, licking his hair until it was soaked through, and nosing at his throat and belly until he screamed aloud again. 'It tickles!' the boy protested. 'Stop it, Mummy!'

Mark moved a pile of papers from an office chair and sat down. He watched as Diana played with the boys, occasionally casting backwards glances at him, inviting him to play. He shook his head, reaching out to tickle between her ears, then settling down to look at her papers, what seemed like a random pile of handwritten notes, computer printouts of statistical analyses, and colour photographs of Julie and Leanne. A hardback book caught his attention, but he realised, when he opened it, that it was a diary, and closed it again, looking over at Diana.

Eventually she relented and Changed, reaching across him to retrieve her underwear, jeans and a black shirt. She dressed without a word, waiting for him to speak.

He cracked. 'I was bored, I thought I'd come and visit.'

She finished buttoning her shirt and pushed her long hair back from her forehead with both hands. 'I'd ask you if you had a home to go to, but you clearly have. You and Katie have made up then?'

Mark remembered that friendly sniff when he'd come in, and smiled apologetically. 'We're sleeping together again, yes. I'm sorry, I should have Changed to kill her scent, but I just didn't expect you to be wolfie at this time of day.' He watched her carefully. 'Diana, why are you mad? You're not jealous are you?'

'No, but I am annoyed. I thought we'd established long ago that you don't come to my home with her scent on you. It's basic good manners.' She took a deep breath. 'Why were you looking at my notes anyway?'

He looked away, realising he'd wanted her to be jealous, just a little bit. 'Just curious about what you do in here. Is there a problem?' He felt wary, unbalanced. He was on Diana's territory here.

Her face softened and she took a step towards him. 'No problem, it's just unusual that's all. I guess I'm still a bit shaky after that attack. It's just weird, you being here with that smell all over you, at this time of day, and looking at my notes.'

Mark shook his head. 'Oh, nothing like that. I couldn't Change at home because the cleaner was in the house, and when I got here I got involved with what the kids were doing. If I'd thought you were going to be wolfie, I would have Changed before I came in. Forgive me?'

He couldn't believe what he'd done. It'd been years since he'd made such a basic mistake with her. He looked at her, anxiously at first, then with a growing amusement that got her attention.

'What?' she snapped.

He stood up and went to her, unbuttoning her shirt quickly. He tugged at the hems on each side, then buttoned it up again – correctly this time.

'So, I missed a button,' she grumbled. 'So what?'

'You need someone to look after you,' he joked, then shrank away from the withering look she gave him.

She looked at the little boys, who were playing quietly. 'I think it's lunchtime. Let's get this lot to the house. If you've got time afterwards, and if I can prise Zoe away from her writing, I'll show you what I'm up to.'

He hoped his regret was clear when he told her he was running out of time, that he could stay to help with lunch, but had to get back to collect Matt and Jake from school.

She nodded briefly. 'OK, come on then, Patrick, Liam,' she called out. She turned to pick up the carrycot, and managed a smile when she saw Mark had already picked it up. 'Thanks,' she said.

'My pleasure. Shall I come back tomorrow?'

Diana's face brightened, then clouded. 'Mark, are you sure there's nothing going on that I need to know about?'

'Nothing, I promise. It's just that Katie's banned John and Andy from the house, and I've not even got a guitar there any more. I'm not working right now, so it's either sit around and kill time or come here and help out. I can't even do stuff around the house because we've got a gardener and a cleaner, and the shopping gets delivered.'

'Ah, so Diana's day-care centre gets another customer?' she mocked gently. 'Yet another benefit of John moving in – we get to see more of you. That's good.'

Mark and Diana walked back to the house. He had his arm around her again, relishing the smooth feel of her muscles under the faded cotton of her shirt.

'You smell good, do you know that?' he murmured. The look she gave him reminded him of how he smelled, and he cursed himself silently. 'Look, I'll be back tomorrow. I'll Change before I see you, I promise.'

She was smiling as they entered the kitchen. John looked hot, bothered, and very pleased with himself.

He bowed as they came in. 'Lady and gentleman, may I introduce John Preston, Superdad! It can be done – a man *can* deal with sixteen children for a whole morning and live!'

'Yeah, and a woman can do it and not think it's worth mentioning,' Diana snapped back, nuzzling at his face with uninhibited affection. 'Where are they all?'

John drew back. 'They're mithering Zoe. Do you really think just anyone could deal with that lot?' he said. His voice was mournful, but his eyes were dancing with pleasure.

Mark watched as the pair touched each other almost unconsciously.

John opened a bag of crisps and fed them to Diana as she started clearing up the debris of lunch.

Mark coughed. 'I did have to have a few words with Meg,' he said, interrupting them.

Diana glanced over her shoulder, her hands full of dirty dishes. 'Hmm? Tell me,' she said through a mouthful of crisps.

John opened his mouth, and Mark glared at him. *I'll tell her*, he mouthed indignantly. John laughed.

Diana looked from one to the other of her mates. 'What's going on here?' she asked. 'Is there something I don't know?'

John started to speak, and Mark broke in.

'Nothing, John's just being a prat, as usual. Meggie's been taking advantage of her sisters' good nature, and getting away with it. I sorted her out.'

'Maybe for a week or so, but she'll bounce back.' Diana opened the dishwasher, saw that it was full of dirty dishes, glared at John, and started to run hot water in the sink. As the water ran she put a tablet in the dishwasher and set it off to cycle.

John winced. 'Sorry,' he said.

'It takes ten seconds to turn it on!' Diana muttered.

John took advantage of her turned back to drag Mark out of the kitchen.

'I'm officially free until Diana and Zoe do the school run. Did you say you wanted to jam?' he asked Mark eagerly.

'Not really, I want to work on that guitar. Come with me to the basement.'

In the small workroom Mark looked at the naked, sanded down guitar; she was ready to be worked on. He bit his lip and looked up at John. 'Stain and varnish? Or paint?'

John caressed the instrument. 'Stain her red ... not chestnut, something lighter, prettier.'

307

Mark looked up at him. 'Like Diana's hair?' he whispered. 'You know, I've not used this old thing in anger since our first proper tour. I was always a bit embarrassed by the crappy job I did of painting her. This is a new start for her. Yeah, I'll play about mixing some stains until I get it right. I'll pick some up tomorrow and experiment on some scrap wood.'

John had picked up a jar of odd screws and was shaking it experimentally. He looked unsettled.

Mark sat down next to him. 'Are you nervous about the wedding?' he teased.

'Wedding? No, I'm fine, we're all fine.' He seemed to make his mind up about something. 'Mark, are you pissed off at me moving in? I mean, you're the Alpha, and I didn't ask if it would be OK or anything. I didn't even think about it, it just seemed like the right thing to do.'

Mark leaned against John's side and gave him a friendly shove. 'Mind? No, it was a good idea. I'm glad you're here, it puts my mind at ease. And another adult in the house is a godsend. It means the women can share the school run and none of the kids are late for school any more. I just wish I could be here too.'

John smiled. 'Really?'

'Well, I think so, anyway. If I could bring Jake and Matt, I wouldn't hesitate. They're what's keeping me with Katie. I just can't believe it's gone so wrong so quickly between me and her.'

'It can't be all that wrong, you're still fucking,' John said.

Mark sighed. 'Yeah, now and again. Habit, comfort in the night, there's still some affection there, and she's not ready to take a vow of celibacy.' He looked at the guitar, stroking where Katie had gouged at it with the wire cutters. 'I still can't believe she did that.'

John didn't reply; he'd learned long ago that his views on Katie were not welcomed by Mark.

Mark nudged John again. 'Hey, is it working out? I mean, you living here.'

His cousin laughed. 'Working out? It's the best thing I ever did. I thought I'd get fed up, you know? After living alone for so long, I was scared of losing my privacy, but it's not like that at all. I feel good about myself, because I can see it gives the women more time to spend alone, and they respect it when I say I need some time out too. It's cool.'

'You don't miss clubbing? Dating?' Mark teased.

'Shit, we're getting on for fifty, who needs that sort of crap? Nope, I've got everything I want – busy days, good company, somewhere to run, Diana and Zoe. I'm domesticated now.' John looked again at the jar of screws, and smiled. 'This is the sort of thing I mean. Look, this belonged to Diana's dad. She assures me that some of the screws belonged to his father. Last weekend I helped the older kids to make a bogey – we used some of the screws from this jar. We're a real family, with real history.'

He saw Mark's face and was instantly apologetic. 'Sorry, mate. I know you'd be here if you could be. I'll shut up.'

Mark stood up and stretched. 'Ah well, can't be, can I? How's the honeymoon plans going?'

'Fine, not your problem.'

'And what about Frank and Bill? Diana was in a tizz about finding condoms in their room.' Mark studied his cousin's face.

John shrugged. 'I talked to them. Yeah, they've both got girlfriends, but they know enough not to bring them home. They're a bit upset because they're running out of excuses.'

Mark rolled his eyes. 'Another problem. How the fuck are we supposed to keep this pack a secret? It puts too much responsibility on the kids.'

John stood up. 'They're OK, they've grown up with it. Speaking of kids, shouldn't you be off?'

Mark smiled wryly. 'Cramping your style, am I? No, forget I said that. You know how it is, I want to be with Diana, but I've promised Katie I won't stay overnight here until the wedding. I'm just being crabby.'

John looked sympathetic. 'Are you going to tell Diana? That you're in love with her?'

His cousin chewed on his top lip for a while, then took a deep breath. 'I was going to, but perhaps not. Not yet anyway. I want to be sure. I don't want to spring it on her, then find out that I'm just on the rebound and she's in the right place at the right time.' He looked helplessly at John. 'I don't want to hurt her.'

With that, he left.

Chapter 28

The next morning Mark arrived earlier. Diana was out, but she'd left him a note with the laboratory keys taped to it: 'Let yourself in, have a nosy around. I'm sorry, Caleb's form teacher wanted a meeting with me. I'll be back for lunch. This week's password is "Alexander". Love, Di.'

He let himself into the lab and turned the lights on. It was a big room, with a walk-in fridge and a big freezer; cupboards and drawers took up a lot of room, and he looked inside them all. Everything was marked with the name of the pack member, and the dates and times of sampling and analysis. Mark noted that a lot of the work had been done at night, after the kids were in bed.

He went to the office at the back of the lab, and turned on the computer, typing in the name of his dead friend. He smiled appreciatively at the well-organised directories, and, on impulse, clicked on his own name. He found a family tree; Diana had speculated that his father was a Shapeshifter, but had marked that down as speculation only. As meticulous as ever, she'd not made any assumptions about Katie's bloodline, and Mark's sons with his wife were accompanied by a 'WO / WW?' notation.

There were files for other Shapeshifters too. Diana had blood samples for all of them, including Laura and Duncan's pack

Mark realised he was scowling at the thought of Duncan, the young Alpha. He realised he was jealous, and that reminded him to Change, to get rid of the scent of Katie that had so angered Diana.

In his wolf shape, the office was a different place, dominated by the scent of the Alpha woman. Other humans had been in the room, mostly small children, but he could smell the Beta woman too; she'd been in there, but had never stayed for long. John was obviously an occasional visitor, but it seemed that Andy didn't visit this room at all.

After he'd investigated the scents, he curled up beneath the desk and dozed. He was woken up by the sound of the door opening. He heard that voice, the one that made him shiver with pleasure: it was her voice, low and pleasant, with a slight Geordie lilt to it. He stretched out and crept from beneath the desk. The door to the office opened and she came in, her scent changing almost instantly when she saw him — chemicals flooding from her that told him he was safe and welcome and wanted.

She fell to her knees and held his head in her hands, looking into his eyes. He was captivated, and held still as she stroked him and spoke to him. He wriggled free and took her jumper between her teeth, pulling at the fabric, grimacing a little at the taste of detergent in the fabric.

She said something; it sounded like a reprimand, and he backed away, still looking at her, his tongue hanging out as he laughed. She undressed, and as he started to lick at her legs, she Changed and he had his love with him, his mate, his partner.

For long minutes the two wolves didn't move: they stayed curled up together, silent, drawing on the warmth and scent of each other for reassurance, then the red female stood on thin legs.

The black male looked at her, at the bright red of her fur, the yellow-green of her eyes, the long plumes of fur that beribboned her legs and throat and tail. He could smell the new life in her: two tiny scraps that would soon increase the pack. He bowed to her, and she bowed back then spun and raced through the door, through the lab, and out towards the woods. He woofed once in excitement, and chased after her. Her lead grew fast. He didn't care, he'd always been able to catch her in a long enough chase.

They ran through the small woodland, following every path twice or thrice, forcing their way through thin scrub. Every few moments the female looked back, laughing at him. He was closer, then closer again, and he began to anticipate the moment at the end of every chase, when she allowed him to catch her, when they'd both Change...

He was so close to her, her scent heady in his nostrils. One leap and he would catch her. He drew himself together, every muscle, every nerve anticipating the feel of her beneath him.

She looked over her shoulder at him and she leaped, higher and higher, her body straightening, lengthening, the fur melting away as her forelegs flexed, as her paws became clever fingers that reached for a high branch and grabbed it.

He skidded to a halt, looking up in astonishment as his mate pulled herself on to the branch and sat there, breathless, grinning down at him. He Changed and stood up. 'I'm impressed,' he told her.

'I've been practising that one,' she admitted, flushed with pleasure. 'So, are you joining me?' She patted the branch.

Mark paced around the tree, looking for an easy climb, then stepped back in frustration. 'You planned this! This tree isn't climbable. How are you going to get down?'

'I'll cope.' She swung her legs, and he was fascinated by the red-gold hairs that glowed in the weak sunshine.

He smiled at the contrast between the dryad above him, and the smartly dressed matron who had entered the lab less than an hour ago. 'What's up with Caleb?' he asked, remembering the reason why she'd been so dressed-up.

'Ah, when that lot get back from school, they're going to get the "don't draw attention" talk. Cal, Frank and Bill are all bunking off games.' She started to inspect her fingernails. 'I think Cal's going through some sort of body image problem. He'll talk to me soon, I can tell. Me or Zoe.'

Mark wandered around the tree again, trying to figure out how to get to her; part of him was listening to her, part of him was half remembering his wolfish plans for her. He touched the rough bark of the tree experimentally. He glanced upwards. She was hidden behind the trunk now; he could just see a ripple of red hair high above as she leaned back. He smiled, baring sharp white teeth. Looking inwards, he started the Change. It was hard when he wanted to do this, when he couldn't just relax and let it take him completely. He opened his eyes and blinked, satisfied with what he'd done, with the sharp claws that tipped long agile fingers and toes. He started to climb the tree, and was soon sitting next to her, admiring his claws.

She inched closer to him, and stroked his hand. 'Very clever. That's what I loved about you, from the very beginning. That control, that ability to hold back.' She made a funny, self-mocking little sound. 'You held back from so much, and that's perhaps what's saved us.'

'*You* saved us,' he said with conviction. 'You kept us all together.' He saw that she was ready to argue, and changed the subject. 'So, what's up with Frank and Bill? I thought they loved sport?'

'They're bunking off to watch the girls play hockey,' said his mate, deadpan. 'It seems the combination of windy playing fields and short skirts is enough to drag our lads away from their football.'

Mark raised his eyebrows. 'I'll have a word with 'em. You're right, they should be keeping their heads down, not attracting any more attention than necessary.'

'Oh Mark, it's hard, they're just kids,' Diana protested.

'You tell 'em, then I'll tell 'em. That should sort it. John was exactly the same: couldn't concentrate on anything if there were girls around.' He gave her an affectionate hug. 'He still can't, can he?'

Diana smile was wicked. 'I don't mind,' she said. 'We're happy.'

Mark's heart fell; John was with her so much. 'It's working out then? You and John and Zoe? Nobody feels left out?' He tried to keep the disappointment out of his voice.

'Are you kidding? I've got my two Betas, John's got his two women, and Zoe's got the two people she loves the most. It makes so much sense for him to be around. The kids feel safer too, having a third adult makes life easier for everyone.'

'OK. That's good.' Mark looked dead ahead. He could feel her body heat, they were sat so close. She was touching him, gently, on his shoulder.

'And you… You and Katie are getting back on track? Helen is fascinated by the whole thing. So, are we all happy?'

He summoned a smile. 'Yes, we're all happy. You've got John and Zoe, I've got Katie. We're all fine. Is there anything else we need to talk about?– I was going to work on that guitar.'

She was quiet for a moment, then he felt her shrug. 'No, nothing else, nothing urgent. Thanks for talking to Andy about the wedding stuff, by the way. When I do it, I'm "nagging" he says.'

'Yeah, when I do it, I'm "telling". He doesn't like that either.' Mark managed a smile. 'Still, it's sorted now. Well, how do we get down?'

'Jump,' she said, suiting action to words, and slipping off the branch. She rolled as she hit the ground, and stood smiling.

Mark looked longingly at the trunk of the tree, and considered shinning down it. She stood beneath him, her eyebrow raised. He jumped, and rolled. He came to his feet, grinning. 'That was liberating,' he commented.

'Yeah, I nearly broke my stupid leg, though.' She looked at him appraisingly. 'Shall we go back and get dressed?' She was leaning against the tree, her hair full of leaves, her skin stained with moss and mud.

He reached out for her. 'Only if we have to,' he whispered, drawing her close.

As they made their way back to the lab, shivering slightly as their sweat dried in the crisp March air, he realised he couldn't let her go, not for three weeks, not for a week. He picked up his clothes from the office floor and headed for the house, telling her that he wanted to shower before he got dressed again. He made his way to her room, and looked through her drawers until he found her passport. He checked it: two years left. He slipped it into the pocket of his jeans. 'I'll stay here with you. I'll make sure it's a holiday for you,' he whispered. He looked at the three pillows on the bed and frowned. Was he too late?

He jumped as the door opened and she strode in, wearing her underwear, her suit carefully folded over her arm.

'I thought you were having a shower?' she said lightly, hanging the suit up and sitting in front of the mirror.

'Wanna join me?' he asked hopefully.

'I do, but I promised to spend some time with the Quads. Oh Mark, look at the state of me!'

'Yeah?' he grinned. 'You look like you did the first time I saw you.' He picked up a hairbrush and stood behind her, gently picking twigs and leaves out of her hair, before starting to work gently on the tangles. 'I wanted to do this then.'

'Liar,' she commented.

'I did!' he protested. 'Among other things.'

She leaned back, silent. He leaned over and kissed her forehead, seeing her face relax. He continued brushing her hair until it shone, then she stood and made him sit, and took the brush and drew it gently through the long fall of jet-black hair.

As it fell on his skin like a whisper, he closed his eyes, wanting this, wanting this every day and every night. When she stopped, he turned and nuzzled into her belly. She stood silent, trembling, then moved away. He watched quietly as she dressed in cords and a heavy cotton shirt.

'Th-that guitar won't fix itself. I won't keep you away from it any longer,' she stammered, and fled.

He looked at his reflection for a long time, then dressed.

John found him in the music room, picking at an acoustic guitar, crooning meaningless sounds to himself.

Mark ignored him and carried on, improvising a tune.

John sighed. 'What's up now?'

'I'm too late. She doesn't want me. She just walked away from me. Why would she do that?' He kept his eyes on his own fingertips, slurring the strings a little.

'You'll never know unless you ask,' John said sharply. 'Look, seventeen years this has been going on. Do you really think she'd change her mind about you after so long?'

'I'm her Alpha, that's all. She loves you. She loves you and Zoe.' He bowed lower over the guitar, cradling it, singing to it and listening to it sing back to him.

'Oh, for fuck's sake,' said John. He left, slamming the door.

Mark looked up; he hated himself. 'I fuck everything up. Every fucking thing,' he said quietly. He gently put the guitar back on its stand, left the room, and drove back to Katie.

He managed to stay away for a week, called back two days before the wedding, by Zoe. He'd been asleep on the sofa, dulled by daytime TV. He was puzzled by the call at first, then shamed. She needed him, the ache of the pack bond growing stronger until she couldn't hold back from contacting him. There was reproach in her voice, and he remembered his promise to her.

She was waiting at the gate for him when he arrived at Silverwood, and led him to her room without a word.

He found it oddly easy to be tender to her, to assure her of his regard for her, and her place in his pack. The first time calmed her need of him; the second brought out his playful side and left him exhausted but deeply satisfied. He realised, almost too late, how fast time had passed and had to leave suddenly, without speaking to Diana. John had disappeared two days earlier, and was reportedly celebrating his last days of official bachelorhood with Andy.

The night before the wedding, John rang him from Silverwood, mildly drunk and highly emotional. Mark took the phone into his study, curling up on the big armchair and talking until midnight, about everything and anything. When he got to bed, Katie was already there.

She tried to reclaim him from the pack, knowing where his heart lay that day. He lay silent for a while under her caresses, faking exhaustion, hoping she would leave him be. At last she stopped, turning away from him with a sigh.

He drifted into sleep.

Chapter 29

Mark barely slept that night; it felt like the first morning of a tour, moving into the mental gears necessary to deal with being away from home, away from Katie and Jake and Matt. He told himself he could always come home at the weekend, perhaps during the day. Seth and Noah were responsible enough to help with the kids, surely? He fretted, gradually becoming aware that Katie was awake.

Her hand took his own, beneath the sheets. She found the reassurance she needed when he squeezed it. She acknowledged their wakefulness.

'Mark, do you have to stay there? For so long?'

'I do. They need me, they're my responsibility,' he said truthfully.

'I don't understand why Diana is going away. It's not her honeymoon.' There was a vicious undertone that Mark heard, and grieved over.

He squeezed Katie's hand again. 'It makes sense – it takes at least two adults to look after the kids these days. If she stayed behind, you wouldn't be happy about me being with her, and Helen wouldn't be happy about Andy being with her. If it's just me and Andy, we'll all be OK, won't we?' Again, he spoke the truth. A demon scampered in his mind, a demon that looked like him and waved a passport at him. Liar! the demon screeched. He ignored it. It was easier to lie if he could believe the lie.

Katie fell quiet. All the arguments had already been gone over, time and again. She had surrendered, accepting that Mark would be gone, for weeks. He'd promised to try to get back whenever he could, if things felt safe enough at Silverwood.

She moved towards him. 'I guess that's it then. When are you leaving?'

'Everything is sorted. I just have to turn up and witness the ceremony. I said I'd be at Silverwood for one o'clock.'

Katie smiled in the darkness. 'So we have some time? Show me you still love me.'

The demon scampered in his head again, listing her motives. Mark banished it. Still, when he lay in her arms, when he touched her familiar curves, he could still pretend everything was fine between them. She didn't cry any more when they pretended to make love. One day, he promised himself, neither would he.

Later he said goodbye to the boys, promising to ring them every day. Matthew was too young to trust with the truth, Katie had decided. This was another of Mark's business trips, so far as they knew. His family were subdued and quiet when he left them.

An hour or so later, in Silverwood, the noise hit him like a hurricane: everyone was talking and laughing. Andy stood in the middle of the big living room, towering above everyone else. His eyes met Mark's and they smiled at each other. Nobody in the room except them and John knew about the honeymoon plans. Mark could see a hint of panic in Andy's expression, and laughed inwardly.

His gaze found Diana; she was in a corner of the room with John and Zoe. Diana was holding hands with Zoe, her other hand touching John's face as she talked to him. John was leaning against the wall, one bare foot extended, his leg entwined with Zoe's, his hand on Diana's hip. Diana turned to look at Mark, smiling, but she made no attempt to move, to join him.

Mark averted his gaze. They didn't even know they were doing it, the three of them, so comfortable together, so right together. He had to do something. He needed to get Diana alone, to convince her he had something to offer her, something other than the fix they both needed. Three weeks away from John and Zoe should be enough.

Andy rounded the adults up and drove to the wedding venue, a private location that they'd booked for the afternoon. They'd booked a private ceremony, at a licensed venue. Mark was standing as best man, and he and Andy would sign as witnesses. Diana didn't want her name written down in the records, and was there as matron of honour. As they waited for the registrar, they stood in a rough circle, staring at each other. The three men wore suits made of the same dark grey fabric, with blue shirts and ties. The cut of each suit was different, made to flatter each of them.

Mark noticed wryly that Diana and Andy were looking at each other with undisguised interest. He couldn't blame Andy: Diana was radiant in a bottle green trouser suit that flattered her figure, and made her look petite and pretty. The amber necklace she wore caught the light, and toned with her hair, which she was wearing loose and long.

Zoe looked beautiful. She'd styled her hair carefully, pinning fresh flowers into it and spraying it with streaks of colour. Mark had heard her grumbling about not having a hair stylist for her wedding, about having to retrieve her hair from its post-Change natural state in less than an hour. John looked besotted; he kept stealing glances at her. Zoe joked that she should have brought a tape recorder – she was getting tired of saying, 'Don't touch me, you'll crease the dress.'

Mark looked at the clock and then at his mates. He coughed gently; Andy and Diana were kissing. They broke off and laughed.

'Sorry, it's just the excitement,' Andy said.

Mark didn't mind. They were all close to each other; it was natural for all of them to want to touch and hold each other. He realised with a shock that it was the first time the five of them had ever been together away from Silverwood, and felt unsettled enough to make his way to Diana for a hug.

The ceremony was a short one. John and Zoe put their hands behind their backs and ostentatiously crossed their fingers when they were asked to make vows of sexual fidelity to each other. Andy looked like he was in grave danger of laughing out loud, but smothered it. After the service, Mark took photographs, and the registrar took some of the entire group. In the corridor afterwards, Zoe and John wanted to hug and kiss everyone.

Back home the kids had formed a reception committee, and Mark relaxed as the gates closed against the outside world. They were ushered into the big dining room, where they had to stand and admire the kids' hard work in decorating the room before they could sit down and tuck into the first course.

At some point, Caleb started to cry, and Diana took him upstairs. They were gone a while, and after five minutes Mark asked Andy if he thought he should follow them.

Andy shook his head. 'Sometimes they just want Mum. Leave 'em be,' he said wisely, pouring another glass of champagne and waving the empty bottle at Alice, who ran up with a full one.

In the room Caleb shared with Sammy, Diana was holding him close, letting him cry it out. It had been a long time coming.

'Mummy, I killed that man. He died. I killed him. Mummy, I didn't want to, but he was hurting Zoe.' He'd regressed: he was talking like a much younger child.

'I know, and you're a big brave boy, and I'm proud of you. He was a very bad man.'

'I wanted to tell you.'

'I know, sweetheart. I was waiting for you to tell me.'

'Mummy, are John and Zoe and the babies going away? Because I killed that man?'

Diana sighed. 'Of course not, honey. What made you think that? Did you think they were going to get married and move out?'

'They said they were getting married, and they decided after I killed that man. My friend at school told me that people leave home when they get married. And they'll take all the little ones with them.'

'Caleb my love, John is going to live with us, all the time. And Mark and Andy will be around more. None of the little ones are going anywhere for a long, long time. Everything is going to be OK. And we're all proud of you and very, very grateful.'

He was still quiet. 'Mummy…'

'Hmm?' Diana said, still holding him on her lap, remembering him as a toddler, appreciating the scent of him, who he was in the pack.

'I mean, Mum, do you love all of us?' She hugged him. She knew what he meant. Ever since the older kids had started to go to school, they'd been fascinated by families with one or two or three kids.

'You mean, do I love *you*, don't you?'

He nodded.

She caressed his hair, thick and black and long. 'Yes, I do. We might have lots of kids, but we've only got one Caleb, and we've missed his jokes and smiles over the last few weeks.'

He looked serious, and challenged her. 'OK, what am I doing at school?'

She laughed, and reeled off his subjects, hobbies, favourite games and position in the Under-14 school football team.

He was still tense. 'Mum, if I didn't do anything wrong, why did Daddy Mark take me away?' This was a real stumper.

Diana frowned. 'Well, it was supposed to be a treat.' she tried to explain.

He looked at her as if she'd gone mad. 'But, Mum, I like being at home. I missed Sam, I missed everybody. I kept waiting for Daddy to tell me off.'

Diana had a sudden mental picture of Mark and Caleb staring at each other for a whole day, trying to figure each other out. She nodded gravely.

'OK then, kid, no more holidays for you. I promise. Now, are you feeling a bit better? Shall we go back to the party?'

She got a bigger smile than she expected, and he said, 'In a minute. Will you cuddle me a bit longer?' She was happy to, until he inevitably wriggled away, and it was time to return to the party.

Mark noticed that Caleb was all smiles when he came down again.

Diana took her place next to him. 'All sorted now. I think we've got our boy back.' She looked at her empty plate in mock bafflement, prompting all her mates to offer something from theirs. She waved them away. 'It's OK, these trousers are tight anyway. I'll settle for soup, ice cream and wedding cake, if nobody minds?'

Zoe made a sarcastic comment, and John hastily intervened before the two women could start a food fight.

Mark watched them all, smiling despite himself.

Diana stopped flirting for a moment, falling silent and looking towards the back of the room, where a real fight had broken out between Nathan and Isaac.

Miranda touched Diana's shoulder. 'Shh, Mum. You enjoy yourself, I'll sort 'em.'

Diana shook her head. 'That's not your job, my love.' She stood up and made her way down the room, grabbing the two five-year-olds by their ears and taking them into a corner where she sat down, a boy on each knee, listening to each version of what looked to be a long and involved story. She spoke to them briefly.

Mark noticed how she stayed sitting for a while after the boys had quietly found their own seats again.

Zoe kicked him under the table. 'What's up, gorgeous?' she asked.

'Oh, just watching Nat and Zak – they're acting up.'

Zoe nodded. 'Every day. They don't change. We'd hoped they'd take after me and Diana, and get on with each other, but they're just like Andy and John – all they want to do is wind each other up.'

'I resent that remark,' said Andy mildly. 'I never wind anyone up. If you want someone to blame, look at that hairy ape you just married.'

'I take your point,' said Mark to Zoe.

His gaze drifted over to Diana, who was standing, a little wearily. She saw him and straightened up, waving as she came back across the big dining room. His heart clenched; she was clearly tired, and a holiday would be so good for her. The demon danced again. A few weeks with her Alpha would be good for her, it said. He glanced at John, who had put down his drink and was gesturing to Diana to come and sit on his lap. Mark turned away, and reached for the champagne bottle. It was empty, again, and he left the dining room, finding Seth and Noah in the big kitchen, drinking red wine and ordering the younger kids around. They hid the bottle hastily behind them when they saw him. He shrugged. 'Just don't get pissed, OK? You're taking over from Frank and Bill on patrol from midnight aren't you?'

'Yes boss.' Seth held the bottle out. 'Want some?' he asked.

Mark nodded. 'I'll get a couple of bottles for the grown-ups. That champagne is too bloody bubbly.' He glanced out of the window, seeing the Kittens on the big playground slide, running up and down, shrieking. 'Are they *drunk*?' he asked, incredulous.

Noah looked guilty. 'Well, Miranda thought they'd be OK with a couple of spritzers. It is a wedding, isn't it?' He glanced at his twin, who frowned at him.

Mark raised his eyebrows. 'Get 'em back indoors before dark, OK?' He looked at the pack's eldest children and smiled. 'You're both doing a good job, I'm proud of you.'

Seth's face lit up, and he looked at Noah, who spoke up. 'Dad?'

'Yup?'

'Can we have driving lessons?'

'Yes,' Mark said instantly.

The twins looked at each other. 'Can we have a car, when we've passed?'

'Definitely,' Mark said. He grinned, grabbed a corkscrew, and left, looking for his mates. He heard Seth, behind him, say suspiciously, 'That was too easy.'

Mark found his mates in the big living room, surrounded by kids. He claimed a chair opposite Diana, opened a bottle of wine and started to drink, watching Diana, who was suddenly sleepy. He heard Seth and Noah come in, pushing the giggling Kittens in front of them. He smiled, watching as Seth stood behind Diana's chair and leaned over, kissing the top of her head.

Diana reached up behind her and held Seth's hand for a moment, then winced as a fat toddler landed on her stomach, quickly followed by his twin. A button flew off her jacket, and she closed her eyes in mock despair.

Mark looked round. Andy and John were sharing a sofa with Zoe, who wore a badly stained and crumpled wedding dress. Each of the men was cradling a grizzling baby, and he could hear Zoe complaining that wedding dresses weren't designed for women with babies to feed.

Mark's attention drifted back to his eldest. Noah was surveying the pack affectionately, asking Seth if he thought they'd ever be as successful as their parents. Mark shut his eyes, pretending that he wasn't eavesdropping, but jumped in surprise when Seth asked Noah, in completely innocent amazement, where Noah had got the idea that they were going to share a pack. Mark's eyes met Diana's; she seemed to be more amused than worried, and he relaxed again. He watched Diana as she cuddled Mikey and Harry closer, getting comfortable with them, slowly going to sleep. When he was sure she was asleep, and that the last thing she'd seen was his face, he yawned and stretched.

Andy flopped down next to him, laying his head on Mark's lap. The tall blond looked up at his Alpha. 'Mark, if we're going to live together for the next couple of weeks, we need to get some things straight. One, separate beds. Two, no snogging in front of the kids. Three— Oof!'

Mark kept the cushion pressed hard against Andy's face for another few seconds, before he relented and released his mate. He rumpled Andy's blond curls affectionately. 'Shut up, idiot.'

Andy sighed and looked at Diana. 'She's got the right idea. I think I'll have a nap myself. Am I OK here?'

'You're fine, I'll make sure the monsters don't get you.' Mark shifted a little until he was comfortable, then settled his head back and went to sleep.

He was sure he hadn't even dropped off properly when his legs were pulled hard. He woke up instantly and jumped to his feet, yelling in surprise. Andy's head hit the sofa, and he woke up with a frown, complaining.

Diana was standing above them, a wicked glint in her eyes. 'Fun's over, time to tidy up.'

Mark looked around. 'The kids did that already, let's just relax.'

Andy shrugged. 'She's right. There's muck everywhere. Diana, when did you last clean that light fitting?'

'The last time *you* visited. I can't see the dirt, I'm too short. You know where the dusters are?'

'Aw, it's a party night,' Andy protested half-heartedly.

Diana sighed. 'OK, OK. I'll do it all myself, tomorrow.'

Mark smiled at Andy. 'It's that last nail that's so hard to hammer in, isn't it?'

'Yeah, women make crap martyrs anyway, no good with tools.' Andy stretched out, getting rid of the kinks in his back.

'I'll bloody tool you,' Diana spat at Andy, earning a wicked grin in reply.

The tall Shapeshifter looked at her seriously, then sighed. 'OK, we'll clean up. Then we'll get the kids to bed, eh?'

Diana smiled her thanks, and the three of them soon had the downstairs rooms clean, apart from several sets of sticky, sleepy young twins.

Mark got a pot of tea and sat back with Andy. They'd been chatting for a while when they realised Diana was gone.

'She's head-counting,' Andy said. 'It's an obsession with her. Sometimes I'm tempted to hide a pair of 'em, just to see what she'd do.'

'Change, and sniff 'em out,' said Mark instantly. 'That's what I'd do anyway.' He blushed as Andy started to laugh. 'Look, they're my responsibility. I have to think about these things.'

Andy stood up, took Mark's hand, and pulled him to his feet. 'Let's go see the kids, eh?'

Mark found Diana in the kids' playroom, where Seth and Bridget were sitting companionably, talking quietly. Diana was lying on the floor talking to Meg and Beth. Mark looked at the scene for a while, and wondered what Jake and Matt were doing. Meg was glaring at him; he still wasn't forgiven, it seemed. He decided it was time she learned that there was more to MarkDad than being punished, and scooped her up.

She looked alarmed for a moment, looking to Diana for reassurance.

Mark announced that he was taking the little girls for a jam session – it was about time they spent some time in the music room. He tucked Meg under one arm, and Beth under the other, and carried them outside.

'We can walk, you know?' Beth said.

He grinned. 'I can walk faster.' He kicked open the door of the music room and put them down. 'Right. Four years old, eh? Let's start with some percussion… Have you guys been in here before?'

Meg started to open her mouth, but a warning glance from Beth shut her up.

Mark laughed. 'I see, not with permission. OK, would you rather shake something or hit something?'

Both girls were adamant that they wanted to hit something. Meg was certain she could deal with the big drum kit perfectly well.

'Oh, honeypie, you couldn't reach the pedals. Let's start with some bongos,' her dad told her. He let them experiment for a while, then started to teach them more formally. The lesson was well underway when his mobile rang. He listened carefully and went pale. 'The little bastards!' he said, then blinked at his daughters and apologised. He put the phone down. 'Your brothers are joining us – we have to entertain them.'

He waited, grim-faced, until there was a timid knock on the door. He opened it, glancing across at the house, where Diana stood at a bedroom window, watching the kids until they were safe with their dad.

Isaac looked the most guilty, and Mark grabbed him by the ear, letting go when the boy winced, remembering it wasn't the kid's first telling-off of the night.

'Come in, the lot of you. First of all, explain why you broke my new laptop.'

Nathan looked at him, the picture of innocence, his angelic face solemn and tear-stained. 'We wanted to know how it worked,' he said. 'We're sorry.'

Mark felt himself softening, and wondered how the hell Nat and Joe ever got disciplined about anything. They had their father's beauty and charm – coupled with their age, it made them irresistible. 'Yeah, well. OK. Don't play with other people's stuff without permission from now on. Understand?'

'Yes, Daddy,' Joe said, his eyes wide.

Mark realised Ian was grinning, and he narrowed his eyes at the boys. These four were a formidable force together – he could sense it already. Meg was whispering to Beth, and he could sense control slipping away from him. It suddenly occurred to him that these children were almost a different generation to the older kids, and had grown up in a different family environment. He pulled himself together.

He found some more instruments – a small guitar, a triangle, a tambourine, a recorder and a xylophone – and arranged the kids in a semi-circle around him, starting the lesson. The kids brightened up straight away. Order was being imposed, a lesson was in progress, and they paid close attention.

Eventually Mark noticed Beth was fighting to stay awake. He glanced at the clock and was surprised to see how late it was. He called the lesson to an end, and waited for the kids to put the instruments away tidily.

Back at the house, all was quiet, and it was clear that the rest of the kids were in bed or getting ready. He picked Meg up and hugged her. 'Come on, horrible, let's get you lot ready for bed.'

Meg burrowed sleepily into his shoulder, barely finding the energy to whisper. 'Gotta turn all the lights off first.'

He frowned, looking round, seeing a dim glimmer of light at the end of the corridor. It looked like the light had been left on in the living room. He carried Meg towards it, followed by the other five kids. He pushed the door open and was surprised to see Diana alone.

She smiled; she looked tired. 'Ah, the last half-dozen. Will you get them to bed? They just need a shower.'

'Sure.' He hesitated, wondering if she'd stayed up for the children, or for him. He was aware of John upstairs, and he suddenly had a vivid flash of memory of the way Diana and Zoe had been with John before the wedding: the three of them laughing together, touching each other almost without knowing it. 'You can go to bed now, they're all safe,' he offered.

She held his gaze for a full minute, then shook her head. 'I'll stay up a while longer,' she said.

He herded the kids upstairs, waiting for each set of twins to get out of the shower, wrapping them in warm towels, supervising as they brushed their teeth and put their pyjamas on, then putting the little girls to bed first, then the boys. As he made his way downstairs again, he heard a door creak behind him. He stopped and turned round. Joe was on the landing, the door open behind him. The blond kid stopped, wide-eyed.

'Where are you off to?' Mark asked. He noticed Nathan was in the doorway, just behind him.

'We want to sleep in Isaac and Ian's room. Mum lets us, honest,' Nat said.

Mark thought about it for a moment, then nodded. 'OK, but be quiet.'

Back in the living room, Diana looked more alert. She was sewing the button back on to her jacket. A half-empty wine glass was on the table beside her. Mark picked it up and emptied it, realising he'd sobered up. He looked at her carefully. 'I'm going outside to check the fences. I guess John and Zoe are waiting for you?'

Diana looked amused, and he pointed out that Zoe was quite capable of tiring John out if she put her mind to it. Diana didn't take her eyes off him.

When she said she wanted him, he felt a spreading warmth of excitement in his belly. He saw his reflection in the mirror: a slight, shortish guy with stupidly long hair, pale skin, lips too thin, nose too long and crooked to let him ever kid himself that he was attractive. 'You really want me? Not John and Zoe?' He looked at her carefully. 'Not Andy?'

'Ah, yes. I think Andy's pinched the second bedroom.' She looked rueful. 'I should have said something to him.'

'Shit, who cares,' Mark managed to say. 'We'll take the third room.'

She stood and winced. 'That bed needs making,' she said.

He could see in her face every job that needed doing, every day of hard work and research and childcare. He thought again about the passport he'd hidden. He felt another guilty pang, telling himself he needed to make her love him again, for the good of the pack.

He held out his hand, and she stood and took it. They went up the stairs together, pausing twice to kiss. They went to the end of the corridor, to the third bedroom, which held nothing more than a long single bed and a wardrobe. The bed was unmade, and Diana was looking underneath for bedding.

'Shh, never mind that, I'll keep you warm,' Mark said, pulling her closer. His hand was beneath her clothes, on her breast; he could feel her heartbeat, fast, excited. She shrugged her jacket off, and he abandoned his caresses to take the hem of her top and pull it off.

She was still wearing the amber necklace. It looked startlingly heavy against her neck. He ran the back of his hand against the black lace of her bra, relishing the heaviness and warmth of her breasts. She was reaching behind her neck to remove the necklace. The move pushed her breasts forwards and he moaned. The necklace was on the floor now, the silver gleaming in the moonlight. Diana had unzipped his flies and his prick was in her hand – she was making tiny, appreciative noises that were driving him wild.

He unfastened his belt and negotiated the complexities of a raging erection, trousers and boxer shorts skilfully. His mate was wild-eyed now, a storm of lust clouded the green, and she dropped to her knees, licking delicately at the tip of his penis, savouring the taste of him so obviously that he nearly came on the spot.

He grunted and pushed her backwards, pinning her to the floor with one arm while his other hand tore at her trousers. The coppery smell of blood hit him, and he looked down at what he was doing; his hand had become a claw, and he'd shredded her clothes, scratching her thigh as he did so. She was kicking now, and he drew back, watchful, until he realised she was merely untangling herself from the ruins of her clothes. His own shirt was gone, beyond repair, and he shrugged the rags off his shoulders.

She'd shifted her attention to his arms, and was kissing and licking at his left forearm. The scent of her surrounded him, and he wriggled down, burying his face in the warmth and wet of her, pushing her thighs apart as he licked at her. The Alpha rush took him, and he bucked and trembled as he came, hot and thick, and sticky on her belly. He watched, dizzied, as she dipped her hand into it, and raised her fingers to her mouth. Her eyes stayed closed as she licked each finger, as she licked the palm of her hand, then returned her hand to her belly, questing for more. The rush of blood to her skin gave him his cue to dip his head once more to her heat. He knew that it was the taste of him that set off her orgasm; his tongue was not the instrument of her pleasure, but the delicate sensor that relayed every tremor from her body to his brain. When she stopped trembling, he raised himself up, wriggling up against her slick body until his lips were on hers.

She was whispering his name, whispering endearments mixed with obscenities as she moved beneath him, rubbing herself against his hard length. 'Inside me. In me. Mark?' she pleaded as he became distracted by the texture of her hair in his hands, of the shape and taste of her eyes under his lips.

'Wait, honey, wait,' he whispered, and his desperate tenderness finally registered with her. 'Look at me. Look at me, Diana,' he begged. 'Be still, kiss me.'

She moaned, half complaint, half desire, and lay still, opening her eyes and looking into his, captured by the infinite depths there, fascinated by a hint of silver deep in the dark, dark brown.

He gently held her face, cupped between his hands. 'Diana, do you trust me? Do you love me?'

'Always.' She sounded a little bewildered. 'You know I do.'

He brushed her damp hair away from her face, kissing her pale high forehead. She was his, she would always be his. There was no need for jealousy, no need to win her back from anyone. He would be happy if she was happy.

She was touching his mouth gently, tracing the contours of his face. 'Are you tired?' she asked carefully. 'Do you want to sleep?'

'No, I want to make love to you,' he assured her. 'But to you, not that wild thing I was with a few minutes ago.'

Diana blushed. 'Yeah. Let's try the bed?'

More comfortable now, they hugged for a while, until Diana took Mark's earlobe in her mouth and bit on it gently. 'I still want you,' she reminded him.

He looked up mischievously. 'I wondered when you'd remember about that.' He rolled on to her, his whole weight on her, his prick nestled between her thighs. He teased her for a while, then gently eased into her, kissing her.

She looked into his eyes and became perfectly still, raising her hips a little to perfect the angle at which he entered her, letting her eyes speak for her.

He stopped twice, drawing back from the edge of his orgasm, watching her carefully until she sighed and shuddered beneath him, he let go then, feeling the utmost peacefulness spread through him.

He dozed for an hour, and woke up to find her sitting up, looking at him.

She looked nervous. 'We've been waiting for the right time to bring you in on this. Me and Zoe and Andy, we were all working on stuff, separately at first, just in case, and then we started talking and...'

Mark listened with growing interest as she spelled out what she'd been working on in her lab, tentatively outlining aspects that might have a commercial angle, expressing her concerns about what would happen if big businesses got their hands on information about the Shapeshifter genome, talking about licences and agents. She spoke for an hour, and left Mark stunned.

'This could make us stupidly wealthy,' he said. 'I don't just mean "don't worry about replacing the car" rich. I mean big business rich. And Andy obviously knows what he's doing – we're lucky to have him. Diana, you know we're on the edge of being found out, don't you?'

She nodded, looking miserable.

Mark bit his lip. 'We'll survive. We have done so far, but these discoveries of yours are brilliant – they can be marketed in so many different ways. And Zoe ... can she market that, do you think? You've obviously talked about it.'

He went downstairs, and came back with a laptop. He saw she'd dragged some bedding out, and was starting to make the bed. He gestured impatiently. 'Don't do that, love. Go and sleep with Andy if you're cold.'

'Yes, boss,' she said, mock demure, putting the sheets back and planting a kiss on his head.

Mark worked through the night, checking out what he'd just been told, making sure in his own head that his mates were on the right track. Andy's business and social connections were going to be desperately important, that much was clear, and Zoe's PR skills would be vital.

He realised it was daylight when he heard the thundering noise of the teenagers running downstairs for breakfast. He switched the computer off and rubbed his eyes. He frowned at the rags of the wedding clothes that still lay on the floor. He left them where they were, and wandered into the main bedroom, which was empty and tidy, the windows open. The bathroom was clean and inviting, and he treated himself to a hot bath before mooching through the wardrobes and finding some clothes that belonged to him.

The house was unusually calm; the Kittens were paler and quieter than usual. Andy and Diana were in the kitchen, sending out platefuls of food to the waiting hordes. Mark stepped over Harry, who was opening and shutting a cupboard door and shouting about something he obviously considered to be of great importance. The Alpha picked up a plate of toast and made his way out, stopping to hug Diana as he passed her.

He found John. 'We've only got a couple of hours to pack,' he said.

John shook his head. 'No, all sorted. I packed their essential stuff a couple of days ago – anything else we'll buy new. It's all in the car. Where the fuck is Diana's passport?'

Time slowed down. Mark looked at his cousin, really looked at him, as he would look at a stranger to whom he was giving responsibility for his life. He saw a man who looked to be in his late thirties, with deceptively innocent dark eyes. Black curls fell unfettered to his waist, framing a strong-featured, heart-shaped face. He was short but well-muscled, thicker around the waist and neck than he had been years ago, but still powerfully built. His skin was golden, his lips full and red. The lines around his mouth and eyes expressed humour and kindness.

Mark sighed. 'Will you look after her? I don't want her to feel left out.'

A shadow of irritation crossed John's face, replaced quickly by a look of such utter understanding that Mark stepped back, embarrassed by his own transparency.

'Put the passport back,' John said. 'What on earth did you think you were doing?'

'I wanted to keep her here, with me,' Mark confessed.

'Way to go, Brains. Katie would have sniffed that one out within days. What were you going to do? Confine Diana to the house?'

Mark laughed a little. 'It was a dream. That's all. She'll be happier with you, I know. I've got the passport in my pocket – I'll give it to her when you're ready.'

John shook his head. 'What about you? Will you be OK?'

'Are you kidding? Me and Andy? All these kids? It'll be like *School of Rock*.'

John shrugged. 'Keep an eye on Liam and Patrick, that's all. They've been clingy since the girls were born, and you might get a dirty protest from them if they can't find their mums. Other than that, everything should be fine. I briefed Seth and Noah and Miranda this morning, they're OK with it. I daren't tell any of the others, they'll let something slip and I'm *not* telling the women until the last minute, or they'll come up with a very good reason why they can't go.' Mark still looked panicky, and John touched his hand. 'Mark, you'll be fine.'

'I'll be fine,' Mark repeated. He sounded a little shaky, then managed a smile. 'I'll be fine,' he said more steadily. He blinked slowly. 'I've just realised, you're taking the babies. Oh hell.'

He went back to the kitchen and picked up Harry and Mikey, then took them up to the main bedroom where Leanne and Julie slept. Zoe found him there, and he almost spilled the beans.

'Aren't you supposed to be going home?' she asked.

He opened his mouth, then shut it again. 'In a while. I don't get enough time with the tinies. Come here and give me a hug.'

She looked a little puzzled, but did, then left again, leaving him with two sleeping babies, the toddler twins and an immense pile of building bricks.

Eventually Andy found him. 'Zero hour. John's got Zoe in the car. We're gonna need you to convince Diana to go.'

Mark picked up the boys, and Andy the girls. He could see John in the garden, talking to Diana. The Alpha woman's taut posture made him smile.

He made his way carefully downstairs and out to the garden, he strolled over to John and Diana, and handed his toddlers to John.

The Silverwood Beta was at his most charming, his eyes were wide and guileless, his hands spread out, but there was a desperate light in his eyes. He looked over Diana's shoulder, appealing to Mark for help.

For the last time, Mark felt the demon rise, telling him that all he had to do was fail to be persuasive. He quashed it, touching Diana's shoulder and instantly getting her full attention.

'Hey, you. Why are you still here? You've got a holiday waiting for you,' he said gently. He listened as she listed the reasons why she couldn't go, then smiled. 'You need a holiday, don't tell me that you don't. More than that, you deserve one. We'll be fine. Here's your passport – I found it a week ago. Andy's packed for the kids, and I got passports for Mikey and Harry sorted. Just go, hon.'

She looked around, asking for Andy and seeing him stride towards her on those long, long legs.

Mark watched as he teased and flattered and threatened until she realised she was outmanoeuvred.

All became still as she looked around at her home, at Mark. Her gaze rested on his face, and Andy excused himself hurriedly.

Mark realised she was beginning to panic again, and embraced her. He wanted to reassure her, but the warmth of her in his arms, the familiar pattern of her breathing, the scent of her hair, overcame him.

'Thanks for last night. It meant a lot to me,' he murmured into her ear. Her arms were around his waist, returning the embrace.

'What are you talking about?' she asked. She sounded genuinely puzzled.

He realised that this was it, he was going to tell her. The blood rushed to his face. 'I'm talking about you and John and Zoe.' Once he'd started, it was surprisingly easy. He let his defences fall, one by one. If she laughed at him, at least she'd be away for weeks, to give him time to gather the shreds of his dignity. He plunged in. 'It's always bothered me. He loves you. He tells you he loves you, you're always laughing and joking with him. But given the choice, you always come to me. I've never understood it. And don't say it's biology. You come to me when I know you can't possibly still need the Alpha fix.'

He realised he was gabbling, and shut up. He took a deep breath. Looking at her face took all his courage. She was reaching up, touching the corner of his mouth gently, her eyes open wide. 'Mark, I love you. Don't you know that?'

The cynic in him mocked gently, reminding him of the way she looked at John, at the way she flirted with Andy. He tried to ignore it, but it had to be said. Already ashamed of himself, he articulated his fear. 'Of course I know. You love us all, it's instinct.'

He felt her recoil, and held her more tightly, pulling her back towards him, his body belying the distrust in his words. She flinched a little, then gathered herself again. He knew she was considering every word before she said it. He wished he'd done the same. He waited, terrified.

Eventually she spoke. 'Mark, I'm *in* love with you. Everything about you. I always have been. How many times do I have to tell you that? Instinct? I don't believe this. All these years, and you still think I'm operating on instinct?'

Her voice had risen, she was going to leave. She was going to leave with John and Zoe, and he'd just insulted her completely and utterly. He felt beyond redemption, beyond any chance of salvation. Yet still she held him, still she stayed unresisting in his arms.

'I'm sorry, so sorry…' he managed to say.

'What? Mark, tell me.'

There was a rising impatience in her voice, and he took a deep breath. He couldn't make things any worse, surely. 'Is it too late?' His voice had fallen. He suspected that he was barely audible. He was reminded of a recurrent nightmare: he was on stage, the crowd applauding madly, John ready at the mike, Andy already posing with his bass, flirting with the front row – and he'd turn to pick up his guitar and find a plastic, stringless toy.

His legs were weak, there was no going back, he was committed to this, with nothing to back him up. Diana was speaking to him carefully, as she would speak to a distressed child. What was he sorry for, why was he so upset? He summoned the little strength he had left – he'd rather be in battle with a hundred of those white wolves than here, now, exposing his heart to a woman he was sure he'd just mortally insulted. He plunged in.

'I do love you. I've fallen in love with you, and I don't understand how or why. All these years and you've been my mate and my Alpha, and I've protected you and we've got all our kids, and yes, I loved you, and cared for you. I denied I loved you, but we knew it was there. But I was never *in love*. You were just there, inevitable.'

He looked at her; she was pale. He winced again. What had he said now? Had he really implied she'd been nothing more than a convenience? He needed time to think. He needed more time with her. He could hear the horn of the car blaring out: John was getting impatient. Fuck him, Mark needed to make her understand. She was turning, looking at John.

'No. Let me finish. I didn't understand how you felt about me. I didn't understand, at all. Then I saw your face when I told Katie I was in love with her, and I began to understand. And it's been on my mind. And I watch you with the kids and … the research you do – it's incredible. I thought you were just messing about in that lab, then I read your notes. And last night, those ideas you had, and how you've drawn everything together with Andy and Zoe. I can't believe how I've treated you. You're amazing. And that's why I wanted Zoe, to try to see if I felt the same way about her. That day, in London, it wasn't a coincidence. I'd followed you all day. John told me where you were going. And last night… John and Zoe waited for you, and you just switched them off and came to me, and I felt like I was drowning. I've been helping John to plan this holiday, and every day I've wanted to tell him that you're not going. I even hid your passport from him. What am I going to do?'

He took a deep breath, and finally drew the courage to look at her again. He was shocked to see tears on her face.

She kissed his throat, wiped at her eyes. She nestled into him and spoke to his chest. 'Mark, you really do choose your moments.'

He laughed a little. It was OK, she was joking. He knew every tone of her voice. He knew she wasn't angry or hurt. He knew, with a triumphant conviction, that she did love him, that if the Alpha desire faded and died, if by some weird chemistry they lost their powers, he would still be the man she desired and loved, and she would be his woman.

He started to say, 'I love you', but she hushed him, her voice trembling a little, assuring him that if he said that now, she'd never leave. That capricious demon teased him, but he overruled it. 'You know, Diana, you know now. Don't ever forget, even if sometimes I forget to tell you.'

She took a deep breath. 'And Katie? Tell me she doesn't know, please.'

He shook his head. 'I'm not stupid. I won't tell her. And I don't want to hurt her any more than I already have.'

That damned horn was still blaring out. There was time for one kiss... She kept her eyes open, and they looked at each other. Her kiss answered all his questions, all his doubts, and at last he could draw back and release her. He took her hand and walked with her to the car. She belted herself in, smiling dazedly, checking that the children were secure. As John cursed mildly and happily, releasing the handbrake, Mark leaned in through the window to kiss Diana for one final time. John revved the engine pointedly, and Mark nodded and stepped back.

He watched the car as it sped up the drive. The gates opened, and they were gone. She hadn't turned around, hadn't waved. He understood. He wasn't sure how long he'd been standing there, looking at the gates, but distraction came in the form of a tentative hand taking his. He looked around.

Caleb looked anxious. 'Where've they gone?' he asked.

Mark swallowed. There hadn't been time to tell the younger kids. 'Just a holiday. Andy and I are going to look after you for a few weeks.'

'Weeks?' Caleb yelped.

Mark grinned. 'Hey, buster, trust us. It'll be fun.' He tugged at Cal's ear. 'They're coming back, don't worry about it.' He watched Cal carefully, making sure not to look too sympathetic.

Cal nodded briefly. 'OK, Dad. OK.' Caleb's phone rang and he answered it. 'Mum? Yeah, it's OK. I'm all right, don't worry about me. You have a nice time.'

Mark put his arm around Cal, and they walked back towards the house. Cal ended the call, and Mark hugged him.

'I'm so proud of you,' he said quietly, and left the boy standing, smiling.

Andy approached him, looking vaguely puzzled as he looked around the garden at the kids who were talking excitedly to each other about their mothers' absence.

'Mark, sweetie, tell me again how John's managed to bugger off for weeks with both women… Because now he's not here to explain it, it suddenly makes a lot less sense to me.'

Mark shook his head. 'And me.' He hugged his friend and together they went indoors.

Chapter 30

Three days into their stay at Silverwood, Andy approached Mark, asking his permission to invite Helen to visit.

'Look, I've not seen her and the girls since the morning of the wedding. She's not going to hurt any of the kids, is she? Come on, Mark, you know her.'

Mark's brain went into overdrive, looking at the situation from every perspective. Eventually he nodded. 'She can come on to the grounds, but not into the house. If the weather's bad, unlock the annexe and use it. It's furnished, it just needs airing. Make sure all the kids are expecting her, and that they know who she is.'

Andy's eyes opened wide. 'Shit, never thought of that. I'll show them pictures of Eva and Naomi too.'

Mark chewed at his nails. 'They're your responsibility, OK? We've not had strangers here before, and the kids might get jumpy. Hell, I might get jumpy. Keep her away from the little ones, eh?'

Andy started to joke, then realised to his horror that Mark meant it, and nodded grimly. 'It's not easy, this, is it? Shall I tell Diana?'

The Alpha's eyes opened wide. 'No! Not until she's on her way back, and make damn sure Helen's gone by then. If she knows, she'll come back straight away.'

His friend teased him gently. 'And you don't want that, do you?'

'Fuck off, Andy.' Mark turned on his heel, and stormed away.

Once the little kids were in bed, he called a family meeting.

'We're getting visitors tomorrow. Andy's other family will be here. His wife is friendly, and if we're nice to his daughters, they will be too. I know all of them, and they're lovely. Helen knows about the furriness, the little girls don't, so no Changing or talking about it. Leave all that to the grown-ups.'

Seth's eyes blazed. 'Dad, the little kids…'

'Seth, I trust Helen. She won't hurt them. But just to be sure, until you guys are comfortable with her and her girls, I'd like the little 'uns to stay in the house if she's outside in the grounds. Just so we don't have any misunderstandings.' Mark locked his gaze with that of his firstborn, fully aware of how strong Seth's protective instincts were.

He continued. 'You aren't going to like the next bit either. We can't let Diana and the Betas know about this. Diana and Zoe will want to come straight home if they suspect Helen's here.'

The expected protests didn't come, although the kids put their heads together and spoke intently to each other for several minutes. Mark found that weird; sometimes he was spooked by the cohesion these children showed, their closeness to each other. He could see they were upset, and that they were reluctant to challenge him. He also understood that, although he would request their obedience, he wanted their understanding and agreement.

'OK, lay into me,' he said.

Eleven kids looked at him, looked at each other.

Seth shifted uncomfortably. 'We don't want to lie to Mum. And we don't want Helen to come here.' He glanced at Caleb as he said it.

Mark nodded, and addressed his attention to Cal, who was sitting cross-legged on the floor. 'OK, Cal, what's the problem?'

'Mum might not come back if ... I mean, she might get mad with us.' The boy was chewing his lip nervously.

Mark nodded. 'She's going to be furious, yes. But she's going to want to come back. And that's why I don't want her to know. They're all having a good time, and we don't know when they'll be able to have a holiday again. So far this is working out fine, with me and Andy minding you.'

Seth broke in. 'So why does this Helen woman have to come? Remember what happened when Mum went to meet her sister—'

It was Mark's turn to interrupt. 'I remember that. Are you thinking that you won't see me again for months?'

There was a blur of motion next to him, and the breath went out of him as Bridget landed on his lap and buried her face in his hair. He hugged her, more tightly than she was used to from him, and he felt her begin to relax.

'Look, all of you, things have changed, things will continue to change. We all have to accept that. Helen isn't a threat to any of you, and nothing on earth will keep me away from you lot for long, ever again.'

Darlene raised her hand, tapping impatiently on the table with the other, scowling at Bridget, who had raised her head now and was facing the rest of the kids. 'I quite like the idea of meeting Dad's other family,' she offered.

Beatrice glowered at her. 'So, ask him to take you to his other house. Mum won't like it if he invites them here. This is *our* home, not theirs.'

Mark cleared his throat, and had their undivided attention. 'Maybe that's something we can talk about when your other parents get home. Dar, you're not to visit Andy's without permission from me and Diana, you understand?' He waited for Sara and Darlene to agree, then carried on.

'Helen *is* going to visit tomorrow. She's going to bring her little girls with her. I don't want *anyone* going wolfie, or talking about it, until Eva and Naomi are sympathetic to us. We have to be absolutely sure they like us, and they understand they've got to keep our secret.'

'Why take the risk?' blurted out Noah. 'I mean, I'm not allowed to bring girlfriends home… Why should it be any different for Andy?'

'Because his wife is my friend, and I've known her since I was your age, and I trust her.' Mark stared hard at Noah, until his son backed down.

The Alpha looked around at his pack. 'Do any of you really think I'd do anything that would hurt you? I'll tell Diana at the end of her holiday, don't worry about that. All I'm asking from you is that you're discreet around Eva and Naomi, and that you don't tell your mothers or John what's happening.'

Seth grumbled again about lying to his mother, and Mark was wildly proud of him. 'Seth, I understand how you feel, but she needs the break. I want to give her this holiday, do you understand me?'

His eldest son looked at him carefully, light dawning in his eyes. 'Yeah, Dad, I think I do. Like you said, things change.' Seth smiled a little. 'I'm glad you're looking after her, but I still think you're wrong,' he half conceded.

'It's my decision,' Mark said firmly. He noted, with a degree of amazement, the acceptance on the faces of his children. Still, even as teenagers, they automatically trusted him. He realised that his leg was going numb, and nudged Bridget. 'Will you get me a drink, hon?'

She got up reluctantly, moving towards the door. 'Anyone else want anything?' she asked.

Mark watched them, waiting for the gathering to disperse, for them to separate and do their own things. They seemed reluctant to move away.

Miranda finally looked up from under a fringe of fine blonde hair. 'Dad, will you hang around tonight? This feels nice, us all together, with you.'

'I could get Andy…' he offered. 'He's just patrolling.'

Bill grinned. 'No, let him do the guard dog thing. He's looked after us loads of times anyway. I can't remember the last time it was just you. Did you ever look after us? Just you?'

Mark thought hard. 'Yeah, a few times, before Zoe moved in, before the family got really big. Sometimes John would take Diana to a party or a gig, and I'd stay in with you. That was before Bridget and Beatrice were born. But yeah, I'd sit in with you. Seth, do you remember? Usually Bill, Frank and the Kittens would be in bed before I arrived, but you and Noah and Miranda would sit up and play for a while.'

Seth grinned. 'Yes, I remember. You always brought pop with you. But this is the first time since the Bees were born?'

'Yeah, I guess. Is it weird?' Mark relaxed into the chair.

Noah shook his head. 'No, it feels good. Will you tell us some stories?'

Mark blinked. 'What kind of stories?'

'Stories about growing up in a normal family?' suggested Caleb.

His father laughed in surprise. 'I don't really have any of those, but if someone gets us some snacks and drinks. I'm open for questions.'

Bill stood up. 'Dad? Can we have beer?'

Seth rolled his eyes, and Mark shrugged. 'It's Friday night, get beer and wine and pop.' He smiled gently, and waited as Seth, Frank and Miranda left on a mission. They came back with a trolley laden with glasses, snacks and drinks.

Mark poured himself a long drink of lemonade, and settled back. He waited until all the kids were settled, then raised his eyebrows. 'So, what do you want to know?' He felt slightly absurd, as if he was being interviewed for a job he'd held for almost two decades.

Miranda was the first to speak. 'Tell us about your first Change. We've heard everyone else's stories.' There was a murmur of approval.

He took a deep breath. 'OK. Well, you guys all knew what was coming, yeah? Even your mother had an idea that it might happen, because her sister was a Shifter, but I was clueless.'

The kids were looking at him, rapt already. 'I don't know much about my family. My mother definitely wasn't a Shifter – I asked her some pretty probing questions when it started happening to me, without telling her exactly what was happening, of course. She never gave me any indication that she knew what I was on about. John and I think that our fathers were Shifters – they were twins. That doesn't make it definite, of course, but it's good enough circumstantial evidence for me. He disappeared when I was a kid. I don't remember much about him, or Uncle Tomas. We don't know why he left. I don't think I missed him. I don't remember missing him. Mum did. She cried a lot, when she thought I was asleep.'

Mark glanced around the room. Seth was staring into a glass of wine with a moody expression. He looked up and they looked into each other's eyes for a moment. Mark winced. 'OK, so I've not been the world's greatest dad either. Maybe it's in the genes?' He regretted it instantly, but recognised his own self in the way Seth glanced protectively around at his younger siblings. Mark hoped with all his heart that Seth would get the chance to do things right.

Miranda broke the silence again. 'Dad? Your first Change?'

Relieved, Mark smiled at her. 'OK. Well, I was a bit of a weird kid. I used to sneak out of the house at night and go down to the beach. If the tides were right, I'd go out swimming sometimes. It was something for myself, you know? Every other thing I did was with my mum, or John, or John's mum. Well, one night I misjudged things pretty badly. I hit my head on something and blacked out. It could only have been a few seconds, but it was enough to half drown me.' He grinned and looked at the kids. 'Being a teenager, I thought I was immortal – it didn't occur to me that I was dying. I got pissed off and started to struggle, then I knocked my head again. The next thing I knew, I was shaking water out of my fur and wondering why the hell I had four legs.'

Noah smiled with recognition, and Mark continued. 'I must have been a very strange kid, because I realised what had happened, accepted it, and dealt with it. If you talk to John, he'll tell you that he freaked out. Zoe decided she was having weird dreams and she was lucky never to get caught, she was so careless. Diana, of course, had a Shifter older sister, and parents who were proud of her. Like *your* parents are proud of you.'

He looked affectionately at Sammy and Caleb. 'It's a huge event, your first Change. That's one of the best things about being a dad, running with your own kids.'

Miranda cleared her throat and spoke again. 'How long was it before John Changed?'

Mark thought back: it had seemed eternal, that time of loneliness, of aloneness. 'It can't have been more than a year. I'd almost given up on him, to be honest. I knew, absolutely, that I had to find more people like me. I read a lot of werewolf stories, and it looked like it was either a family thing or that I'd been infected. I was pretty sure that if I'd been bitten by a wolf, either I'd remember it or my mum would have mentioned it.' He fell quiet, to allow Bill and Frank to giggle at that.

He shrugged. 'Well, John's older than me by a few months, but, around that time, he looked a good couple of years older than me. He was like Bill and Frank: growing up fast, but not fast enough for his own liking. He was already talking about forming a band, going round the country. We never, for a minute, considered the possibility that we'd ever be apart. We were like brothers. I suppose we were pack brothers, even then, before his first Change.

'When he did Change, it was after a fight with me. I think I was really pissing him off at the time, because I was smaller and weaker than he was, and he felt mean if we did fight. He was on a hair trigger: everything either annoyed him or sent him into rhapsodies. Anyway, we had an argument, and he stalked off rather than beat me up. He growled. He actually growled as he left the room, and it was the most beautiful sound I'd heard in my life.' He smiled.

'So I followed him, up the street and around the corner to Auntie Miriam's. By the time he hit the stairs, I could see his ears Changing. It was a bloody miracle that his mum didn't notice. I chased after him, and got into his room just as he went furry. I think that's when I realised I was happy to be what I was, to be what we are. If I was half as beautiful as John was, then it was worth it. I just held him, until he Changed back, and then I got the chance to really talk to someone about what had been happening to me for the last year. It brought us together, even closer than before.'

Caleb spoke up. 'ZoeMum said that when we found her, she was so lonely she was ready to die. Was it ever like that for you?'

Mark shook his head. 'No, I wanted to find others. But then I was young, I had hope that John would be like me. Zoe had been living with her secret for fifteen years – she'd tried to live a normal life, and that had gone wrong.'

Darlene looked up. 'Is it true that you didn't want her in the pack?' she asked cautiously.

Mark shifted uncomfortably. 'Yes, it is. I was wrong. Diana was right. I wish they were both here now, I miss them.' He noticed how Caleb opened his mouth and broke in, 'But that doesn't mean that you're to tell them to come home, OK?'

Caleb nodded, and Mark relaxed.

Chapter 31

Mark and Andy decided to wait until late afternoon to introduce Helen to the pack. As soon as the last of the schoolkids had been ferried back through the gates, Andy took his car and went to collect his other family.

From the moment Andy left Silverwood, Mark could feel tensions rising. He reminded the older kids to control themselves and to not Change, and reminded all the little kids that new friends were coming to visit, but they weren't to talk about wolves to them.

The Ransomes arrived to a spookily quiet Silverwood. Mark stood outside, waiting to greet them. In the big house, curtains twitched. Andy got out of the car first, stretching his long body luxuriously, showing no hint of any tension. He looked across at Mark and raised his hand in a lazy salute, before walking around the car and opening the door for Helen. She looked across at Mark and gave him a little wave, almost shy, before opening the back doors of the car and encouraging her daughters to get out.

Eva was a tall, skinny eight-year-old. Mark had known her since the day she was born, and his eyes automatically went to her knees to check for sticking plasters. She'd always been a tomboy, and prone to infections in the many cuts and scratches she picked up – the carrier syndrome showing its colours.

Naomi was six months younger than her half-brothers, Nathan and Joseph, and looked uncannily like them. Her hair was still a fine white blonde, long and unbound.

Mark moved forward to greet his guests. Eva ran to him for a hug, but Naomi held back, overawed by the new place. He scooped Eva into a bear hug and held her for a minute, before setting her gently down and looking up at Helen.

'Damn it, Hel, can't you shrink a little?' he half joked.

His old friend shook her head. 'Sorry, mate, not without cutting bits off. Where are the kids then?'

'Hiding. Did Andy explain that the older ones are a mite protective of the babies? We want to do the introductions slowly, partly for their sake, and partly because we don't want to overwhelm you and your girls.'

Helen nodded curtly. 'Yes, I get it. Are we safe?'

Mark hesitated. 'You are under my protection, they understand that. I'd be very careful around the very little kids though: no sudden movements if their big brothers and sisters are around. When we were attacked, there was a kidnap attempt too, and the whole pack is fairly keen on the idea of not losing siblings.'

Helen's laugh was rich and sweet and natural, 'I wouldn't hurt a hair of their heads – or tails! Bring them out, I want to meet them.'

The Alpha grinned, despite himself. 'OK, but we'll take it slowly. I'll introduce you to our eldest children. I'll bring Miranda out, shall I?'

Helen paled. 'She's Xan's daughter? Oh, I'm not sure now. Maybe we should wait until we're a bit more settled, until I've met more of your family?'

Andy wandered over. 'I think it might be an idea if I spend an hour or so in the house. Mark, can you show Hel to the annexe?'

Helen glanced quickly between the Alpha and his Third. 'I forget this is Andy's second home. That's weird. Yeah. OK, Mark, could you show me around?'

He took her to the annexe first, which had been aired and cleaned, and was warm and dry. She asked Mark if the girls could explore the house, and when they'd gone, she followed him into the kitchen.

He shrugged. 'We didn't know if it was worth bringing supplies in, but there's stuff for making tea and coffee, and some biscuits and fruit...' He gestured around.

Helen took his hand. 'Mark, I know this has got to be hard, but thank you.'

His smile was warm and open. 'Hel, I wouldn't do this for anyone else ... *anyone.*'

She raised her eyebrows. 'Katie?'

He shuddered a little, enough for her to notice. 'No.' He put the kettle on and set out a couple of mugs. He glanced through the kitchen window and picked up three more. 'Hel, you have visitors.'

She turned and looked. Three teenagers were walking across the lawn from the main house: two lads with dark red hair, wearing jeans and Ts, and a tall blonde girl, who wore a long crimson velvet dress that swept the ground. The boys walked just ahead of her, something about them suggested they would protect her with their lives. Mark smiled.

'Open the door then, Hel,' he said gently.

'Oh, yes.'

Mark leaned against the wall, watching as Helen welcomed the eldest pack children to the annexe. Miranda followed her brothers to the living room, hesitating at the doorway. Mark's gaze flicked from his daughter to his friend; Helen was pale but composed, and she invited the three teenagers to sit.

Miranda took a seat on the sofa, and before Helen could move to sit next to her, the twin brothers hurriedly sat down on either side of her.

Mark coughed. 'Noah, help me with these drinks,' he said.

Noah stood reluctantly, and Helen sat on the arm of the sofa. Noah glanced backwards, almost frantic with worry, but Mark pushed him into the kitchen. 'Noah, be polite,' he muttered.

'She's staring at Miranda,' the boy objected.

'Your sister is the image of Xan, who Helen loved. Have a bit of sympathy, the poor woman's in shock.' Mark made his voice a little gentler. 'Just make that tea, OK? And the little girls are around somewhere, if you see them, be nice.'

Mark went back into the living room, watchful and quiet. Miranda and Seth were holding hands, something they'd often done as children, but rarely did now. Seth was restless but silent. Miranda seemed to be excited and happy.

Mark spoke. 'Are you all too shy to introduce yourselves? Kids, this is Helen Ransome, Andy's wife and a good friend to me and John. Call her Hel, everyone else does. Hel, this is my eldest son, Seth, and my eldest daughter, Miranda.' He raised his eyebrows at Seth, who hurriedly stood up and shook hands with Helen.

'Seth Foster, pleased to meet you,' he blurted out.

Miranda took a deep breath. 'I'm Miranda Kendrick Foster,' she said quietly. 'It's really good to meet you at last. I've heard a lot about you.'

Helen was giving Miranda a quizzical look. 'Kendrick Foster? You have Xan's name?'

Miranda blushed. 'Not really, it's just what I call myself. Mum says it's all right, as long as only the family know. Mum wants us all to be called Preston, but she also says that would be like taking out an advert in the newspaper linking us to our dads. She doesn't want that.'

'She doesn't want to be associated with them?' Hel asked carefully.

'No! She doesn't want attention! We go to different schools, and we try not to be seen together.'

Mark broke in. 'Diana's protected and hidden the pack for a long time – we all trust her to make the right decisions. She's getting impatient though. The newest babies are Prestons. I even registered my youngest sons under my name, and John did the same for his baby daughters. It's not blatant, John and Mark Preston aren't unusual names. We're getting tired of lying and hiding, and we're trying to work out how to come out into the open. The wedding is the start of it.'

Helen reached out her hand to touch Miranda's hair, and stopped when she saw Seth's face. Behind her, she could sense Noah glaring at the back of her head. She forced herself to relax.

'Mark, you've got my support. I've already promised Andy that I'll keep your secret, but when it's time to come clean, I'll do whatever I can to help there as well.' Her eyes were drawn irresistibly back to Miranda. 'Honey, do you know how much like your father you look?' she asked.

Miranda blushed deeply. 'Andy's told me that, but I've seen pictures. He was beautiful, I'm not.'

Mark laughed aloud. 'She's fishing!'

'I'm not as pretty as the Kittens,' Miranda objected.

Mark grinned. 'No, not like the Kittens, like yourself!'

Helen was looking at Miranda thoughtfully. 'You know, a little eye make-up, a shorter haircut, a touch of blusher and some nice new clothes, and you could be a heartbreaker. I could show you...'

Miranda shook her head. 'Zoe keeps saying that too. I like my hair long, and I'll wear what's comfortable. I have to wear a uniform at school, I won't at home.' She muttered something quietly. Mark heard it and winced.

Hel moved closer. 'What did you say, hon?'

Mark sighed. 'She said that Xan says she can wear what she wants. She "sees" him.' His tone conveyed his opinion on the matter, and Miranda flinched. Seth was waiting, and squeezed her hand companionably.

Helen was stock-still. 'Xan always used to say he could see ghosts, when he was in his teens. Andy and I teased him about it until he shut up. Miranda, did Andy tell you about that?'

The girl shook her head. 'No, but Xan did.' She raised her chin defiantly.

Mark rolled his eyes at Seth, who responded with a small smile.

Miranda continued. 'I don't care if you don't believe me. My father looks after me, and he loves me.' She looked at Mark and added hastily, 'All my fathers do.' She was rewarded by a small smile, and she relaxed again.

Noah spoke up. 'We all do. Mum says that Miranda's our treasure, and we all look after her.' His glance at Helen said everything.

The woman smiled. 'Noah, I'm here to get to know you, and to make new friends. Speaking of family resemblances, you are the image of your mother.'

Noah nodded. 'We know. We've got darker hair, and we've got brown eyes like Dad, but she always says that we look like our granddad Foster, but shorter.'

'Maybe you'll grow…' commented Helen, without thinking, then hurriedly added, 'Not that you're short!'

Mark was laughing. 'Hel, you said the same thing to me and John when you met us!'

Miranda and Helen exchanged a grin, and Noah snorted and handed out the teas. Mark relaxed; something had just changed in the room, and the kids were off guard now. He hoped they'd picked up on the warmth between himself and Helen. Noah was offering a mug of tea to Helen, and she accepted it gladly.

There was a thud from the hallway, and Eva and Naomi burst into the room. Eva stopped suddenly, and Naomi ran into the back of her.

'Twins!' Eva said, awed. 'Are you really twins? I love twins.'

'Then this *is* your lucky day.' Seth grinned. 'Which one are you? The pretty one or the clever one?'

Eva was startled, and looked at her mother anxiously.

Helen shrugged. 'Answer the boy, or shut your mouth, kiddo.'

'I think I'm the clever one,' Eva managed eventually, earning herself a kick from her sister, who was looking from Noah to Seth and back again.

'How do you know which one you are?' Naomi said to Noah, who took a step back and looked at his twin with something that almost looked like confusion.

Mark laughed aloud. 'Ask the twins who's the pretty one and who's the clever one,' he suggested.

'Miranda,' both boys said instantly, looking affectionately at their sister, who nodded.

'It's true,' she said, deadpan.

Helen couldn't resist reaching out, pushing Miranda's hair back from her forehead. 'You really are Xan's child. Oh Mark, you shouldn't have kept her from me for so long – she heals my heart.'

Mark found his voice. 'I'll leave you all together then. Seth, when you're satisfied that Helen is a friend, send the others over in twos and threes. I'm going back to the house.'

He looked back once. The light was on in the annexe, and it occurred to him that he liked the thought of the old house being lived in. As he ran through a mental checklist of chores, he decided that it was good to have Helen around, and wondered how he could persuade Diana to accept her as a visitor.

The next couple of weeks passed in a blur. Mark managed to get back to Katie's once or twice, to see Jake and Matt. Katie was there, and together they put on a show of being a united family, taking the boys out for the day. Each time, he left after the evening meal, visibly worried about having left the pack unguarded but for Andy.

Every day he spoke to Diana. She set the tone for their conversations on the first call: a jokey rundown of what had been happening on the cruise, and later, in Canada. Every day she looked different. For the first week, she was more relaxed every day, especially after listening to Mark's report on how good things were at home. After the first week, Mark recognised the signs of Alpha withdrawal kicking in. She said nothing, but although she was still cheerful and relaxed, her physical condition was starting to fail. He was attuned to every sign; he felt the same way, and they were used to this. Diana seemed to have aged by five years, and was making references to coming home soon. She implied that Zoe was missing Mark too, but that the fun of the holiday was making up for it. Mark just wanted them all to come home. Diana never referred to their last conversation before she'd left, and he was beginning to wonder if he'd dreamed it. John spoke to him every day, increasingly aware that their time away from the pack was limited, that every day apart from the Alpha was making the women weaker.

He was in the music room, observing Bill at drum practice, when his phone buzzed in his pocket. There was a message from Darlene:

> *Dad, check your laptop. Mum*
> *wants to talk to you. It's my*
> *fault, I didn't think. I*
> *mentioned Eva. I'm really*
> *sorry.*

He quickly accepted the video call, and knew from Diana's face that she knew about Helen. He could see that her eyes were blazing in her bloodless face, her lips drawn into a pale line.

'Oh god, I love you,' he whispered, the acknowledgement a pain in his guts. He braced himself for the whirlwind. She spared no time on pleasantries.

'Mark, what the fuck is going on back there?'

He swallowed. 'Helen rang just after you left. She was upset, her girls were upset. Andy asked me if it was OK for them to come down. It's the best solution. I can't cope with all the kids alone, and neither can Andy. We didn't know how to tell you.'

'So Helen is looking after my children?' Her voice was cold. Mark realised that he'd staggered back under the impact of her fury, and drew himself together again. He raised his hand, begging patience, but stepped back again under the onslaught of her next words.

'Katie was right, you are a deceitful treacherous bastard. You planned this. Get me and Zoe out the way so that you can get your wives over and play happy families in the big house? Get the monster women out of the way. Was that the plan?'

He could see beyond the fury, beyond the accusations, to the deep hurt that fuelled her anger. He knew she believed what she was saying, and grieved over it, wondering if there could ever be a way to convince her otherwise.

'No, Diana, believe me. Katie's not here. Perhaps a year ago, I would have asked her but … it's different now, I don't want her here.' He paused, staring at her. 'I want you here.'

'Just tell me this. Has she been there?' she demanded.

Mark shivered. The force of her personality spilled over across thousands of miles, and he almost forgot that she wasn't physically present with him. He understood, without any doubt, that she knew him well enough to recognise a lie.

He took a deep breath. 'No. I promise. I've been back to her, every few days. She knows I have to be here, but she doesn't like it. When she found out that Helen was here, she wanted to come too. She doesn't really want to meet the kids though, she just wants you to know she's been here. She thinks I don't know her motivation. Oh, this is crap. I hate feeling this way about her. Please, come home. You have no idea how much I want you.'

Every word straight from the heart, and he was emptied, standing, waiting, looking at the clear image of the woman he loved. He leaned closer to the screen, wanting the image to be real, wanting to touch her, hold her.

She blinked, just once, and the fury was gone. There was no softening of her gaze though; she kept herself contained. She spoke quickly, decisively. 'Mark, I'm coming home. I'll leave immediately. Meet me at the airport.'

He smiled. 'I love you,' he said.

'I know,' she said. 'Now, can you find Helen for me?'

'I'll get her,' he said, and left.

Helen was in the annexe, working at a laptop, her hair tied back loosely. She looked up as Mark walked in.

'Jesus on a broomstick, what the fuck has happened? You look like death warmed up,' she said.

'Diana knows you're here. She's on her way back, and she wants to talk to you. She's on the laptop in the music room.'

Helen nodded. 'Sure, I can handle that.'

The two women stared at each other from across thousands of miles of ocean.

'Hey,' Diana said.

Helen smiled. There was no triumph in it, just an open friendliness. 'Your kids are lovely. And my Eva is quite taken with Billy and Frankie.' She paused. 'This wasn't planned, I promise you. It just seemed like a good idea. I was missing Andy so much, but he wouldn't leave Mark by himself with the tribe. When I heard you were gone, I decided I wanted to meet Sara and Darlene, and Miranda, and the little boys. How could Andy refuse?'

'Is Katie there?'

'Don't you trust Mark to tell the truth?' There was a hint of malice there. Diana respected that.

'Is she there?' the Alpha repeated.

'No.' Helen laughed, 'Do you trust me more than you trust him?'

Diana didn't answer that, but went straight to the point. 'Where are you sleeping?'

'I'm in the annexe with Andy and our kids. Don't worry, I've barely been in the house.'

Diana nodded. 'I'm coming home early—'

'And you want me gone? I understand.'

'No, stay. You're right. I've always thought it would be nice if our kids could know each other, but it's a difficult situation, after all. Perhaps this way is for the best.' Diana was determined to show that she too could be cool and friendly.

'I know. But *we're* not kids any more. We should be able to work it out.' She paused, and Diana could see solid determination in her expression. 'When you come back…'

Diana smiled, understanding. 'I know, I can't expect to see much of Andy. How did my girls take it?'

Helen knew which girls. 'Oh, I think it's going to be OK. They had a few moments of jealousy, but Samuel has developed a bit of a crush on Eva, and the Kittens think it's hilarious. I love that name for them, they are very catlike, aren't they? All four girls have bonded. It's scary. They're competing to see who can be most like their father. I've got to admit, the first time they joined us in the annexe, I couldn't handle it. I walked down to find Andy on the sofa with two gorgeous leggy redheads sprawled all over him. And Darlene knew exactly what she was doing – she gave me such a glare.'

'I know that glare. I get it too. They're Daddy's girls and they don't want to share.'

Helen giggled for a moment. 'You know, I was right to trust him, you lot are no threat to us. I just wish he'd told me earlier. I really think we could have been amicable about it.' She saw Diana's expression. 'Oh, I know. Perhaps not, but like I said, we're older and wiser now.' She sobered up. 'I won't tell a soul, I promise. I know how much danger you're in, it explains everything.'

'Helen, I've never really had the chance to apologise. I knew he was married. But they come as a pack, I couldn't pick and choose.'

'I know. He explained. It was his choice, not yours. It's OK now. Really. We never had a terribly conventional marriage anyway, not as long as Xan was around. Look, it's cold here, I'm going back to the annexe. I'll see you tomorrow.'

Helen cut the connection, and Diana sat, stunned. She had to get home.

Mark was still wondering how Diana's conversation with Helen had gone when John rang less than an hour later, to tell him when and where the plane was arriving.

'Take a big car – she's got all the kids with her,' he said. 'She's gone into ultra-Alpha mode. I pity anyone who gets in her way.'

Mark smiled. 'Have fun, but come back soon, we're all missing you.'

'Oh hell, it's almost stopped being fun: the girls were both pining for you, and we're all missing the kids. I reckon I've got a week left, tops, before Zoe snaps.'

Mark spent the drive to Manchester alone with his thoughts: Diana clearly felt betrayed by Helen's presence at Silverwood and blamed him. She hadn't mentioned Andy at all, which he found a little unfair. How long would she be angry for? He stopped once, pulling off the motorway and driving on back roads for a while until he found a small cafe where he determinedly stoked the fires of his increasingly fast metabolism. It was the usual Alpha withdrawal: he was burning fast, but wasn't in the slightest bit hungry. He arrived at the airport with an hour to spare, and spent most of it sitting in the car. It would be stupid to go to the arrivals lounge to meet Diana and the kids: he would be seen – the risk was too high to take. He put the seat back and tried to relax, imagining the plane getting closer, almost persuading himself that he could bring it in to a safe landing by the sheer force of his own willpower. The arrival time came, and he still sat there, his eyes closed.

He messaged Diana, to tell her where he was, with an apology for not meeting her at the barrier. He imagined her getting off the plane. He visualised her charming the stewards into helping her with the children. He sat up, and shook his head, barely remembering to lock the car door behind him in his rush to get to the arrivals lounge.

As he got to the barrier, he checked the clock: she'd still be collecting her luggage; he was there in plenty of time. He glanced at the tunnel, entirely focussed on the moment when she'd appear at last, willing her to be there.

He almost missed the moment when two small boys on long reins came charging through the doors.

One of them looked straight at him and yelled, 'Dada!' at the top of his voice.

The woman next to him laughed, and complimented him. She was saying something about him being glad to see them again, and he said something polite and noncommittal back to her. She fell silent as Diana appeared behind the boys, holding on to the reins, the baby girls slung in carriers around her. Diana was seven months pregnant and looked every day of it. She so clearly did not expect to see him at the barrier, and it was Mikey's yelling that alerted her to him. She gave him one brief, dazzling smile, then composed herself and walked up to him, offering her cheek to be kissed. She glanced at the woman, who was clearly intrigued by the two sets of twins, and said coolly, 'I'm sorry about Mikey, he calls most men Dada. Thank you for coming for me.'

Her eyes flickered to one side, and Mark took in the photographer lurking to one side of the arrivals lounge. He smiled distantly, his face a mask, and took the baby girls, carrying them to the car while Diana looked after the boys.

Mark settled the children, spending longer than he needed to making sure that they were safely buckled in, finding out that the boys had tripled their vocabulary in the three weeks they'd been away. Back in the driving seat, he looked at Diana, who had closed her eyes.

'No luggage?' he ventured.

'John and Zoe will bring it. I just wanted to get home. The kids wouldn't sleep on the plane, so I'm going to rest now.' Her meaning was clear, and he didn't say anything.

She was asleep straight away, waking once when Mark stopped at a service station to take the boys to the toilet. He brought back drinks and chicken sandwiches and sweets, which she accepted silently and devoured. Before they set out, he touched her face, dying to hold her again; they were so close, but still separated.

'Be careful,' she hissed, and his hand fell back, cheated.

As he drove through the gates of Silverwood, Diana gave a huge sigh, kissing him lightly on the lips, lingering for a moment, then drawing back regretfully.

'We'll sort the kids out, then talk,' she said.

There was no sign of Andy or his family, Seth was the first of the children to the car, opening the door for

Diana before Mark could get out, leaning in to hug her tightly.

She got out and was surrounded by the older kids. Each of them got a hug, and a few words, before she handed the baby girls to Seth and Noah, who carried them straight into the house. Mark had got the toddlers out of the car, and couldn't help grinning as they were snatched away by the teenage girls, who bore them away, making them giggle and yell. It was obvious they'd missed their younger brothers. Diana was still hugging Frank and Bill, telling them that the Betas would be home soon, and she'd give them all the news as soon as she'd caught her breath.

Frank shrugged. 'Well, tomorrow's soon enough. I expect you'll want to catch up with Mark ... and stuff?' The boy glanced from one Alpha to the other, anxious to know what was happening.

Mark acknowledged him. 'I'll be freshening up. Your mum'll know where to find me,' he said.

Caleb and Sam were standing close by, waiting for Diana to finish talking to their older brothers. Mark went to the house, stopping at the doorway to glance back. Diana was following him, her arm around Caleb, who was almost as tall as her. Sam was on her other side, grinning broadly, while the two older boys flanked them, competing to be heard.

Mark went upstairs, waiting in the bedroom, annoyed by Diana's coolness, suspicious of the time she'd spent with John and Zoe and, most of all, frustrated by the situation they were in: the web of lies that had prevented him from greeting her at the barrier as he'd wanted to. He heard light footsteps on the landing, and turned to face her as she stepped through the bedroom door. She looked at the room critically. A few weeks away gave her a fresh perspective, and Mark could have sworn she was going to start talking about redecorating. He knew he would scream if she did.

She opened her mouth then closed it again, looking at him at last, really looking at him, drinking in the sight of him as if her life depended on it. Then, at last, she was in his arms, surrendering to that Alpha kiss they'd been so desperate for. Just a kiss. Not enough to sate the mutual need, but enough to reassure their desperate bodies that they were back together again. He knew that soon he would have to leave her again. The idea of being away from her was crazy; it ran against his deepest feelings, the desires of his body, mind and soul, but he could see no way around it. He would have to return to Katie, maintain the mockery that his marriage had become.

'What are we going to do?' he asked.

'I want to run,' she said, deliberately misunderstanding.

'Yeah, later, but what are we going to do?' He nuzzled at her throat, it was so white, the skin almost translucent. He could feel the pulse of life in her artery, and rested his lips there for a second, knowing in a rush of sentiment that if that pulse ever stopped, *his* life would be over too. She was speaking, and he struggled to listen to what she was saying.

'Mark, I don't know why you're coming over all *Brief Encounter*. What do you mean? We'll do like we've always done: you'll get here when you can, and stay with Katie when you can't. Nothing has changed.'

'Everything has changed,' he murmured, licking delicately at her earlobe, wondering why he'd never noticed before that it was the most perfect shape possible.

She shivered in his arms, but drew away almost forcibly, looking into his eyes. He knew that she was starved for him, but she spoke steadily, sensibly, telling him she felt the same about him as she always had, that although she understood he loved her, she was worried his feelings would compromise their safety. He wasn't surprised by anything she said; it was Diana, she was supremely sensible, and he loved her for it. He needed that reassurance though, more so than ever, and he asked her again if she loved him.

She kissed him before she replied, and left him in no doubt about her feelings. He accepted it – it was there, between them. Before he could relax, he had to get something out in the open, something that had bothered him for months, something that had been triggered again by the sight of Caleb and Sam waiting patiently for Diana's attention while she spoke to Frank and Bill.

He started to pace the room, trying to get his thoughts in some sort of order.

'You don't realise how much I've figured out, over the last few months. I know why you favour Frank and Bill, and Susie and Nancy. It's not just because they're John's, is it?'

She flushed, and protested that she didn't have favourites.

Mark held his hand up, shushing her gently. He smiled, telling her that he wasn't judging or complaining. He desperately needed to make up for the lost years, and this needed to be said. 'John loved you, heart and soul, when you made them together. You know that, and you treat them differently. Could you try to imagine, now, that I felt the same when we made our babies? Because I wish I could do it all again, and be your man, not just your Alpha.' He paused. 'I was beginning to love you, truly, when we made these two…'

For a split second, as he caressed her, his mind drifted back to those few stolen minutes in a drab thicket of trees, the sounds of passing cars rising and falling, a flash of halogen headlamps briefly illuminating her face as he'd undressed her and fucked her, still believing that was all she needed from him, an Alpha fix. He'd known, even then, that things were changing, that he was allowing things to change. He played the scene again and again. It had left both of them scratched and bruised, and he couldn't remember a single moment of tenderness between them, just a blind need fulfilled.

She was speaking again. 'Mark, these two might not be yours. I didn't realise, with the fight and the arguments and … and they might be John's.'

Mark stilled. He'd known she'd gone back to Silverwood; he'd known she'd needed comfort, and it was obvious she would go to John – he'd always been there for her. He found that he didn't care, he loved her, she was his Alpha, her babies, as always, were his. She was looking at him anxiously, and he realised that she was waiting for his reaction, wondering if his new feelings for her would translate into a new possessiveness, a new jealousy. He was amused by the idea. She was their Alpha, that would never change. He kissed her again, finding something gorgeously new when their lips met, almost hidden by the increasingly insistent Alpha rush, but it was there: a new tenderness he realised was a direct response to the way he was touching her.

She was a new world for him to explore, but he had all the maps in his head, every curve and shadow was subtly changed by the way he felt about her now, and at last, his whispered declarations of adoration were answered, and they wrapped themselves around each other in the darkness of their bed.

He woke up, her hair in his face, and her legs entangled in his. The curtains were open, and a river of sunlight crossed the bed and bathed them. For a moment, he felt perfectly at peace with the world. The kids were awake; he could hear noises from downstairs. He looked at her again, and she was awake, grinning wickedly, already reaching for him.

His phone rang. He leaned out of bed and fished it out of his pocket, and peered at the number. 'It's Katie,' he said. 'I can't deal with this.'

'You can do anything,' Diana stated, with absolute certainty. 'Sort it.'

He went into the bathroom and answered the phone.

'Where are you?' his wife spat.

'Silverwood. You know that.'

'The bitch is supposed to be in Canada. Why is she back?'

Mark blinked, then recovered. 'She came back yesterday … something came up here.'

'I bet it did. You know damn well our deal does not include you being seen in public with her.'

Mark fought to stay calm. 'I had to pick her up from the airport. I couldn't expect her to manage four babies by herself. Not in her condition.' He heard Katie suck in her breath. He'd hit the target, and was instantly ashamed.

'Look, I'm coming home today. I'd planned to do that even if you hadn't found out that Diana was home. Who told you?'

'The same person who told several million other people. It's in the newspaper,' Katie spat.

Mark shook his head. 'Which one? Katie, believe me, we were very careful, nobody could read anything into me picking her up.'

'You should have told me. It's humiliating to be asked where my husband is, and then to be told that he's with someone else. Do you get that? Do you have the slightest idea what you're doing to me? You could, at least, have told me!'

The Alpha was silent, then he switched the call to video. 'Katie, turn the vid on,' he said quietly. He waited a moment, then the screen lit up, and he saw Katie's face, streaked with tears.

'I'm coming home, we'll sort it out. I understand our agreement, and I don't want to hurt you. Where can I find this article?'

Katie told him, and he said goodbye, taking the article through to Diana. He watched as she read it carefully.

> *Family man and ex-Hearts guitarist Mark Preston shows his caring side by picking up an unknown pregnant woman and several dark-haired children from the airport. The mystery*

> *redhead, who is believed to be in her early forties, had been holidaying with Mr and Mrs John Preston after their recent marriage. When this reporter rang Dr Kate Preston for comment, she was unaware of her husband's whereabouts, and assured us that he was staying with friends.*

Diana shrugged. 'We did our best. I'll talk to her.'

Mark glanced at her, half frowning. 'You will? You've never done that before.'

'You didn't love me before. Things have changed.' She smiled sadly. 'I won't hurt her, don't worry about that.'

Mark was gloomy. 'She says she won't be publicly humiliated. What do we do?'

'I'll sort it.' Diana repeated, and picked up Mark's phone. It was answered immediately.

Katie's eyes opened wide for a second, but she composed herself quickly.

'Katie,' Diana said.

Katie scowled out from the small screen. 'You're not due back for a week. What are you playing at?'

'I changed my plans. I'm allowed to do that. Look, he's on his way back. We can sort this out, if you'll co-operate.'

'Why the fuck should I co-operate?' Katie hissed.

'Because if my pack is exposed, it will affect your sons. I assume that's sufficient reason?'

Katie shook her head. 'I'll make sure my boys are protected.'

Diana shook her head. 'If you're going to take that attitude, I have to tell you that I'll do everything in my power to make sure they're exposed to the same media attention as my own kids. If you blow the lid off this thing, you won't get away unscathed.'

'How dare you threaten me!' Katie gasped.

'I'm not making threats, I'm making sure that you understand the situation. It suits us both to share Mark, and to hide his relationship with me. This is not irretrievable, but I'll have to talk to John to explain what's going on. We need to make it look like I'm a close friend of the family, and that you know me, and trust me.'

'I'd win an Oscar for that performance,' spat Katie.

'Me too.'

Diana's voice was dangerously sweet, and Mark winced. He listened as the women made their arrangements, and looked at Diana as she hung up. He smiled weakly. 'It's a good job you two aren't friends, together you'd be dangerous.'

'Fuck, yeah. She's not the first person I would have chosen as an enemy. I admire her a lot, you know?'

'Me too.' Mark smiled wistfully. 'You're lucky, you've got me, John and Andy without any complications.'

The look she gave him was half amused, half exasperated, and she invited him to share his definition of 'complicated' with her. She was already on the phone, briefing John and Zoe. Mark rang Katie again, telling her where and when to meet them.

The Alphas spent the morning at home, Diana taking ten minutes to go to the annexe and have a cuppa with a very cautious Andy and Helen. She was quiet when she returned to the house. Mark asked her if she was OK, and she shrugged.

'It's happened, I've got to accept it. She seems OK. So long as she stays away from the main house, I'm cool. They've agreed to help us with Katie.'

It was a quiet morning: the Alphas did nothing but sit in the big family room together, sharing a comfortable sofa. The children all found their way to them as the morning went by, and a peaceful calm settled over the house. Eventually Diana stood and held out her hand to Mark, hauling him to his feet.

'Let's do this,' she said, sighing.

She looked at her clothes, deciding that they were sufficiently neutral and dowdy, then let Mark lead her to the car. They stopped off at a busy cafe, waiting until Mark had been recognised and the grapevine had been given time to work. When they left, they had two journalists tailing them.

Katie met them in another cafe, this time in the middle of Manchester. She embraced Diana and gave her a carefully gift-wrapped package, saying something loudly about presents for John's children. Diana smiled her thanks, and left. Mark didn't watch as she got into a taxi.

Katie got up to leave, and Mark took her hand and guided her back to the table. 'Stay for a while. We'll have something to eat.' He saw his reflection in the window, and was surprised at how calm he seemed. They ordered a meal, and made conversation.

At some point, as Mark had predicted, a young woman sat down nervously at the table next to them, then leaned over.

'You're Mark Preston, right? Could I ask you a few questions?'

Mark raised an eyebrow. 'Well, if you have to,' he drawled.

'There's been some talk that you're having an affair.' The newshound didn't look at Katie.

Mark laughed and turned to Katie. 'Have you been starting rumours?' he asked.

Katie shrugged. 'You should keep me informed! This is all because you went to collect Diana yesterday, someone saw you, and jumped to the wrong conclusion.'

Mark allowed himself to appear distressed. 'Look, the lady in question doesn't like to be talked about. She's got nothing to do with the band; she's a family friend.'

The young woman nodded. 'And the friends your wife thought you were staying with?'

Mark took satisfaction in outstaring her, then relented. 'Andy Ransome and his wife. Andy and I are producing an album together for the Puce Punk Quartet, so I stayed with him for a few days. Oh gosh, Diana stayed at the Ransomes' last night too. Is that too shocking to deal with? What do you think? Any more questions?'

The girl checked her recording equipment. 'Whose are the children?' she asked.

Mark's face was stony. 'You're pushing it too far. If you must know, the babies are John and Zoe's, the older ones are Diana's. Goodbye.' He returned his attention to Katie, who had stood and was reaching for her coat. Mark picked it up and helped her to put it on.

Back home, he rang John and Zoe, telling them about the developments.

Zoe nodded. 'I've been expecting this. They're bloody jackals, the lot of them. Is Andy singing the right tune?'

Mark confirmed that he was.

Zoe thought hard for a moment, then made her mind up. 'I'll handle this one, Mark. I think things have gone too far to expect it to be dropped. I'll make a firebreak, to separate you from Diana. That's all we need, isn't it?'

'Yeah. Katie handled things OK this afternoon, but she's not happy.' Mark knew that his voice was weary.

'OK, leave it to me. You've got enough on your plate. We'll be home in a week.' Zoe grinned, her eyes wide. 'And then you'll have even more on your plate, wolf boy.'

'I'll take that as a promise,' Mark replied, summoning a smile for her. He rang Andy next. 'Do whatever Zoe advises,' he said. 'And ask Diana to ring me as soon as she gets home.'

All was quiet that night. At eight, Mark sent Matt and Jake to bed, and went to the phone. He rang Silverwood. Seth answered, he was obviously worried. Diana wasn't home yet, and hadn't rung. The kids were alone in the house, and getting restless. Mark spoke to Andy, asking him to spend the night in the house rather than the annexe.

'Andy, there's no way I can come back tonight, Katie would hit the roof. Have you any idea where Diana could be?'

'I've already rung Duncan and Laura – they've not seen her or heard from her. I can't think of anyone else that she would go to. Is she upset?'

Mark lowered his voice. 'Andy, I'm having a hard time dealing with this. We should all be together, not scattered around the planet. Diana feels the same way. When she gets home, do whatever it takes to cheer her up.'

Andy's eyes widened. 'Mark, Helen is *here*,'

'And Diana is your Alpha, and she needs you,' said Mark. 'Ask her to call me the minute you hear from her.' He put the phone down, and went to sit with Katie, getting more agitated with each passing hour, until eventually she went to bed alone. He sat up, waiting with increasing panic for the phone to ring.

By dawn, he was sure that it was over. That Diana was dead or dying, that there had been some awful accident. Katie came down with the boys to find him hollow-eyed and frantic. For the first time, she was unsure of how to deal with him, but settled for making him breakfast, which remained untouched.

Mark rang Silverwood, where the mood matched his own. Andy had sent the older kids to school and college in taxis, figuring that it would be a distraction for them.

The day passed horribly slowly. Mark rang the hospitals, and scoured the news, but could find nothing. He had no energy; he could barely stand. Mid afternoon a taxi drew up, and he jumped to his feet, but it was just Jake and Matt home from school. Whey-faced, he made a meal for them, going through the motions before sinking back on to the sofa.

At last the phone rang. Andy's voice was joyful. 'She's home. She's wolf, and she's worn out and footsore, but she's home. She's in a sulk, that's all. The main thing is that she's safe.'

A sulk? Mark fled to the bedroom. How could she do that? How could she disappear for so long, make him believe that she was dead? He wanted desperately to go to her, to Change and lie beside her, run with her. But Jake was at the door, looking at him curiously.

'Are you back for a few days?' he was asking. There was a carefully concealed hurt about the boy that Mark recognised instantly.

He beckoned to his son, and when he was close enough, wrapped him in a hug. 'This is where I live, isn't it?' he said.

'Are you going to leave?' Jake asked again.

Mark took a deep breath. 'I don't know. If I do, will you come with me?'

Jake shook his head. 'I like it here. But you'll be able to visit, won't you?'

Mark shuddered. 'I've had enough of "visiting".' He hugged Jake again. 'Don't start buying spare toothbrushes yet – I'll be here for a long time. I'll tell you if I ever have to go.'

Katie came home. She asked him in a neutral voice if there'd been any word, and nodded when he said that Diana was home safely. She went to shower and change, and left a tabloid newspaper on the table in front of him.

'Page seven,' she said.

Mark read it aloud. 'Hearts front man reveals secret love triangle.' He blinked and read the story: three hundred words where John told the world of his long relationship with Diana, their frequent break-ups, her relationship with Zoe, and how Diana had introduced him to her girlfriend, who was now his wife.

> *"Basically, we're all dead happy together, we have been for ages. Nobody's getting hurt, so I don't know what all the fuss is about. I'd have married Diana years ago if she'd agreed, but she didn't. Anyway, we'd appreciate it if everyone let her be — she's a very private person."*

Further along in the article, John mocked the idea of Diana and Mark being together.

> *"Credit her with some taste!" he'd laughed. "No, she's like everyone else who knows me: she puts up with Mark because I love him to bits. He's hard work, you know?"*

Mark put the paper down, smiling. John wouldn't mind a bit if the entire world knew that he was living with two women. He rang Silverwood. Darlene answered.

'Dad, will you, please, come home! Mum is *still* wolfie, and nobody can get through to her. She's just wandering around whining, and it's getting very annoying. And those poor babies have nobody to nurse them, and Miranda's at her wits' end trying to get them to take formula!'

He pushed his hair back. 'Darlene, if I could come home, I'd be there now, and we wouldn't have a problem.

I have to stay here for a few more days, at least. I know your mother is upset, I'm not doing too well myself, but we've just got to ride it out. My wife is at the end of her rope, and if I come home now she'll snap.' He chewed on his lip. 'I'll get John and Zoe home, and you make sure the lads do their share of looking after the babies. If necessary, get Andy to tell them. That includes Bill and Frank. Make sure your mum gets plenty to eat, and sleeps somewhere warm and dry – she's still pregnant, even if she's wolf. Other than that, I can't help. I'm sorry. Look, can I speak to Andy?'

She barely hid her scowl. 'I'll get him,' she said.

Andy came to the phone. 'I saw the paper – Zoe's a good 'un. I've had a few calls, and I just played innocent, said I thought that all John's mates knew about Diana. Mark, I've never seen her like this. What the fuck is wrong?'

Mark shook his head. 'More lies, she's sick of them. She wants me at Silverwood. I want to be there, but Katie's in control. The worst part is that I have to pretend I want to be here.'

Andy glanced behind him. 'Look, we've got our own PR queen in-house; someday this whole thing is going to blow sky-high anyway. We should be plotting the angles right now, not hiding away and hoping that it'll never happen. There's too much that we can't control. Duncan's pack is growing fast, and they've got living relatives who are going to talk about their grandkids. We've got more carrier-born teenagers turning up every year, and they're already asking me to put them in touch with each other – in four or five years there'll be another half-dozen nascent packs, minimum. We need to start planning ahead.'

Mark growled. 'We need to get Diana up on two legs. How long can she stay wolf?'

Andy rubbed at the back of his neck. 'I don't know. She's OK as she is, for now, although Helen is getting extremely pissed off. If I don't get some help around here soon…'

'John has to come back, simple as that. He'll sort Diana out. Is there anything I can help with? Bearing in mind that Katie is on a knife-edge.'

Andy shook his head. 'Just speak to the kids as much as you can. They're not happy. Yesterday morning they had their Alphas at home with them, and tonight you're miles away and Diana's a wolf.'

Mark nodded. 'OK, put Seth on, he needs to know that it's the situation that's pissing us off, not each other. Keep an eye on Miranda too, she'll try to take over, and end up making herself ill. I'll speak to you tomorrow.'

He spoke to Seth, grateful for his eldest son's pragmatic common sense. The boy looked cool and contained.

'Dad, how long do you think we'll have to manage like this?' he asked. There was no reproach there; Seth was gathering information.

Mark smiled his approval. 'John and Zoe will be back soon. I don't know how long your mother will sulk for, but I promise you that she's not angry with me. Things are better between us than they've ever been. The problem is, I can't be with you for at least a week. I want you all to carry on going to school, leave the little kids to Andy.' He managed to smile. 'Seth, this isn't your problem, it's mine, I will deal with it. It won't hurt your mother to be wolf for a day or two, it might be good for her after being away from home for so long. Andy is your dad too, and you're safe with him. If there's a real emergency, I will come straight away.'

He realised that Seth wasn't looking at his face, and he glanced over his shoulder. Jake was standing in the doorway, looking at the screen. He came closer, looking at Seth with interest. 'Hiya,' he said.

Seth's eyes flickered to Mark, then to Jake. 'Hiya, squirt. What's your name?'

'Jake. I know who you are.'

Seth smiled. 'Tell me then.'

'You're my brother,' Jake said, glancing at Mark nervously. 'I don't know your name.'

'It's Seth. Pleased to meet you.'

Mark broke in. 'This is lovely, but I'm sure Seth has homework to do.' He winked at his eldest son, then said goodbye and broke the connection. 'You're a nosy wretch,' he observed, taking Jake's hand and pulling him closer. 'What do you think of your brother?'

Jake shrugged. 'Dunno. Are you and Mum fighting again?'

'No, the fighting's stopped – we've got a truce.' He relaxed, realising that he'd managed to convince himself that things would be OK. 'Come on, kid, we'll cook tea for Mum and Matt.'

By the end of the third day, Mark was getting anxious. John and Zoe were on their way home, having decided not to cut short their holiday; in light of the current press interest in them, any unusual move would be suspicious.

They flew back on time, and went straight back to Silverwood.

Mark shut himself into the spare room with a phone. Andy spoke to him briefly; he was pale and had lost weight. For the first time since the attack on the pack, he looked anxious.

'Mark, something's got to give here. She's wandering off, she has no interest in any of us unless we go wolf. Caleb's heartbroken because she just sniffs him and walks away, and the little ones are upset. We need her back. The only good thing is that we're managing to bottle-feed the tinies.'

Mark smiled wanly. 'If John can't sort it, I'll come home, but I can't speak for Katie's actions – she's still fuming about the airport incident. Look, you go, get Cal. I'll talk to him.'

He spent an hour chatting to Cal, teasing and listening in equal measure, earning a smile from him eventually. They were interrupted by Miranda, who rushed in, a huge grin on her face.

'Mum's back. John and Zoe got home and went wolfie straight away. They've all been in the woods. They've brought her back. She's crying but she's OK.' Her lip trembled, and she burst into tears.

Mark stood up, helpless. 'Miranda…' he whispered, but Caleb was holding her, looking back at the screen.

'I'll look after her. I'll send someone to talk to you,' he said, looking much older than his years.

'If Sam doesn't mind, ask him to come for a chat, OK?'

Caleb grinned, and Mark hurriedly used his other phone to call Andy.

'She's back!' yelled the Third.

Mark nodded impatiently. 'I'll talk to her as soon as she's ready. Make sure she knows that I'm here all night for her, will you? Oh, gotta go, Sam's here.'

Sam's face came on the video screen. He wanted to talk about old Hearts albums; he was taking more of an interest in the band than any of the other kids but Miranda. Mark found himself talking guitar with the kid, almost forgetting himself as he got carried away with enthusiasm. Sammy told him that Caleb was interested in guitars too, but was too shy to talk about it. Mark fell silent for a moment, and Sam looked anxious, worried that he'd said the wrong thing.

Eventually Mark spoke again. 'Sam, which guitar do you use?'

'One of the practice ones in the music room. Mum says if we touch your stage guitars she'll cut our hands off.'

They shared a smile, then Mark said, 'Yeah. Look, Sam, if you go down the basement, to the workshop, there's an old guitar there that I've been working on. I've finished staining it, and it's ready for restringing. Andy or John can show you how to do that…'

'I can do that,' Sam said a little indignantly.

Mark beamed at him. 'That's my boy. Anyway, it's yours, and Cal's of course.'

Sam blinked. 'Honest? That was your first guitar Dad! It was on the front cover of your first album!'

'Ah, it's just a cheap guitar. I was only a year older than you when I got it – it's seen some heavy action in its time. I'll get you both something much better for Christmas. Hell, the practice guitars are better than that old thing.'

Sam was grinning from ear to ear. 'I don't care, it's a real stage guitar. Wait until I tell my friends…' he tailed off. 'I can't, can I?'

Mark shook his head. 'No, you can't. One day, maybe, but not yet.' He felt an old grief become real and immediate. Sam must have seen something in his face, because the boy looked troubled. Mark was about to reassure him when he saw the door open behind Sam, and a pale, thin figure walk in.

Diana bent to kiss Sam on the forehead, then dismissed him.

'Thanks, Dad,' the boy said as he left.

Diana sat down, looking hungrily at Mark. 'I'm so sorry,' she said quietly. 'That was unforgivable of me.'

'I reckon I owe you a lot of forgiveness,' he replied. 'Welcome back. You look awful, by the way.'

'Yeah, I feel like shit. Andy's been a lifesaver, I would have been over the hills and far away but for him. It all hit me at once, you know? This is so much crap.' She swallowed hard. 'I dreamed about killing Katie, you know.' She shuddered. 'I dreamed about Joyce. I dreamed about the fights. I just wanted to get away from the pack, to find you and take you away with me, far away, and never be human again. I would have left the kids and our mates without a thought.'

Mark reached out, forgetting for a minute that she was just an image on a screen. 'I don't believe that,' he said gently.

She pushed her hair back, then folded her arms on the table and put her head down. He waited. When she straightened again, she was more composed. 'No, my love, you're right.'

He glanced behind him, aware of Jake's curiosity. The door was firmly shut. He kept his voice low. 'I would have gone with you, you know. If that was what you really wanted.'

They looked into each other's eyes for a full minute, then she grinned. 'I can see it now, two lovesick middle-aged wolves prowling around the barnyards and allotments of Lancashire, on the run from the law like a furry version of Thelma and Louise.'

'Butch and Sundance,' Mark said soberly. 'I can't see myself as Thelma or Louise.'

'So you think I'd make a good Sundance?' she shot back. 'I thought you loved me?'

'Oh, I do,' he said fervently. They were quiet again, then both spoke at once. She waved her hand, and he continued. 'It'll be another fortnight, before I can see you again. Katie's got my days and evenings planned out, social events galore. It's her way of pointing out to the world that we're a couple. There's no way I'll be able to spend more than a day with you for a long time.'

'I've survived worse.' She looked bleak for a moment, then summoned a smile. 'I'm sorry, I really am. I must have put you through hell when I went missing. I got out of the taxi somewhere on the moors, paid the guy, and wandered off. I just remember being miserable. I hope I buried my clothes somewhere out of the way, that's all. It's all a bit of a blur really.'

'It's done now.' Mark shrugged. 'Where do we go from here?'

'Keep our heads down, as usual,' she said.

'No! I've had enough of it. Things are going to change, but we can talk about that later. By the way, you're officially John's concubine, or mistress or something. You'd better speak to him or read the papers.' He mustered a smile as she raised an eyebrow in surprise. 'We had to tell the press something, so you're his long-term squeeze. It was a good story because, just as we went public with it, some lass from John's past went to the press with a story about having recognised you from years ago, when you went to parties with him.'

Diana sighed. 'OK. Anything else I need to know? How many kids do we have?'

'That's undetermined. Zoe's threatened to bring down the sky on anyone who investigates your private life, but it's still a good thing that you registered the kids in different districts. Useful lies.'

For the first time the anxiety fell away completely. 'When will I see you?' Her tone was wistful.

'In two weeks. It's a Wednesday night, I'll be there at teatime, and back here the next day. Katie has it all worked out. She says that I start to look too ill to be presentable after three weeks. Thank God for the Alpha withdrawal, eh?'

'Does she know?' Diana's voice was quiet.

Mark paused. 'She knows that things have changed. She thinks it's because you're pregnant again, which, by the way, she is extremely pissed off about.'

Diana dismissed Katie's feelings on that matter with a gesture. 'Keep her sweet, OK?'

'I am doing.' He frowned. 'She's not some ogre, you know? She's not hard to live with, and this isn't her fault.'

His Alpha sighed. 'I know, it's all my fault. I know now you would have left her, right at the start, if I'd asked you to. But, at first, I didn't have enough faith in our relationship, and by the time I was sure that we couldn't be separated, I'd realised that I needed to stay out of the limelight. She's right to hate me, I used her.'

Mark shook his head. 'Don't blame yourself. I was the one lying to her for God knows how long – I could have refused to go along with it. I stayed with her because I wanted to, not because it was convenient for you.'

'I know,' his mate answered. 'I do know that.' She looked at him, her eyes suspiciously bright. 'And now I know that you want me, and that you're with her for *her* convenience. Fuck, this is her revenge, isn't it?'

He moved closer to the screen. 'No, it's not. She doesn't know how I feel about you, I swear it. I can hide that as long as I have to.'

'Where is she now?' Diana blurted out.

'Downstairs. She's doing a dinner party for some people from work. I've got ten minutes before I have to make myself presentable.'

She stood up. 'We'll talk tomorrow. Will you give Miranda those ten minutes, she's fretting about us? I'll take you through to her room.' She smiled, and was gone.

He waited for a few seconds, then the screen changed to a wall filled with pictures of Xan. The angle changed again, and he saw his eldest daughter peering at the screen.

'Dad! Mum's OK!'

'So I see. How are you, hon?'

'OK. I've just been saying goodbye to Helen, she's taking the girls home.'

'That's sweet of you.' He smiled.

'I was wondering … if I could go to visit her sometime?'

'If your mother and Zoe are OK with it, yeah, sure, it's all right with me. But I want Andy with you if you do, OK?'

She was playing with her hair. 'Dad, have you and Mum made up?'

'We didn't fall out,' he said firmly, then changed the subject. 'How are John and Zoe?'

'I've not seen much of them. They were holed up with Mum, then Zoe sent for the babies, and I think they're asleep.' She must have seen his anxiety, because she grinned. 'Dad, it's OK. Mum's back, she can run the pack blindfold.'

'She can, can't she.' He shook his head. 'I've got to go. Are you OK, honey?'

'Me? I'm good. Are you and Mum really all right?'

'Really truly, I'm her number one fan.' He grinned. 'But don't tell her that, or she'll get big-headed.'

'Oh yeah, and she's ever so humble as it is!' Miranda waved at him. 'Bye, Dad.' And the screen went dead.

Mark went downstairs. Katie was in the kitchen, putting the last touches to the dessert. She looked at him.

'Everything all right? Do you have to go?'

He could have sworn there was a touch of sympathy there; it confused him. Nothing was ever clear-cut. 'Diana's fine now, I knew she would be as soon as John got back.'

Katie was more relaxed than he'd seen her for ages. She kissed him on the cheek. 'I thought she would be. He's the right one for her, it's a shame she didn't see that at the beginning. Now, give me a hand with these vegetables, our guests will be here in an hour.'

Chapter 32

He found the next two months bizarre. He seemed to be moving in a dreamworld, where everything was exactly as it had been for years, where Katie was warm and friendly to him on the surface but made it quite clear what the situation was if he tried to get too close to her. Their sex life faded away. She was drawing away from any need of him she might once have had, betraying her grief and loss only occasionally. Whenever that happened, he held her and assured her that he loved her, that she was beautiful and desirable and that he only wanted things to be good again between them. He was sickened by himself, partly because it was half true, and partly because he couldn't bear the thought of causing her so much pain.

After one particularly harrowing night, when she'd accused him of making her life a lie, he shaved off his hair in a fit of self-loathing. Oddly, it seemed to please her, but Diana stared at him as if he'd grown an extra head. After a Change, it was back to its usual length. Diana muttered something about self-image, and reminded him that Zoe had been bleaching her hair for her adult entire life. Without thinking about it, he went home without cutting his hair again, and Katie freaked out completely. It was the first time since his initial confession that she'd been confronted with blatant evidence of his Shifter-self. She was almost hysterical, and wouldn't calm down until he'd cut his hair again. He let it grow back slowly, finding himself having to note his hair length before each Change and cut it back to that length afterwards.

Jake settled again, and Mark watched him carefully, knowing that while he was ready to leave Katie, he didn't want to lose his sons. He spent as much time as he could with Jake and Matt.

The call that demanded his presence at Silverwood came early in the morning, as expected. Diana usually gave birth at dawn, and he'd been waking early every day, expecting her summons. Katie had been sweet, and hadn't complained when he rolled out of bed. She offered to pack an overnight bag, and he almost pointed out that Silverwood was his home too and that he had everything he needed there. Just in time, he accepted her gesture and waited patiently while she packed underwear and T-shirts and toiletries for him.

It didn't delay him for long, and Diana was still walking around when he arrived. She was wearing an ancient green sweater that John had bought for her years ago. When he saw her, she was leaning forwards against a kitchen chair, breathing deeply. Zoe was fussing, and Mark saw that Diana was getting pissed off. He asked Zoe to leave. The Beta glanced at Diana, who nodded and smiled grimly.

'Are you ready?' Mark asked, trying to keep the excitement from his voice.

'Mark, something's wrong, it hurts,' Diana whispered.

He nodded and started to rub at her back, stopping when she growled at him.

'I don't mean it hurts, I mean it *fucking hurts!*'

He looked at her carefully. 'What's wrong?'

'I don't know,' she spat.

'I'm taking you to the hospital.'

'I'm not going anywhere,' she hissed. 'I didn't tell Zoe because I thought she'd do exactly what you are doing. Mark, I'm staying here, I'm just telling you that something is very, very wrong. If it goes wrong in the hospital, they'll want to do tests, and I can't risk that.'

He was still. 'What do you want me to do?' he said eventually.

'Stay with me, keep Zoe and the others away. Get the Bees to help you – they've not seen a birth yet, and they won't know that there's anything different about this one. Get John to distract Seth and Miranda – they know me better than any of the other kids, and will pick up on this and panic.' She looked at him. 'Mark, don't go away and, whatever happens, don't let anyone take me away from Silverwood.'

He found a chair, and his voice. 'It's serious?' he whispered.

'It's never been this bad before. I don't know if I can deliver them safely. I've never been scared before.' She winced, and what little colour there was drained from her face. 'They're coming.'

He carried her up to the bedroom, summoning Bridget and Beatrice and instructing them to bring him a steady supply of towels and hot water to bathe and soothe Diana.

Andy arrived after an hour, walking into the room and expressing merry surprise that he wasn't too late. He fled under a torrent of abuse from Mark, chastened.

Mark turned to Diana anxiously, and found that she was giggling. 'I've never heard you speak to Andy like that before,' she managed to say, before another contraction took her away from him.

He decided to intervene, feeling inside her and finding the problem: a tangle of arms and heads. Something inside Diana was bleeding, which had the positive effect of providing lubrication. He concentrated and identified which arms and heads belonged together, telling Diana that these twins were fighting even before they were born. He gently pushed back on one tiny pair of shoulders, then put his finger and thumb around the second head, and pulled gently.

'There's a lot of room in here,' he murmured.

'I'm working on it,' Diana answered wearily, and he snapped his head up, realising that she was using her Shapeshifting powers as much she could. Blood flooded out in a sudden rush, soaking the towel that he had underneath her. He changed it calmly for a fresh one, and Bridget came forwards again and washed Diana's face.

Diana registered her daughter's troubled expression, and managed to smile. 'It's not usually this bad, sweetie. Don't let this put you off having babies of your own. These twins are going to be trouble from the start, that's all.'

'Here we go,' muttered Mark. 'Push now.'

The second twin arrived within seconds of the first. Diana moaned as the afterbirth came out much too quickly and with far too much blood. Mark quickly cleared the babies' airways, and grinned in satisfaction as they took their first breaths simultaneously, unleashing twin yells that brought the other pack parents rushing into the room.

Mark passed the babies to John without further ado, and concentrated on Diana, who was still bleeding heavily. He looked at her. 'Hospital,' he said decisively.

'No,' she said firmly. 'I'll be fine, the pain's stopped. It was bad, but I'm healing already, I can feel it. Give me a minute or two.' She tried to stand up, and he helped her to the bed.

'Rest!' He took the babies from John and passed them to her, looking at them for the first time. 'Girls, redheads!' he cried, and she laughed at him, at his obvious delight. 'Faith and Joy, my daughters,' he said firmly.

She looked at him curiously; he'd never been so quick to name the children before, but she liked the names, and lay quietly and happily, encouraging them to nurse. Zoe was anxious, looking at the bloodied sheets and towels, and Diana was speaking reassuringly to her. Mark stood to one side for a while, watching with a huge grin as their packmates fussed over Diana and the new babies. At last, he caught John's eye, and his cousin moved aside to let him sit by Diana. He took her hand and kissed it.

She bit at her lip. 'Mark, I think this is it. I'm forty-five, I've been pregnant thirteen times. This last time was hard. It's enough. I'm sorry.' She closed her eyes. 'Zoe's only thirty-seven, if you ask her—'

Mark interrupted. 'No. If you're done, so am I. John and Zoe can grow the pack now. Thank you for these girls. Now rest, I'll be here when you wake up.'

Andy came back. He'd been shopping, and brought lots of sweet treats for Diana. 'Helen's here,' he told her. 'She's waiting in the car.'

'Let her come in. She's not pack, but she is family,' Diana told him.

Mark frowned, but kept his peace. He suspected that Helen had been the one to buy the chocolates, and that was confirmed when she arrived with flowers. She cooed at the babies, and Diana observed her taking a damn good look at them.

'Mark's babies, this pair,' Diana said.

They settled down again, wary but prepared. Another year came to an end. Then, six months after the wedding, their world changed forever.

Chapter 33

A normal enough day. John had been away for a few days on business; he wanted to put out a solo album, and was checking his contacts to try and gauge the mood of the market. He'd just got home, and was asleep on a sofa, recovering from his late nights. Andy had dropped by for the afternoon and been ambushed by Frank and Bill, who wanted a quick guitar lesson, then by the Kittens, who wanted to know if he could be at their sports day. He explained once again why he couldn't do that.

Mid afternoon Mark rang. 'Turn the TV on.'

Diana put a news channel on: a famous actor was on a podium, addressing a crowd of journalists.

'And it seems that she just changed into a wolf – we don't understand how or why…'

'Who?' Diana asked.

'Her fucking stepdaughter!' Mark replied, half giggling.

Diana found herself fighting the same overwhelming desire to laugh. 'OK, that's it. Plan A goes, now. Oh, Zoe, get in touch with that actor, say something supportive and positive without letting her know who we are. I'll ask Duncan to contact her tomorrow. Andy, be a love and ring all the baby Packs, tell them tonight's the night.' She booked a function room for that night, rang around the genetics labs of all the major universities, and rang the press. Her presentation was ready at all times; she updated it several times a month.

Zoe drove into town for a haircut, and rang her publicist. The guys booked a different function room, and crashed every Hearts forum they knew of, publicising a livestreamed gig in Manchester later that night.

Mark had a long and difficult conversation with Katie. The kids moved to the annexe, and practised their fighting skills. The pack hoped it wouldn't come to that, but knew they were better safe than sorry.

Diana made her way into the function room. It was packed. She estimated about thirty scientists, all looking very sceptical. The rest were press. She took the podium and started her presentation.

'I'm here to present my findings on the genetic basis for Shapeshifting.'

There was a mild uproar. She stared them down.

'Before I start the presentation, I have to say this. I'm not a doctor, or a professor. I have a BSc, and have been researching this alone for years. I worked as a research assistant before that. None of this work is peer-reviewed, for what should be obvious reasons, but my notes have been made available to several different research groups as of 8 pm tonight. Any business interests here should be aware that my family has taken out protective patents on my research, and linked lines of enquiry. We will be working closely with Nathaniel Ransome of Ransome Industries on this. That means our abilities are not available for exploitation by anyone but ourselves. I am a Shapeshifter, I speak of what I know.'

She continued with the presentation: two hours of complex genetics. Many of the reporters were from science journals, and followed it. Some needed the ten-minute precis at the end. Many of the questions were not genetics-related, and were more social in nature.

At about that time, phones in the audience started to vibrate. Zoe was doing her job. And the men were doing theirs.

A science journalist from the *Guardian* stood up. 'You might be aware that another Shapeshifter gave a press conference earlier. Do you know Zoe Preston?'

Diana smiled and looked at the door to the function room. Zoe was making a grand entrance, looking stunning. The women nodded to each other.

'Gentlemen, ladies. This is Zoe, my packmate for the last eight years. She will be taking questions now.' The room was in an uproar. Phones were ringing everywhere.

'Zoe! Your husband is John Preston of the Ransomed Hearts. Is there any link between tonight's announcement and their decision to play a gig for fans here in Manchester tonight?'

They couldn't have managed it better. Diana smiled and switched on the display screen, which had a live feed from the gig.

The guys were magnificent on stage, and clearly had the handpicked audience in their pockets. In line with their plans, they stopped and made their timed announcement. Andy went into full motormouth mode, and made his views on anyone who didn't support full werewolf rights quite clear.

John took the stage, he was glowing, energised. The crowd screamed.

'This is our new song, for the woman who has been our life for the last eighteen years. It's called "Red Girl" and it's a loud one.'

Diana was caught off guard. Zoe was in on it, and was smiling. The reporters were going barmy. Zoe turned off the lights, and let the music speak.

Diana was in tears. Zoe guided her out through the back door, where a hired security team escorted them back to Zoe's car.

Back at the function room, three short videos were screening. Diana hadn't watched them beforehand, but had insisted they be recorded months ago, when they were making plans. Zoe had made copies, and put them on a mobile DVD player for Diana to watch.

Andy first, Helen sitting next to him, looking cool. 'I'm Andy, you probably know that … well, if you're watching this, everything has gone sky-high, hasn't it? This is the truth, at last. Helen and I are still together, the pack is part of our lives, and I love my children and my packmates. But my first loyalty is to my wife, who has trusted me more than anyone with more than two brain cells ever should. Helen is not part of this, but supports me in it. She's an amazing woman, and the love of my life. That's all I have to say.'

John next. 'Er … my name is John Preston, and I'm a werewolf? Mark? Can I start again, that was lame … no? OK. Well, I'm a werewolf. I've got loads of kids, and I'm happy, and I love Zoe, and Diana, and Andy and Mark. And Hel is cool as well. Hiya.'

Mark: 'OK, I'm Mark Preston. This is my responsibility, and mine alone. I know what you want to ask, and yes, my marriage is over. It's not something I will be talking about, so there is no point in asking. No more lies. Take me as I am.'

Diana and Zoe got home a few minutes before the men did. The house was in uproar, and the word was 'No more secrets, no more lies, take us as we are.' Some of the kids were crying, some were watching their parents on TV, looking at them, then looking at the TV again.

Bill just kept saying, 'Awesome gig, Dads.'

Around the country, young Shifters contacted their parents and grandparents, and told their own truths. In pubs and clubs and kitchens, people took in this new information about the Shapeshifters who lived among them, and talked about how they felt about it.

And in an underground war chamber deep in Bavaria, Harald listened to his adviser's report, and laid his plans.

Characters in alphabetical order of first name.

Alice Foster. Shapeshifter. Fourth daughter of Diana and Mark Preston. Twin of Jane.

Andrew Daniel Ransome (Andy). Normal, then successfully infected to become Shapeshifter. a.k.a. The Changeling. Bass player with the Ransomed Hearts. Married to his cousin, Helen Townsend. Diana's Third, along with Mark and John Preston. Father of Eva and Naomi Ransome (with Helen Townsend), and of Sara, Darlene, Nathan and Joseph Foster (with Diana Foster).

Anne Foster a.k.a Nancy. Shapeshifter. Second daughter of Diana Foster and John Preston. Twin of Susie.

Anthony Aubin a.k.a Anthony Preston. Shapeshifter. Twin of Tomas. Father of Mark Preston (with Frances Shepherd).

Arthur Kendrick. Normal. Minister. Father of Xan Kendrick.

Beatrice Foster a.k.a Trixie. Shapeshifter. Eldest daughter of Diana Foster and Mark Preston, twin of Bridget Foster. Together Beatrice and Bridget are known as 'The Bees'.

Bridget Foster a.k.a Bee. Shapeshifter. Second eldest daughter of Diana Foster and Mark Preston, twin of Bridget Foster. Together Beatrice and Bridget are known as 'The Bees'.

Caleb Foster a.k.a Cal. Shapeshifter. Third son of Diana and Mark Preston. Twin of Samuel.

Chloe Stephenson. Shapeshifter. Mated to Duncan Moss and Laura Matlock.

Darlene Foster. Shapeshifter. Eldest daughter of Diana Foster and Andy Ransome. Twin of Sara. She and Sara are known within the family as 'The Kittens'.

Deborah Foster aka Debbie. Shapeshifter. Seventh daughter of Diana Foster and Mark Preston. Twin of Leah.

Diana Foster. Shapeshifter, daughter of Jane and Gerald Foster. Geneticist. Mated to Mark Preston, John Preston and Andy Ransome, and Zoe Bradwell. Mother of Seth, Noah, Bridget, Beatrice, Caleb, Samuel, Jane, Alice, Margaret, Elizabeth, Deborah, Leah, Henry, Michael, Faith and Joy (with Mark Preston), Miranda (with Xan Kendrick), William, Francis, Susan and Anne (with John Preston) and Darlene, Sara, Nathan and Joseph (with Andy Ransome). Alpha female of the Silverwood Pack.

Duncan Moss. Shapeshifter. Discovered as a teenage werewolf by Diana Foster. Mentored by Andy Ransome. Mated to Laura Matlock and Chloe Stephenson.

Elizabeth Foster. Shapeshifter. Aka Beth. Sixth daughter of Diana Foster and Mark Preston. Twin of Margaret. Together with Louise, Tara and Meg, the Quadettes.

Eva Ransome. Half-blood. Elder daughter of Andy Ransome and Helen Townsend.

Evelyn Townsend. Normal. Helen Ransome's mother.

Faith Foster. Shapeshifter. Ninth daughter of Diana Foster and Mark Preston, Twin of Joy.

Frances Shepherd. Half-blood. Daughter of Eddie Shepherd and Dorothy Marsden. Wife of Anthony Preston. Mother of Mark Preston.

Francis Foster a.k.a. Frankie. Shapeshifter. second son of Diana Foster and John Preston. Twin of William Foster

Hannah Byrne. Shapeshifter. Teenager being monitored and mentored by Diana.

Harald Guntherson. Shapeshifter. Alpha of the White Pack.

Helen Townsend. Normal. Married to Andy Ransome. Mother of Eva and Naomi Ransome, with Andy Ransome

Henry Foster a.k.a Harry. Shapeshifter. Fifth son of Diana Foster and Mark Preston. Twin of Michael.

Ian Bradwell. Shapeshifter. Second son of Zoe Bradwell and John Preston. Twin of Isaac. Together with Nathan, Joe and Isaac, the Quads.

Isaac Bradwell aka Zak. Shapeshifter. Eldest son of Zoe Bradwell and John Preston. Twin of Ian. Together with Nathan, Joe and Ian, the Quads.

Jacob Preston, aka Jake or Jakie. Half-blood. Eldest son of Mark Preston and his wife, Katie.

Jane Foster Sr. Half-blood. Mother of Joyce and Diana Foster.

Jane Foster Jr a.k.a Janie. Shapeshifter. Third daughter of Diana and Mark Preston. Twin of Alice.

Jen Conway. Normal. Singer with Oaf Uckitt, had a one night stand with Xan Kendrick and was present at his death.

John Preston. Shapeshifter. Son of Miriam Hartnell and Tomas Preston. Mated to Diana Foster and Zoe Bradwell, along with Mark Preston and Andy Ransome. Singer with the Ransomed Hearts. Father of William, Francis, Susan and Anne Foster (with Diana) and of Isaac, Ian, Tara, Louise, Patrick, Liam, Julie and Leanne Bradwell (with Zoe). Beta Male of the Silverwood Pack

Joseph Foster a.k.a. Joe. Shapeshifter. Second son of Diana Foster and Andy Ransome. Twin of Nathan. Together with Nathan, Isaac and Ian, the Quads.

Joy Foster. Shapeshifter. Tenth daughter and youngest child of Diana Foster and Mark Preston. Twin of Faith.

Joyce Bridget Foster. Shapeshifter. Daughter of Jane and Gerald Foster. Sister of Diana Foster.

Julie Bradwell. Shapeshifter. Third daughter of Zoe Bradwell and John Preston. Twin of Leanne.

Katie Crawford. Normal. Married to Mark Preston. Mother of Jacob and Matthew Preston (with Mark Preston).

Laura Matlock. Shapeshifter. Mated to Duncan Moss and Chloe Stephenson.

Leah Foster. Shapeshifter. Twin of Deborah. Eighth daughter of Diana Foster and Mark Preston.

Leanne Bradwell. Shapeshifter. Fourth daughter of Zoe Bradwell and John Preston. Twin of Julie.

Liam Bradwell. Shapeshifter. Fourth son of Zoe Bradwell and John Preston. Twin of Patrick.

Louise Preston. Shapeshifter. Second daughter of Zoe Bradwell and John Preston. Twin of Tara. Together with Tara, Beth and Meg, the Quadettes.

Margaret Foster aka Meg. Aka Meg. Shapeshifter. Fifth daughter of Diana Foster and Mark Preston. Twin of Elizabeth. Together with Louise, Tara and Beth, the Quadettes.

Mark Preston. Shapeshifter. Son of Frances Shephard and Anthony Preston. Guitarist with the Ransomed Hearts. Married to Katie. Alpha male of the Silverwood Pack with Diana Foster, Zoe Bradwell, John Preston and Andrew Ransome. Father of Seth, Noah, Beatrice, Bridget, Caleb, Samuel, Jane, Alice, Margaret, Elizabeth, Deborah, Leah, Henry, Michael, Faith and Joy (with Diana Foster), Jake and Matthew (with Katie Crawford).

Matthew Preston. a.k.a Mattie or Matt. Half-blood Younger son of Mark Preston and Katie Crawford

Michael Foster. Aka Mikey. Shapeshifter. Sixth and youngest son of Diana Foster and Mark Preston. Twin of Henry.

Miranda Foster. Half-blood. Daughter of Diana Foster and Xan Kendrick.

Nancy Foster. Shapeshifter. Second daughter of Diana Foster and John Preston. Twin of Susie.

Naomi Ransome. Half-blood. Second daughter of Andy Ransome and Helen Townsend.

Nathan Foster. a.k.a Nat. Shapeshifter. Eldest son of Diana Foster and Andy Ransome. Twin of Joseph. Together with Joe, Isaac and Ian, the Quads.

Nathaniel Andrew Joseph Ransome. Normal. Father of Andy Ransome, husband of Pippa Ransome.

Noah Foster. Shapeshifter. Second child and Alpha bond twin of Mark Preston and Diana Foster. Twin of Seth Preston.

Patrick Bradwell. Shapeshifter. Third son of Zoe Bradwell and John Preston. Twin of Liam

Phillippa Ransome aka Pippa. Normal. Mother of Andy Ransome.

Raj Drake. Shapeshifter. Teenager being monitored and mentored by Diana.

Samuel Foster. Shapeshifter. Fourth son of Diana and Mark Preston. Twin of Caleb

Sara Foster. Shapeshifter. Second eldest daughter of Diana Foster and Andy Ransome. Twin of Darlene. She and Darlene are known within the family as 'The Kittens'.

Seth Foster. Shapeshifter. Eldest child and Alpha bond twin of Diana Foster and Mark Preston. Twin of Noah Preston.

Susan Foster. a.k.a Susie. Shapeshifter. Eldest daughter of Diana Foster and John Preston. Twin of Nancy.

Tara Preston. Shapeshifter. Eldest daughter of Zoe Bradwell and John Preston. Twin of Louise. Together with Louise, Beth and Meg, the Quadettes.

Trisha Harrison. Shapeshifter. Friend of Joyce and Diana Foster

William Foster. a.k.a Billy, a.k.a Bill, a.k.a Willum. Shapeshifter. Eldest son of Diana Foster and John Preston. Twin of Frank

Xan Kendrick. Normal. Deceased. Drummer and original lyricist with the Ransomed Hearts. Distant cousin and lover of both Andy Ransome and Helen Townsend. Friend and companion of Diana Preston. Father of Miranda Foster (with Diana Foster).

Zoe Bradwell. Shapeshifter. Beta female in Diana Foster's Pack. Mother of Isaac, Ian, Tara, Louise, Patrick, Liam, Julie and Leanne, all with John Preston.

Children of Silverwood

Seth and Noah (Diana and Mark)
Miranda (Diana and Xan)
Billy and Frankie (Diana and John)
Darlene and Sara (Diana and Andy)
Beatrice and Bridget (Diana and Mark)
Jacob (Katie and Mark)
Caleb and Samuel (Diana and Mark)
Eva (Helen and Andy)
Janie and Alice (Diana and Mark)
Susie and Nancy (Diana and John)
Matthew (Katie and Mark)
Nathan and Joe (Diana and Andy)
Isaac and Ian (Zoe and John)
Naomi (Helen and Andy)
Margaret and Elizabeth (Diana and Mark)
Tara and Louise (Zoe and John)
Deborah and Leah (Diana and Mark)
Patrick and Liam (Zoe and John)
Harry and Michael (Diana and Mark)
Julie and Leanne (Zoe and John)
Faith and Joy (Diana and Mark)

Acknowledgements

Thank you to Adrian, this couldn't have happened without his support.

Thank you to everyone who has read the first two books and given me feedback and encouragement. I always wanted the world to meet the Hearts.

Thank you to Fiction Feedback for their editing and critique work.

And thank you to Jon, who is a brilliantly creative and intuitive cover designer.

Jeanette Greaves

Printed in Great Britain
by Amazon